Blood Price

A Blood Grace Novel

VELA ROTH

FIVE THORNS PRESS

Copyright © 2022, 2020 Vela Roth

All rights reserved. No part of this book may be reproduced in any form or by any electronic or mechanical means, including information storage and retrieval systems, without permission in writing from the publisher, except by reviewers, who may quote brief passages in a review. For more information, contact: velaroth@fivethorns.com

This is a work of fiction. Names, characters, places, and incidents either are the product of the author's imagination or are used fictitiously. Any resemblance to actual persons, living or dead, events, or locales is entirely coincidental.

ISBN 978-1-957040-15-8 (Ebook)
ISBN 978-1-957040-13-4 (Paperback)
ISBN 978-1-957040-14-1 (Hardcover)

Edited by Brittany Cicirello, Suncroft Editing

Cover art by Patcas Illustration
www.instagram.com/patcas_illustration

Book design by Vela Roth

Map by Vela Roth using Inkarnate
inkarnate.com

Published by Five Thorns Press
www.fivethorns.com

Visit www.velaroth.com

CONTENTS

Content Note vii
Map ix
A Sword in the Ground 1
A Bird in the Storm 6
The Last Thing of Value 17
A Thousand Lilies 25
The Bride of Spring 36
The Wedding Feast 47
Bluebird 60
The Fire Dance 69
The West Field 77
The Sacred Offer 90
For Good or Evil 99
Essential Magic 109
The Greatest Reward 127
The Only Cure 137
Into Hespera's Realm 146
The Hidden Goddess 157
The Pillars of the Sanctuary 169
A Better Hesperine 183
Alkaios and Nephalea 194
The Taste of Sunset 205
Cherished Shadows 214
To Stay Anthros's Hand 227
Light's Benediction 237

Shadow's Reign	246
No Walls of Stone	259
An Arrow in the Grass	274
Glossary	277
Acknowledgements	285
About the Author	289

For the mourners

CONTENT NOTE

BLOOD PRICE portrays medieval fantasy violence, death, and mental health struggles with grief, including references to terminal illness. Chapter Ten discusses women's fertility and miscarriage.

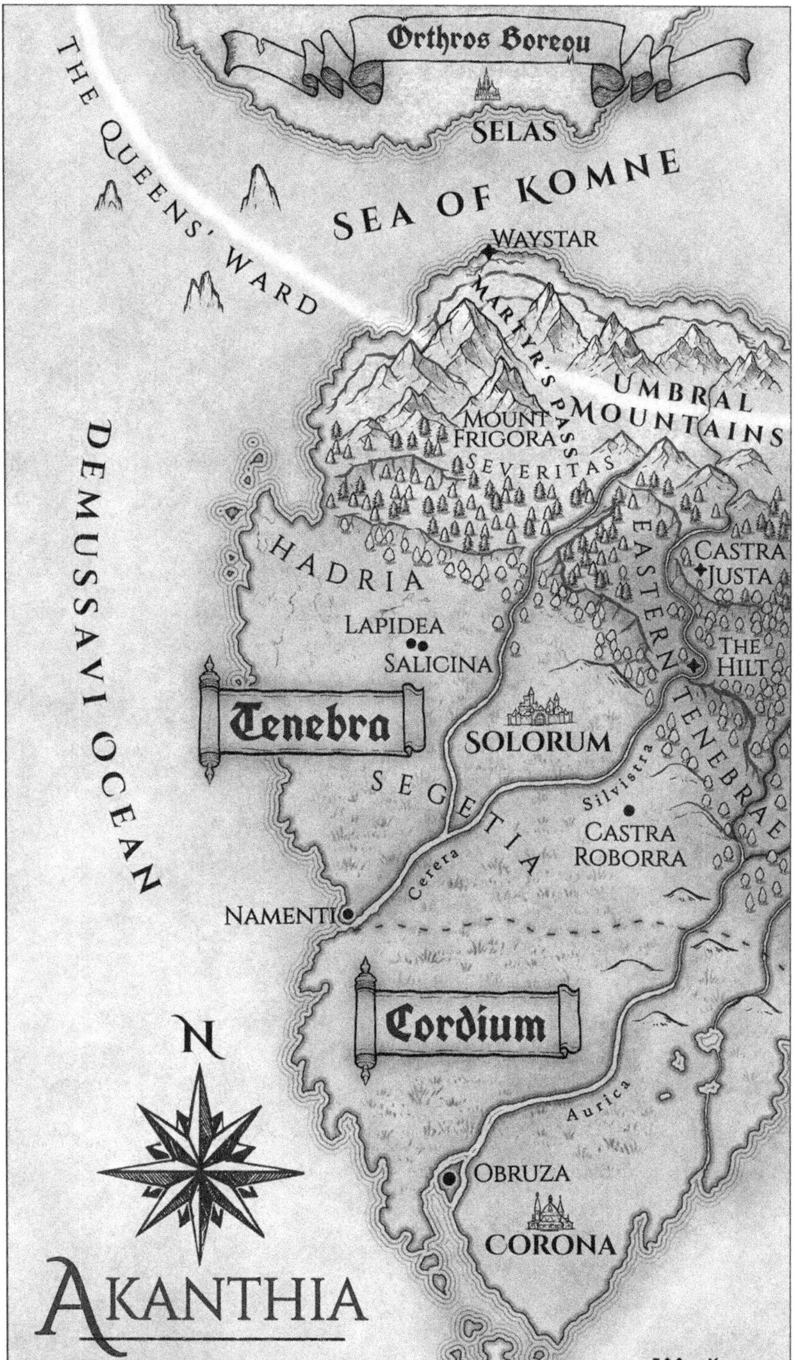
Orthros Boreou
SELAS
THE QUEENS' WARD
SEA OF KOMNE
WAYSTAR
MARTYR'S PASS
UMBRAL MOUNTAINS
MOUNT FRIGORA
SEVERITAS
DEMUSSAVI OCEAN
HADRIA
EASTERN TENEBRAE
CASTRA JUSTA
THE HILT
LAPIDEA
SALICINA
Tenebra
SOLORUM
SEGETIA
Silvistra
CASTRA ROBORRA
Cerera
NAMENTI
Cordium
N
Aurica
OBRUZA
CORONA
AKANTHIA
Eastern Hemisphere
500 miles

prologue

A SWORD IN THE GROUND

WHEN THE LADY KNELT beside him, all the pain stopped. He could no longer feel the agony in his belly. The cold mud and blood under his back faded from his awareness. He couldn't hear the rain.

Moonlight shone on the pale oval of her face, and night shadowed her deep-set eyes. Her hood gleamed as if woven of black gossamer.

She was beautiful, but not like Maerea.

He was already breaking his vows to Maerea. He was leaving her. Nothing could stop the pain of that knowledge. He squeezed his eyes shut, clenching his teeth.

The lady brushed his hair back from his brow. Her skin was soft, her hand strong. He turned his face away from her.

"Do not be afraid." Her voice was a velvety contralto, luring him into ease. "What is your name?"

He answered without thinking. Or tried to answer. The words gurgled in his throat as he choked on his own blood. She touched his brow again, and the discomfort faded.

"Alcaeus," she identified him, without him needing to say it. "Do you know why I am here?"

Hers was not the face he longed to see above him, the voice he wanted to hear in his last moments. But she was here, and he was not dying alone.

Finally, he looked at her again. Her full, feminine lips parted, revealing what she was.

She had fangs.

He recalled what he'd overhead after the battle had ended. He hadn't understood through the pain at first. Now everything made sense.

"My lord, shall we let his people collect him now?"

"No. Make sure no one comes for his body."

"Shouldn't we at least call a mage to give him his rites?"

"Say nothing to the mages."

"But—my lord—! There will be no one to stop…them. The creatures of the darkness. They always come for the dead."

"Let them use his corpse however they please. Let him pay for all of our losses. Leave him for the Hesperines."

Hesperines. Fanged, immortal, inescapable. They haunted the night, flocking to abandoned battlefields to scavenge for fallen men. Humans were nothing to them but blood to feed on or corpses to use in profane rituals.

Alcaeus stared up into the beautiful, horrifying face of his fate.

"I am Iskhyra," the Hesperine said. "I promise you will not feel any more pain."

Fear for himself gripped him for the first time that night. He had faced his enemy in combat without hesitation. He had done his duty and fought to the last. His only worry had been for his family.

Now the Hesperine was here. There was no shame in fearing what she would do to him. She would corrupt him. He would not even have the consolation of dying by the sword in honorable combat. No warrior deserved this. To fade into darkness, borne on a Hesperine's seduction.

He wanted to fight her, but his strength was spent. And no amount of strength would protect him from her. A Hesperine could rob a man of his will with her dark arts. She had such sorcery, she could do anything she wished to him. He was at her mercy.

At last it came, a grimmer messenger of his end than the Hesperine herself. Despair. "Leave me be. Please. My honor is all I have left. Leave me that."

She took his hand. "It is a great honor for battle to deliver you to the one you worship. You are devoted to Anthros, the god of war, are you not?"

"What would you know about devotion, heretic? Your kind worship the goddess of night." Hespera, outcast of the gods. He did not invoke her name aloud. He couldn't stop her creature from destroying him, but he wouldn't make it easy.

"Hespera is my goddess, but if you wish to meet Anthros tonight, I will not stand between you and your god."

There came a clank, and something hit his palm. He closed his stiff fingers around the hilt with a gasp. The family sword. He held it to his chest.

A sigh escaped Alcaeus, almost a sob of relief. Part of his hazed mind wondered if he could believe the Hesperine's words. She had just handed him the answer to that question.

"I found your sword driven into the mud," she said, "just out of your reach. A cruel insult to you and your blade. Your foe was not worthy of you."

"He," Alcaeus wheezed, "isn't dying."

"That does not make him the victor."

He held fast to the sword and the image of Maerea in his mind.

"Are you ready to depart?" the Hesperine asked. "To go to your afterlife in Anthros's Hall and join his company of eternal warriors? Are you finished with your work in this world?"

"This world is done with me."

"I am not." She closed her hand around his where he held his sword. "I have the power to keep you here, if that is your choice."

He swallowed. "You want to turn me into one of you."

"Only if you wish it. The magic in my veins can restore you. I can offer you the Gift, Hespera's blessing of immortality. Do you understand?"

"Yes," he choked.

He could become a Hesperine, powerful and undying. He could escape death for a half-life in the darkness, surviving on blood.

Her grip on his hand was bracing. "I know this is a difficult decision for you. Whatever choice you make tonight will be the right one. You have lived with honor. You have no cause for regrets."

"I do regret…"

"What? Did you want revenge against your enemy?"

"No. I just wanted Maerea." Her name escaped him, a prayer, he knew not to whom. "She gave up everything for me. Now she will have nothing."

"I can make it possible for you to help her."

"How, if your goddess demands my service?"

"Hespera makes no demands. She gives. She will not change who you are. She will grant you the power to finish what you started. Power as you have never had before."

"I don't care about power. Only about Maerea."

"The Gift would give you a second chance with her."

Alcaeus realized his choice was very simple. He could die in battle and go to Anthros's Hall, leaving Maerea. Or he could forfeit the god of war's favor for all time, accept Hespera's taint on his soul, and save Maerea.

What honor mattered more? Honor in battle? Or honor to his lady?

Alcaeus had made that decision already, the day he had chosen Maerea over a declaration of war.

"Does it take long?" he asked.

"You have strength and discipline, and Maerea is a powerful motivation. I expect you'll need fewer nights than most to learn to use your power. The transformation itself takes mere hours. However, know that the Gifting—the change from human into Hesperine—may or may not be easy. It will test your conscience."

He grimaced. He had lived by Anthros's laws. What would Hespera make of his conscience? "How so?"

"I withhold nothing from you so you can make your choice wisely. During your Gifting, you will relive moments of your life with empathy you never had before. You will see your experiences through others' eyes. You will feel their joy or pain, the consequences of your kindness or cruelty. If your deeds caused suffering, you will suffer. This empathy breaks the spirits of the depraved, and they perish before the transformation is complete. But those who have learned…those who have loved…their spirits endure, and they are reborn with new strength."

Alcaeus had never imagined he would have to submit his soul to Hespera's judgment instead of Anthros's.

But from the moment he and Maerea had met, he had known he would risk everything for her.

"I will survive this night," he vowed. "I will not abandon Maerea. Do it. Give me your Gift."

"Hespera hears your sacred request. In her name, I cannot refuse you. It is my honor to convey her Gift to you."

As if he were light as a child, the Hesperine picked him up. She carried him through the rain, as smoothly as if she floated, and bore him away from the field where generations of his and Maerea's forefathers had slaughtered each other.

He faded in and out of awareness. The rain stopped. They were somewhere quiet and dry. Low light bathed his face. The Hesperine supported him with one arm, lifting his head. He watched her raise her arm toward her face. When she lowered her hand, his senses sharpened again.

Blood gleamed on her wrist, vivid against her pale skin. Bile rose in his throat.

Anthros would not forgive him. His family would fear him. He could have no future with Maerea, not as a Hesperine.

And yet, he would meet his fate knowing he had done the right thing.

He braced himself and let the Hesperine touch her wrist to his lips.

He didn't taste the metallic tang he knew from getting blood in his mouth on the battlefield. He felt as if he'd downed a cup of raw courage. It warmed him from within and braced him for action. His vision faded. But he *sensed* Iskhyra, a commander just out of sight in the heat of battle, turning the tide of his inner war.

Now at last he beheld Maerea. In his mind flashed an image of her smile. She never smiled, except at him. He'd thought he could no longer smile, until he'd found her.

He would never forget the day they'd met. But she had not been smiling then.

chapter one

A BIRD IN THE STORM

Thirteen Days Earlier

MAEREA REFUSED TO BE afraid.

Rain spat in her face. At any moment, the storm would drive in through the window, and she would have to close the shutters. But she needed just one more breath of fresh air.

She could still smell the sickroom. Could still hear her father's last words.

My only regret…that bastard Aemilius will outlive me. I should have killed him…

Her brother had said nothing. Not as he had leapt to his feet and taken Father's sword in hand. Not as he had rushed out of the sickroom, leaving her with the remains.

Gerrian hadn't spoken to her until he returned hours later to tell her that Lord Aemilius the Elder, their father's lifelong rival, was dead.

Father had departed this life, the weak and wizened shadow of a warrior, on a sickbed. Lord Aemilius had departed as a weak and wizened shadow on the end of Gerrian's sword.

Perhaps that was why Gerrian had killed Lord Aemilius's son, too.

Aemilius the Younger had been a warrior in his prime, with years more experience than Gerrian. She might have had to plan her father and brother's funerary rites that day. But Gerrian had come back alive.

Only to depart again, this time to seek allies, he said. Leaving the castle without a lord to defend it. The perfect opportunity for their surviving enemy, Lord Alcaeus, to avenge his father and elder brother.

From here in her chambers, high in the keep, Maerea could see far. But not far enough. On the other side of the rain lived the enemy, close enough to march an army here in a matter of hours.

She caught sight of a bird in the storm. On sopping wings, it flew against the wind. It wavered, soared, wobbled, but did not succumb.

A flicker of motion drew her gaze down to the steep road that approached the castle. Her heart jumped in her chest. A lone rider ascended the treacherous path, his horse sure-footed despite the rain.

"Come away from the window," said Bria.

The rider couldn't be Lord Alcaeus. He would not come alone, if he came.

When he came. With his superior forces and provisions. If it was a siege he wanted, he could trap Maerea and her people inside these walls with their dwindling supplies and…

Maerea took one more deep gasp of air before Bria secured the casements. The room plunged into gray gloom. Maerea wiped the rain from her face.

Bria took a warm cloth to Maerea's hair. "There, there."

Maerea sat back in the window seat, leaning against Bria. "I'm so glad you're here."

"And where else would I be, after serving as your mother's handmaiden since she and I were girls? I promised her I would take care of you." She went over to the hearth to hang the damp cloth in front of the fire. Her soft, round face, now harrowed by age and lean years, creased in a smile. Her hair was now a silvery aura shining out from under the edges of her kerchief, but showed no signs of ever turning white. "I'll always be here."

Maerea swallowed a laugh that threatened to turn into tears.

The rider had not been Lord Alcaeus.

"We have work to do," she announced. "We'd best get on with the spinning. We need every scrap of yarn we can get from this year's combing."

"Aye. And we'll mend the old blankets to make them last awhile longer. It will be enough."

"At least until those allies my brother is courting bring us new prosperity."

Bria neither smiled nor frowned in response, her expression that calm one that filled Maerea with both comfort and dread.

"Tomorrow," Maerea went on, "or as soon as the rain lets up, I'll make my rounds to our people. See who needs food from our kitchens. Don't say I'm too generous. We won't starve. They will, if nothing gets done."

Bria set out their distaffs and spindles by their chairs in front of the hearth. "You're not too generous. You're so like your mother was."

Shouts from beyond the window made Maerea jump.

Bria's gaze went to the closed casements. "We'd best stay here."

For a heartbeat, Maerea sat there in her dark room, with walls and armed men between her and the unknown threat outside. With nothing but a few walls and armed men holding together her home, her people, everything that was left of her family's legacy.

She refused to be afraid.

She got to her feet. "No. I will see what the commotion is."

"We ought to stay here where it's safe."

"Would you get started on the spinning for us? I'll be back to help you in a moment."

"I'm not letting you out of my sight, dove." Bria covered Maerea's hair with her warm woolen headdress and bundled them both in shawls and capes.

They left the hearth room and went down through the deserted corridors and stairwells. Just inside the old oak doors of the keep, the commander of the guard halted them. He had been here as long as Bria and was almost as stubborn. "We'll see to the matter, my lady."

"Who is it?"

"The enemy."

Bria clutched Maerea's hand.

Maerea put her other hand on the wall for support. A chill seeped into her from the stone. She forced a breath into her tight chest. "He came alone?"

The commander shared a look with Bria. "My lady must stay in the keep."

Bria tugged on her hand. "Come back to the fireside, dove, and let the men see to the defenses while we start the spinning."

"Commander, did my brother give you orders about what to do if Lord Alcaeus arrived during his absence?" Gerrian never told Maerea anything these days.

"Yes, my lady."

She waited.

The commander sighed. "He gave orders to prepare for a siege, not…this."

"A siege is not what Lord Alcaeus has in mind. He wants to challenge Gerrian." Another duel. Another chance she might lose her brother.

"It would seem he knows my lord is not here, for he asked to speak with he who holds authority in Lord Gerrian's absence."

"What? Then he has been watching us. He waited for Gerrian to leave and plans to take advantage of the situation." She spoke with confidence, even as fear made her cold. "I must speak to him."

The commander moved to one side, blocking the door more completely. "My lord charged me with keeping you safe at all costs, my lady."

"Does Lord Alcaeus carry a bow?"

The commander hesitated. "No, my lady."

She raised her brows. "Or any throwing weapon that can reach over the walls, do you suppose?"

He sighed. "Nay."

"I will find out what he intends—from a secure position atop the gatehouse."

The commander bowed, but did not move aside. She waited, her hand still braced on the unyielding wall.

Her palm sweating, Bria released Maerea's hand. "Our lady is the one who holds authority."

At last, the commander pushed one door open for her. He held his cloak over her and Bria as they crossed the courtyard in the downpour. Bria marched up the stairs to the top of the gatehouse alongside Maerea, breathing not a word of aching knees.

Maerea clutched her skirts with icy fingers and strode to the edge to look down over the parapet.

The lone rider waited below, perched at the top of the stony road, just out of reach of the archers on the walls. He gave her a courteous bow from the saddle. When he spoke, she could hear surprise in his words. "My lady."

So he had manners and a pleasant voice. What did they conceal?

Despite the weather, he threw his cloak back, revealing an astonishing fact.

She stared. "You wear no sword."

"I did not come here seeking violence."

The rain eased, merely licking at her cheeks, the clouds lightening now that they had spent their spring storm. His wet hair might be light brown when it was dry. His face might be handsome up close. He was younger than his late brother, older than hers. Perhaps her age. Twenty-four was ancient for an unmarried woman like Maerea, but for Lord Alcaeus, it meant he was a young, strong warrior.

A rising, powerful threat.

"Lord Alcaeus of Salicina, what brings you to Lapidea this day?" Maerea congratulated herself on the steadiness of her tone, when she already dreaded his answer.

"Lady Maerea," he called up, "you have nothing to fear from me."

She rested her hands on the parapet, straightening her spine. "I refuse to be afraid."

He sat back in his saddle. "Then so will I."

"And what has a warrior like you to fear from me, my lord?"

"My brother's son is five. Until he is old enough to take over his responsibilities, it is my duty to protect him. I promised his mother, my brother's widow, she can rely on me. On their behalf, I intend to return home alive."

It could have been Maerea planning two funerary rites. But she wasn't. Aemilius's widow was. "If it is not a battle you desire, then why are you here?"

"To satisfy the law." He spoke with dignity and a raw edge in his voice. "Your brother challenged my father. My brother sought justice for that deed. Now it falls to me to seek justice for him. Under the laws of the Kingdom of the Tenebrae, I ask that Lord Gerrian compensate my family by paying my brother's life price."

In the silence after his announcement, Maerea could hear drips of water and the chime of his horse's tack.

Then Bria whispered to her, too low for Lord Alcaeus to hear from below. "He must know Lapidea cannot afford a farmer's price, much less a lord's."

"A ploy," the commander murmured. "He seeks to use this demand to gain easy entry into the castle."

"And should he gain it," Maerea returned, "what could he accomplish without an army? Without even a sword?"

"It matters not," the commander answered. "He will not have the chance to try."

"Do not fear, my dove. Our soldiers will never allow the enemy near you."

If he wanted a siege, he could starve them out while Salicina's fields ripened. If it was a duel he craved, Gerrian would love to give it to him.

A man who wanted a siege brought an army. A man who wanted a duel came when his enemy was in residence—and brought his sword.

Maerea did not know what to make of this man, who approached foolishly without a blade and kept himself wisely out of reach, who asked for the money his enemy did not have when the lady of the castle was here alone for the taking.

"Lord Alcaeus, the law allows you to demand a life for a life. No one in your position invokes the second option and claims a life price instead."

"Hence the generations of feuding between our families."

"Will monetary compensation truly satisfy your need for justice?"

"It will satisfy me for my sister-in-law and nephew not to suffer the terror of another battle, and for Salicina not to waste our hard-earned prosperity on a war. Let us mourn in peace."

She recognized that plea. It was her own prayer. "I am sorry for your losses."

He went still. As if he really listened to her simple words of sympathy. She realized they were bold words. "My condolences to you, Lady Maerea."

He did not want a siege. He did not want a duel. He made a far easier and more painful demand. He offered her a chance to buy the safety of her people and her family with something other than blood. And she had not a coin to give him.

She thought fast. Gerrian should return no later than six nights hence with reinforcements…and the gifts they might offer to seal the new alliance. She could use those to pay Lord Alcaeus.

"Would you return in half a fortnight to collect what we owe you? I ask only for your patience for seven days while I consult with my brother's master of accounts regarding the funds." Lord Alcaeus didn't need to know there was no master of accounts, only Maerea herself counting the scraps in the larder.

"Thank you, Lady Maerea." He bowed again and looked up at her for a long moment. "I will return to you in seven days."

He turned his horse around and started the ride back down the ridge. Before he was out of sight, he paused and looked over his shoulder at her. Then he disappeared between the hills toward Salicina, and the only living thing moving over the stony landscape was that bird, flying high now that the rain had lifted.

WHEN HER BROTHER STRODE into the great hall, Maerea's spirits rose, then sank. He was alone.

His allies would surely arrive later. She held her hands out to him. His harsh expression lightened for a moment, and he almost looked like himself. He pulled her close.

He smelled of steel and long days in the saddle. Not like he used to, of the spruce that grew around the yard where he had sparred with Father. But his embrace still made the world feel right again.

His dark brown hair was windblown, his oft-mended clothes begrimed from the road. Restless energy animated him. His blue eyes seemed keenly focused upon some goal she could not see.

He pulled back the chair at his right hand for her. Mother's chair. Maerea still thought of it that way, although she had been sitting in it for almost ten years now, ever since Mother's illness. He sat in Father's chair for the first time.

A draft blew down the long table, and the wine in his goblet shivered. After intense debate with herself, she'd opened the very last bottle of his favorite. She'd had it secreted away to surprise him on a special occasion. They couldn't afford such luxuries anymore.

"Here." She pushed the wine a little closer to him, trying to smile. "Your favorite."

He drained it in a few swallows.

"Let us celebrate the alliance," she said to the empty goblet.

"We'll celebrate when I return." Gerrian set into his dinner.

It looked like he would want another plate of food after this one. She would have to rearrange her meal plans. "You're leaving again?"

"Father's old comrades to the north are greedy cowards. They won't honor our families' past alliance. All they care about is profit, not the quality of the warriors they call friend. As if skill like mine isn't worth a lord's ransom. I've no use for that fickle, craven lot. Good riddance. Tomorrow I ride south."

Would the southern lords be any more willing to ally themselves with a family that had fallen on hard times? Would their old promises be any less likely to perish with Father?

She wrapped her hand securely around the wine bottle and refilled Gerrian's goblet.

Gerrian had no allies. No one to reverse their fortune. When Lord Alcaeus returned tomorrow, she could not pay. The law would demand blood.

The grasp of Hypnos, god of death, would once more close around Lapidea. He would take many of her people in a siege. Or her one and only family in a duel.

But she could send her brother out of his reach for now.

The longer she kept the two men apart, the longer she could prevent violence, and the more time she would have to deal with Lord Alcaeus herself.

"You must go immediately," she said. "There is no time to waste. You have not exhausted our options by far. I know you will find worthier allies among others of Father's old friends."

"My sword will restore us to our proper place. With my prowess in battle, other men will be quick to align themselves with me. They know I bested Lord Aemilius and his heir. I'll catch a few hours' sleep, then leave at first light."

She refilled his goblet once more, the bite of the wine's fragrance making her eyes sting.

～

Maerea awaited Lord Alcaeus's return on her knees before the statue of her patron goddess, Chera. No prayer came to her today.

"My goddess…" she tried.

She looked to Chera's statue for inspiration, as if she might peer through the Mourning Goddess's gray veil and glimpse her hidden face and unseen tears. Maerea touched the hem of the Widow's weeds. Generations of petitioning hands had worn the stone smooth there.

What should I do about Lord Alcaeus?

Now his name was at the end of the question she asked her goddess every day. *What should I do about…the empty larders? The sick farmers? The crumbling castle?*

She couldn't leave her fears at Chera's feet. Each time she departed her family's stalwart little shrine, she must carry her burdens back out with her. But after consulting her patroness, she always felt a sense of solace. And she always found a way.

She would find a way to pay Lord Alcaeus.

The rustle of robes alerted her to Master Eusebios's approach. "I thought I would find you here."

"I wish I had flowers or candles to spare to make better offerings." She placed another cracked spindle at Chera's feet atop the many others broken beyond repair.

"The Widow sees your troubles and your devotion, child. Know her heart aches for you…as does mine." The old mage took a seat on a nearby prayer bench, and she was no longer waiting alone.

She glanced up from the corner alcove, which housed Chera's statue, at the large sun disk that dominated the room. The bronze circle was so tarnished, it brought little glory to the god of war. "Thank you for allowing my patroness here in the shrine of Anthros."

"Of course." The mage sighed, his bony chest rising and falling within his faded red-gold mage robes. "You need a place here at Lapidea for your feminine devotions. It is a shame the shrine of the Mother Goddess Kyria is at Salicina, where it is unsafe for you to worship."

Maerea had never been in the shrine of Kyria, the harvest goddess, Anthros's happy Wife. She wouldn't know what to pray before a statue of the harvest goddess, who jubilantly held a sheaf of wheat and a shuttle in her hands, her belly heavy with child.

Chera knew pain. Chera knew loss. Anthros had broken her power when he had struck down her husband Demergos, once the god of agriculture, for disobedience. But the Widow still fulfilled her duties, nurturing the fields as the goddess of rain and easing mortals' passage into the afterlife as the Mourning Goddess.

How would Maerea fulfill her duties? How would she buy the safety of her people, who looked to her for rescue? Of her only remaining family member, who was beyond price?

The commander's boots crossed the threshold of the shrine.

Maerea stared at the pile of spindles. "He has returned?"

"I'm afraid so, my lady."

She was out of time.

"I will stand by outside." The commander's boots retreated.

It was an effort to rise to her feet.

Master Eusebios stood with her. "Would you like me to speak with Lord Alcaeus? Perhaps my involvement would diffuse tensions. When the temple sanctioned this shrine all those years ago, they assigned me to serve this entire area, including both Lapidea and Salicina."

"It's all right, Master Eusebios. Lord Alcaeus knows you have always been closer to our family."

"Feuds have no place in shrines. I regret that I have failed in stopping the conflict at the gods' door."

Maerea touched the widow's hem again, beseeching. Her hand slowed as she considered Chera's gown. "I am ready."

"Go with her voice."

"Although I must speak to Lord Alcaeus myself, perhaps we could hold our negotiation here."

"A wise course. Despite everything, this is the only place that resembles neutral ground."

"I will return shortly." She put her hood up and departed the shrine, braving the downpour. Chera was also the goddess of rain, after all. This weather reminded Maerea her patroness was with her.

The commander's eyes narrowed. "My lady, I haven't seen that look in your eye since that winter you had us take down the ancestral tapestries so the farmers' children could use them as blankets."

"Needs must. Invite Lord Alcaeus to the shrine of Anthros to collect what Lapidea owes him."

"Allowing the enemy anywhere near you is out of the question!"

This was not a negotiation she could conduct with an arrow's distance between her and Lord Alcaeus. How she presented her offer was everything. It would require a close inspection for him to see any value in it. "No one will start a battle under Master Eusebios's nose. It is the best place for Lord Alcaeus and me to negotiate. When my brother comes home long enough to be unhappy about it, you may tell him it was all my doing."

The commander had given her that same look about the tapestries, right before he'd ordered his men to do as she said and wrapped up the first child himself. "Yes, my lady."

Now she had a plan. It was good to know what she must do. It didn't matter how hard it was, when it was what she had to do.

chapter two

THE LAST THING OF VALUE

Alcaeus approached the shrine of Anthros, praying he would survive to leave it. Mages were forbidden to take sides in the feuds, but that still left him surrounded by Lord Gerrian's men. Their commander looked as if he'd rather feed Alcaeus to the hounds than let him breathe the same air as the lady of Lapidea.

But Lady Maerea had invited him to holy ground.

He'd not known what to expect from Lord Gerrian's sister. It would have been unjust to judge her before he met her. But he hadn't expected her to appear on the battlements and face him with such courage.

I refuse to be afraid.

He had never imagined her bravest words of all.

I am sorry for your losses.

The only thing her brother wished to give Alcaeus was a sword through the heart. But she had agreed to pay Aemilius's life price. She was Alcaeus's only hope of finding a solution without further bloodshed.

And so he staked whether he would return home alive on Lady Maerea's invitation. The commander and the guards escorted Alcaeus around the outside of the castle walls. They crossed a short distance of muddy, clear-cut ground to the lonely shrine. The worn arches and crumbling stones looked more like a crypt. But he made it through the doorway with his heart still beating.

It leapt at the sight of her. The distant goddess from the gatehouse was astonishing to behold up close. As he approached her, he scarcely felt the commander's gaze. He barely noticed the mage of Anthros at her side.

Her hair was the color of spring sunlight, her eyes the blue of a reflected sky. There were dark smudges under them and lines of strain around her mouth. Dressed in a heavy cloak and simple woolen headdress, she bore herself with composure, her dignity evident through the mask of her exhaustion. She was the most beautiful woman he had ever seen.

"That's close enough," said the commander, "my lord."

He hadn't realized he had gone so much nearer. He felt irrationally safe in her presence.

"My lady." Alcaeus set his pack before him and swept a deep bow.

She gave him a curtsy and looked him up and down. "He is unarmed. Stand down."

The commander retreated, but watched from across the small shrine. The guards, waiting outside, left a clear path from the door to Alcaeus's horse. But if he had to escape, it might still go ill for him. He could only pray Lord Gerrian's men wouldn't start a battle in a place of worship. Would an aging mage, a dull sun disk, and Chera's silent statue be enough to inspire their consciences?

If not, their lady ought to be. "I have an offer for your consideration, Lord Alcaeus."

"First, allow me." He gestured to the pack.

She touched a hand to the blue glyph that glowed upon the oilcloth. "A seal of Kyria?"

"To reassure you I did not poison the contents. It is basic courtesy for a guest to offer the lady of the castle a gift of food."

She opened the pack and rifled through the provisions inside. She shook her head at the cured meat, wheels of cheese, and jars of preserves. "The customary gift is a single hen."

"That wouldn't go very far among your hungry people."

"Why does it concern you if our people are hungry?"

"They did not kill my father and brother."

She looked away. "Commander, have this taken to the castle so the kitchen mistress can prepare a basket for every family."

Once Alcaeus's peace offering no longer stood between him and the lady, he felt less safe. She did not even offer him a thank you as a shield.

She pushed off her cloak and let it fall to the floor. Holding out her arms, she turned slowly in a circle.

Alcaeus strove to be a man of honor, but he was a man. Beholding the view she gave him, he forgot she was his enemy's sister. He forgot his own name. The contours of her breasts beneath blond velvet. Her slender waist, bound in a golden girdle, the perfect place to rest his hands. The ends of her hair teasing the tops of her hips. Deprivation had sculpted her thin body, but pride made her carry herself with grace.

She halted, facing him. "There is nothing more valuable in this domain. It is yours, if you will have it."

Priceless. His.

He realized what she meant and brought his mind back from where it longed to go. "My lady, I have no intention of taking the gown off your back."

"Fabric like this is costly. You will get plenty of coin for it, or ample goods in trade, I assure you."

"I did not come here to extort valuables from a woman."

"You could have. Why didn't you?"

"You did not kill my father and brother."

"My brother did."

"And let him pay the price."

"Perhaps it is not clear. This is the last thing of value in Lapidea. I've already sold the rest of my gowns to feed our people. I kept this one only because an advantageous marriage would have brought more benefit to them. If revenge sweetens the bargain, I'll have you know it was my mother's wedding dress."

"I'm not interested in revenge."

"Lord Alcaeus, you and I both know you have asked for a price my family cannot pay. When we fail to meet your demand, by the laws of the Tenebrae, my brother's life will be forfeit. Gerrian is all the family I have left. This gown is all I have to buy his life. Please. Take it."

He reached out across the distance between them. The commander stood at attention, and the mage's eyes widened. But when Lady Maerea did not back away, neither man stopped Alcaeus from taking her hand. She startled.

Her fingers were cold. He wrapped her hand in both of his and kissed the air above her knuckles. "That gown should not leave this castle until you leave wearing it—for a new and better life, I hope. Lapidea could pay the price with some timber from your lands, perhaps. Or the right to fish in your river. I'm certain you and I can think of something. The only payments I will not accept are your gown—and your brother's life."

"Please, let us settle this without a battering ram. Our dependents shouldn't die for our families' rivalry."

"They are blameless in this. I have no intention of subjecting your people or mine to the hardship of a siege."

"I don't understand. You *must* want revenge."

"Revenge is why my father and brother are dead. Revenge will only get your brother or me killed. What will revenge avail you or my nephew and sister-in-law? If your family pays my brother's life price, honor and the law will be upheld, and the bloodshed can stop. If you help me, we can stop the feud this very day."

She let out a sigh, almost a laugh. "Just like that? Generations of feuding between our families, swept away in one day? How are you and I any different from our forebears?"

He longed to hear what her genuine laughter sounded like. He ached for a glimpse of her smile. "I don't think any of them ever tried to stop it. But we're willing to try. At least, I am. Aren't you?"

She studied his face. "I believe you."

He did want something, but not revenge. He wanted her trust. That would be a prize worth more than a purse full of jewels. What he saw in her eyes now gave him hope it was not impossible to win.

"Walk with me," she said. "I'm certain you and I can think of something."

Why did Lord Alcaeus's nearness make Maerea feel warm all over?

She couldn't explain it. She needed the chill wind to clear her thoughts.

He joined her on the path outside the shrine, leading his horse, her guards close behind.

Details about him kept distracting her. He had long legs and a loose, masculine stride. His prominent nose had been broken in the past. She thought it lent an honest ruggedness to his face. The way he moved beside her was as courteous as the way he spoke. He never stood too close, but responded to her every cue.

"So," he began, "about that timber."

She pointed out across the bare ridge they traversed. "There is none left, my lord. It has all gone to firewood or shoring up the old castle. Our lands are clear cut."

He winced. "Let us consider fishing rights in your river, then."

"If we allow it to be overfished, our people will starve faster."

"Your brother shares the bounty of his fishing rights with the peasants who work his land?"

"Fishing is not foremost in my brother's thoughts."

"I would accept reasonable limits on what my family can catch."

She thought hard, going over the numbers in her mind again, but shook her head. "I reevaluate the fishing limits every month. I can't see how we could spare any without disaster."

He rubbed his chin. The day was wearing on, and his after-battle shadow had appeared, a stubble of light brown that emphasized his jaw. "I would ask about hunting your game, but after the way you looked at the provisions I brought, I don't think you've seen any bacon in some time."

"You have no idea how long it's been since I had a pork chop. The way our kitchen mistress used to season them for festival feasts…" She sighed. "Not that such things are of any importance now."

They roamed the desolate slopes and farmholds surrounding the castle. Wearing her people's fortune in fabric, she had tucked the train of her gown in her girdle to protect it. As she and Lord Alcaeus ran down the list of possible payments, she could not avoid revealing the true state of the household accounts. In a single hour, he educated himself about the estate more than Gerrian had in years.

She observed Lord Alcaeus, analyzing everything he said, searching for traps. But there was no glint of calculation in his brown eyes. Only kindness and regret. She kept arriving at the same conclusion. He was really what he seemed to be.

Honorable. Astonishing. Rare.

The wind had pulled a lock of his light brown hair out of its horsetail. The strands swept across one high cheekbone. "I knew you'd fallen on hard times in recent years, but I didn't realize the extent of your distress. Lady Maerea, if I may ask, how has your family's plight come to this?"

She stared at him. "Don't you know?"

He shook his head.

"Your father laid claim to the West Field."

"Yes…my father took it back from your family. Your father's father had taken it from us."

"We were raised to believe that it belonged to my family before yours ever came into this part of the kingdom."

He frowned. "My father taught us it was unclaimed when our forebears settled here and began to farm it."

"The gods only know who really has a right to it. But it was Lapidea's only arable land. We could never recover from that loss."

"Wait—your *only* arable land?"

"We tried our best to cultivate the rest. That was another reason Father had so much of the timber cleared. But it's too steep and rocky, the soil too poor."

He hesitated. "We have more fields to the south."

"A great deal more. I know."

"I'm sorry, Lady Maerea."

"You didn't take the West Field."

She paused on a cliff that overlooked the sharp drop behind the castle. She gestured to the smudges of brown fur that dotted the opposite bluff. "We still have the goat farms. We can keep those stubborn creatures alive out here, and their milk, meat, and hair keep us alive. As long as we keep the herd sizes under control. Between the goats, the river, and the bit of gardening we squeeze in pockets of decent soil, we get by."

"While you are calculating herd sizes, setting fishing limits, and squeezing in pockets of gardens, what is your brother doing?"

She pulled her cloak closer around herself. "My mother was an excellent household manager. It was difficult for my father after he lost her. I started assisting him. Then age brought on his slow decline, and I took more and more duties off his shoulders."

"Where was your brother, Lady Maerea?"

She looked out at the ravine instead of the man beside her. She seldom had so much difficulty deciding what to say. Gods knew she had been free with her words, filling her father and brother's ears with unwanted advice, everything Mother would have said if she were here. For all the good it did, Maerea would keep saying the words Gerrian didn't want to hear, because the alternative was to sit and watch everything fall apart.

But she struggled for words with Lord Alcaeus. Because it would be too easy to speak the truth, and she must not, not to her brother's enemy.

"Forgive me," he said. "It is wrong to press you for details about your brother's affairs. Your silence on his behalf does you credit. I will not dishonor you by speaking ill of him in your presence. But I will ask about you."

She couldn't keep her gaze from returning to him.

He leaned his forearm on the low stone wall that bordered the cliff, and the posture brought him closer to her. His was a lean, rangy strength. He was tall, with broad shoulders that shielded her from the wind. "Did you wish for your brother's help, when you grew weary of making life and death decisions about the fish in that river, to which he gave no thought? All the hours he was in the training yard instead, becoming expert with the sword, did you miss him?"

Why was it so hard not to be honest with Lord Alcaeus? Why was it so tempting to speak to him?

"My brother regards his swordsmanship as his best means of improving our lot. Our father was very dedicated to training him." There. That was simply a fact. Neither a critique of her beloved brother, nor a defense that would insult the man whose family Gerrian had just killed.

"Did you weep with frustration when he overhunted the game?"

"He…was trying to do his part to feed everyone."

"Did you explain the truth of the matter to him, when he lacked the foresight to realize he was doing more harm than good?"

That was why she could so easily open her mouth and confess her very heart to this man. It was because, if she did, he would actually *listen*.

He had listened to everything she'd said. He had considered her words fairly and judged them honestly. As if she had a head on her shoulders and was not just a nagging noise and a pair of wringing hands.

She searched his face. "Do you listen to your sister-in-law like this?"

He blinked. "I should hope I listen to her. It's my responsibility to take care of her now. She knows she can always tell me what she needs."

"I am not your responsibility. Why do you listen to me?"

That look came to his eyes again, the one she'd seen on his face in the shrine when he had taken her hands. She found herself wishing to feel his warm, strong, calloused hands again.

"You are worth listening to," he said.

Grief was a wild beast. It chose that moment to bring tears to Maerea's eyes. She blinked hard, swallowed, and willed herself not to weep for all her unheeded words and failed plans and impossible obstacles. For Mother. For Father. For her brother, who had become a stranger. For her future, which had long ago gone the way of the barren stones she lived among.

For the first time in a long while, she remembered that mourning was not supposed to last forever.

And something happened that never happened anymore. A vision of her future flashed in her mind.

Air seemed to fill her lungs. The castle that loomed nearby seemed lighter. A smile came to her face.

Lord Alcaeus looked at her as if captivated. And then he was smiling at her. Her heart gave a thump. His smile was as kind as his heart and as handsome as the rest of him.

It was the lengthening shadows around them that stole his attention from her. His smile faded. He drifted a step closer. "I ought to take my leave of you. My sister-in-law will worry."

There was a family waiting for him at his home, fearing he would not return alive from hers. "Go and reassure those who love you."

"I will come again tomorrow."

"You must. We have yet to decide how my family will pay our debt to yours."

He nodded, but it was not grief she glimpsed in his eyes as he took his leave. It was the promise of another smile.

chapter three

A THOUSAND LILIES

THE NEXT DAY, ALCAEUS walked willingly into his enemy's great hall, just as he had willingly risen from bed to face the morning. One day had changed so much.

Lady Maerea had changed everything.

She waited for him before an empty table. The firepit struggled to fill the space with warmth, but the barest touch of firelight made her shine. She wore her mother's wedding gown again. There were only half as many guards as the day before. She gave him a hint of the smile he had beheld on her face yesterday.

He would make her smile at him again today. Really smile. She deserved it. And he wanted it.

"Welcome, Lord Alcaeus." Her curtsy gave him a view of her neckline.

He bowed, pinning his gaze her hem instead. "Thank you for your hospitality once again, Lady Maerea. Imagine my surprise at your invitation to enter—and your guarantee of safe passage."

"You have my word no harm will come to you, and that you will ride home in peace with whatever price we negotiate."

"Thank you." He reached into his cloak and withdrew what he had carefully sheltered there.

At the sight of the pristine white lily, she gasped in delight. "A gift is only customary upon your first visit, and food is all that's required."

"This is just for you." He couldn't help smiling.

Then suddenly she was smiling. There. He had done it. Won the gift of her smile even more easily than he had hoped. It lit up her eyes and softened her gaunt face. Her cares seemed to disappear from her for a moment. And she was looking at him. He would bring her a thousand lilies.

"Where in the world did you get a lily?"

He gave her a rueful, conspiratorial look. "The local mage of Kyria has a way of coaxing them to bloom for us."

She drifted closer. "Ah, that explains it. We haven't seen her since my parents' wedding decades ago. She's always had a soft spot for your family. No wonder she let you in on the secret."

"Yesterday was the first time I'd seen the local mage of Anthros since my brother's wedding."

"Master Eusebios comes by most evenings for a pint with the commander."

Alcaeus held the flower out to her. "I hope the fact that even the mages take sides will not spoil your enjoyment of this."

"It's not the flower's fault the mage who grew it never comes here." Miraculous. Her smile hadn't disappeared yet. She beckoned to him. "We mustn't let such a lovely thing wilt. We'll put it in some water. Please attend me in my hearth room."

"It would be an honor, my lady." She trusted him enough to invite him there. The one part of a lady's chambers a man might honorably set foot, where she received those of the world outside. She would give him a glimpse into her domain.

The corners of her mouth twitched. "Tell me if you still feel that way after my mother's handmaiden scrutinizes you."

He chuckled. "I see. You are fortunate in those who are loyal to you. She may put me to the test as much as she likes, and I will still consider her a welcome escort after enduring the commander's assessment yesterday."

"Don't be so sure." Amusement danced in Lady Maerea's eyes.

Two of the guards followed them at a discreet distance. She led Alcaeus out of the great hall and through the passages of the keep. No rugs. No tapestries or banners. Seeing the sudden tension in her shoulders, he didn't comment. He wanted to ask her if she was cold, but that would only draw attention to the state of her home.

Firelight spilled out of one door ahead. When they reached it, the two guards posted themselves just outside. She left the door open and ushered Alcaeus into her hearth room.

He stepped over the threshold. This room was a refuge with one rug and worn, but fine oak chairs. A gray-haired woman sat by the fire, her spindle turning, turning at the end of the thread she spun. But it was him she studied. She halted the spindle midair and rose to her feet.

Before she could give the expected curtsy, he held up a hand and gave her a slight bow. "Please, Mistress, do not disturb yourself on my account."

"My lord." She had a sweet face with the sort of loveliness age could not diminish. But the calm in her eyes could only come from tempered inner strength.

"Bria, look at this. We must put it in a pitcher."

Mistress Bria's gaze arrested on the flower. She uttered a soft, "Oh."

"Have you ever seen such a beautiful thing?"

"I remember them from the shrine of Kyria."

Lady Maerea gave her a curious look. "You've been there?"

"Your mother used to worship there, before…well, in happier times. I always went with her."

"Those must have been happy times indeed." Alcaeus held the flower out to Mistress Bria with a smile.

She hesitated, then leaned close, breathing in a deep whiff of the flower. "Do not let it wilt."

Lady Maerea disappeared into the next room, presumably her bedchamber. Alcaeus heard her footsteps and the rustle of fabric. He felt so aware of her, moving about that intimate space, just out of his reach.

She returned with a simple stoneware water jug and placed the vessel on a side table near the chairs, smiling at him in invitation. He drew closer to her again and slipped the lily into the water. For an instant they stood together over the flower. But Mistress Bria's gaze made Alcaeus step back.

"Please, join us." Lady Maerea had a seat by the fire.

Alcaeus took the third chair, finding himself on the opposite side of the hearthrug from the lady. Mistress Bria sat between them and gave her spindle a turn. It twirled midair, dangling from her thread. Formless gray wool moved between her fingers, emerging as fine yarn.

No interrogation came. Her silent attention was far more intimidating. He didn't know if anything he might say or do would ruin his chances of winning her approval.

Lady Maerea did not start spinning right away, her attention focused on him. "Thank you again for the provisions you brought yesterday. You should have seen the children's faces. It gave their mothers such joy for them to have full bellies."

"I'm sorry I can't do more."

"You've done a great deal."

He spread his palms. "I have two idle hands. Might they be of use to you?"

He had surprised her again. "You are our guest."

"We are neighbors. No need to stand on ceremony. What can I do?"

She rested one finger beneath her lower lip. Only his awareness of Mistress Bria made him tear his gaze away before he looked too long.

Lady Maerea was quiet long enough that he feared he'd offended her. Or was the list of matters her brother left unattended that long?

Alcaeus was just one man, and every day she admitted him here was one more than he'd hoped for. He would repair the castle from towers to cellars if he could, but there was so much here that he alone could never fix. He hated that he must make her choose just one thing from her list of grievances.

At last she shook her head. "We have already established that I have no men to spare to repay you in labor. I will not add to the debt by accepting your offer, kind as it is."

"Then let me help you with something that will not add to your brother's debt. Let me do something for you." His gaze roamed her hearth room, assessing the state of her domain. It was spotlessly clean. He couldn't help with the patched drapes or cushions in need of restuffing, but…

His attention settled on the windowsill where she kept a small, beautiful chest of carved and inlaid oak. The latch hung askew, warped so it couldn't be closed or locked. He pointed. "May I?"

She hesitated.

"Ah. I should not have asked. Forgive me if I intruded upon something private."

"The damage grieves me. Could you repair it without looking inside?"

She had assigned him a test of honor. That was a challenge he welcomed. "Yes, Lady Maerea. I will make it good as new without a glimpse within. You can rely on me."

"I swear there are no jewels in it—"

He held up a hand. "You need not explain."

She rose from her chair. Sitting there across from her, he felt like a petitioner before a goddess. A goddess whose hand he longed to take in his, to turn over so he could kiss the soft skin of her palm. Whose hair he longed to free from its sensible knot, so he might run his hands through her sunny tresses. A goddess whose body he wished to—

Some devout he was. He envisioned latches and locks. How they worked. The properties of various metals. He must not fail her test.

She went to the window, the train of her mother's wedding gown sweeping behind her, and retrieved the little chest. She didn't hesitate to place the box in his offered hands. But once she had done so, she stilled.

"I'll take good care of it," he promised.

"I know." Her reply, so quiet, felt like a declaration.

He let his fingertips brush hers. As if that was what she'd been waiting for, at last, she withdrew her hands.

He settled the box on his lap. The lid bore a beautifully carved and painted bluebird in flight. He studied the loose, mangled latch, careful not to disturb the lid. "How did it break, if I may ask?"

"It wore out over the years from too much use."

"My lady, may I withdraw a small work knife from my boot? The blade is not a weapon, but I do not wish to alarm you."

Mistress Bria patted her distaff. It was a sturdy stick, and she had loaded the top with more than just wads of fluffy, unspun wool. She had extra spindles tucked in there. Some of them looked sharp. "Go ahead and draw your butter knife."

Alcaeus exchanged a glance with Lady Maerea, seeing his own suppressed laughter reflected in her eyes. Even Mistress Bria's lips twitched.

"It seems you have permission," Lady Maerea said.

He pulled out his knife and set to work. She picked up her own distaff, which was dressed with blue wool. Tucking it close, she selected one of her spindles that already held the beginnings of blue yarn.

When she twisted the spindle with one slender hand, he couldn't help watching. Her graceful fingers guided and caressed the new thread, spinning it tighter, stronger.

Their gazes met. She looked away. He checked that the lid of the box was shut, if only to reassure her he was taking care to keep his promise.

It wasn't the last time he caught himself watching her work. Or caught her watching him. He realized she wasn't looking at the box, but at his hands. Or his face again. Or the leg he had stretched out before him.

With great effort, he didn't smile at her each time. If he didn't let on he was aware of her notice, perhaps it would continue.

As they whiled away the afternoon, she didn't stop looking.

~

MAEREA TRACED A FINGER over the straight, secure latch of her bluebird box. It was even better now than before it had been broken. Waiting in the window seat, she looked down at the road. Lord Alcaeus would be here any moment for their next meeting.

"You should have plenty of gowns to wear," Bria groused, "and a castle full of suitors."

She looked over at the dear, laughing. Not bitterly, as she would have a few days ago. "Where did that come from? We have long since lamented and accepted my destiny as a spinster."

"Lord Alcaeus isn't the only young man in the world, but he's the only one in *your* world. How would you know any different?"

"What are you talking about? He's not…" She couldn't even say the words. *A suitor.*

That was an impossibility. There was no point even thinking about it.

But still the question came to her lips. "What do you think of Lord Alcaeus, Bria? You have had time to form an opinion of him."

Worry often darkened Bria's expression, but it was a different kind of worry today. "He's a man who gives bread before flowers and would sooner draw a repair knife than a sword. He's the sort who won't open your treasure box unless you let him. That's why he's so dangerous. He makes it very easy for you to let him."

"There's nothing in here." Maerea ran a hand over the carved bird again. "Nothing that would mean a thing to anyone but me."

She caught sight of him riding toward the castle. His horse leapt up the dry road through the rays of sun that peeked through the clouds.

Maerea stood and headed for the door, stopping to pat Bria's shoulders on the way out. "Thank you for keeping up with the spinning while I negotiate with him. I promise I will make up for lost time with my work this evening."

"You always do. Why don't I come with you?"

"We'll never finish everything in time for Weaving Day if we don't take turns working on it. I'll spin tomorrow while you let the kitchen mistress make a balm for your knees."

Bria waved a hand. "I don't need my knees for spinning. Where are you taking Lord Alcaeus today?"

"To have a look at the beans. Those count as mine, not Gerrian's."

Bria snorted. "Men don't know beans."

Maerea laughed. "Lord Alcaeus oversees crop rotations on his own lands. He'll have some useful suggestions."

She didn't tell Bria she would talk to Lord Alcaeus about more than that. He was full of ideas about many matters, but equally willing to listen to hers. She had already devised some new solutions to problems just by thinking aloud with him.

New solutions meant new hope.

But it was strange for there to be anything she didn't tell Bria.

"I'd sooner you brought him to the hearth room again," Bria said.

"Don't worry, dearest. The commander will be with us every moment."

Bria settled in her chair again, clearly under protest. "There are some things the commander is no protection against."

"He is equal to Lord Alcaeus's butter knife, I'm sure," Maerea teased on her way out the door.

Bria did not laugh. "Be careful."

~

The commander's face seemed frozen in a frown these days. She forgot him and the guards as soon as Lord Alcaeus rode into the courtyard. Once he'd handed his horse off to her men, he offered her a bow and the two gifts he brought her each day: a smile and a lily.

Smiling back, she lifted the flower to her nose to enjoy its elusive fragrance. "I am collecting a bouquet."

"This one is not for your vase."

"No?"

He shook his head. With the knife he had used to repair her treasure box, he shortened the stem of the flower. His fingers brushed hers in a touch more fleeting than the flower.

But the look he gave her lasted longer. His gaze roamed over her hair, her face. He tucked the lily behind her ear. His thumb slid lightly upon her cheek. Had that been an accident?

The thought that he'd done it on purpose did not alarm her. It should.

"Your gown is too fine for the bean plots, my lady."

She really shouldn't wear her mother's wedding gown out there. But all her other clothes were worn, faded remnants. More than that, the wedding gown felt as necessary as his smile and each lily. A piece of their ritual. Another impossible feature of these few, impossible days, a time separate from her life, from anything she'd known.

"I won't get it dirty." The corner of her mouth turned up. "You'll be doing all the work, my lord."

His laughter was so pleasant. Like something from another world. It drifted up, escaping the walls.

"Besides," she added, "there's another place I wish to show you, and this gown is appropriate for there."

Curiosity lit his face. "Lead on, my lady."

They took their walk outside the walls, this time to the bean plots in the lee of the castle. He didn't hesitate to kneel in the dirt, studying the mangy but resilient plants. Maerea couldn't remember Gerrian or her father ever giving beans a passing glance, except the ones on their plates.

"An ingenious solution," Lord Alcaeus said. "The castle shelters this area from the cliff winds, and these ledges form natural terraces. It was your idea to plant the beans here, wasn't it?"

"Yes." Chera help her, how she warmed at his praise. One would think he'd showered her with poetry about her hair, not complimented her beans. But unlike pretty locks, beans saved lives—and he knew it. "These broad beans can withstand our poor soil and will give us harvests throughout the summer."

"Beans also restore the soil, instead of taking from it."

"Then I should plant them everywhere they'll grow. Perhaps they can revive some of our land."

"Here, where they've been growing for several seasons, you could rotate them with other crops to add more variety to your people's diet."

"That's wonderful news."

They continued to trade ideas, facts, and opinions, peppered by the occasional jest. They moved on from the bean plots to a tour of all her other farming projects. It often seemed spring had forgotten to come to Lapidea, but here were the hard-won proofs that Chera's season prevailed, and life would return each year.

By the time they arrived at Maerea's tiny stand of currant trees, the sun was low on the horizon. "Will your sister-in-law worry if you stay just a little longer? There's one more place I want to show you."

"The place you wore the gown to visit?"

"Yes."

He offered her his arm. The natural gesture suddenly reminded her how unnatural this was. She was once more aware of her brother's fully armed men watching them.

But her touch counted as hers. Not Gerrian's. She rested her fingers in the crook of Lord Alcaeus's arm.

She set off, strolling away from the grove with her gaze on her hem. But her heart raced, and inside, she felt full of something too powerful for these simple actions.

She led him away from the castle, the crops, and the guards, although the men followed some distance behind. As she and Lord Alcaeus neared the bluffs, the harsh winds became their allies, stealing their words from the guards' listening ears.

"A little farther. Right here." She halted him on a high point where the rock curved out over the ravine. She pointed to the east. The sun was setting behind them, somewhere over the West Field, unseen. Before them, the eastern horizon turned rose, lavender, and periwinkle. "Everyone wants to look west when they watch the sunset, but the most beautiful colors appear farthest away from the sun."

After the words were out of her mouth, she realized how fanciful they had been, how silly all this was. She was showing a hardened warrior a sunset while she wore a wedding gown.

There were few treasures in Lapidea. She tried to never squander a sunset. But he wouldn't understand that.

He lifted her hand, placing a kiss on her knuckles this time. Brilliant warmth and something soft and dark sank through her, as if the sun were going down within her. She bit back a gasp, looking up at him.

"Beautiful," he whispered, his voice a match for the wind. "Thank you for showing me."

"My home must seem wretched," she tried to explain. "I wanted you to see there are good things here, as well…things worth saving. I know the same sun shines on all of us, but…"

"Of course it's worth saving. It's your home."

She put her other hand to his where he still held her fingers. "You do understand."

"You shouldn't have to do all this alone." He wore no sword at his belt, but for the first time, she could hear his blade in his voice. The saturated colors of dusk cast his face in fiery light. She had never seen him angry until this moment. She knew without a doubt his righteous fury was for her sake.

"Thank you," she said.

"You don't have to do it alone. Not anymore."

It was the only promise anyone had made her in years. Long years of keeping all her promises.

That promise from him counted as hers.

He gave her yet another. "We'll think of something."

"Yes," she believed. "Yes, we will."

The sky had gone to indigo. Twilight draped around them and turned all the harsh edges of the valley below into soft folds.

A crunch of rock warned her that the commander approached. She held up a hand. He gripped the hilt of his sword and halted as if straining against a tether. When she did not relent, he took a step back. But he lit a lantern and set it down nearby. As if she were staying out too late with…

A suitor.

Impossible.

He makes it very easy for you to let him.

There's nothing in here. Nothing that would mean a thing to anyone but me.

But it did mean something to Lord Alcaeus.

"What more can I do to help you?" he asked.

Take me away from here.

The unvoiced longing shocked through her, leaving her speechless.

Take me out of here before I die.

She clamped her mouth shut on the plea that wanted to tear from her throat.

But he saw it. He leaned closer. "Anything. Name it."

She drew in a long breath, trying to steady herself, to put the pieces of the world back into place. She couldn't afford longings. If she didn't keep a clear head, other people would die.

She had withheld nothing from him. He could confirm there was no life price to be had. He had put aside his own immeasurable grief to offer her this chance to secure peace between their families, and she could give him nothing.

Or could she?

There is nothing more valuable in this castle. It is yours, if you will have it.

She knew in that moment what she must do. For the first time, it wasn't hard.

chapter four

THE BRIDE OF SPRING

GERRIAN DESTROYED EVERYTHING IN his path. Alcaeus had watched it happen to his father and brother. Now he knew it had been happening to Maerea for years, just out of sight.

No longer.

He hadn't been able to save his father and brother. By the gods, he would save Maerea.

"My lord." The way she said the courteous title, here in the near-dark, made it feel intimate to him.

She was a lady who would never beg for help. He knew he must offer and prove she could trust him to deliver. Now, at last, he might have succeeded.

"I have a question for you." She sounded determined.

Promising. "Yes?"

"May I ask if a betrothal promise binds you?"

He held her hand closer, like the treasure it was. Like the treasure her question was.

In recent days, he'd given no thought to a wife and family of his own, only to his brother's widow and child. Now that he thought of it, he had even less to offer a bride than before. His inheritance was the same, his responsibilities greater.

And yet he was so glad for the answer he gave to Maerea. "No."

He heard her swallow. "It is surprising to me that a man of your rank and character has no wife."

"I am not so much in demand. It's not as if I have a seat on the Council of Free Lords, with influence over the king."

"Salicina enjoys prosperity rare in these times. Surely many ladies would see the advantage of marrying into your family."

"I was born a second son. My prospects were fewer. I had less to offer a wife."

Lady Maerea shook her head. "That's not true. You have so much to offer. You have…you."

His sister-in-law had predicted he would one day find a lady who would value him more than an inheritance. She had been right.

"There have been possibilities," he admitted, "when I traveled on behalf of my father and brother to uphold our alliances and allegiances."

She arched a brow at him. "I dare say there were. After you fought their battles, were there not eligible daughters at the victory feasts?"

"Fine ladies, all. Ready to bring honor to their families with a good marriage. But…their hearts were not in it."

"No lady has laid claim to your affections?" she asked.

That lady stood before him. Asking him if his heart was free.

He had seen how she looked at him. Would she dare admit it? "I do not have an understanding with any lady."

"In that case, I have a suggestion that could solve our dilemma. As you can see, this gown really is all I have to bargain with."

His heart sank. She was still trying to sacrifice all she had left for the sake of her worthless brother. What did she think to do? Give him her gown for his future bride? "I have laid down my terms, my lady. I will not take your gown."

She drew a deep breath. Her slim, soft hands held onto his rough one. "Not even if I leave wearing it—for a new and better life?"

"Maerea." He said her name, no titles, for the first time.

Although he stood between her and the wind, a little shiver went through her.

"What are you saying?" He had to be sure.

"Take me," she bade him, while her hands beseeched.

With two words, she broke down the fortress he had believed would always separate them.

She trusted him with what was most precious—herself.

He could gather her into his arms right now. Carry her away and make everything right. Have her sound counsel and her clever ideas for the rest of his life. Make her smile with a lily every day.

Make her his. Touch her. Taste her. Know her.

When she had been unattainable, he had lain awake at night with need for her. Now his body tightened at the thought of making his imaginings real. He kept his hand gentle while desire gripped him.

But nothing had changed. He could never accept.

He waged a battle to withhold the words he longed to say. The silence lengthened between them while he mastered his voice and his body.

Slowly, she withdrew her hands and took a step back. Turned away.

"Forgive me." Her words sank into the darkness beyond the lantern's reach, while her bright gown stood out in the night. "How could I ask such a thing of you? To give your marriage vows to me after what my brother did. How could I think my life could pay for your father's and brother's? I'm so sorry."

He closed the distance between them in one stride and caught both her hands, turning her to face him. "I would give *you* any vow, Maerea."

She lifted her gaze to his, and the lantern light caught a glint of hope there.

"But I will not accept you as a sacrifice to pay for your brother's deeds. That you would make yourself my brother's life price—it sickens me. You have labored for your brother's domain like a debtor. I will not have you do the same for me."

A gleam came from the horizon. The moons rising. They showed him her tears.

"How many tears do you weep that no one sees?" he wondered.

She squeezed her eyes shut, but the tears escaped her lashes.

He put his back to her guard and cupped her face in his hand. She turned her face against his palm, her tears sliding down their skin together.

"I came here wanting only one thing from you," he said.

"What can I give you?"

"Your trust."

"Will you not accept more than that?"

"I will. Something that will not pay your brother's debt. Something for you."

"I cannot think of me."

"Why not, Maerea? Why do it for him, but not for yourself?" His certainty wavered, and he almost withdrew his hand. But this might be the last time he could touch her. "Is he the only reason you would wed me? If there were no feud, no life price…if there were only you and me, would you still wish to be my wife?"

"Of course I would. I long ago resigned myself to the bitter knowledge that I would never have the husband and children I hoped for. I grieved for that family I would never know. I thought I would live and die alone inside these walls. Then you came. A finer man than any I imagined. You were right here all along, and the feud denied me—denied us any chance."

"But now it has brought us together. I would do anything to change those moments that cost me my father and brother. But I will not regret meeting you. You are the blessing the gods have seen fit to bring out of this curse."

"Do you really see me so?"

"That's exactly how I've seen you since the moment I first beheld you."

"I cannot bring them back, but I can try to bring you comfort."

"You are my comfort. You need not try."

"I would be a good wife to you. I—"

"Shh. You need not try."

"You would have me?" she ventured. "If there were no price to pay?"

"That is the only way I would have you."

"What of justice for your brother?"

"That is your brother's responsibility."

"What of the law? If you were to take me to wed, and my family waived the bride price, it might balance the debt."

"No. I will not accept your gown, your brother's life—or you as payment." He took a step closer, lowering his head. She tilted her face back, her lips parting. "Will you not come away with me? Bring your treasure chest and your gown and forget everything else."

"I cannot forget my people." She pressed her lips together, and the longing on her face gave way to hollow weariness. "You cannot have me without the rest. We are both of us entangled in the feud, although it was not of our making."

It was her honor alone that stayed her from doing as she wished and accepting him. Far from cooling his heels, it only made him admire her more.

"I will pay your bride price, Maerea. I will give the West Field to your brother. Then, once the land has restored your prosperity, he can pay my brother's life price."

Her eyes widened, and her breath caught. "You would do that?"

"For you, my bluebird."

She slid to her knees before him and pressed her forehead to his hands.

He knelt with her, looking into her face. "No. You are not my supplicant. I am yours."

"Anything," she said fiercely. "Name it."

"Marry me."

Her entire face lit up with a smile, unlike any even the lilies had brought to her face.

"Child, are you certain?" Master Eusebios's question echoed within the shrine.

"I'm afraid she is," Bria answered.

"This is the right thing to do," said Maerea. "My honor demands it."

Master Eusebios shook his head. "These are the affairs of men. You should not have to bear their burdens. I don't want to see you come to harm, caught in the middle of their feud."

"Lord Alcaeus wants only peace. That is a cause I will gladly champion. Together, he and I can restore both our families."

"I don't like this for you, child. You should have your Autumn Greeting and a proper promise dance and all the celebration that entails. A betrothal in winter, agreed between your brother and the man in question. Then a spring wedding."

She looked around at the dull sun disk behind the weary mage, the benches empty of celebrants, the worn arches devoid of garlands. Bria stood at her shoulder, her attendant for her wedding day, looking as if she had come for a funeral.

But none of it dimmed the bright, exhilarating thing fluttering in Maerea's chest.

After all these years, how she got married mattered not a whit to her. She just wanted to be married as soon as possible—to Alcaeus. She had only one heart's desire, and he would join them in the shrine at any moment.

"I don't need dances. I will have my spring wedding this very day, to a worthy man."

"Worth leaving your home?" Master Eusebios asked.

"Our people know I am not abandoning them, that I am doing this for all of us. I have arranged for everything here to continue as it should. I will bring safety and prosperity to our people once more."

"Always thinking of everyone else before yourself," said the mage.

She tried. But close to her heart, she held the truth. She wanted Alcaeus for reasons that had nothing to do with honor or duty.

"Come here, dove." Bria shooed the mage away, then sat Maerea down on one of the prayer benches and took both her hands.

"I will be all right, Bria."

"I have seldom had cause to question your judgment. You have more sense than the rest of your kin combined, thanks to no one but your good mother."

"You consider me an excellent judge of character, do you not?"

"Lord Alcaeus's character is not in question. His family is all that will matter to your brother. You don't need me to tell you what will happen if you go through with this."

Maerea bowed her head. "I know, Bria. I know. It will be…the hardest thing I've ever done."

"Are you sure you're prepared?"

"My brother has not been himself since father died. He doesn't know how to grieve except with his sword. His retaliation will be terrible. But it would be so if I did not marry Alcaeus. The only thing powerful enough to temper my brother is the vow I will make to Alcaeus today. The only thing powerful enough to shield him from Gerrian is—me."

"When has your brother ever listened to you, Maerea?"

"Never. And yet I have managed to shield him from himself all these years. You know how strong my influence is over him, in spite of himself. I will bring him around, as I always do."

"What's at stake today is not timber or fish or game. *You* are at stake."

"The one thing that has not changed is Gerrian's and my love for each other. That has withstood every trial we have faced over the years. He will eventually accept this marriage and the end of his feud—for my sake."

"Giving a man a choice between his family and his family feud is a dangerous endeavor."

"He and I are all that's left of this family. Once he sees that we can turn from the path of our own destruction, that his sword is not our only hope of survival, he will be glad for what I've done."

Bria held her gaze. "Are you sure?"

"Yes."

A long sigh escaped Bria.

"Don't worry," Maerea pleaded. "Be happy for me."

"Maerea…do you love Lord Alcaeus?"

Trust Bria to be the only one who asked her that question. Maerea whispered the treasured secret to her friend. "Yes."

"Goddesses preserve you, my dove. Loving across the feud is a thankless fate. I don't want this for you."

"You do not think me selfish?"

"I think that after your many years of selflessness, you deserve all your heart's desires. But why must it be him?" Bria shook her head, her eyes gleaming with anger like Maerea had never seen in her. "Why must love always grow in the most dangerous places? Why must the feud always ruin it?"

"Only the gods know why. But love that grows in hostile ground is the strongest of all, don't you think?"

"It never withers," Bria murmured, "for better or for worse."

"Does this mean I must marry without your blessing?"

Bria blinked hard. "No, dove. Never that. No matter what happens, I will take care of you."

Maerea embraced Bria, holding her friend close.

"Would that I could protect you from everything," Bria said.

"Having you with me is enough." At length, Maerea drew back, wiping her eyes. She couldn't hold back the smile that came to her face. "I'm getting married today."

"So you are, dove."

"Today I get to say the bridal prayers."

Maerea lowered her veil over her face and went to the alcove. Kneeling before the statue of Chera, she touched a hand to the worn place on the Widow's gown.

She murmured the traditional prayers of a bride. The same words her mother and grandmother had once sent up to the goddess. So had Alcaeus's mother and sister-in-law, and all the women who had taken on this sacred role before.

Before Chera had become Demergos's Widow, she had been the Bride of Spring. Every woman belonged to her in these moments before becoming a wife under Kyria's auspices.

Maerea would always be Chera's, for the Mourning Goddess had brought her through her trials to this moment.

When she heard a footfall, she knew it was him. Excitement flitted down her back, and the shrine seemed full of his presence, of her awareness of him. She looked up. And there stood her betrothed, in a golden velvet tunic, ready to pull her to her feet and into their future.

~

His bride knelt in a pool of golden skirts, resplendent in the gown she would at last wear for her wedding. Their wedding. She had made his lilies into a flower crown upon her veil.

But he longed to see her face. He could not make out her expression through the fabric that hid her face and hair.

He offered her his hands. "Are you ready?"

She gave his fingers a squeeze as she let him help her to her feet. "I can hardly wait."

The happiness in her voice banished his concerns. She was not having second thoughts. This very day, she would be free of her brother, safe under Alcaeus's protection. She would be his wife. The law itself would be on their side, empowering him as her husband to shield her from all things, even her own family.

Gerrian would not be her liege lord anymore.

Alcaeus wished he could give her a grand festival to celebrate their union. She deserved so much more than this abrupt ceremony. But right now, what mattered most was getting her away.

They would have the rest of their lives for him to shower her with everything she desired.

He brought her hands to his lips, kissing each in turn. "You are so beautiful. I've wanted to tell you that since the moment I first saw you."

"I can scarcely believe I am to marry such a handsome man."

He smiled at her praise. "Everything is in order. Our mage of Kyria has come with me."

He turned with Maerea to find Daughter Pherakia and Mistress Bria facing each other in the aisle.

Daughter Pherakia's bright blue robes and veil left only her eyes visible, but the mage had no trouble conveying her meaning with a single prickly gaze. "Bria."

Bria did not appear the least cowed. "Rakia."

"How long has it been?"

"Since you delivered Maerea."

"After the birth, you didn't come to the shrine of Kyria for the customary rituals of thanksgiving."

"I was not aware I was welcome." Bria lifted her chin.

Daughter Pherakia crossed her arms. "Well, here we are, thanks to her wedding."

"Yes. You never come for funerals. We've had many more of those."

Mother bears came to Alcaeus's mind, and he wondered if the soldiers outside were the greatest threat to his and Maerea's impending wedding. He cleared his throat. "Mistress Bria, I assure you, you are not only welcome, but to make yourself at home with us. I have a donkey waiting to carry you to Salicina in comfort."

Mistress Bria gave him a dignified curtsy, despite the wobble in her knees. "Thank you for your consideration, my lord."

"You are Lady Maerea's dearest companion and will be treated accordingly. If there is ever anything you need, you have but to ask."

Daughter Pherakia turned away from Bria to look Maerea up and down. "Well then, introduce me to this bride of yours, Alcaeus."

She had dispensed with his title when he was a lad picking her sacred flowers to make poesies for his pony. After his mother's death, she had filled the void in her own way. But he would not let her or anyone else treat Maerea with disrespect.

He took Maerea's arm, ushering her a step forward to face the mage. "Daughter Pherakia, this is Lady Maerea—soon to be *my* lady."

"Thank you so much for coming to perform the ceremony," Maerea said graciously.

"A wedding can't take place without a mage of Kyria and a mage of Anthros." Daughter Pherakia's tone was grudging.

Alcaeus laid his hand upon Maerea's arm, trying to reassure her. At least Daughter Pherakia was here. Her loyalty to her duties and her affection for him outweighed her misgivings that much.

"It's lovely to meet you at last," was all Maerea said. His diplomatic lady. Her fingers tightened on his arm, as if to say she was not so easily deterred.

They had known each other for such a short time, and yet all it took was a touch for him to understand her. He'd never been so in accord with any person, even those he'd known for years. They were two of a kind, him and his bluebird.

He could search to the ends of the world and find no one so well suited to him. Thank the gods he would snatch her today, before anyone could part her from him.

The two mages faced each other on opposite sides of the sun disk. Bria took her position just behind Maerea's shoulder. Now was their chance.

As Alcaeus escorted his bride down the aisle of the shrine, his ears played tricks on him. He kept thinking he heard hoofbeats approaching through the rain outside.

Nonsense. Her brother couldn't possibly make it back for another few days, at least.

The mages began chanting in the Divine Tongue, the secret language of the temples. Even though he couldn't understand the words, he should pay attention to all the reverent details of his own marriage rites. But he barely heeded the mages' ministrations with oil and sheaves of wheat and all the sacred symbols of Anthros and Kyria's joining.

He was only aware of Maerea's hands in his and his own alertness, as if he kept watch on the walls, awaiting a siege.

chapter five

THE WEDDING FEAST

AT LAST IT CAME time to say his vows. The back of his neck prickling, he recited every sacred word, building her safety with each one. "…that my sword will ever serve you…that I will be your shield…"

"…that I will be your bounty…that I will be your warmth…" With sweetness and passion, she promised him everything and freed herself.

He parted her veil, draping each side over her shoulders to reveal her face at last. She looked up at him with shining eyes, her joy stark on her face.

Daughter Pherakia presented him with the headband that would signify Maerea's status as a married woman. Mothers always made them for their daughters. Alcaeus was glad Maerea's mother had had time before her death to fulfill such a cherished tradition.

He smoothed the embroidered golden velvet over her forehead, just under her flower crown, and tied it behind her head.

Twin sighs escaped them, the clouds of their breaths mingling in the chilly shrine.

They were wed.

His relief was so powerful, he felt almost giddy. Or perhaps that was just the knowledge that this marvelous woman was his.

There were no trumpets or cheers, only the silent mage of Anthros watching them go. No weeping mothers, only Daughter Pherakia and

Mistress Bria walking out at arm's length. No procession, only his horse and armed escort. But as he lifted Maerea onto his saddle, she looked down at him with such radiance that he regretted nothing.

He swung up behind her. Arranging her on his lap, he put his arms around her. His bluebird. His wife.

When he urged his horse into motion, a laugh flew out of her. Her prison receded behind them.

∼

Maerea first glimpsed her new home through the gentle fall of rain, with her husband's warm arms around her. He had pulled the hood of her cloak up to shield her lily crown from the weather.

How strange that his ancestral castle, Castra Salicina, was built of the same stone as Castra Lapidea, Maerea's family's fortress. Their dueling ancestors had quarried their strongholds out of the same cliffs. That was the only resemblance, though.

They approached through a busy village that had overflowed the outer palisades. No gaunt, tired faces here, like she saw among her farmers every day. Healthy, energetic folk lined the main lane to bow and call out ritual blessings for their lord and his bride. Maerea almost didn't notice Daughter Pherakia turning her donkey away from their procession without a word, Bria gazing after her.

Maerea relaxed a little more against Alcaeus. It boded well that his people were willing to make such a show of loyalty to him, even if he had married the enemy's sister.

"Our people will come to know you," he said in her ear. "You will have no trouble winning their devotion."

Our people. He meant his and hers. "I will do right by them."

"I know. They will soon realize how fortunate we are to have you."

There were even more soldiers on the walls of the castle than she had predicted, all in golden livery. The gates were open by the time their procession neared the curtain wall, and they rode through the deep gatehouse to the cheers of his men.

Maerea knew the look of men who gave loyalty out of fear or memory.

She had seen many of her own people look at Gerrian that way. She also knew what real loyalty looked like. She saw it on her people's faces every day.

Although all of this was rightfully his nephew's, it was clear everyone supported Alcaeus as their lord and the protector of their future liege.

"They are fortunate in you," she said. "I can see their faith in you."

"Thank you, Maerea. That praise means the most coming from you."

Another fortified gate let them through the shield wall. In the inner courtyard, he dismounted and handed her down from the saddle, while one of his men helped Bria off her donkey. A hostler led their mounts away to the nearby stable. Maerea caught a glimpse inside at several well-fed, well-bred horses.

A little girl ran up to her and scattered petals at her feet. "Welcome, my lady," she said in her sweet baby voice.

"Thank you, my dear. I'm so happy to be here." Maerea smiled and touched the child's head. "What a pretty girl you are."

The girl blushed and skipped away to her mother. "Mama, the lady says I'm pretty."

With a smile, Alcaeus scooped Maerea up in his arms. Her cloak fell back, and with a laugh, she clutched at her lily wreath. He carried her through the courtyard and up the front steps of the keep, her gown never trailing on the ground. She wrapped her other arm around his neck, listening to his people's well-wishes.

Here were the flowers and the cheers. She hadn't expected or asked for them. That made them all the sweeter.

Alcaeus carried her over the threshold. The doors of the keep swung closed behind them, and she could no longer hear the people's happy voices.

～

It took a great deal to make Alcaeus angry, but when he saw the bare table in the great hall, his temper flared, fast and hot. This was not the welcome Maerea deserved.

He set her on her feet, but kept her close to him. He put on a relaxed, pleasant expression while his blood boiled. "We must have made better time on the ride here than we realized. Our wedding meal is not even on the table yet. I'm sure my sister-in-law has planned something marvelous, as I asked her to before I came to get you. Perhaps you would like to rest for a short while before the feast."

"Bria and I wouldn't mind the chance to catch our breaths, would we?"

"I'm right behind you, dove. My lord's men assured me they'll bring up our things in a moment."

Alcaeus rested a hand on Maerea's lower back. "I'll show you to the chambers I had prepared for you. Your rooms adjoin mine."

He guided her out of the great hall, then down the short corridor and up the flight of stairs that took them directly to the family rooms. Her gaze roamed everywhere as they went, taking in the carpets and tapestries, shields and urns, and the views from the windows.

"Your home is beautiful. So warm and inviting."

"Our home."

She smiled at him. "Our home."

They came to the door of her rooms. The lovely, empty rooms that had sat next to his all these years, in anticipation of a wife. "The hearth room here gets good morning light. Perfect for weaving, I'm told. I'll have a new loom made for you."

"That sounds wonderful."

With his hand on the latch, he hesitated, thinking of dinner missing from the table. "Wait here just one moment. I'll make sure the drapes are open, so you can get the full effect."

She obliged him with an affectionate glance. He left his bride and her companion stranded in the hallway and went in to inspect her chambers.

He took one look at the closed drapes, untouched layers of dust and blankets still draping the furniture, and covered his face in one hand.

Gods. He had known his sister-in-law disapproved of his decision, but he had not expected this. She was such a loving woman. How could she treat Maerea this way? How could she not feel even a little female sympathy with a fellow lady who had suffered at Gerrian's hands?

What was he going to tell Maerea?

He put that ridiculous pleasant expression back on his face and rejoined her and Mistress Bria in the hall, shutting the door behind him. "I apologize. It's taking them a little longer than expected to get your rooms ready."

Mistress Bria gave him an all-too-knowing look. "I would be happy to help make ready for my lady."

No, he would not have Mistress Bria and her knees take on that task alone after a long ride. "I'm sure you want your own opportunity to settle in. I'll see to it the kitchen mistress surrenders her room to you until your place in Lady Maerea's chambers is prepared."

"As much as I appreciate that, my lord, I doubt it will endear me to my new household. I'd like to begin here on the kitchen mistress's good side."

"Ah. All are welcome in the guest chambers at the shrine of Kyria, and they are most comfortable. If you can bear a few more minutes on the donkey, I can have one of my people show you there."

Mistress Bria exchanged a look with Maerea. "Do you need me nearer, dove?"

Maerea squeezed her friend's hand. "I must also make my first impressions."

Mistress Bria gave a nod, then folded her shawl more securely around her shoulders. It reminded him somehow of a soldier girding himself for war. "I will go to the shrine of Kyria."

Alcaeus hailed a page, and while he made arrangements, Maerea and her companion murmured their farewells, however temporary.

He found himself alone in the corridor with his wife. Thank the gods she was not in tears yet. "Would you be comfortable in my rooms for the time being?"

Maerea slid her arm in his again, the caress of her hand more intimate this time. "I'd like to see your rooms."

"Very well. The next door is mine."

His new wife had suffered neglect and parted from her one friend here, and now the only place for her to find refuge was a male domain. Until yesterday, he'd been an unmarried man, and had expected to remain so for gods knew how long.

She drifted inside his solar, looking around. He'd left out a sword and oil after cleaning the blade when he could not sleep. Piles of pledge tokens, correspondence, and household accounts cluttered his desk.

"You'll be warmer in the next room." He ushered her into the bedchamber, wincing at the sight.

Clothing spilled from his trunk after his haste to dress appropriately for their wedding. He also happened to know that his four-poster was smaller than the bed in her rooms, because a considerate man always visited his lady.

At least his people kept a fire burning in the hearth, but that was the only comfort his chambers offered a woman. There was just one chair by the fire, a pair of his boots beside it.

She turned to him, pure affection in her eyes. "You spend most of your time in the saddle or among the soldiers, when you're not playing with your nephew or attending your sister-in-law in your hearth room. It has been so for some time, because you have put your duties to your family ahead of personal concerns. You were so invested in serving your father and brother that the chambers for your future wife lay untouched."

He opened his mouth to come up with some excuse to smooth things over, but she reached out and touched her fingers to his lips.

The intimate touch scattered his thoughts. For a moment, all that mattered was that his lips were upon her skin.

"Your sister-in-law does not want me here," Maerea said. "I'm sorry, although I'm not surprised. I knew nothing about this would be easy. But we will sort it all out. Together."

He turned her hand so he could place a kiss upon her palm. "I am so sorry. I thought I had everything arranged—"

"Of course you did."

"You deserve a warm welcome. A feast. Rooms that can be a refuge to you after everything you've endured. Today was supposed to be the start of our new life."

"It is. I have everything of importance right here in front of me. The rest can wait."

He eased her toward him. She came without hesitation. As he had longed to do last night on the cliff, he wrapped her in his arms. "Maerea. My bluebird."

She leaned into him, resting her face on his chest.

It felt so good to hold her. To offer her his strength and comfort.

To take comfort in her.

"You do not hold my brother against me," she said, "but I cannot blame your sister-in-law for doing so. She mourns her husband, the father of her child. Grief like that is blinding. I will do everything in my power to open her eyes. I will devote myself to healing the wounds Gerrian has dealt."

"You have nothing to atone for. I will see to it she does not hold you responsible."

"Be patient with her. I do not wish to cause a rift between you."

"Let me speak with her. After that, I will see to it you have everything you need."

She took a step back. "A meal right here in your rooms would suit me just fine."

"You are a goddess, Maerea."

She blushed at that. The pretty flush pinkened her pale cheeks. Was that what her face would look like when she flushed for other reasons?

The urge to kiss her came over him. Here he was, alone in his bedchamber with his wife for the first time. To Hypnos with everything outside the door.

Their gazes held. The moment lengthened. He pulled her close again. Her blush grew brighter, and her lips parted.

One kiss. Just one.

And he wouldn't want to stop.

"Make yourself comfortable. *My* doors are open to you." He pressed his lips to her forehead and withdrew.

"Domitia?" Alcaeus called softly, approaching his sister-in-law's hearth.

She slumped in her chair, opposite the empty one where his brother had always sat to watch her weave. Her black curls hung limply around her face. Her round cheeks were pale, her eyes puffy. In the days since Aemilius's death, her ample figure had begun to wear away. Domitia did everything with her whole heart. Being a wife. Motherhood. Grief.

He stood by his brother's chair. "Have you eaten today?"

"Tell me you didn't do it. Tell me you're returning to me a free man, and we're all safe."

"We are much safer now than we were this morning, thanks to Maerea's and my vows."

Domitia let out a wail and covered her face in her hands.

It was no use trying to reason with her when she was in the grip of one of her tempests. But the same passions that reduced her to such despair made her the loving woman she was.

The men of their family had ever been willing to do anything for her happiness. After a difficult birth claimed the life of Aemilius and Alcaeus's mother and new sister, many cold years had gone by. Then Domitia had brought life back into their home.

Now Alcaeus was the only one left to dote on her. As he often had in recent days, he knelt beside her chair and ran a soothing hand up and down her back. She always saved her tears for when they were alone.

She wailed as she had at Aemilius's funerary rites, each sound shredding Alcaeus a little more.

Grief like that is blinding.

Maerea understood. If only Domitia saw that. He must do everything he could to help Domitia understand Maerea.

He waited. And waited. At last she was wrung out, and her sobs quieted.

"All is well, I promise," Alcaeus said. "When you meet Maerea, you'll see. She is eager to be a good sister to you."

"She's *that man's* sister."

"She isn't to blame for her brother's crimes."

"She's his blood."

"She is my wife." Alcaeus took a deep breath, reigning in his anger. "I wish you had prepared her rooms and a wedding feast as I asked."

"You expect me to entertain the enemy? Make a place for her in our home?"

"Today was my wedding day, Domitia. I thought that might be worth celebrating."

She looked away.

"Maerea has risked everything, given up everything to place her trust in us and seek refuge here. She arrived with very little, after the hardship she has faced. And she's having to wait in my rooms, with none of what a woman requires."

"You put her in *your* rooms?" Domitia hissed.

"What did you expect me to do?"

"Take her back!"

"This is her home."

"She's been in your rooms. Now it's too late. If you'd just come to your senses at the door and taken her straight back, we might have been able to undo the damage."

"I just made sacred, lifelong vows to her."

"Oh, Alcaeus. You are a man of your word. What have you done?"

"I've wed the woman I want to spend the rest of my life with."

"You expect me to tolerate her under my roof, permanently? Allow her in the same home as my son? I thought you would do anything to protect him!"

He sank back on his heels. "You really believe Maerea would harm a child? That's what you think of her?"

"She seduced you! Her brother put her up to it, so she could sneak into our home and harm my boy. My Aemilian."

"Domitia." He weighed his words, taking her hand. "You are a woman who has suffered because of Lord Gerrian. You know better than anyone the pain he can cause. Now imagine living under his authority. Consider what he has been doing to Maerea all these years. I had to help her escape him. And in accepting rescue from me, she has provided our rescue. She wants peace just as much as I do. Our marriage will end the feud."

"I've always known you were kind-hearted, Alcaeus, but I never imagined you were so naïve."

"Maerea is trustworthy."

"It doesn't matter what kind of person she is. When her brother finds out what you've done, his anger will be terrible."

"More than anything, he wants to restore his fortunes. He won't be able to refuse the bride price I'm offering him."

"A bride price? After everything he's taken from us?"

Alcaeus decided it was not the best time to explain that the price he had in mind was the West Field. "If it will stop him from taking more, yes."

"He deserves your sword in his gut, not payment."

"You and Aemilian need more from me than just my sword arm."

"I don't know what we'd do without you. I hate that you had to marry that harpy, our enemy's get—"

"She is my wife. I ask that you treat her with the respect she deserves."

"And what about what you deserve? All those years, you worked so hard for your father and brother, securing my boy's future. Never taking a moment to build your own fortunes or woo a wife for yourself. And now you're bound to her for all the rest of your days. I wanted to see you happy."

"I am happy."

She fell silent, as if he had slapped her.

He continued to hold her hand. "Maerea is the woman I always hoped to find. If I could choose anyone, I would have none but her."

Domitia snatched her hand away. "That witch. She's pulled the veil over your eyes. Wrapped you around her finger. Even a man like you can fall for such wiles."

"Domitia—"

She held up a hand, turning away from him. "Don't expect me to leave my chambers while she's in the house. I won't let Aemilian out, either, until the danger has passed. I can only pray you, our only protector, will come to your senses so we'll be safe in our own home again."

Alcaeus stared at her, feeling as worn out as after a battle, but not physically. He got to his feet and left her, shutting the door as quietly as he could.

MAEREA CURLED UP IN Alcaeus's chair, enjoying the vision of him sitting here for long hours by firelight. She loved how his rooms smelled like him. Like leather and horses, fresh rain and clean stone, and the fragrant, masculine oils he bathed in.

He returned a long while later, carrying her tray himself. He directed two strapping lads where to place her trunks, then dismissed them. The door shut, and they were alone.

He set the tray on the table by the chair. "Your feast, my lady."

He had brought two goblets and a bottle of wine, a basket of fresh bread, and…a platter heaped with the fattest, juiciest pork chops she could ever imagine. She stared at them.

"I don't know if our cook seasons them the way you like, but…"

She caught his hand. "You remembered something like that."

He knelt before her. "I want you to have everything you love."

"You're a very wise man. You understand that the way to a woman's heart is through pork chops."

The earnest, fraught expression on his face cleared, and he laughed.

"You will share them with me, won't you?" she asked.

"Come to think of it, I am hungry."

He sat back against her skirts. They ate the pork chops in their hands, licking the juices from their fingers. She made herself eat slowly. She could have devoured them if she let herself. Four bites in, she felt that primal sense of wellbeing that came from a plate full of meat. The pork was so delicious, so deeply satisfying, her toes curled in her slippers.

She caught him regarding her and felt herself blush again. But she saw no censure on his face. He appeared to enjoy watching her eat.

She felt so very indulgent, eating rich food and drinking wine with her handsome man at her feet. The entire affair felt like a festival picnic. She could never have enjoyed herself at a formal feast in the great hall, trying to make an impression on Domitia and reassure little Aemilian that the adults were not angry with him.

"This is the most wonderful wedding feast I could have imagined," she said. "I mean that."

He rested his head on her knee. "I confess, I relish it, too."

A little closer, and his head would be in her lap. She wanted to run her fingers through his hair, but stopped herself. Her hands were still sticky.

He brought her hand to his mouth and licked one of her fingers. Slowly.

Pure heat awoke through her entire body, all teeming toward her deepest center.

Then he released her hand and got to his feet. He went over to the washbasin to clean his hands, then brought her a damp cloth.

She wiped off her hands, the water chilling her skin. "Where must you go now?"

"To set your chambers to rights, if I have to dust every stick of furniture myself."

She hung the cloth by the fire to dry, then sat down again and patted her skirts in invitation. "Why don't you leave it for tomorrow? You've done enough for today."

He halted just out of arm's reach. Why was he standing so far away? "Today has been…trying for you. I want you to have somewhere to rest."

"You…are planning to rest here?" The other words she might have said caught in her throat. Quiet fell.

He stepped closer. Oh, if only he would come closer still…

He cupped her face in his hand, as he had after sunset on the cliff. But this time, her guards were not watching. There was no one to stop him from touching her. It was all right—in fact, entirely right for him to touch her.

His calloused palm teased her cheek as his thumb rubbed a tantalizing circle over her skin. "Although we married in haste, I have no intention of rushing now that you are my wife."

The thought of taking their time brought many things to her imagination. Thoughts she didn't have to push away. She was a married woman now. And he was her husband.

Alcaeus was hers.

"I am a patient man. I will not place any demands on you tonight." His hand slipped from her face. He was retreating across the room.

"Alcaeus."

He turned back to her. "Yes?"

"Although our union serves our families, you know I meant our vows. I intend to be your wife in every way. Is that…what you intend for us as well?"

"I meant every word I said to you before the gods. And I intend to make you mine in every way. But we can take some time to grow comfortable with each other."

He was a man. Surely it would be more uncomfortable for him to refrain. He was trying to be patient for her sake. "I waited for you for years."

"And now we'll have years together."

Silence chased his sweet assurances. They had both seen how swiftly loss could come.

Before she knew it, she was on her feet. She dare not admit what she wanted. It was unseemly for a woman to be too eager. And she didn't know how to describe the weakness in her knees and the warmth low in her belly. "You don't have to ready my chambers."

"I think I must, for if you stay here tonight, I'll not be able to keep my hands off of you."

"You don't have to…" she whispered.

At last his arm came around her waist. He pulled her against him, sliding his other hand into her hair. "Maerea."

chapter six

BLUEBIRD

WHEN HE HELD HER and spoke her name, it was the most intimate thing she had ever experienced. Until he lowered his lips to hers.

His kiss was as gentle as his hands had been the first time he had touched her. Sensation and warmth cascaded over her skin and down her spine. Leisurely, he caressed her lips with his, a little deeper each time. Finally, he kissed her lips apart, and she felt the warmth of his mouth.

At last. This was what it was like to be kissed.

Anthros's fire burned within her temperate husband. When his tongue slid inside her mouth, her entire body melted against him of its own accord. The texture of his tongue stroked over hers. Liquid heat traveled down through all of her.

She didn't know how long they stood like that, trading breaths between kisses. Speechless and heady, she never wanted the moment to end.

But then he kissed her jaw, then the skin below her ear, then her throat, his stubble scraping her skin. She almost whimpered, but swallowed the indecent sound.

"Maerea," he murmured against her neck.

"Yes."

"Do you trust me?"

"With my whole heart."

His voice was warm and low in her ear. "And your body?"

"Yes," she breathed.

His fingers played with the ends of her hair. He rested his large, long hands at her girdle, framing her waist. Then his hands slid up, slowly upward over her ribs…

He cupped her breasts through her gown. The thick fabric felt like nothing. Her cheeks burned as heat coiled deeper within her.

"You're so beautiful," he told her.

She drank down his praise. It didn't matter that her bloom had faded. He thought she was beautiful.

Her breasts were just the size to fit in his palms. He massaged them, making an appreciative sound in his throat. "Maerea, I'm not the sort of husband to make love to you with a minimum of ceremony while you're fully clothed."

"Claim your marital rights as you wish."

His eyes gleamed, the corners of his mouth turning up. "How very dutiful of you. But I'm also not the sort of husband who wants you to come to me out of duty."

She was still trying to find a response that wouldn't betray her when he kissed her again. A giving, worshipful, demanding kiss. By the time he let her up for air, she had wrapped her arms around his neck to hold herself up.

He smiled down at her, his expression stark with desire and his gaze soft with affection. "As the lord of the house, I have only one rule for our bedchamber."

"Yes?" she asked, eager to please him.

"No duty is permitted in this room. I require that we leave it at the threshold before entering."

Laughter leapt out of her. He laughed with her, running his hands up and down her back, pulling her against him as if he could not get her close enough.

The firm ridge of his desire pressed into her belly. An answer echoed in her body, a quiver between her legs. How could they laugh and lust together at the same time?

"It could be dangerous to allow your wife to be undutiful, my lord."

"I find I have a taste for danger."

She meant only to lean into him, to show her trust, but her hips shifted against his arousal. What looked like pain flashed across his face, but she knew it must be pleasure.

He steadied her against him with one hand. With the other, he took a fistful of her gown and drew her skirt upward. Deftly, he slid his arm under the layers of fabric and flattened his hand on her outer thigh.

It was a shock, his skin against hers. His calloused hands moved up, then down the outside of her thigh. He tucked his fingers behind her knee and pulled her leg around him, parting her, opening that place of hers that was already throbbing. She looked away from his face, only for her gaze to land on her bared knee, gripped in his big hand.

"I'd like to see all of you." He kissed her beneath her ear again. "May I?"

"Of course."

"Would you like to see all of me?"

She blushed again, even as her womanhood tightened. "Of course."

He chuckled low in his throat and gently set her leg back down, stepping back from her. He knelt before her, her gallant champion, and gathered her voluminous skirts so he could lift her gown off of her.

She helped him, and together they freed her from the heavy tangle. With great care, her randy husband draped the garment over the chair before turning back to her.

His gaze skidded over her, slowing upon her ankles and the peaks of her nipples showing through the fabric of her tunica.

He slid the loose neckline down over her shoulders, his fingers brushing her skin, and let the tunica fall to the floor.

She stood there in nothing but her wedding veil. As he lifted the flower crown from her hair, the scent of lilies drifted around them. He placed the ring of blossoms on the chair with her gown.

At last, he pulled away her veil, baring her head to him for the first time. With the full length of her hair uncovered before his gaze, she felt more naked than she ever had in her life. And yet with him, it seemed natural. She felt safe, and she felt dangerous.

He kissed her marriage headband. "Come to our bed."

She let him lead her away from the hearth, over to the four-poster. He turned back the bedclothes for her. Slipping her bare bottom onto the linens, she lay herself down before him.

He stood over her, the fire naked in his eyes now.

"I really would like to see all of you," she said.

He flashed her a grin and pulled his shirt over his head. Tossing it aside, he slid his braccae down his legs.

The fire behind him outlined his silhouette in burnished gold, defining every line of muscle. Lean. Hard. Strong. This man she had yet to see with a sword was every inch a warrior.

He knelt in front of her on the bed, his weight pressing down into the mattress. The light shifted over him, revealing his manhood.

She took in the sight. Her skin flushed, whether with modesty or at the boldness of her own curiosity, she was not sure.

"What *are* you thinking, bluebird?"

She swallowed. "I am more fortunate in my choice of a husband than I knew."

He burst out laughing and came to her, propping his hands on either side of her to support his weight. She reached up and tucked his hair behind his ear. She hoped they would always laugh in bed.

"I will be gentle with you," he assured her.

"I know." She smiled. "I may have been isolated, but my mother imparted much womanly wisdom while she was with me. I am not unprepared."

She could see his relief. As she recalled all of her mother's advice, her smile turned to a grin. Alcaeus really was finely equipped. That meant Maerea would enjoy this even more.

Her smile turned shy, though, as he lowered his body over hers. The hair on his chest touched her nipples. He brought his mouth to hers again and plunged his tongue inside. Even as she opened her lips for him, she pressed her legs together.

His thumb found the seam where her knees were locked tight against each other. Coaxing her apart, he placed his hand on the inside of one of her knees, as if staking a claim.

He eased her legs farther apart with that hand until there was room for his body between them. She was still savoring this new closeness when he released her mouth. She gasped as he exhaled, his breath sweeping warmly over her bare breasts.

When he put his mouth to her breast, her head snapped back on the pillow, and she had to clench her teeth to keep from making a sound. He performed the same adulations upon her nipple as he had upon her lips.

His tongue swirled around the peak, then lapped at it. Then he was sucking her, drawing at that raw point of pleasure over and over again. She focused on trying to breathe.

Her back arched, and he slid an arm under her so he could hold her to him. Draped over his arm, her breasts served up to him, she let her head fall back, her lips parted in wonder.

He started on her other breast. Her hands found purchase on his shoulders. Her legs tucked together again, this time tightening around him. The pleasure he sparked at her breast flared to life in her womanhood, and her hips lifted, molding against his body. A long moan escaped her.

"How sweetly you warm to me," he said.

Warm? She was aflame. He seemed to know, for his hand slipped between them and ran, unerringly, up the inside of her thigh toward the center of her need. He slid his finger and thumb up and down the lips of her womanhood, teasing sensation through her curls, and flicked his tongue over her breast.

It was even more than she had imagined. If she just wouldn't ruin it by wanting it too much. He would think less of her if she was licentious. Everything was going to so well. She could not bear to lose his admiration.

She trembled and squeezed her legs tighter, bracing herself against his body. He was obviously enjoying tasting her breast and touching her curls. She could keep her head while he did so.

But then he slipped a finger into her folds. The tender invasion felt strange and thrilling. His finger explored her, as if getting to know her and introducing her to the feel of him. She gazed up at the ceiling, pressing her lips together over her panting breaths, while she marveled. His touch stirred her everywhere, but when he roamed over certain places, the intensity shocked her.

His finger settled near the top of her sheath and swirled around a tiny spot there. Oh, goddess. *There.*

Not even her mother's frank guidance had prepared her for this. Something that she'd never known was inside her now awoke with a vengeance. Her entire body came to life. Her head tossed, and she bit her lip hard.

He teased the little bud of flesh with quick, rhythmic flicks of his finger, then circled it slowly, applying a touch of pressure. She swallowed the moans that wanted out of her.

His thumb joined his finger, and he rolled that point of pleasure between them. Her hips leapt up, pushing into his touch. She tightened her hands on his shoulders, fighting to regain her self-control.

But his touch was relentless. He worked that sensitive spot. The pleasure built and built inside her. Her limbs went taut as bowstrings. Her inner walls tightened to a sharp ache.

She held on. Long, immeasurable moments passed of their rough breaths and the crackle of the fire and the pleasure. Tears trickled from the corners of her eyes. It was unbearable, but she wanted it to last forever.

When his fingers slid out of her, they trailed a warm, damp path over the inside of her thigh, smearing her skin with her own fluids. He moved up her body, the firelight playing over the angles of his face and the planes of his chest.

Now, at last, he would join with her and seal their union. She would know how it felt. It would be over soon, and she would come through it with her dignity intact.

It would be over soon. But they would do it again.

He studied her face. "You're crying."

Oh, no. No, she would not ruin this. "It doesn't hurt."

"I promised to stop your tears. What did I do?"

"Everything you've done has been… I'm fine." She tried to swipe away the betraying tears, her womanhood still coiled painfully tight. If only he would keep touching her.

"Then why the tears?"

She could feel her blush spreading up her forehead and down her collarbone. A slow smile spread across his face.

His sudden touch upon her point of pleasure took her by surprise before she could collect herself. She cried out. Then just as quickly pressed her hand to her mouth, biting down on her finger.

But he didn't look shocked. His smile widened. "I'll carry you over the edge yet."

With his free hand, he pulled hers from her face. He put the finger she'd bitten into his mouth and sucked, drawing it slowly out again. She watched him, mesmerized by the dueling sensations from one end of her body to the other.

He lowered his mouth to hers once more. The rhythm of his tongue matched that of his hand. Then he was kissing his way down her body. Her throat. Her breasts. Her belly. Claiming her with his mouth everywhere his hands had touched her.

He kept going. Downward. Downward. When she thought he would stop, his breath swept over her skin below her navel.

"Do you trust me?" he asked once more.

"Yes."

He braced his palms on the inside of her thighs and spread her legs wider apart. She let him, wanting to oblige him, hungry for the feeling. And it felt so good to lay like this, open and throbbing.

"You only need more pleasure," he said. "I'll give you as much as you need, until it's enough."

His mouth descended upon her womanhood. His lips soft, his stubble rough, his tongue plumbing her. She gasped, then the breath rushed out of her on a moan as he fastened onto her pleasure point and suckled her.

Whatever control she thought she had evaporated in a haze. She rolled up onto her elbows, her hands bunching in the bedclothes. Her heels skidded over the bed, while he held her legs down.

He picked up his pace, ravishing her with his mouth. Her jaw dropped, and the tears flowed freely from her eyes.

The spear of tension inside her let fly. She called out as her body heaved against his mouth. Wave upon wave of pleasure arced through her, throwing her back onto the bed. Long, hard spasms released something from deep within her, wringing her out, rocking her hips against his hands.

He sucked and licked her through every tremor, driving her into the next. And the next. Ragged cries of relief tore out of her, one after another.

At last she became aware of the damp bedclothes under her, her sore throat and limp, trembling limbs. She breathed in the quiet darkness with her husband's face resting on the inside of her thigh.

He slid up next to her in the bed with a cocky smile she'd never seen on his face. "I think my lady enjoys the pleasures of the marriage bed."

She turned her face away. "You must think me wanton after that display."

He turned her chin so she looked at him again. "I think I am more fortunate in my choice of a bride than I knew."

She gasped, then they laughed together. He positioned his body over hers once more. They were still chuckling and smiling at each other when he slid inside her.

So natural. The pinching pain was so brief compared to all the long, wearying pain she had endured in her life. And then they were one.

She felt her body stretching for him. He felt even larger than he looked. Smooth and measured, he stroked in, then back, in, then back, never fully withdrawing, but easing himself deeper into her.

He watched her face, as if vigilant for her tears. But they had dried.

She smoothed her hands over his hair and shoulders, savoring the look on his face. Fierce. Determined. Hungry. "Husband."

"My wife."

He was almost buried to the hilt. She pulled her knees up higher to give him room, and his hips bunched, pressing down. Their bodies slid into a perfect fit, hers cradling him, his covering her. She could see on his face that he felt it too.

That fit became a perfect rhythm. They rose and fell together, sighing into each other's mouths. This time the sensations building inside her were sweet. They overflowed all at once, and her body found release again. He thrust into the undulations of her hips as she voiced her astonishment with every sigh.

His hard length moved easily through her wet, languid channel. But each motion made her hum tighter inside. Her body's resistance increased, and with it, the pleasure. Each time he pulled back, expression eddied over his face, and his muscles tensed, before he sheathed himself fully in her again.

"You don't have to hold back," she rasped.

"Your first time should be gentle."

"It doesn't hurt. You don't have to go slowly."

A smile flickered across his face. He shut his eyes, his hair falling across his forehead with the motion of his body. "Are you asking me to make love to you harder, Maerea?"

She gave up, arching into him in invitation. "*Yes.*"

He grimaced in pleasure. Her desire pleased him. He wanted her. Wanted her to want him.

His strokes became long, hard thrusts, his muscles rippling as his body worked upon her. She matched him, bracing her feet on the bed and rocking her hips to meet him. Goddess, the way he rubbed her point of pleasure…how deeply he penetrated…the weight of his body upon her…

"Enough?" he asked.

"More?" she wondered.

He pumped into her in rapid thrusts that pinned her to the bed. Beyond making a sound, she could only pant beneath him, writhing on his erection. The bedposts shivered with his every move.

She fell hard over the peak, her womanhood clamping around him. The grip and release, so good with him filling her, with him to hold. He gave an exultant shout and drove down into her once more, his body rigid upon her.

But what erupted inside her was warm and soft. Life, flowing between them. His seed, filling her womb.

He collapsed on top of her. She relaxed under his weight. In a moment he bestirred himself and rolled to the side, tucking her into his embrace.

He checked her face for tears again, and seeing none, let her rest her face against his chest. He ran his hand through her hair. "I never expected you, my bluebird."

chapter seven

THE FIRE DANCE

MAEREA LAY ENTWINED WITH him, skin to slick skin, reveling in every ache and exhausted muscle. A confession bubbled out of her. "I hope I'm with child already."

So this was what contentment looked like on Alcaeus's face. "There's a fine image. You with our child in your arms."

"I know we're getting a late start. But we've time enough. I'll bear you a strong line."

"We don't have to worry about a strong line, bluebird. Just a happy one."

Thoughts from beyond his embrace intruded. She didn't want to let them in. But there was no denying their children would be born of both sides of the feud. The nieces and nephews of his father and brother's murderer.

"You'll be happy for me to be the mother of your children?"

"You'll be a wonderful mother."

The feud was not what he saw when he looked at her.

He framed her face in his hands. "I won't have our children raised to feud. Anyone who fills their head with such will learn the error of his ways, and I will teach him with my sword, if I must. I want peace and safety for you and ours. You won't have time for sad memories if you're too busy chasing our brood around the house."

He pulled her back into their visions of the future. "I've always dreamed of a house full of children."

"I'll give you as many as you like. You have but to ask."

She grinned. "Keep on like this, and I won't have to ask. We'll have children aplenty."

"A fine plan." He ran his hand over her hip. "After you are no longer sore."

But the rest of the night satisfied them in a different way. She had never imagined they would spend so much of their wedding night just laughing and whispering to each other. They had both been alone so long. It would be a long time before they got enough.

She hoped he never got enough. How she hoped this would last.

It would last, she vowed. She would devote herself to this, to him, and they would build a lifetime of something real out of this dreamlike day.

He pulled her back against his hard chest, tucking her buttocks into the curve of his body and her thighs against his muscular ones. He stretched an arm out over her, pointing out the window. "Look there."

The eastern horizon was awash in rosy hues.

"This is the eastern side of the castle," he said, "the perfect place to watch the sunrise…but an even better one to watch the sunset."

"It's more beautiful than the view from the cliffs."

They lay fondling each other and watched the sky turn slowly to dusky blue.

"There's something I want to show you," Maerea said.

When she got out of bed, he made a playful protest and grabbed for her. Laughing, she skipped away from him. She went to one of her trunks and retrieved her bluebird box before hurrying back to bed and the warmth of his body.

He sat up next to her against the headboard, wrapping his arm around her. He grinned and nuzzled her temple. "Are you going to show me what's inside your treasure box?"

"You just plundered all its secrets. I might as well show you what's in this box, too." They shared another burst of laughter.

She opened the latch he had repaired to raise the lid of the box. She ran her fingers through the bright red scraps inside. Little squares and diamonds cut from long lengths of ribbon. She smiled at the memory of them twirling and dancing around her on the breeze.

"Festival ribbons," he said. "Tokens from a treasured time?"

She nodded. "Right before my mother's illness. She and Bria took me to the Garland Festival to celebrate my womanhood."

"That's one of Chera's most sacred holidays. I know how much it must have meant to you."

"We had such fun. It seemed these ribbons were floating on the air everywhere. I filled my hands with them, as if I could capture it all. This box was a gift from Mother that day. She was so happy."

"And so were you."

"It seemed I could feel my entire future ahead of me, and all of it so bright."

"I'm sorry you had to wait so long. But the future you sensed that day? It has finally begun."

ALCAEUS HAD THOUGHT HE would spend their first night as husband and wife burning for Maerea and keeping company with his honor. Instead, he had enjoyed the miraculous discovery that they were a match in bed, as in everything else. Actually, he had enjoyed many miraculous discoveries as he had acquainted himself with her body. But she would still be sore this morning.

"Are you certain you feel like riding today?" he asked.

She gave him a private smile. The wind dipped into the courtyard, trying to pull her hair from her headband. "I don't mind."

"I will have to keep an eye on you, to make sure you aren't putting on a brave face for my sake."

She laughed. "I am not."

"No more brave faces for you. No more grief or shutting your hopes in a tiny box. I will make you happy."

"You do," she said, low and warm.

He whispered in her ear. "Is bed one place I can do that?"

She turned her blushing face away from the bystanders in the courtyard. "I think you know the answer to that."

"Hmm. I may need you to show me the answer again." And again and again, until he released all the unrequited longings she had harbored for so many years.

She raised an eyebrow at him. "Are you certain *you* wish to do this sort of riding today, my lord?"

"Alas, duty calls." Grinning, he handed her up onto the mare he had chosen for her. He swung up onto his tall riding gelding, and they set off. "Thank you for being willing to tour the domain with me so soon."

"I'm looking forward to seeing your work."

He took her along the road that circled through the village, putting on another display. She smiled and waved, receiving bows and greetings with her characteristic grace. The people might find her even more impressive in the plain blue gown she wore today, which made her look like the hardworking lady she was. He couldn't keep his eyes off her. Let that send its own message to everyone.

He tried not to consider the painful contrast between his sweet, open wife putting herself before strangers and his sister-in-law, weeping in her rooms, shut away from their people.

"Can I do aught else to ease your worries this morning, husband?" Maerea asked.

"Remember what I said, bluebird. You needn't try. Tell me, do you like the mare?"

Maerea stroked the horse's neck. "She's lovely. You must thank whomever I am borrowing her from."

He had bought the pretty chestnut palfrey for breeding, but was even happier to provide her to his wife. "She's one of my horses. And now yours. She's sweet-natured, but strong. I think you two will get along perfectly."

"Oh, Alcaeus. A horse like this is a magnanimous gift."

"She hardly counts as a gift. Everything that is mine is yours."

She reached over to touch his hand. "Not all husbands see it that way."

"They should."

"With you, I feel like everything is a gift."

The entire day felt like a gift to him. He acquainted her with as many of Salicina's affairs as he could on their first day. She listened with interest and understanding. Even when he waxed on about crossing grains to get new varieties, which always bored everyone he knew. She had many insightful suggestions, just as he'd known she would. She didn't hesitate to speak her mind, either, clearly relishing the possibilities of having so much more to work with.

"No wonder you didn't marry before now," she said as they rode through the apple orchard. "You've been too busy."

"Starvation is the exception, rather than the rule in recent times. It takes vigilance to ensure our people don't meet that fate. I'm grateful we've been able to secure the prosperity we have."

"The feuds have left many fields trampled." She looked around at the peaceful, orderly trees. "Strange that our reprieve came as a result of our fathers' age and infirmity."

"My father always seemed surprised, but peace is profitable."

"We will make my brother see that."

He halted his horse at a fork in the path. "Shall I show you the West Field?"

She gave a solemn nod.

He urged his horse to a faster gait, and she kept pace with him. In silence, they covered the ground. Moving in tandem with her across the land, too slow for haste, too fast for conversation, he could easily forget what they raced toward.

He brought them to the low ridge that bordered the field. They drew rein, and she looked out at it, the infamous center of all their troubles.

Both their grandfathers had died here. So had his father and brother.

The midday sun shone down on the green field, lighting up the hints of gold that were appearing in the ripening wheat. Men, women, and children were hard at work rooting out any weeds that might threaten the crop. They expected an excellent harvest come autumn, gods willing. The low stone fences and copses of trees Alcaeus had added around the field continued to protect the soil year after year. The rich land and all it yielded to feed hungry mouths belied the blood that soaked the soil.

Maerea reached over and took his hand. As if by unspoken agreement, they sat there together and observed a moment of silence. For both their fallen.

Then her gaze lifted beyond the field, to the tiny gray castle in the distance. "Castra Lapidea looks so small and far away from here." Her shoulders relaxed, and the lines of tension on her face all but disappeared.

She would be happy here. With him. "What else would you like to see?"

She turned to him again. "Show me your favorite place on your land."

"It will be a perfect spot to stop for a meal. Are you hungry?"

"Ravenous."

They left the West Field behind, circling back toward the castle in a wide arc that took them to the old willow tree. They settled their horses to graze nearby, and he slung his saddlebag over his shoulder. When he reached for her hand, she smiled at him, banishing all his solemn thoughts. Hand-in-hand, they strolled into the shelter of the willow's low-hanging branches, which brushed the ground.

"Our festival pavilion, my lady." He spread out the blanket for them, then unpacked wine, bread, and a length of sausage. "Not tired of pork yet, I hope?"

"Never!" She lit into the meal with the same enthusiasm as the night before.

He would gladly watch her feast like this for the rest of their lives, knowing he could ensure she never went hungry again. Also, it was a pleasure to watch her eat. It brought things to his imagination. Maerea had proved enthusiastic in bed, eager to please and be pleased. He suspected she would enjoy trying many things.

She caught him watching her and blushed again. He loved knowing she blushed all the way to her nipples in the heat of passion. Everything—the wine, the food, the air—tasted sweeter, now that he knew the taste of her.

"This is a beautiful place," she said. "No wonder it's your favorite."

"We've come here for many occasions over the years. Riding lessons, tree climbing—broken arms."

She made a sympathetic noise.

"When my arm healed, Father brought my brother and me out here together and showed us the best way to get as high in the tree as you can, which his father had shown him." Alcaeus's throat tightened suddenly, his eyes stinging. He forged ahead anyway. "My brother and I used to spar out here. Whoever won the match was 'Lord of the Tree.'"

That feeling ambushed him, like he would never breathe again.

And Maerea was there, sliding under his arm, soft and close against his side. Strong enough to lean on. "How many tears do you never weep?"

"Too many people rely on me. I don't need tears, just work."

"So I have said to myself for years. I had to learn it's not weak to let them fall. It's wise."

He didn't want tears when he could have her instead. "We hold all the festival dances here."

"The first day of summer is only three days away."

He and Maerea had never danced together, he realized. "I wish we hadn't canceled the Summer Solstice festivities this year."

"You're in mourning." Such gentle fingers combing through his hair.

He let his head fall to rest on her shoulder. "No one comes out here anymore."

"We will come here together."

He seized her hand again and pulled her to her feet. "Dance with me. Here and now."

She took his other hand, completing the ring of their arms. "The wind shall be our minstrel, and the sunset our festival bonfire."

He spun her into the Fire Dance. They twirled and clapped, pranced and leapt as if Summer Solstice were already here and with it, all the warmth of the season. She gazed upon him as if he had won every contest at the tournament, and she would kiss his wounds when they were alone. With no one watching, they wove the ritual steps tighter and tighter, turning the sacred into the intimate. They danced within the circle of each other's arms, then body-to-body, and they moved together in perfect tandem, as they had in the night.

They danced and danced until peace stole over him, as he had never expected to feel again. As he had never felt it before.

"My lord. My lord!" The sound of hoofbeats and a soldier's voice reached them across the field.

Alcaeus gritted his teeth. The afternoon was warm, the woman in his arms more so. He felt the unfamiliar urge to ignore the summons and hide with Maerea here under the tree.

She drifted to a halt, her face tired again.

"I'll see what the matter is." He held her an instant longer, then released her and strode to the edge of the willow branches. But she did not wait for him under the tree. She stayed at his side.

A mounted guard awaited them, he and his horse both winded.

"What's the matter?" Alcaeus asked.

The young man leapt down from the saddle and bowed. "A messenger has come from Lady Maerea's brother."

She wrapped her arm around Alcaeus. "Gerrian is back already?"

Alcaeus pulled her closer. "Did he return to Lapidea alone?"

"It appears so, my lord, according to our scouts."

No new allies, then. The only good news. "Have the messenger wait in the great hall, and offer him our hospitality."

"It will be done, my lord." The guard mounted and raced back toward Castra Salicina.

Maerea gazed after him. Her face seemed made of stone.

"Don't be afraid, bluebird. However Gerrian reacts, we will weather through this. You are my wife now, by law and in the eyes of the gods. He can't take you from me."

A breath rushed out of her. "How you banish my worst fear with a few words. You're right. I have nothing to be afraid of."

He held her tightly despite his reassuring words. She clung to him, despite her brave ones. The hours ahead were the edge of a knife.

chapter eight

THE WEST FIELD

When Alcaeus entered the great hall with Maerea on his arm, Gerrian's messenger watched their display attentively. Good.

She spared the young soldier a benevolent smile. "How is your mother's rheumatism?"

He came to his feet and bowed, sneaking the last bite of his food in his mouth. "Getting better, as the days get longer, thank you, my lady."

Alcaeus tucked Maerea closer. "With more blankets and firewood, I hope this winter will be easier for her."

"Thank you for your generosity, husband." She touched his arm.

He looked at the messenger. "What message does your lord, my brother-in-law, send to us?"

"My lord has been informed of your marriage. He wishes to meet with both of you this very day, in peace, to discuss the terms of his lady sister's bride price."

Alcaeus exchanged a look with Maerea. The hope he saw in her eyes pained him. Gerrian had best do right by her. If he did not, he would learn what Alcaeus did to men who failed to treat his wife as she deserved.

The messenger went on, "My lord invites you to enjoy the hospitality of his hall to celebrate his sister's marriage."

Her hand tightened on Alcaeus's arm in warning. In agreement, he covered her hand with his. This could be a trap. He would not deliver her into her brother's grasp that easily, or risk getting himself ambushed by Gerrian's men. But Alcaeus couldn't invite the bastard here, either. He wouldn't let that man under the same roof as Domitia and Aemilian ever again.

There was only one solution. "Tell your lord we are grateful for his hospitality, but I am eager to deliver my lady's bride price as a show of goodwill. Would he meet us in on the border of Lapidea and Salicina, where we may make amends before celebrating?"

"I will deliver your request to my lord and return with his answer."

"Give my brother my love," said Maerea. "Tell him that once he and my husband meet in celebration, my happiness will be complete."

As soon as the messenger left, Alcaeus turned to Maerea. "Do you take Gerrian at his word?"

"No. He will come prepared for conflict. He won't trust your intentions. But when I talk with him, I'll be able to make him see the reality of the situation. Once he understands who you are to me, we can negotiate."

"He must see that the West Field will give him a foundation for better fortunes, which will win the attention of new allies, which will improve his status."

Maerea gave a nod. "We have the advantage. We hold everything he desires. He'll realize it is better to lay down his sword."

How Alcaeus prayed she was right. "I have preparations to make."

―――

Maerea could do nothing but sit in the great hall and wait. The hour stretched on, unbearable. The servants offered her something to eat, but she declined, her belly roiling. Instead, she asked them about their families and their roles in the household. At last, the preparations for possible battle called every one of them away.

In the quiet hall, Maerea heard the barest scuff of a little foot. She glanced toward the sound. Rosy cheeks. Curious eyes. That's all she could glimpse before the child ducked under the far end of the table.

As quietly as she could, Maerea rose from her seat. She tiptoed to the little fellow's hiding place and bent to peer underneath the table.

He gasped and froze. Light brown hair. A tunic too fine for a page. He had a miniature version of what must be the Salicinian nose. His father and uncle must have had that in common.

Maerea fought the overwhelming urge to gather the child into her arms and hold on for dear life. Instead, she straightened and gave him a curtsy. "Lord Aemilian."

After a moment's hesitation, he scrambled out from under the table, then stood up with as much dignity as a dusty, mussed boy could achieve.

"Your Uncle Alcaeus never stops talking about you, he is so very proud of you."

"He…he is?"

"Doesn't he tell you so?"

"Well, yes, but…"

Maerea knelt down on Aemilian's eye level. "You are an honorable young man who tries hard to do the right thing, I can see. You love your uncle very much, don't you?"

Aemilian's hands tightened into fists. "I will never let anything happen to him. What powers do you have, my lady?"

"The same ones your mother has. We ladies can be fierce when defending our families."

"Then…you are not a witch?"

Maerea bit back a sigh and gave his serious question a serious answer. "No, Lord Aemilian, I am not a witch or a sorceress."

Aemilian scratched his head. "My mother has said my uncle married a witch. That doesn't sound like something Uncle Alcaeus would do. Unless you're a good witch."

"I have not a drop of magic, but if I did, I would use it for good, like Daughter Pherakia. I am sure your mother and I can clear this confusion when we become better acquainted."

Aemilian gave her a pretty bow and kissed her hand. "Welcome to our home, my lady."

It was Aemilian who seemed to have magic. All the trials and coldness of her arrival at Salicina vanished, dispelled by his guileless touch. "Would you like to call me Aunt Maerea?"

"Uncle Alcaeus said you were good and kind, and that you are my aunt now."

She took both Aemilian's hands. Such little hands, which must grow strong enough to do a warrior's work one day. If only they could stay this soft forever. "You and I have something very important in common, Aemilian. I will also do anything to protect your Uncle Alcaeus."

Aemilian glanced around them. They were still alone. "Then you know why I had to come and see you for myself. Please don't tell my nurse. Mama said I was not to leave my rooms."

"You were only trying to protect your uncle. You and your secret are perfectly safe with me. But next time, you must mind your mama, all right?"

"Yes, Aunt Maerea."

Alcaeus's tread, already familiar to her, announced his return. The man who had worn no blade as he courted her, who loved nothing better than to talk of wheat varieties, entered fully armored. He wore gleaming mail and a golden surcoat embroidered with the eagle of Salicina, and he carried a sword in its scabbard.

Her husband was also this warrior she now saw before her. He usually wore his strength beneath his kindness, but today, his strength must show on the outside.

"Aemilian," he said with surprise.

Maerea winked at the boy. "Lord Aemilian came to the great hall to welcome me. Wasn't that noble of him?"

The boy stared at Alcaeus's armor. "Where are you going, Uncle?"

Alcaeus came to their sides and scooped up Aemilian, balancing the boy on his hip. "Maerea and I are going to celebrate our wedding with her family."

"Why aren't we celebrating here?"

"We will. When Maerea and I come home, we'll have a wonderful feast, I promise." Alcaeus hid his face in the boy's hair, clutching him close.

Maerea rose to her feet and slid under Alcaeus's other arm. Aemilian smelled of honey cakes and his bath, Alcaeus of steel. His scabbard bumped against her skirts.

"Thank you for helping your Aunt Maerea feel at home." Alcaeus looked into his nephew's face. "I'm so proud of you."

Aemilian sat up straighter in his uncle's embrace. "I'll take care of Mama while you're gone."

"Thank you." Alcaeus was quiet for a long moment, just holding them. At last he seemed to force his words out. "I just spoke with your mother. She'd like it if you keep her company until Maerea and I return."

It didn't sound as if Alcaeus had succeeded in making peace with Domitia. The looming confrontation with Gerrian must have made matters worse. Her son was surely her only comfort in this hour.

Alcaeus set Aemilian down. The boy clung to his leg a moment longer, before turning around and darting out the door to the family wing. Alcaeus watched him go.

"Alcaeus…was Aemilian there…when Gerrian came?"

He hesitated so long, she knew the answer before he said it. "Yes."

"Gods." Her gaze fell to the sheathed sword in his hand. "I tried to stop him. But even I didn't know what he planned to do, I swear it."

"I know."

"Tell me what happened that day."

"I have no kind words for Gerrian, and I wish only to speak kind words to you."

"I need to know."

His gaze swept the room, as if looking for ghosts in the corners. "We were here in the great hall. The entire family together. Gerrian arrived at the gates in some kind of rage. We didn't know what to make of that. We'd heard nothing from your family in years. Then suddenly here he was, issuing a challenge. And my father…he laughed. Told them to bring the whelp in, so he could teach him a lesson in manners."

"Oh, gods."

"My father won his last duel with yours, when he took the West Field. He assumed Gerrian's skill would be the same, his experience less."

Her brother had taken out his grief on a poor old man. Gerrian must know, deep in his heart, there was no honor in that. Did he really have it in him to target a child next?

"My father *let* Aemilian watch." Alcaeus's voice faltered.

She touched a hand to his lips. "But it was my brother who *made* him watch."

Alcaeus's gaze fell. "Gerrian's messenger returned just now, while I was assembling the men in the courtyard. He has agreed to meet us."

The moment was upon them. "Is my horse ready?"

"I would rather you stayed here."

"What? We already agreed we would meet him together."

"I can make our case to him. Petition him for your hand, as I ought."

"I must be there to reason with him. He'll listen to me."

"You would be safer here, if anything goes wrong."

"If anything goes wrong, my place is at your side." She took his hand in both of hers.

She couldn't believe that mere days ago, she had not known this man. Now their vows felt like invisible cords in the air between them, unseverable. What they had done with their bodies felt like an imprint on her flesh.

And a mark somewhere much deeper. "I will not be parted from you."

How gently he spoke the worst truths. "This encounter could easily turn violent. I would do anything—have done everything I can to prevent crossing swords with your brother. But he may cross swords with me."

"I won't let that happen. You and I did this together, accepted the risks together. I will see it through."

"I promised you no more grief, bluebird."

"You have given me nothing but happiness." She willed her tears away. She had wept enough. Today, she would act. "I am coming with you."

He clasped her to him, his hand behind her head, and kissed her. In that kiss, she could feel all the fears he would not speak. She couldn't hide her own. But she could show him her love with her mouth and tongue and touch.

He rested his forehead on hers. "We have a plan in place in case you need to escape. You must promise me you will follow it. Promise me. If I have to fight, I must know you're not in danger."

If her safety distracted him for even an instant, it could cost them everything. "I promise."

He held out his sword to her. "This was my father's. My brother took it up the day he died. I had it placed in the armory for Aemilian, but it falls to me to wield it this day. Will you put it on for me, my lady?"

She opened her hands. He rested the sword across her palms. She felt the weight of it travel up her arms.

His father had fought for his life with this sword. This was the weapon his brother had taken from their father's body and also died wielding. Against her brother.

Now Alcaeus asked if she would arm him with it.

"It is in the most honorable of hands." Letting him see the pledge in her eyes, she strapped his sword on him.

～

Maerea tried to take the clouds as a sign from her patroness. One of Chera's storms was gathering over Salicina, dimming the god of war's light. But the change of weather seemed to cast a morbid air over the fields that had been so sunny earlier that day.

She shook the feeling off and sidled her horse closer to Alcaeus's. The border drew nearer.

He hadn't brought enough guards to throw down the gauntlet, but Gerrian would take their escort seriously. More of Alcaeus's men waited just over the hill, hidden in the orchards, should he need them.

He wouldn't. She must see to it. Her brother and her husband would not do battle this day.

She broke the silence of their procession. "When I was nine, I went out to gather wild plants for medicines and recipes. I took a nasty fall in the ravine and couldn't climb back out. Gerrian slid down through an entire patch of fire nettle to rescue me, then carried me out. His skin was raw for weeks afterward. And then, when I was fourteen, and Mother…" The pall over the landscape made her skin crawl. "He didn't leave my side for…I don't know how many days. We spent every waking moment together, and he slept in my hearth room with his sword across his knees. As if his blade was some use against illness and grief."

As if her reminiscences had conjured him, she saw the familiar figure of her brother ahead. He waited on horseback, flanked by guards in faded gray that had once been Lapidean silver. His escort appeared comparable to theirs in size.

But they had not waited at the border. They had positioned themselves in the middle of the West Field.

Alcaeus swore under his breath. "We must enter the field to get within speaking distance."

"Where are the workers?"

"I sent them home earlier…just in case."

"But that still leaves the harvest vulnerable." Maerea didn't take her eyes off Gerrian. "I think it would be most beneficial if I speak to him first."

"I trust your judgment," Alcaeus replied.

Gerrian and Alcaeus were about to meet.

Her husband's party rode toward her brother's. They halted, facing each other. A gust of wind swept through the wheat.

Maerea had no sword. She wielded a smile. "Brother. It's good to see you."

"Imagine my astonishment when you were not at home to see me upon my return."

"Forgive our haste. I waited so long for marriage. Can you blame me for my eagerness?"

His horse shifted restlessly under him, flicking its tail. She would know the look on his face anywhere. That anger could lash out of him as quickly as his sword could leap from his scabbard.

She kept her smile out. "Did you imagine you would ever see your sister married? Will you not congratulate me?"

"Your husband has said he wishes to make amends before we celebrate. A wise offer, as I did not promise you to him, and he paid no bride price."

Alcaeus bowed from the saddle. "Well met, brother-in-law."

Gerrian's jaw clenched.

"Your sister has made me the most fortunate of men. A woman of her grace and character is worth any sacrifice. I am prepared to put all our differences behind us in the name of my union with Maerea. For her bride price, I offer you the West Field."

"Imagine what we can do with this land, brother. Our people will never go hungry again. My husband has even been forbearing enough to defer his brother's life price for seven seasons, so we may first restore our fortunes."

"He has extracted the highest price from you, sister. I do not see how I owe him anything."

The whir meant nothing to her ears at first. Not until she heard the impact. One of Alcaeus's men dropped from the saddle, an arrow in his chest. She ducked low against her horse's neck, her gaze darting to her husband.

He was unharmed, his sword in his hand, silver against the gray sky. "Maerea, ride."

Every instinct in her screamed that she should stay with him. But her part of the battle was over.

She had failed.

She spun her horse around. The mare was as strong as Alcaeus had promised. She stretched out her neck, forging back through Alcaeus's soldiers as they charged forward to meet Gerrian's. The stone fence ahead. Once over it, they would ride hard for the castle.

She cleared the fence and let mare run as fast as she dared down the ridge. The orchard there. She could hear Alcaeus calling for his reinforcements.

The men who surged from the trees wore green, not Salicinian gold. Their blades were bloodied. They surged toward her. She swerved her horse to dart around them.

They swarmed on all sides. One snared her mare's bridle. Another clamped his arm around Maerea's waist.

As they yanked her from the saddle, she screamed a warning. "Alcaeus! He has allies!"

"Maerea!" Her name. His war cry.

The strange soldier dragged her back up the ridge. She called out their numbers, position, and movements the entire way. She fought, trying every trick she'd seen Gerrian use in all the hours she'd watched him spar with Father. But the soldier was twice her size and well trained.

When he handed her up to another man, she found herself hauled across the commander's saddle. "Let me go!"

"I'm taking you home, my lady."

"This is my home."

The man who had protected her since the day she'd been born said nothing more. His grip was as strong as ever. He rode through the chaos.

Bodies. Shouts. The clang of steel. The wheat fell with a whisper. The horse's hooves flung up bits of the precious soil. She looked through the melee for a glimpse of Alcaeus.

There. In the middle of it all, still on his horse. His family sword arced and struck her brother's.

It was her husband's name that came to her lips. *"Alcaeus!"*

"Maerea!"

Someone she loved would die today. Whatever she said now would be the last words she ever got to say to him.

"Gerrian, don't do this."

"I'll kill him for touching you."

"Alcaeus, do what you must! Survive!"

The commander rode beyond the fray, and she lost her chance to say anything else that was in her heart.

⁓

Maerea watched the road from her window. She could see nothing through the dark of night.

Her body hurt from throwing herself against the door of her hearth room. It was no use. The commander would obey her brother's order to keep her "safe."

Her hands ached with cold. She couldn't tear her gaze from the window to stoke the fire. She had never felt so useless. The lady sitting in the tower while…

Thinking of what might be happening on the battlefield made her mind go blank and her stomach roil.

There. Torches. Figures on the road. A column of soldiers. At the head of the company…

Gerrian.

Sweat broke out on her skin, even as the wind chilled her.

The next few moments were a blur. Then suddenly the door was opening. Gerrian was there. He limped in and halted by her hearth, his face splashed with mud and blood.

She surged to her feet. As she advanced on him, his eyes widened, and he took a step back.

"Does my husband live?"

"Dead by my hand, like his father and brother before him."

She wanted to hurl herself at him. Take that sword, the blade that had killed Alcaeus, and swing it wildly. But she swayed on her feet. She groped behind her for her chair and sank into it.

The words dropped out of her, one at a time. "I am a widow."

"You are safe now. I have freed you from him."

"Safe?" She must have shouted, for he flinched. "I was safe with Alcaeus."

"This never should have happened!" her brother bellowed. "You should never have had to sacrifice yourself to one of them! A Salicinian—and *my sister*—! I would have killed him before he set foot here if I'd known you would be the cost. All I could do was make it right now."

She sat there, still as stone as he raged. At last her voice emerged again, a hiss she didn't recognize. "Is that what you think?"

"The commander and the mage assured me he didn't force you. That you did it because you thought to save us." His face twisted. "You didn't have to do it, Merry."

That name he used to call her when they were children. He hadn't said it in years. The sound of it made her throat close and her eyes burn.

He knelt before her and took her hand. In that moment, he felt like her brother who had always loved her. The feeling made her sick. That hand had killed Alcaeus.

She pulled away, clutching the arms of her chair.

Something like pain flickered in Gerrian's eyes. "If you'd only waited one more day…I was returning with the ally we need. Lord Drusus will honor his father's agreements with ours. He has come to court you."

"What? You were brokering a marriage for me? You said nothing."

"I didn't want to get your hopes up if I failed. I didn't want to disappoint you."

She slumped back in the chair, her head spinning.

"It's not too late," Gerrian said. "You can still marry Lord Drusus and have everything you wanted. Tell me the enemy didn't touch you. It doesn't matter if you were in his home. I'll believe the truth and silence anyone who questions your reputation."

"He was my husband." *Was.* The word dried her tears' final attempt.

She was done mourning.

She was angry.

She rose to her feet over Gerrian. "You never listen to me."

He knelt there, looking up at her, as if confused.

"Listen to me! You left me alone, with the enemy within riding distance. He could have done anything. Laid siege to us. Burned what little we had left. But when he came here, all he asked for was the life price. We agreed to negotiate."

"You should have told me he'd been here. I would never have left you again. I would have—"

"I know what you would have done! Why do you think I wanted you to go? You would have dueled him, and one of you would have died! Everything I did, I did to keep him from battling you. I couldn't bear the thought that I might lose you."

Gerrian sat back on his heels. "It's not your duty to protect me, Merry. I protect you."

"We didn't need protecting from him. He would have given you the West Field so we could prosper again. He would have let you repay him in time. We would all have had enough, without the need for violence."

Gerrian clambered to his feet. He loomed over her now. "There was always going to be violence. What do you think I needed allies for? I was always going to end his line. When his domain is mine, we will never want for anything."

She took a step back from him, her knees coming up fast against the chair, trapping her.

His hand closed around the hilt of Father's sword. "You didn't have to protect me. He could never have defeated me, just as his father and brother could not. My swordsmanship is all I have, but it's all I need."

She didn't recognize his voice. The look on his face. She had never seen them in her hearth room. Had they always been there in the drills with Father, in the hours when he was among the men?

"Did you doubt I would fulfill Father's last wish?" Gerrian asked. "His lifelong cause. I was born for this. He honed me for it every day of my life. When Alcaeus was the only one standing in my way, why would I stay my hand?"

She voiced one more plea, watching for a glimpse of her brother in the hateful man before her. "I thought you would stay your hand for me."

"I've done everything for you."

She shook her head. Then she reached out and drove her palms against his chest. He staggered back, and she could move again.

"I *chose* him, Gerrian. I wanted him. Because he was a good man. We consummated our marriage, and everyone at Salicina and Lapidea knows it. Tell Lord Drusus he can go to Hypnos, where he helped you send my husband. Now get out. *Get out!*"

chapter nine

THE SACRED OFFER

Iskhyra stood at the edge of the cliff and let out a cry of frustration. Centuries of clues. Years of painstaking research. Nights and nights of searching. All in vain.

Her shout echoed up to the stars and down across the ravine, for her ears alone. No one would hear the voice of a Hesperine wrapped as she was in veil spells. Her magical concealments ensured she would go unnoticed by mortals and her own people alike, whether she shouted or whispered.

Only her Goddess heard her. Hespera was her only companion on this quest. This had been Iskhyra's solitary calling since the night she had undertaken it. If anyone could turn this lost cause into a victory, it was she.

And yet, she had failed again.

She cast her auric senses out around her one more time, grasping for any hint of the magic she sought. It *had* to be here. She knew she was close. She had cross-referenced the written and oral accounts so carefully, and they all pointed to these cliffs.

But no blood magic answered the call of her own. What arrested her senses was a thread of pain.

The sudden touch of agony made her gasp. Someone was suffering, near enough that she could sense them in the Blood Union that connected Hesperines to everything with a beating heart. She opened her senses wider, pushed them farther, seeking the person whose distress had reached her like a plea for help.

A mortal presence. Fading. His heart wouldn't beat much longer.

Focusing on him, she stepped, letting her innate Hesperine power take her to him in the blink of an eye. A familiar stench hit her sensitive nose. Death.

She stood under a line of trees that bordered a field. Here was a scene she had beheld far too many times. Mortals lay slaughtered by their own countrymen. The air was heavy with sweat and fear. The soil was thick with their blood. Not the rich, living blood that tempted and sustained her. This was blood shed by violence, which only filled her with disgust and regret.

Tightening her veil spell around herself, she kept to the shadows and quickly assessed the situation. The battle was over, yet no one picked their way across the carnage to collect their comrades' remains or search for survivors. If no one was coming to rescue these men or give them their rites, it was allowable for her to intervene.

It was her sacred duty. Her personal quest must wait. The quest of all Hesperines fell to her tonight—to offer the Mercy to fallen mortals.

It was not for her to judge whether these men were innocent or guilty, friend or foe. Tonight, they were all her sacred charges, and what mattered was providing them as much dignity as she could.

With a heavy sigh, she waded through a stand of wheat, then levitated over bare, blood-soaked mud. She approached the man whose heartbeat was weakest. Rain slashed under her hood as she bent over him.

"Do not be afraid." She lowered her veil spell to reveal herself.

White rimmed his dilated pupils. His terror at the sight of her screamed through the Blood Union.

"Shhh. I mean you no harm. How can I make this easier for you? Do you wish to go swiftly to your gods—or do you seek a way to remain longer in this world?"

"Witch! Hypnos take you!"

She retreated, unwilling for the man to spend his last moments in fear of her. She left a blanket of magic over him that would soothe his pain. At least she could do that for him.

She went to each failing heart in turn. Their accusations hounded her across the field. Just like always. They shouldn't be able to get under skin as thick as hers.

She sank to her knees beside the last man, blood and mud soaking through her robes. The field was silent now, except for their two heartbeats and the rain. It was him. The one whose suffering had drawn her here.

As her magic came between him and his pain, his shallow breathing eased. She examined his belly wound. She knew a fatal injury when she saw one. No magic in the world could save him now, except Hespera's Gift.

"Do not be afraid," she tried one last time. "What is your name?"

He couldn't speak through the blood in his throat, but his name drifted to the surface of his thoughts.

"Alcaeus. Do you know why I am here?"

Thoughts, emotions, little shards of his life scattered and sliced through the Blood Union. She gathered that the victors in this battle had deliberately left the fallen for any Hesperine to find, intending it as a final indignity. Honorless vultures.

She would keep trying, even if Alcaeus was unlikely to understand she was not here to torture him, as mortals believed. She introduced herself, to help him see her as a person, not a specter. "I am Iskhyra. I promise you will not feel any more pain."

She tasted his fear in the rain, and his despair seeped into the ground. "Leave me be. Please. My honor is all I have left. Leave me that."

Goddess. Was there nothing she could do for him? She could endure blood and death, battle and pain. Just not helplessness.

Her gaze fell to the sword nearby. The sight went straight to her heart.

She restored his blade to him and helped him keep hold of it. She kept talking, trying to fill these moments with what mattered to him. His sword, his honor, his god.

But all his emotions centered on one image. Her strength and beauty seemed to fill the Blood Union, radiant in his memories. So there was someone he loved.

Love was powerful. Alcaeus's was not spent, it seemed, nor was his Will.

And so she made the sacred offer, although he would refuse. "The magic in my veins can restore you. I can offer you the Gift, Hespera's blessing of immortality. Do you understand?"

"Yes."

"I know this is a difficult decision for you. Whatever choice you make tonight will be the right one. You have lived with honor. You have no cause for regrets."

"I do regret…"

"What? Did you want revenge against your enemy?"

"No. I just wanted Maerea. She gave up everything for me. Now she will have nothing."

Maerea. So that was her name. "I can make it possible for you to help her."

"How, if your goddess demands my service?"

She shook her head, cursing the mages and their false teachings. "Hespera makes no demands. She gives. She will not change who you are. She will grant you the power to finish what you started. Power as you have never had before."

"I don't care about power. Only about Maerea."

"The Gift would give you a second chance with her."

He went quiet, although his emotions churned and his mind wrestled. Iskhyra waited, the rain slipping down her cheeks.

She had done all she could.

"Does it take long?" he asked.

Something burrowed under her skin. She almost didn't recognize it.

Hope.

It had been a long time.

She must help him be sure. She explained the Gifting as best she could while his blood slipped away.

He spoke at last, as if making a vow. "I will survive this night. I will not abandon Maerea. Do it. Give me your Gift."

He wanted her to Gift him.

She had to remember the ritual response. From some unused corner of her mind, the words came, strong and true. "Hespera hears your sacred request. In her name, I cannot refuse you. It is my honor to convey her Gift to you."

She gathered the fallen warrior in her arms and lifted him. So much lighter than most of the burdens she carried these days.

She had to get him to a Hesperine refuge. But she couldn't step with him. His body was too damaged to withstand magical travel.

Even Hesperine speed wouldn't get them to the nearest safe place for hours. Did Alcaeus have that much time? Goddess, she couldn't lose him when he had just chosen to live.

She wouldn't lose him.

"I am your Gifter now. You can rely on me."

She bared her fangs and heightened her senses. They didn't have time for interruptions. The first mortal, whether soldier or mage, who tried to get in her way tonight would find he had made a grave mistake.

Her heart pounded, a contrast to Alcaeus's fading pulse. "Stay with me. Maerea needs you. You have the strength."

He didn't respond.

"Stay with me!"

That was when she felt it.

It called to her, a whisper in the night. A sliver of light, an elusive shadow that promised deliverance.

Sanctuary magic.

She grasped at the faint power. Instead of slipping away, it bloomed. The inseparable duality of light spells and shadow wards unique to Sanctuary magic was as familiar to her as the blood in her veins.

There was only one place it could be coming from. The very one she sought.

The magic guided her like a beacon. She levitated away with Alcaeus, past trees and over fields, back toward the cliffs. To the very place she had been standing earlier when she had first sensed his pain.

Ancient power opened wide, as if it too understood his need. She beheld stately archways and columns carved into the bluffs. A tall stone door appeared in the cliffside and swung open before them.

The long-lost Hesperine Sanctuary had surrounded her all along.

She carried Alcaeus inside, where no living person had set foot in over fifteen hundred years.

─────

Alcaeus tasted blood. He smelled it, richer than wine. He felt it on his skin, more tempting than death.

But there was no battle here under the willow tree. Except the cheerful clang of his and his brother's swords.

Aemilius gave a breathless laugh. "You'll never win against me."

Alcaeus's arm ached from the new weight of the heavier sword father had recently awarded him. "It's been an hour, and you haven't won, either."

"Give me one more hour," Aemilus threatened with a smile, "and you'll be flat on your back."

Alcaeus grinned. "We were both still standing after two hours yesterday. But today is your temple day. Mother will never forgive us if we're late for the feast. Should we call it a draw?"

"A draw?" his brother scoffed. "I'm twelve now! Too old to surrender, especially to my little brother. I'll race you to the top of the tree. Whoever makes it to the highest branch first is the winner."

They sheathed their swords and ran for the trunk, each scrambling to get the best handholds. Alcaeus shimmed upward along the route he'd practiced, careful not to let his scabbard tangle in the branches.

Aemilius was stronger, and Alcaeus's sword was heavy. But he was lighter, faster. He overtook his brother quickly. At dinner, how proud he would be to tell Father he had won, even with his new blade.

The thrill of his imagined victory faded. This was his brother's temple day. It was Aemilius who should get to boast at the feast.

But if Alcaeus did not fight his hardest, Father would disapprove. And if Aemilius knew Alcaeus let him win, he would be furious.

Only one thing could be worse. The look of disappointment on Aemilius's face if he lost on his own temple day.

Alcaeus knew it was wrong, but he let his sword catch on a branch.

"Ha!" His brother shimmed past him and seized the highest limb.

Alcaeus hid his smile.

"I am Lord of the Tree and one day, of all Salicina!" Aemilius drew his sword and held it high, crowing over the rolling fields. Sunlight caught and gleamed on his blade.

But the world darkened, throbbing in time to Alcaeus's racing pulse. A tide of shadow and blood washed away those golden years and left him standing in the West Field.

He watched his brother fall, saw the soft green wheat part to embrace Aemilius. The powerful man lay still on the wet ground, rain spattering on his armor. Domitia threw herself over his body, her cheers during the battle now turned to wails of grief. Daughter Pherakia cradled his head on her lap, shedding silent tears over the wounds too dire for her to heal.

Aemilius had been Lord of Salicina for less than an hour. Now his body lay beside their father's.

Alcaeus looked from the sword in his brother's hand to the blade Gerrian held aloft in triumph.

"Take up the family sword," Gerrian demanded. "I will bury you next."

If Alcaeus did not fight his hardest, his father would disapprove.

"Will you stand there and hand me victory?" Gerrian taunted. "Avenge your father!"

If Aemilius knew Alcaeus let him win, he would be furious.

Gerrian sneered. "Your brother was no coward. Are you?"

Shame drove Alcaeus to his knees. Rage closed his hand around the grip of the sword.

"How will I tell him?" Domitia wailed. "How will I tell our son?"

She needed Alcaeus to tell little Aemilian that his father and grandfather were gone. The boy needed his uncle to make him feel safe when this day was through.

Alcaeus let go of the sword. He rose to his feet.

He was no coward. He was simply the last man standing between the enemy and his family, between Salicina and another war.

Alcaeus thought it was wrong, but he knew it was right as he let his sword lay on the ground.

He faced Gerrian. "Go."

Gerrian stood frozen, his gaze locked on Alcaeus's.

Alcaeus had left his sword and his honor in the dirt. All he had left was grief. So why did he see fear in Gerrian's eyes for the first time that day? What did the enemy see in Alcaeus that struck such terror in his heart?

No, sorrow was not all that remained in Alcaeus. He had the Will. To live. To protect.

"Go!" Alcaeus commanded.

Gerrian turned and fled.

Do what you must. *Survive.*

He had made the right choice.

The realization emerged like a pearl from a sea of blood.

Blood. Pounding under his skin, raging through his veins, running down his throat. Sickening and wondrous.

He had forgotten his body. Now it was awake.

Was he dying after all?

"Drink," a voice commanded.

Another vein, another swallow. How could warmth put out the fire? But it did. He needed more. It would take so much more to fill what he had lost.

"The worst is past. All you have to do now is drink."

No, the memories had not been the worst. This thirst. This was agony.

He could have done the easy thing. No more pain. No more effort. Sweet rest, eternal.

Do what you must. Survive.

He had made the right choice. He had survived.

For…her. Maerea.

He was alive. He could see her again.

His gums throbbed. Something sharp sliced his lip. With a roar of triumph, he bit down on the wrist pressed to his mouth, and his new fangs pierced his Gifter's flesh.

"Well done, warrior."

Iskhyra watched her newgift fall into his first Dawn Slumber. Alcaeus's face relaxed into hard-won peace.

What was she going to do with a newgift? How long would he need her? Where would he go once he was strong enough to leave her?

She had lost a lot of blood, and her quest was blown to bits like a spell had just exploded.

So why did she find herself smiling in wonder?

She touched a hand to the newborn Hesperine's brow and worked a cleaning spell. Glimmers of light traveled over his hair and skin, dissolving the mess of the battlefield and his first drink of her blood. She pulled a blanket over his naked, remade body.

At last she looked around her at the Sanctuary that had opened to his suffering. The spell lights still shone. Not a cobweb hung between the pillars. And from floor to ceiling, scrolls and more scrolls filled the shelves, fragrant of paper and ink, without a whiff of decay.

The answers she had sought for so long were here.

She had a little time before the Dawn Slumber claimed her as well. She should go out and seek the Drink from the animals and replenish herself. Alcaeus would need more blood when he awoke.

Instead, she dragged herself to her feet and started near the door. She would identify as many of the scrolls as she could before the night ended.

chapter ten

FOR GOOD OR EVIL

When the bleeding started, Maerea almost fainted on her way from her chair to the bed. She managed to get the rags she needed, but didn't dare take another step, even to beg the guards at her door to send for a healer.

Maerea curled in on herself, gritting her teeth against the knife of pain in her lower belly. She lay alone with her fear, trying to lock the dreadful truth out of her mind.

She wasn't sure how late it was when her bluebird box appeared in her hands. She stared at it. How had it gotten here? She lifted her gaze to see Bria sitting on the bed beside her.

"Oh, my dove." Tears made her voice waver.

"Bria? How did you escape? If anyone at Salicina harmed you—"

"Lady Domitia let me leave in peace with what I could carry."

"I'm so glad you're all right. I'm so glad you're here."

"I'm here, dove."

"I need a healer. Please. Can you convince the mage of Kyria to come, if not for my sake, then for Alcaeus's?"

For the first time, Maerea found the words for a prayer to Kyria. *Mother Goddess, don't let me lose his child. Please, Goddess, please.*

She must have lost consciousness, for she woke to the mage's cool palm on her forehead and Bria's warm grip on her hand. A strange force seemed to course through her, like soothing water running under her skin. Magic?

"You're not miscarrying." Daughter Pherakia's voice was matter-of-fact, but not unkind. "It's just your courses. Are they always this difficult?"

"No." No miscarriage. But no child.

Death had claimed everyone. Life couldn't even take hold inside her own body.

"Grief, then," Daughter Pherakia said. "Such an ordeal can make you bleed too much, too fast. My magic has returned things to normal now."

Maerea drew in a shaky breath. "Has the mage of Hypnos arrived yet?"

"Don't worry about that now, child. Try to rest."

"I can't miss my husband's funerary rites."

"There's no way to get you out of this castle. It was hard enough to get me in."

Maerea swallowed. "Put a lily on his tomb for me."

※

Maerea lifted her head from the pillow. Heavy. Dizzy. "Bria, how long have I been asleep?"

She might have slept through his burial.

"Rest is what you need now, dove." Bria had pulled her chair in next to the bed, along with her distaff and spindle. Maerea knew the look of a woman trying to keep busy to keep from going mad.

Maerea reached across and took her friend's hand. "I'm so sorry I had to leave you behind when they dragged me back here."

"If only I had the power to be in two places at once. I'm sorry you were alone here for even a moment."

"I was so worried about you. What if Domitia had taken out her anger on you? I might have lost you, too."

"You'll never lose me, dove. I made a promise, and I'll keep it."

"Was she very awful to you?"

Bria sighed. "She let me go unharmed."

"With nothing but what you could carry. Did she expect you to walk all the way back?"

"My knees and I might have had to make a go of it, if not for a donkey from the shrine."

"I begin to see the mage does have some Kyrian charity in her heart."

"Do not judge her by her harsh exterior. She has been hardened by… life's disappointments. Rakia is a good woman…one of the best."

Maerea blinked at her friend. Bria's use of the mage's shortened name didn't sound like an irreverence, as Maerea had first imagined. "You speak as if you know her well."

"We were close once." Bria's practical voice held a rare note of wistfulness. "I was not so hardened myself then. In those days, the shrine of Kyria truly was neutral ground where the feud could be forgotten. Rakia and I enjoyed those times."

"What happened?"

"Salicina took the West Field."

"The feud ruins everything." Maerea felt listless suddenly, as if she might waste away, a dry, weightless thing in this heavy bed. "Help me out of bed."

"You need to stay off your feet and drink." Bria pressed a cup of water into her hand.

Maerea sat up on her elbow and drained the tasteless fluid to reassure her friend. "Keeping vigil in my chair is useless. But it would feel less useless than lying in bed."

Bria shook her head. "*He* is in the hearth room. I don't think you want to see him."

Maerea stumbled to her feet, caught herself on the bedpost, then made it out into the hearth room.

There he was, sitting in the chair where he had spent every night after their mother died. The washed-out afternoon light gleamed on the blade across his knees. She closed her hands over the back of her chair to hold herself up.

He lifted tired eyes to her. "Maerea. Thank the gods. The healer wouldn't tell me what was wrong."

"Get out."

"I need to speak with you."

"There's nothing you can say."

His jaw tightened. "Lord Drusus is willing to overlook your indiscretion with Lord Alcaeus. He will take you as a widow."

"I am in mourning."

"Everything depends on this alliance. Imagine his anger when he arrived here and another man had taken the bride I promised him. I've smoothed things over with him, though. He knows that his role in rescuing you makes you rightfully his. As long as you're not with child, he'll have you. As soon as we know, we can plan your marriage to a proper husband."

Daughter Pherakia hadn't told him. Maerea wished she could thank her. As long as Gerrian didn't know, she could stall.

"I know you asked the mage, Maerea. Did she tell you you're with child or not?"

"She said it's too soon to tell. Grief made me ill."

"Don't waste your tears."

"Get out."

He stood, his sword in hand. "Our forefathers died for this. I will see it through. I expect you to do your part."

His hand darted out, quick as lightning. His fingers raked her forehead, and her hair pulled. Before she could stop him, he had torn her marriage headband from her.

She lunged toward him. He backed away, crumpling the headband in his fist.

She could claw and pry at that fist, and it would never open.

"Our generation is just like the last," she cried. "Our blood in the ground, and nothing to show for it but barren fields. You have won nothing, Gerrian."

"Not yet. But the enemy's domain will soon be mine. We have already laid siege to Castra Salicina. With no lord to defend them, the widow and her brat stand no chance."

"What are you going to do to Aemilian?"

Gerrian turned from her.

"Is that what you've become?" she called after him. "A murderer of children?"

He left her, and the guards shut and barred the door.

It was easy to feign continued illness. Her spirit was deathly ill, and if it ever recovered, she would wonder what was wrong with her. She kept the casements closed to shut out the arrival of summer. She wanted none of Anthros's season.

After a few days, Gerrian finally consented to let the mage of Kyria come again. But he stayed on guard in the hearth room.

Bria shut the door, standing there next to Daughter Pherakia. "Thank you for coming again."

"Now is not the time for old squabbles." After a moment's hesitation, the mage touched a hand to Bria's arm.

With a startled expression, Bria watched Daughter Pherakia cross the room.

Maerea sat up, dropping her sickly act. She kept her voice low. "I know you have little enough reason to care what becomes of me, since I am not to be the mother of Alcaeus's child. I can only try to tell you, with the gods as my witness, that I am still faithful to him."

The mage sighed and took a seat on the side of her bed. "It would be easy to blame you for what happened to him. I wish I could. But I saw how happy he was with you." Her breath hitched. "Thank you for making his final days happy ones."

Alcaeus, laughing at sunset. Grinning as he whispered in her ear. Holding her as they danced and all the cares disappeared from his face. "My loyalty is to him. Now and always."

She looked to Bria. Her friend nodded.

Maerea turned back to the mage. "I wish to declare my allegiance to Alcaeus's family. Would you intercede for me with Domitia? Tell her Bria and I humbly beg her to give us refuge. I will devote myself to her and Aemilian. I will tell her all my brother's secrets and strategies so she and her soldiers can use the information against him. I will serve her in any way possible, if only she will have me."

"I'll give her your message." Daughter Pherakia hesitated again. "I should warn you, I doubt her answer will be what you hope for."

"Please. I must try."

"Yes. I will do what I can to sway her."

"Bless Mother Kyria for your kindness."

"I'll tell your brother I must return to check on you tomorrow, and I'll give you her reply then." The mage touched a hand to Maerea's. That sensation of cool strength flowed into her for an instant. Then Daughter Pherakia released her and went to the door.

She paused beside Bria. "You wish to return to Salicina."

"I am trying."

"So shall I."

"Lady Domitia's answer is no."

Perched on the edge of her bed, Maerea stared at Daughter Pherakia. She was out of disappointment, it seemed. Alcaeus was gone. Everything else was just an afterthought. "Thank you for trying."

"I'm sorry."

She had won the mage's sympathy. But not Domitia's.

Bria leaned forward in her chair and held Maerea's hand. She and Daughter Pherakia looked everywhere but at each other.

"I can't blame Domitia," Maerea said. "She surely fears Gerrian's retribution more than she values the information I could give her. She is alone now, with lives in her hands. She has to base her decisions on that." Maerea knew what that was like.

But the image of little Aemilian pierced her numbness. She also knew what it was like for him to call her Aunt Maerea.

He was fortunate to have his mother's protection. But what would he do without Alcaeus? What would Domitia or Maerea do without him?

"Tell her I'm sorry for her losses," Maerea said, "and that my heart is with her and her son, come what may."

The mage turned to leave. Maerea's last hope was about to slip away. She had nothing. No allies, no power. She would sit uselessly by her window, the silent widow, while Gerrian laid waste to everything.

No.

She still had her mind. That's what had kept this domain running all along. If she could keep Gerrian's carelessness from starving their people, she could keep his sword from hurting anyone else.

Something uncurled within her. It had been lurking always, and now it rose, stretched, and drew its claws.

She got to her feet. "Wait."

Bria looked at her with pride in her gaze. The mage halted, her hand on the door latch, and looked over her shoulder.

Whatever was inside of Maerea must show somehow. She put all the new authority into her voice. "I understand that my sister-in-law will not accept my help directly, but I still intend to support from here. There are certain things I can accomplish in my position."

The mage turned to face her again with considering eyes.

"I ask for no loyalty from you, Daughter Pherakia. I will not ask you to place yourself in that position. However, I know your affection for Domitia's family. Would you be willing to aid a plan of mine for their sake?"

"I'm listening."

How easy it turned out to be. Speak like you had power, and suddenly you had an ally. Where should she apply her power first? Where would her influence have the most impact, do the most damage? What was Gerrian's weakest point?

"My brother has many weaknesses—and I know them all."

She had coddled him over the years, making up for his lack, cleaning up after his mistakes. Remove her strengths, and he would fall. But she could not let their people fall with him. She had to disarm him, not cause more destruction.

"My brother's alliance is tenuous—and dependent on my marriage to Lord Drusus. However, he'll only have me if I'm not carrying another man's child."

The mage's eyes narrowed. "I see."

"If I lie and say I'm pregnant, it will weaken the alliance. If Lord Drusus abandons Gerrian, Lapidea's forces will once more be inferior to Domitia's."

Bria stood. "You must be very sure you are willing to do this. If your brother believes you are carrying his enemy's heir, you won't be safe."

"I'll be all right."

"If I must protect you from my liege lord, I will. I remember when he was just a terror of a little boy, running your mother ragged. He doesn't frighten me."

"No, Bria. You are more vulnerable to him than I. I can't let anything happen to you." Maerea looked to Daughter Pherakia. "If all goes ill for me, I want to make sure Bria has a safe place to go."

Bria cast a flinching glance at Daughter Pherakia. "Not a word about funerals being all that will bring me back to Salicina."

"No, Bria. You will always have a safe place at my shrine."

Bria turned to her. "Do you mean that, Rakia?"

"I will not let you get yourself killed. That young cock who calls himself your lord isn't worth it."

Bria smiled, and despite everything, a laugh escaped her.

"She is right," Daughter Pherakia told Maerea. "This will be very dangerous for you while he believes our misdirection—and when the truth comes out, as it eventually must."

"It would be months before a pregnancy would become obvious. That will buy us valuable time."

"Time for Domitia's allies to arrive," the mage admitted. "Thanks to Alcaeus's foresight. He sent for them the day he…faced your brother in battle."

Maerea swallowed. "His actions are still protecting those he loved."

"So is his widow. I appreciate the risk you're taking."

"It is no small thing, to betray my brother. But he betrayed everything—his honor, his responsibilities to the people of this land. My husband did not, and so I will honor our vows."

The mage gave a nod. "I'll tell your brother you're with child."

The three women went out into the hearth room together to face him. Bria made a show of settling Maerea in her chair and fussing over her.

Daughter Pherakia crossed her arms at Gerrian. "Out of loyalty to my calling as a mage, I must tell you the true state of your sister's health. My spells have shown she is with child."

He was silent, his face ruddy, his knuckles white. He looked like a petulant little coward. Maerea discovered she was not afraid of him or his anger.

"Is it a boy?" he demanded.

"Only the gods can know yet," Daughter Pherakia answered. "However, out of a more personal loyalty to her late husband's family, I must tell you this. If the child proves to be a boy, he and Lady Maerea will not remain under your roof."

"Like Hypnos, they won't."

"Don't think your invocations of the god of death can intimidate me, boy. I settle down to chats with the gods all the time, and you wouldn't want to know what they think of you. I advise you to take excellent care of your sister and her babe. If you don't, you'll have more than swords to worry about."

Sweat broke out on Gerrian's brow, and he tugged on the collar of his tunic. What trick was the healer playing on him? Could she cause disturbances in the body as well as repair it?

Daughter Pherakia took a step closer to him. "Do you understand?"

"You may go." If he was trying to sound imperious, he failed. His voice was tight and desperate.

"Do you have further need of me, Lady Maerea?" the mage asked.

"No, Daughter Pherakia. Thank you for your care."

"I'll come again soon." She hesitated, looking at Maerea, then longer at Bria. But they all knew she must leave them to face Gerrian.

As soon as she was gone, he leapt out of his chair. He looked as if he might lunge at Maerea. She sat there impassively and lifted her chin.

"My sister," he spat, "that man's harlot. I never imagined."

"No congratulations for me?"

He stalked back and forth in front of her. "You will not leave your rooms. You won't breathe a word of this to anyone. The first person who gives a hint to Lord Drusus will lose their tongue."

"I see. You'll turn me into a prisoner and then a mute. What brotherly love."

He halted in his tracks. "I do love you! You'll see. Everything I'm doing is for your good." Calm returned to his face. "We'll wait and see. His get might not be viable, and then all can return to how it was." He paced away from her. At the door, he paused and looked over his shoulder at her. "Not a word." He slammed the door behind him.

Maerea didn't jump. But reflexively, she put a hand to her belly. If she had been with child…

Gerrian had just wished death upon her babe.

"Who is he?" she wondered. "Was he ever the man I thought he was?"

"When the gods put us to the test," Bria replied, "we must draw strength from our better or worse natures. See which one he picked."

"I hope my better nature is my strength."

"It is, dove. It always has been."

As much as Maerea treasured Bria's faith in her, she had to wonder. It was a question only she could answer for herself.

Would she wield these claws inside her for good or evil?

chapter eleven

ESSENTIAL MAGIC

When Alcaeus surfaced this time, his first waking moments were not torment. Thirst no longer sucked him dry. He needed more blood, all right, but he could bear it. His mind was clearer than it had been in…how many nights?

It was over.

He tried sitting up. A blanket slid off of him, but he caught it before it left him bare. His armor and clothing were gone. Only his sword rested next to him, within easy reach.

"Good moon." Iskhyra sat on a cushion at a low table nearby.

He got his first good look at her. She wore simple, long black robes. She'd put her hood back, but a black scarf hid her hair. Her face was a perfect oval, her mouth full and feminine, her skin as flawless and white as the Light Moon. But her ethereal beauty did not affect him the way Maerea's chapped lips and frequent blushes did.

He took in his surroundings. Iron sconces held orbs of spell light. By their soft, warm glow, he beheld more scrolls than he'd ever seen in his life. Stone pillars ringed the chamber, carved in designs of sinuous beasts with fangs and feathered wings.

In a central alcove was a votive statue carved from the same stone. A voluptuous goddess clothed only in her long hair. Blood-red petals, long dried, lay scattered at her feet.

Hespera.

Alcaeus looked away. He was on a soft carpet, and there was a pillow where his head had rested. He didn't see any stains. It was a lovely setting for the bloodbath he'd just come through. Even his blade was clean.

"Good…evening." Far from the hoarse croak he'd expected, his voice emerged clear and strong. He sounded like himself.

"How do you feel?"

"Like myself." He clutched a hand to his chest, feeling the familiar reality of hair and skin and bone. Was this some strange Hesperine deception making him believe all was well, when he had become something other?

"You *are* yourself. More yourself than you've ever been. That is what the Gift does. It does not change who you are. It helps you become your best self."

Perhaps it was just the strange bond he now had with her. But when she spoke, her words carried weight. He couldn't help but believe her.

It was eerie to realize he had swallowed the blood in her veins. It had become a part of his body, transforming his flesh. What did that make him to her, and her to him?

Thirst prickled in the back of his throat. Now that the instincts of his transformation no longer drove him, he didn't want blood. Not yet, not again. "Where are we?"

"Drink first, then we talk."

"Must I already?"

"Now that your Gifting is complete, you could go for years without blood and not starve to death, but you would suffer for it. With time and training, you'll develop greater stamina for resisting the Thirst for blood. I think it's a little soon to test your endurance, don't you?"

"Denying the Thirst won't kill me, but it will weaken me?"

"Right. To remain at full strength, you need blood every night."

He had to be strong for Maerea. But he didn't want to face Iskhyra wearing nothing but his skin, even if she had just put his body back together. He wrapped the blanket around his waist before joining her.

She stretched her arm out on the table between them, wrist up. Offering him her vein next to pretty pewter cups and a pot of some aromatic brew. "What did you expect? A crypt?"

"Not a tea party."

"It's coffee."

He shrank back a little. "What is that?"

"A delicacy from far beyond the Tenebrae. I don't drink heretical alchemical concoctions in front of the children." With her free hand, she poured herself a cup of the dark brown liquid, then took a leisurely sip. All while her wrist lay on the table for him, as if this were normal. "In Orthros, we have coffeehouses where our people meet for drinks like this."

"In Orthros? The Hesperine homeland?"

"The most dangerous things there are the pastries."

"You…eat normal food?"

"We gain no nourishment from it, but we enjoy it. People have been known to choose immortality just so they can eat their fill of our meatless mincemeat pies."

"That is…not how I envisioned Orthros. At all."

"The mages devised the tales of horror for their own benefit. There are no profane temples dripping with the blood of our sacrifices. No vortexes of pure night that swallow men alive. No humans in cages getting tapped and tortured."

"What is Orthros really like, then?"

A hint of expression crossed her face. "Beautiful. Safe. Unchanging. You will get to see for yourself. In the meantime, I will do my best to make sure your introduction to Hesperine life isn't entirely devoid of culture, although conditions are rough here Abroad."

It was getting harder to concentrate on her words. Her pulse seemed loud. With some sense he couldn't define, he could feel the flow of blood in her veins. Before he knew it, he was lowering his mouth to her wrist.

When he bit down, his mind told him it should disgust him. But nothing about it *felt* unwholesome. It was like taking a swig of strong spirits from a comrade's flask while out on patrol in the cold night. The kick. Then the warmth, all the way to his toes. But then vital energy spread through his every vein, as no alcohol or food could provide.

When the Thirst abated, he sat back. Wetness trickled down his chin. He slapped a hand over his mouth.

Iskhyra passed him a stack of black handkerchiefs. "Nothing to be embarrassed about. It takes practice to drink without getting messy.

These are best to start with until you learn cleaning spells. Black doesn't show stains."

What would Maerea think, if she knew he was here with another female, wiping blood from his lips?

Iskhyra rested her hands on her knees. "I have a great deal of life experience and education, both practical and scholarly. I should hope all of that has given me some measure of wisdom. You have questions. I will answer."

So many questions. They swirled in his mind, and he would rather leave them in that tangled confusion than examine their implications.

But whatever he had been or was now, he would never be a coward. He made himself lift a hand to his teeth. He touched his canines.

"Your fangs came in very fine. You can feel proud of those."

They were…larger than he expected. And sharp. He hissed and pulled his bleeding finger away from his own teeth. He watched the wound heal before his eyes.

Suddenly everything around him felt strange, disorienting.

"You'll grow accustomed," Iskhyra said. "Imagine that kind of healing on the battlefield. A wound that would put you out of the action becomes a scratch."

"A mortal wound becomes an inconvenience."

"Precisely."

"How much damage can I sustain without dying?"

"Excellent first question. You've seen battle. I take it you don't want me to mince words."

"No. Facts my life depends on are best delivered bluntly."

She sounded like a drill commander, but a forgiving one. "There are only five ways to kill a Hesperine: starvation, exsanguination, excardiation, decapitation, and immolation."

"You said it takes a long time for us to starve."

"Years. Bleeding to death takes nights. It's rare for an enemy to excardiate one of us, because to remove our hearts, they must first restrain or subdue us. That's a challenge, given our superior strength and magic. Heart hunters are famous for trying, though."

Warbands of heart hunters with packs of fighting dogs roamed the northern borders of the Tenebrae, guarding against Hesperine incursion from Orthros. Alcaeus had seen them as humanity's protectors. Now they would want to excardiate him. "Do they occasionally succeed?"

"With the aid of their liegehounds, yes. Those dogs are always a threat. They're the only animals that don't trust us. Centuries of nature magic have crafted them into the perfect weapon against Hesperines. Tenebrans have bred and trained them to hunt and destroy us."

"Understood. Decapitation?"

Iskhyra took another sip of coffee. "A human has to be quick to achieve that, but your head is more vulnerable than your heart. You must learn to guard your neck at all times."

"Shouldn't be a problem. Even mortal soldiers must do that."

"Mortal soldiers don't have to fight Gift Collectors. They're necromancers and experts with blades, and they love going for our heads. They serve no one but Hypnos, and they earn bounties for taking our immortality and delivering us to their god."

He was now on the wrong side of the god of death's own assassins. Any Gift Collector would take one look at him and see a purse of gold. Wonderful. "Let me guess. I also need to watch out for war mages who want to immolate me as a sacrifice to Anthros."

"You won't run into fire mages in the Tenebrae. As you know, anyone born with war magic is sent south to be trained in Cordium, the land of the Mage Orders. You still need to watch out for people with torches, though. It's not impossible for someone without war magic to set a Hesperine on fire."

"Does poison harm us?"

"We're immune to most things that are poisonous to mortals. But certain magical poisons can weaken us."

"To make us easier to excardiate?"

"Right."

That still left a very long list of things that wouldn't kill him. "What about losing a limb?"

"Anything besides your head or your heart will grow back." She raised her brows. "Yes, anything."

"That sounds…miserable."

"The worst is regrowing your fangs."

"That happened to you?"

She sighed. "Name it, and I've had to grow it back."

"Does sunlight harm us?"

"The mages wish. But day does put us into a deep sleep. No matter where we are, the Dawn Slumber finds us, and nothing can wake us until nightfall. Not nightmares. Not pain. So make sure you're out of harm's way."

He shuddered at the thought of meeting an enemy in the oblivion of sleep, without even a fighting chance. "If I get myself immolated, I'll make sure I'm awake for it."

She did not laugh.

He changed the subject. "Can we fall ill?"

"Only one thing can sicken a Hesperine." She set her coffee down and looked at him.

He had never felt unsafe in her presence. But that gaze seemed to cleave him deeper than any weapon, to lay him bare like the darkest whispered confessions. The spell light shone back at him from the depths of her reflective Hesperine eyes, turning the warm glow to icy silver.

"It is our greatest strength and our greatest weakness. In all the centuries since the origin of our kind, the mages have never learned of it. Are you going to have second thoughts about your transformation, run to the local mage of Kyria, and give up our secret before letting her call the temples' wrath down upon you?"

One of the laws of his new world became clear to him. He could hide nothing from Iskhyra. He did not flinch away from her gaze. "A heap of ash is no use to Maerea, so no."

Her gaze softened. "The greatest blessing you can look forward to in your Hesperine life is Grace. It is a magical bond that can occur between two lovers, as eternal as the Goddess who grants it."

Hesperine lovers? "I've heard enough."

"No, you must understand. When you find your Grace, you will no longer need mortal blood to survive. The two of you will sustain each other for all time, and you will avow each other before our people. But such power comes at a cost. If ever deprived of each other's blood, the two of you will suffer the Craving. This is the one illness that can befall a Hesperine. It is incurable, agonizing, and ultimately fatal."

"Well, I won't have to worry about that. Ever. If that's required to achieve my full power, I'll make do with whatever Hespera saw fit to give me upon my transformation, and no more. The temples may consider a heretic's vows to his wife null, but I do not. Do Hesperines?"

"Tenebran marriages aren't recognized in Orthros…but love is, Alcaeus. You don't need the mages to make your devotion to Maerea sacred in the eyes of our people."

"Then I won't be expected to take a Hesperine mate?"

"It's not an expectation. Grace just happens to you, when the time is right."

"Grace won't happen to me."

"It happens to all Hesperines…eventually. Or so we believe."

He glanced around the deserted Sanctuary. "You have no Grace?"

"Hazard of the profession."

"What exactly is your…profession?" he finally asked. "Who are you? Why are you in the Tenebrae?"

"Do you know the Equinox Oath?"

"That ancient truce that was supposed to keep the peace between Hesperines and mortals?"

"It is the official treaty between Orthros and the Tenebrae, which still governs our relations."

"I suppose we all know of it, but it must have been broken a long time ago. Hesperines and mortals sitting down for peaceful negotiations? It sounds like a fantastical tale."

She framed her coffee cup with her fingers. "Many Tenebrans consider the Equinox Oath dead. But Orthros still holds it in reverence. It lays down the acceptable conduct of Hesperines errant in human lands. As long as we abide by those limitations, the Oath is also supposed to grant us protections. Not that mortals often respect that."

"I'm afraid I'm not very familiar with the terms of the Oath."

Iskhyra's voice took on the cadence of a prayer, and he realized she must be reciting the Oath word for word. "'Hesperines shall have the right to children who have been exposed, abandoned, or orphaned without anyone to take them in.

"'Hesperines shall have the right to the dying whose own kind give them no succor and to the dead whose kin and comrades fail to collect their remains.'"

Words he'd rarely considered were now the reason his heart still beat.

"'Hesperines shall be permitted to exercise any power on convicted criminals or miscreants acting in clear violation of the law to the detriment of honest people.

"'Hesperines shall not take to them children who are still under the care of their elders, regardless of the elders' treatment of the children.

"'Hesperines shall not disturb the dying who await mortal aid or the dead whose kin or comrades are coming to claim them.

"'Hesperines shall not set foot in temples, orphanages, or places of burial.

"'Hesperines shall not, under any circumstances, intervene in conflicts between the Mage Orders, the Council of Free Lords, the King of the Tenebrae or his enemies, or in any way attempt to influence worship or politics in the Tenebrae.

"'So long as Hesperines hold to these terms, they may traverse all lands under the rule of the King of the Tenebrae without fear of persecution. Should they in any way violate this Oath, then they forfeit the king's protection from mages, warriors, and any subjects of the Tenebrae seeking to exact justice.

"'Finally, each King of the Tenebrae, upon his accession to the throne, is to reconvene the Summit and reaffirm this Oath with the appointed representatives of the Queens of Orthros.'"

"I think I see," Alcaeus said.

"We don't roam the Tenebrae stealing children and turning fallen warriors into our minions. The tenets of the Oath are our Goddess's sacred practices. We seek to give orphans safety and care. We try to mitigate suffering and grant dignity to the dying—or give then a new life. You know the choice I gave you."

"If I had asked, would you really have let me die?"

"Yes. I would have respected your wishes. I would even have hastened your departure for you, if you wished. But I would have been sorry to let you go." She paused. "Are you having second thoughts?"

"No."

"I'm glad." The side of her mouth lifted. "I've been doing this a long time. I usually work alone, but I rather like you."

He'd never thought about any of this from a Hesperine's point of view. "It must take its toll, what you do."

"We are immortal. Death always feels like a failure, even when it's natural and right."

We. The two of them.

Alcaeus was immortal.

His awareness of mortality lingered, like a phantom pain in a lost limb. Would that, too, heal in time? "Death felt that way to me when I was mortal, too."

"I'm sorry about your father and brother. Your grief run in my veins."

The expression of sympathy was unfamiliar, but he understood it. "That's true, isn't it? When you gave me your blood, you saw my memories of my family…of losing them."

"Yes." A heartbeat passed between them. "I lost a brother in battle, as well."

Hesperines had family. Hesperines mourned. Of course they did. And not only because they had all been human once. He just hadn't realized it until Iskhyra had carried him off the West Field.

"I'm sorry." He put a hand to his heart. "Your grief runs in my veins."

"Thank you, Alcaeus."

"Has it been long?"

"Mortal lifetimes."

This was what it meant for the afterlife to be out of reach. He would never see his father and brother again. "Forever is a long time to outlive your family."

"I'm afraid so."

"May I ask how long you've been a Hesperine?"

"Tactful. But I still won't tell you how old I am."

He bowed from the waist with a flourish. "Forgive my impertinence, my lady."

"There. I knew you had some good humor in you. We'll have to nurse that back to health, too. Eternity is a very long time, and laughter helps."

"Before I can contemplate eternity, I have to make plans for right now. I must get back to Maerea." Pain washed over him. His nearly indestructible body didn't make his emotions hurt any less.

"Let us make a plan."

"Us?"

"I am your Gifter. I have a sacred responsibility to support and guide you not only through your transformation and your first nights as a Hesperine, but always."

Now they came to it. He was bound to her—forever. "And what are my obligations to you?"

"It doesn't work both ways."

"I don't understand. Do I not owe you some sort of fealty? At the very least, a life debt."

"Hesperines don't practice fealty or debts. Only bonds of gratitude. You and I both made a choice the night you faced death. We both gave to each other. Free will and generosity are the purest and most powerful ties, and they place us on equal footing."

"I don't see what I have done for you."

"You gave me your trust."

He had countless other questions about Hesperines, Orthros, and what awaited him in this new existence. But they could wait. "You've treated me with nothing but honor. You've saved my life and pledged to help me rescue my wife, all without asking for anything in return. You saw many of my memories during the transformation, so you know me rather better than I know you. But I also felt what you felt the night you found me."

"You experienced it in Blood Union with me."

"I have tasted the truth of who you are in your blood. You do have my trust, as well as my gratitude."

She offered her hand. When he reached out, she clasped his wrist with a firm grip. He mimicked her, wrapping his hand around his Gifter's veins.

"You're going to be all right," she said. "Master your new power, and soon no threat to Maerea will be a match for you."

"Train me."

"You can't learn magic with a blanket for a loincloth."

"I would like to keep what little pride I have left."

They stood over a large travel trunk Iskhyra had stashed between two columns. She waved her hand, and the lid flew open.

Alcaeus eyed the contents doubtfully. Shiny, embroidered robes? "Did none of my gear survive the battle?"

"I had to dispose of most of it. Your mail might be reparable, though." She pointed.

She had draped his armor over a lectern with surprising care. It gleamed, free of blood, as if she had cleaned it somehow. He touched a hand to the mangled links where Gerrian's sword had penetrated his defenses.

A pinpoint of pain. An impossible sight. That dreaded sword, thrust against his belly. Just the tip, biting him. Then more pain, and the sickening warmth that told him how bad it truly was…

Alcaeus snatched his hand back with a hiss, trying to clear visions of the battlefield from his mind.

"Memories take longer to heal than wounds," Iskhyra said.

"My father underestimated him. My brother was not wearing armor. I had a measure of his skill and a full coat of mail. And still I failed. He should never have been able to bring me down with just a sword."

"It was perfectly logical for you to expect your mail to protect you from a sword."

"He didn't even have an axe, or a mace. His archers left me to him. But the very tip of his blade broke one link on my mail…and…that was the beginning of the end."

Why was he panting? It was over, and *now* he had a bout of cowardice? He was a godsforsaken Hesperine. Nothing could hurt him now. Except these images, sensations, smells.

"You'll heal faster if you do not blame yourself." His Gifter's voice snapped him back to the present.

He blinked. When had he picked up his sword? "Will being a Hesperine give me superior strength in battle?"

"Strength, speed, and agility that will make any mortal powerless against you."

"That doesn't seem honorable."

"That is why most Hesperine warriors are sworn to fight with nothing but their fists. Only a handful of Hesperines in our history have wielded weapons, and they have always held to a very strict code of honor."

"Will you teach me this code?"

She put a staying hand on his where he held his sword. "To be a Hesperine warrior is a very particular calling. Our nature makes it difficult for us to harm others. To study the Hesperine battle arts is to shoulder the burden of violence on behalf of our entire people. You must first learn to be a Hesperine, then you can decide what role war is to play in your new life."

He regarded his sword, then laid it across the lectern with his armor.

Iskhyra gripped his shoulder. "Meet me outside when you're ready."

Once she had left, he rummaged through the trunk. Eventually some plain, golden-brown fabric caught his eye, and he fished it out. A simple, knee-length fighting robe, as depicted in statues of the mage-warriors of old. An ancient garment with an honorable history. It looked like it would fit.

He dropped the blanket and donned the fighting robe. Still, he felt naked, going to any kind of training session unarmored and unarmed.

Alcaeus walked out into the world he had left as a mortal. He recoiled from the glaring light. Jagged stones tore at the soles of his feet. A deafening screech made him cover his ears. Smells assailed his nose, and his head spun.

Iskhyra took hold of his shoulders. "It will pass. Try not to breathe. That will lighten the load on your senses."

He couldn't seem to make his lungs stop. They gasped for breath.

Her soothing voice was the only thing that didn't hurt. "It's an instinct left over from being mortal. But nothing will happen to you if you stop breathing. Your heart works without air."

He tried holding his breath.

"Better," she approved. "Now focus on one thing at a time. That little bird ten paces up the cliff from us, for instance."

Did she mean the shrieks coming from above? As much as it hurt, he tried listening to them. One heartbeat. Two. The cries resolved into pleasant birdsong.

"Now open your eyes—slowly."

He forced his eyelids open. It was night, he realized. That stunning light came from the moons.

Iskhyra moved aside, turning him to face the fluid crimson Blood Moon and the glossy white Light Moon. "Meet the Goddess's Eyes. From now on, Hespera watches over you from her night sky. You will come to learn the names of every star. But first, learn yourself. You are blood magic. Blood magic is you. You are your spirit and your body. You are your power and your veins. You are shadow and light. You are twofold, forever in Union."

A frisson traveled over his skin, and his heart leapt in his chest. Something deep within him answered to the gleam of the twin crescents.

As his eyes adjusted, he recognized the moonlit ravine. He had once savored this view at Maerea's side. "We can't be far from Castra Lapidea."

"This is a Hesperine Sanctuary. As long as you don't go beyond these columns, no one will ever be able to find you."

He and Iskhyra stood on a porch of rock that extended from the cliff, ringed by pillars and half sheltered by hewn arches. Behind them, the Sanctuary's massive doors stood open, as tall as three men.

"There's a mage a short hike from here," Alcaeus said.

"That pebble tosser at the shrine of Anthros? I won't even call him a stone mage. He wouldn't sense us if we strolled in and used his sun disk for a coffee table. Not that we would enter a shrine and violate the Oath," she added hastily, her tone suddenly stern.

Alcaeus's brows rose. He knew the tone of a new parent unaccustomed to having their every move set an example for an impressionable child. "I don't think I'll be revisiting the place I got married anytime soon."

Iskhyra winced. "No offense."

"None taken." He couldn't really hold irreverence against a heretic, could he? He was one now.

"In any case, even if Master Eusebios had greater skill, he couldn't detect us using magic within a Sanctuary ward. This is a very safe place to be a new Hesperine."

Well, that ruled out Master Eusebios as a threat—but also said little for Maerea's trusted spiritual adviser. "What about outside Sanctuary wards?"

"Hesperines have two ways of using magic. One is active casting, like mages. That draws attention, although there are ways we can hide it. The second way is essential magic, the innate abilities all Hesperines have. Only experts can tell when we use such power. Who do you suppose has the skill to detect that?"

"Aithourian war mages and Gift Collectors?"

"Two out of three."

He frowned. "Liegehounds?"

"They can scent us through our concealments."

"I see what you mean about not underestimating them. Very well. Which am I learning today—active casting or essential magic?"

"I'll teach you to use your innate abilities first, while we wait to see what affinity you manifest."

"Affinity? As in, an aptitude for healing or agricultural magic, which requires training as a mage? I don't have magic."

"You didn't as a mortal. Many who weren't mages in mortal life develop magic after the Gifting. Those who were mages as humans usually keep their affinity as Hesperines."

What dark magic could he now wield? What unnatural power was now a part of him? He must come to terms with it. It was the power that would help him save Maerea.

"The foundation of the Gift is healing," Iskhyra said. "As a result, we mature slower than humans and eventually stop aging. You're already familiar with our ability to regenerate." She cocked her head. "Do you hear that?"

"I hear...so many things."

"Which one sounds wrong?"

A flutter of wings. Too slow, mismatched. That call was a cry for help. "The bird up the cliff is wounded."

Iskhyra nodded. "Wait here."

He had no time to do anything else, she disappeared and reappeared so quickly. She returned with the injured songbird. The little gray-brown thing nestled in her hands, an image of trust.

"Put your tongue to the wound," she instructed.

He frowned. The creature's feathers were soft and resistant against his tongue. He tasted its blood and the taint of the wire that had torn its flesh. Then all he tasted were feathers. It fluttered against his face and took flight with a jubilant cry.

"I—I did that?"

"Hesperine bodily fluids share our regeneration with mortal creatures."

How easy it seemed. Why couldn't he have flown from the West Field, happy and whole, back to his bluebird? "I don't understand."

"You can heal only small wounds with your tongue. Sometimes injuries are so severe, the Gift is the only power great enough to save a life." Her voice thickened. "If there was anything else I could have done, Alcaeus, I would have."

He watched the bird. It darted back and forth above their heads and chattered to them. "I know."

He had to learn this. Lives depended on him and his new power. He must deal with his regrets later. "So I can heal a bite with my tongue. It should be possible to drink blood without killing anyone."

"It's impossible for a Hesperine to bleed someone to death. Our saliva enters their blood and heals them as we drink. Now tell me, how do you think that affects animals?"

"They aren't frightened of us, so they probably don't mind. And it would actually strengthen them."

"Very good. They are an important source of sustenance for us. For this is one of our most important tenets: never drink from a human without their consent. That is the rule you do not break, Alcaeus. The freedom of the Will is sacred. I believe I can rely on you not to abuse your power. Is that true?"

"Yes, Gifter."

She tilted her head back, gazing after the bird as it finally soared away. "Can you feel that? Like a part of you is taking flight?"

Alcaeus was not really a man of letters, but he found himself trying to describe it. "I can hear its song with something besides my ears. It's like wings in my chest. It…gives me a bit of joy, too."

"That is the Blood Union. You can sense the emotions of every creature with blood in its veins, as if its feelings are your own. It is a visceral empathy. Use the wisdom it grants you with compassion."

"I'll never be able to eat fowl again. Or anything else that has emotions."

"Hence the meatless mincemeat."

"Hesperines aren't cruel, as mortals have long believed. How could we be, when we feel what everyone feels?"

"Now you begin to understand."

When he saw Maerea again, what would she feel like to his new senses? When she learned he was a Hesperine, would her emotions be his deepest wound yet?

Iskhyra's palm made impact between his shoulder blades. He stumbled forward. His toes teetered at the edge of the cliff. He flailed out his arms, grasping at his balance for one sickening moment. Then solid ground slipped away.

Free fall. Pure panic froze his thoughts and exploded his pulse.

Thought cut through. His flip-flopping belly was full of blood. His racing heart was immortal.

But those jagged stones rushing toward him were going to hurt like Hypnos's nails. If this was Iskhyra's way of demonstrating Hesperine healing, she had a nasty sense of humor.

Anthros's bollocks, he had just survived a sword to the gut. He didn't have time to regrow his bones. He had to get back to Maerea.

His descent swept to a halt so fast his stomach turned over again. He hovered, as if a great cord had roped his heart and dangled him from the stars. He heaved a breath, even though he didn't need it. "Thank you?" he called up to Iskhyra.

"Don't thank me. Thank your instinct for levitation, which has just awoken in record time. Well done."

He was doing this? He glanced down at his feet. The sight of the fall into the ravine made him shudder. But the longer he looked, the more giddy defiance overtook him. "Can I control it?"

"Try."

"How?"

"An act of Will. Choose an outcome and apply your determination to it."

He decided to go up. That invisible cord yanked him skyward. He let out a yell. Iskhyra laughed, hard.

"Curse you," he shouted as he passed her.

He had a warrior's discipline. He could do better than this. He envisioned himself in the last minutes of a training session, when his limbs burned, sweat stung his eyes, and he *must* finish one more round of sword drills. He Willed himself down. His feet landed gently on the porch next to Iskhyra.

She was still snickering at him. "You just learned essential movement. Congratulations."

He gave the powerful immortal sorceress who had saved his life a shove on the shoulder.

"You told me you didn't want to waste time," she said innocently.

"How high can I levitate? Can I move forward and backward, like flying?"

She let out another peal of laughter. "Very high, until the astronomical force of the sun begins to interfere with you. Yes, you can all but fly. But there's a faster way to travel."

She disappeared before his eyes again. He felt her tap him on the shoulder. He spun to face her, but she was already gone. He spotted her crouched over the doorway of the Sanctuary like a gargoyle.

He had seen mages attempt such and end up bedridden for days. "Did you just traverse three times in a row?"

"Traversal is how mages get from place to place, and it costs a great deal of power. What I did was simply *step*. Stepping is essential movement and second nature to Hesperines."

"Imagine the look on the enemy's face if I could move like this in battle…"

"Add veil spells, and you will be the invisible enemy." She leapt down, landing neatly before him. She moved a hand in front of her face. She wavered out of sight, as if a curtain had been drawn over her, revealing the columns behind her.

"I must learn how."

"We'll devote most of our training sessions to stepping and veils."

"Wait. There's one more thing you haven't mentioned."

"Patience, you rowdy fledgling."

"But it's the reason I am here at all. I must know my responsibilities toward the fallen."

Her humor faded. "Ah."

"How did you stop my pain on the battlefield? How do we…give the dying their due?"

She bowed her head. "The Mercy. I do not intend for you to need that magic yet. I will teach you one day…but not tonight."

"The magic might need me."

"I would teach you the joys of this life first. Can you blame me?"

He sighed, and his smile slowly returned. "No. And…thank you."

A wicked grin came to her face. "Let us play a game of veil and step."

chapter twelve

THE GREATEST REWARD

Sixteen Nights Later

Maerea's hearth room looked even dearer to him now. There were the patched curtains and the windowsill where her treasure box had sat. There was Mistress Bria in her chair, as if she had never left. A scene from another life. The glow of the dying fire seemed, to his Hesperine eyes, to cast an enchanted copper gleam over it all.

But the embers sent uncomfortable heat over his skin. He edged back.

"She can't see or hear us," Iskhyra said.

"I feel exposed, standing this close to Mistress Bria with my fangs showing."

"You don't have to whisper." Iskhyra took his chin in hand and peered at his mouth. "The extra veil you put on your fangs is holding. So why do you carry your power uncomfortably tonight?"

"The walls of a fortress were once the strongest things in the world. Now they're no barrier at all."

"Fortunately. Are you ready to reunite with your wife or not?"

His heart picked up its now-eternal pace. How would she react when she saw him?

"Tell Maerea only what you must," Iskhyra said. "Once she's free of this place, you'll have plenty of time to make the truth clear to her. Right now, all that matters is persuading her to leave with you."

"I won't take her with me on false pretenses."

"We're here to rescue her. This is not the time for explanations."

"She has a right to know what she'll be giving up if she comes with me."

There was a flash in Iskhyra's aura, but her voice was calm. "It's your decision, but I strongly advise you not to tell her what you are until we've gotten her back to the Sanctuary."

"It is my decision."

"I'll be right here, should you need me." She posted herself just inside the hearth room door, a good distance from the fire.

Alcaeus took one step toward the bedchamber. And he heard it for the first time with his new ears.

Maerea's heartbeat.

A quiver of the most delicate wings. The pounding rhythm of a festival dance. The pulse of their bodies together.

She was so beautiful. There was so much of her he had never sensed as a human.

He entered her bedroom on silent feet. The scent of her hit him and went to his head. Thirst and lust shocked through him. That fragrance was her blood. His wife's *blood.*

He pressed a fist to his mouth, self-disgust rising in him even as his thoughts strayed to the question…

If she smelled this exquisite, what would she taste like?

He levitated backward to get himself away from her as quickly as possible.

Iskhyra halted him with a firm hand and eased him to the floor again. "You've known the Thirst, the need for blood. What you're feeling now is the Hunger."

He didn't need her to elaborate. The scent of Maerea's blood made him hunger for her body. The sight of her body made him hunger for her blood. How could he let his bloodthirst taint the desire they had shared as husband and wife? "What if I lose control?"

"I won't let you do anything you'll regret. Besides, you can't hurt her."

"How can…what I'm tempted to do…not hurt her?"

"As I've told you, it's not painful. In fact, with the right person, it can be pleasurable."

"Physical hurt is not the worst pain I could cause her."

"You won't. Three things stand between you and what you fear. Your discipline, your honor—and your vows to her."

"This is the greatest test of my discipline I have ever faced. But you're right. On my honor, and by our vows, I will not fail her." He strode forward.

Once again, he entered the cloud of fragrance in her bedchamber. The shadows in the room loved her form, but he wanted a better look at her. As soon as he thought about opening the curtains, they parted.

Hespera's moonlight touched the wife he had wed in Anthros and Kyria's name, and the names of all gods fled from his mind. He took a step closer to her. He had never seen the layers of gold and silver in her hair, the luminescence of her skin. He could imagine how her body would feel wrapped in the new strength of his arms. How warm she would be. He could almost taste the skin at the base of her throat, where a river ran, beckoning…

Discipline. Honor. Vows.

He planted his feet and forced himself to stop breathing. Better, although the flavor of her scent lingered in his mouth. The human instinct to panic without air faded before the relief of his temptation to sink his fangs into his wife.

He eased down to sit on the side of her bed. He reached for her. It was an act of Will, but he did nothing more than touch her hair.

HER HUSBAND'S TOUCH FELT so good. Maerea lay there and smiled. It was all so new, but she belonged here in his bed.

Her husband.

Alcaeus was dead.

The realization shook her awake. It happened every night, all night. She would jolt out her sleep and remember the truth. He was gone, except from her dreams.

But now she was fully aware, and she could still feel his hand in her hair.

Who was in her room? Who was touching her the way he had? Her eyes flew open, and she scrambled to sit up.

"Shhh, bluebird. I'm here."

She stifled a cry. His touch. His voice. She must be mad with grief. He was just an apparition of her mind sitting there, handsome and whole.

He held out his hands. "I'm here."

She shouldn't try to touch him. He wouldn't be solid, and she would lose him again. But even so, she reached out to take his hands.

His fingers wrapped around hers, warm and strong.

She gasped a breath, then clenched her teeth on a sob. "How?"

"I survived."

She threw her arms around him. Real. There was his broad shoulder to rest her head on, his neck to hide her tears. There were his arms around her. Oh, gods. He was holding her. This was real.

He rocked her as she wept, murmuring comforts in her ear. The world slowly, groaning, wonderfully righted itself.

"You're alive." She said it aloud, a whispered, triumphant war cry.

"I did what I had to do, so I could come back to you."

"Gerrian lied. He told me he killed you."

"He left me for dead. But someone found me and put me back together."

She drew back just far enough to see his beloved face. There was something different about him. It didn't matter. They had been through so much. Of course he had changed. So had she.

She framed his face in her hands, stroking him, and a smile came to her face. She had to stifle a laugh.

Secrecy was imperative. No one must know. "How did you get in? Nevermind. It's too dangerous. If Gerrian finds you—"

"He won't."

"What's our plan?"

"To get you away from here, now."

At last. Her ally, her best and truest one. She was no longer alone.

Time and danger pressed in on them, but she pushed back and brought her mouth to his.

It was like kissing her for the first time. The layer of mortality had been stripped away, and now he could really feel her.

But she too had transformed since that day on the battlefield. He felt it in the way she held him to her and devoured his mouth. Her same sweetness was now sharp with demand. Her same softness, tempered to strength.

With that kiss, she did something he'd believed impossible. She worked a miracle.

He loved her more.

Discipline. Honor. Vows.

Vows couldn't prevent his fangs from shooting out of his gums. Maerea didn't seem to notice. Bless Hesperine veil spells. He repositioned his mouth, gentling the kiss. Acrobatics and prayer kept him from pricking her. She only seemed to enjoy what he was doing with his lips and tongue.

He had to tell her. Rescue her. Escape.

He pushed her down to the bed.

She stroked him everywhere she could reach. The robe between his skin and her hands didn't dampen the effects of her touch, only teased his new senses more. His body responded as his fangs had.

She kissed her way from his jaw to his ear. "There were so many things I never said. It was too soon, I thought. Then it was too late. I thought you died for me, and I never even told you…"

"You can tell me now."

She looked into his eyes. Something rippled out of her aura, then flowed, then surged through their Union. He gasped, shuddering, and drank it down. There was a force inside her more sustaining than blood, more powerful than pleasure, that made him need her.

"I love you, Alcaeus. I fell in love with you the moment you took my hand. I married you for love."

He squeezed his eyes shut, touching his forehead to hers.

She loved him. The greatest reward of his human life, the greatest joy he had ever known. He was too late for it.

The Gift revealed it to him fully and robbed him of it in the same heartbeat.

But one thing had not changed. "So did I. I love you, Maerea. I will always love you."

She captured his mouth again, so giving, so hungry. She still lived in that world where he was human and they were together again. The truth would destroy her world a second time.

But not yet. He drew out this fleeting instant of eternity. He kissed and stroked her, trying to profess his love with his body, to give her the adoration she deserved. With her every touch, she destroyed his control a little more. Her hips found his erection, and she ground against him through the bedclothes.

It would be so easy to tear the blankets out of the way, push up her tunica, and discover how it felt to bury himself inside her now.

He yanked himself back, taking her hands and pushing them away.

Thankfully, she didn't resist or tempt him further. She sat up again, pushing her hair out of her face. Her look of determination was a sight to behold. "Let us away. Then we'll make plans for breaking the siege."

"Siege? I saw no army outside Lapidea."

"You haven't been back to Salicina?"

"No."

"You came for me first?"

He wanted to kiss her again. To take Iskhyra's advice and just spirit her away without explanations. To let her have her joy a little longer. To let himself have her love for just a few moments more. That wouldn't be right. She deserved to know the truth.

"I'm sorry, Alcaeus. Gerrian and his new ally have laid siege to Salicina. They have Domitia barricaded. We have to stop him."

Aemilian must be so frightened. But not for long. Hesperines were a match for an army. "There's something you should know first."

Her brow furrowed, and she took his hands again. "What?"

"I told you someone found me."

"Was it Daughter Pherakia? If she healed you, and she didn't tell me—"

"Not a mage."

"Whoever they are, I will repay them for your life in any way I can."

"Don't say that. Not until you know."

"If they're on the wrong side of the law…there are worse things. If they're allies, I will be forever in their debt. If they're holding something over you, they will answer to me."

She *had* changed. Her ferocity was beautiful. Her strength shone in her aura, purer than the glint of steel. And here he was, a coward, stalling with hints and empty words.

He took her hands. Was this the last time she would tolerate his touch? "Maerea, I want you to understand. I had a choice between abandoning you or accepting the only power available to me. I did what I had to do."

"You're alive. That's all the matters."

He took a breath to speak, and her scent mocked him. "You know who roams the battlefields, once mortals are done with each other."

Her hands went still in his. Her fingers were like ice.

"A Hesperine found me."

⁓

The moonlight gleamed on his fangs.

She jumped back without thought. The headboard stopped her.

He grimaced. "You deserve to know."

Nothing felt real. Not the pristine white canines extending from her husband's mouth. Not their perfect sharp points. Not the way he held out his hands in reassurance.

What brought her back to reality was the anger. She had just gotten him back. Only to discover this wasn't him at all.

The husband she loved was long gone. If only he had died with honor on that field and gone to his rightful place in Anthros's Hall, as she had believed.

They had both deserved better than this.

She had nothing that would protect her from a Hesperine. Lapidea didn't keep liegehounds anymore. She herself had declared them too expensive. To think, she had sealed her own fate.

It had already been over for her the moment he came back for her.

"I know how hard this is for a devout woman like you. You take the mages' teachings to heart. But you have nothing to fear."

Oh, she knew the teachings well. New Hesperines, mindless with bloodlust, returned to the scene of their mortal lives. They found their families and drained them dry. If the family was fortunate. If they weren't, the monster that had once been their loved one subjected them to the horrific transformation into one of the goddess of night's creatures.

"You know *me*, Maerea. You are safer with me than with anyone. The power I have now can protect you from any danger."

He sounded so sincere. He must truly believe what he was saying. He still saw himself as her protector, although he was about to kill her—or worse.

How strong were his memories of his human life? Could she reason with him? "Please. I am Domitia and Aemilian's only hope. You don't want Gerrian to harm them, do you? You mustn't take my blood, or I won't be able to help them."

"Maerea. I would die before I let any harm come to you. I'm not here for your blood. I won't lay a hand on you, unless you wish it. Just let me get you away from Gerrian."

"I'm afraid I cannot go anywhere with you. I need to stay here, so I can protect Domitia and Aemilian as much as possible."

"You'll be able to do more for them if you come with me. There is a…sort of stronghold where we can regroup and plan. With the help of…an ally."

He must mean the Hesperine who had done this to him. He would not attack her, then. He was trying to lure her back to the one who had created him. Perhaps to feed his new master.

That Hesperine would pay.

"I'll explain everything," he said, "as soon as I take you to safety. If you believe nothing else, believe this: all I've ever wanted to do is protect you. Think how hard I worked to earn your trust when we first met. You found faith in my despite the feud. Will you do that again now, despite heresy?"

A plan was already forming in her mind. She must make him believe he had her trust.

"Did it hurt?" She infused her voice with concern. That was easy. What was hard was keeping her tears at bay.

"The transformation?" Surprise flashed across his face, and he hesitated. "I would do it again, if I had to. I don't regret my choice. It was the only way I could survive to come back to you."

The words went straight to her heart. She must resist the urge to believe what she wanted to hear. Hesperines were cunning, persuasive. They hid their bestial natures under their otherworldly beauty.

To think, she had kissed him moments ago. Touched him and welcomed his touch. She had come so close to joining with him right here. He could have done anything to her.

He had only stopped because his master had plans for her. "The Hesperine who changed you is…your ally now?"

"Yes. I owe her my life. She is more powerful than even I understand, and she will aid us."

Her. A Hesperine seductress had taken Maerea's husband from her.

He laughed. "I can tell you're jealous. That's entirely unnecessary, I assure you. It's nothing like that between Iskhyra and me. You can trust her."

Maerea would have to hide her reactions better, although her words felt like poison in her mouth. "I'm sorry. I should be grateful to her, not envious."

"You have every right to be angry and afraid. There will be time for that. But what matters right now is escaping."

She had passed so many points of no return. She wasn't afraid of this one. "I will come with you."

He heaved a sigh. "Thank you, Maerea."

"I cannot go tonight, though. I need to settle my affairs here. I have to make sure everyone will be taken care of."

"I know you fear how they will suffer under Gerrian, but…there will be time for sorting that out, too. Later." He cocked his head, as if listening to something she couldn't hear. "We must go now."

"Not without saying goodbye to Bria."

"What will you tell her?"

Maerea swallowed. "That Gerrian lied, and you didn't die, and I'm running away with you."

A ghost of a smile crossed his face. "The truth, then."

"Yes."

"Shall we tell her now?"

"No, come back for me…tomorrow night. That will give me time to do what I must."

"I don't want to leave you here another hour. I came as soon as could. It took time to adjust to this unfamiliar form, but I have enough command of my power now. Please, Maerea. Don't wait."

If she pushed him too far, would he take her by force? She had to risk it. "I can't. Think of my people."

"They might suspect you're planning to leave."

"No, I'll act as though I'm laying out our usual plans for making ends meet. They'll believe me."

"You have to be sure. I won't risk Gerrian retaliating against you." Alcaeus's eyes glinted, and his fangs lengthened. "To think, I considered myself well-armed against him when I had a sword and marriage laws. He'll rue the day he ordered his soldiers to leave me to the Hesperines."

"He what?"

"You deserve the truth, Maerea. Gerrian forbade them to call a mage of Hypnos to give my rites, and he ordered them to remove all the Anthros's fire and sunsword that would have warded off Hesperines. He wanted them to make me suffer in my last hours and desecrate my body. He has no idea how wrong he was."

"No. No, he doesn't." Gerrian thought Maerea was under his control. He believed his greatest obstacle was the castle he hurled his forces against.

"I will never let him hurt you again." Alcaeus knelt beside the bed and put a hand over his heart. "I will do everything in my power—the power I have now—to earn your trust. To prove to you I am still the person you married. And the only price I will not accept is your blood."

Not even her anger was enough to armor her against that echo of his promises to her. He looked like himself. He sounded like himself. He spoke to her exactly as he always had.

"Come back for me tomorrow," she begged, and she didn't know if she was trying to banish him…or secure his promise that he would return.

"I will." He rose to his feet, so tall and powerful and beautiful over her.

He disappeared before her eyes. She couldn't stifle a gasp.

What she was about to do would be the greatest challenge she had ever faced. The worst danger to her was not his fangs or his magic or even his Hesperine mistress. It was her own treacherous heart.

chapter thirteen

THE ONLY CURE

"OH, MY DOVE. ANOTHER nightmare?"

"I wish it was. But it's real."

Maerea fell to her knees and hid her face on Bria's lap as if she were still a little girl. She allowed herself that for one moment before she made herself lift her head. "Did you know Gerrian left Alcaeus to the Hesperines?"

The answer was there in Bria's gaze.

"Why didn't you tell me?"

"Gerrian has taken enough from you. You needed to mourn Alcaeus in peace. Your grief was one thing I could protect. Who was cruel enough to rob you of that?"

"Alcaeus told me himself."

Bria pressed a hand to her chest. "Mother Kyria protect us. Rakia promised me…she said there were ways she could try to keep him at bay…"

"She didn't tell me the truth, even when I asked her to put a lily on his tomb. Who else knows?"

"When there was no body to recover, everyone knew. Even Lapidea's soldiers do not have the heart to gloat. Every heart at Salicina is broken. Rakia blames herself that any Hesperine got close enough to take him. She is determined their kind will never come near us again."

"We need to speak with her and Master Eusebios."

Bria stood tall, drawing Maerea to her feet. "Don't be afraid, my dove. I won't let anything happen to you."

Maerea pounded on her door until the guards agreed to carry a message to Gerrian. Just before dawn, he strode in as if he were lord of her hearth room, the last corner of her domain that belonged to her. He was already dressed for the battlefield.

She looked at the man who had doomed Alcaeus for eternity.

"I hear you have a request," Gerrian said.

"I want to go to the shrine."

"I think not."

"You would even deny me the comfort of prayer?"

"Consider your condition, sister. You should go back to bed."

Her fury sharpened. "Then bring the healer here again. You wouldn't want anything to happen to me, would you?"

He crossed his arms over the stained hawk embroidered on his surcoat. "I don't like letting her through our lines."

"She's a mage of Kyria, for goddess's sake. Do you really think she's smuggling siege secrets in her tonics for feminine ailments?"

"When my power is secure, I'll see to it we have our own mages."

"We have one of our own mages. If you will not let me go to our shrine to worship, at least let Master Eusebios come to me."

Gerrian's eyes narrowed. "I suppose that's appropriate. You would want his counsel. Take this as an opportunity to examine your conduct, sister. I am sure the mage will help guide you back onto the proper path."

He left at last, and the ferocious anger inside her curled up again. For now.

She sank into her chair by the fire and waited.

Bria patted her hand. "Well done, dove."

Master Eusebios arrived quickly. If possible, he looked thinner than he had the day of her wedding.

The last time she had seen him, she had been marrying Alcaeus.

The mage sat down across from her. "I would ask if you're all right, but I know the answer. I tried so hard to reason with your brother. I made your feelings about Lord Alcaeus very clear to him."

"It's no use, Master. He is beyond reason."

Daughter Pherakia entered the hearth room, shutting the door in the guards' faces. "Feuds make men think with their blades, not their minds."

"And make them forget they have hearts." Bria looked across the fire at the mage of Kyria.

"Bria." She gave a nod and joined them by the hearth. "Lady Maerea. And Master Eusebios. This resembles a council of war."

"Alcaeus was here," Maerea said.

"Father Anthros!" Master Eusebios's signed a glyph of Anthros in the air. "God of War and Order, God of Sword and Fire, guard us from the creatures of the night and preserve us from Hespera's chaos."

There was only sadness in Daughter Pherakia's eyes. "I'm sorry I did not warn you, Lady Maerea. Bria and I agreed it would be better this way."

"We have done our best to ward him off," said Master Eusebios, "but blood magic is formidable."

Maerea closed her hands around the arms of her chair. "You are surely well-versed in means of countering Hespera's corruption. Is there a cure for what he has become?"

Master Eusebios's gaze darted around. "These topics will be very shocking, I'm afraid."

"Oh," Daughter Pherakia snapped, "stop wringing your hands and make yourself useful."

"You'll find that women have strong stomachs," Bria said dryly.

"I have survived the shock of seeing a creature of the night that used to be my husband. I will not weep useless tears while a Hesperine sorceress holds him in her sway. I will free him from her."

Master Eusebios and Daughter Pherakia exchanged a long look.

"We will set him free." She crossed her arms.

He sighed. "There is one way to cure Hespera's Curse."

"There has to be," Maerea said, "although it must be a closely guarded secret. I know the war mages don't want to cure Hesperines, only to burn them for heresy. But this is Alcaeus. You know what kind of life he lived. He deserves better." She looked from one mage to the other. "You must promise me you will spare him. He is worthy of a cure, not immolation."

"No one will notify the war mages about this." Daughter Pherakia's tone brooked no argument.

"Certainly not," Master Eusebios agreed. "Bringing them into our affairs would do more harm than good. Nor should we summon a Gift Collector."

"No!" Maerea leaned forward. "A necromancer would ensure Alcaeus's destruction."

"That's out of the question." Daughter Pherakia glanced at Master Eusebios again. "We will take care of this matter ourselves."

He gave a nod. "After failing to protect a man under the care of our shrines, we must make things right. I am no war mage, to be sure, but I believe I should be able to handle one newly turned Hesperine."

Daughter Pherakia snorted. "You'll need me."

Bria folded her shawl around her shoulders. "Don't expect me to sit by and watch."

There was hope. But they must first administer the cure to a dangerous Hesperine. "I promised Alcaeus if he would come back for me tonight, we would run away together. He said he wants to take me to his 'ally'—the Hesperine who turned him."

Master Eusebios signed another glyph. "You came so close to falling into their clutches! How brave you were, child, to talk your way out of that. When he comes again tonight, we will face him together."

"What must we do?" Maerea asked. "How do we reverse his transformation?"

Daughter Pherakia put a hand on her shoulder. "Just keep your agreement to meet with him. We will do the rest."

"It is all a magical process," said Master Eusebios.

"I want to help you—to help him," Maerea protested.

"You are," he assured her. "But the magical part, we mages must do ourselves, and I'm afraid my vows prevent me from revealing Anthros's holy secrets."

"Of course, Master. Forgive me."

He shook his head. "You are a good woman, Lady Maerea. I wished for better for you."

"There is yet hope for me."

"Hold on to your faith," he said. "You will need it tonight."

Daughter Pherakia went to the window and surveyed the view. "We need the advantage of surprise. We'll watch your window from the shrine of Anthros. Leave a candle burning here on the sill, and when Alcaeus comes, put it out to signal us. I'll traverse us to you."

Master Eusebios gaped at her. "You can traverse?"

"With her power," Bria answered, "she would have become head of her temple one day, had she not chosen her shrine instead."

Daughter Pherakia crossed her arms. "Independence is a far greater reward than influence and the backstabbing that comes with it. I prefer managing my garden to managing a temple."

"Fortunately for us." Bria leaned down and put her arm around Maerea's shoulders. "You have powerful allies tonight, dove. Your only task is to stall him until we arrive."

She nodded. She could do that. She would do anything to get her husband back.

※

Tonight, Alcaeus would take Maerea beyond Gerrian's reach forever.

He looked around the chamber above the Sanctuary. The scribe's cell was basic, but warm, the spell lights welcoming. He'd added all the extra blankets to the narrow bed and brought the trunk upstairs.

His wife's circumstances would be reduced from a lone warrior's rooms at Salicina to a heretic's underground bedchamber.

But she would be free.

He left the room and levitated down the steps hewn into the wall of the Sanctuary, rejoining Iskhyra in the library. "Let's go."

She rose from the coffee table. "Alcaeus, what did you sense in Maerea's aura last night?"

He halted. "She is appalled."

His Gifter's sympathy reached out to him through the Blood Union. "There's more to it than that."

"She feels frightened and cheated and very, very angry."

"What do you think she'll do about her anger?"

"I don't know. I just hope there's still a chance I can convince her I'm not a monster."

"That will depend on what happens tonight."

"She agreed to leave with me. Surely that means it's not too late."

"Did you get the impression that she trusts you?"

"Not much. She is willing to let me help her escape Gerrian, at least. Even if it is desperation that drives her to take her chances with me instead of him."

Iskhyra sighed. "Your feelings for her would make it difficult for you to see. I'm concerned that leaving with you is not what she has in mind."

"What do you mean?"

"She was telling you one thing while intending another."

"Maerea doesn't have a deceptive bone in her body."

"No, she is clever, capable, and brave. I admire that she seems to have a plan, instead of giving into her fears. But that may not be to your advantage."

"Of course she has a plan. She'll do as much as she can to protect her people and mine from Gerrian in the short time she has before she leaves with me."

Iskhyra paused. "I have more experience interpreting the Blood Union than you do, so I suggest you consider what I'm saying. Be prepared for anything. I will stay by your side."

"She's already having difficulty accepting me. We should wait and introduce you to her when we return here, as we agreed."

"She'll never know I'm with you."

They stepped to the hearth room under the cover of their veils. Maerea waited alone, pacing back and forth in front of the dying fire. She already wore her cloak. From underneath, golden velvet gleamed. Her wedding gown.

The moment he entered, she halted in her tracks. She couldn't see him. She could *sense* him. That warmed him in a deep and unexpected way.

He let his veils fall. She turned to face him, her aura a fraught tangle of emotions. Worry. Guilt. Fear. Determination.

When he approached her, she didn't back away. He reached out. Eased her into his embrace. She melted against him, just as she had when he was human. Her cloak slid back, and he filled his arms with his wife and velvet like sunlight.

Hope became an ache in his chest. "Everything will be all right now. I know it doesn't seem so, but it will."

"Yes. As long as we're together."

It wasn't too late. What might this sweet encounter lead to when they made it back to the Sanctuary? "Are you bringing anything with you?"

"Just this." She showed him her bluebird box, then returned it to an inner pocket of her cloak.

He ran a tentative hand down the back of her gown. "I worried that you had to leave these behind at Salicina."

"When Bria returned to Lapidea, she brought them to me."

"I know you will miss her."

"We've said our goodbyes. She's in the kitchens getting a balm for her knees. No one can accuse her of helping us escape."

"I understand how it feels to have to leave your people. But we'll find a way to do right by them. Are you ready?"

She checked her pocket one more time, then looked around. "Just let me put out the candle."

She went to the window, pulling him along with her as if she couldn't bear for him to be out of reach. Iskhyra was wrong. Maerea wasn't planning anything except to keep him as close to her as she could. Right where he wanted to be.

She paused at the windowsill. "I can't help thinking about when I used to sit here watching for you to arrive."

Her longing pulled at him. "You left everything you knew for me once before. You won't regret doing it again, I promise you. I'm still determined you will be happy, bluebird."

Reaching for the candle, her hand halted midair. Her eyes sought his, gleaming in the candlelight. Their gazes held. Her lips trembled.

He couldn't resist. He lowered his head. Slowly, to give her the chance to pull away.

She didn't.

He captured her lips. She tasted of stone and anger. But her mouth softened under his kisses, and he caught the flavor of passion. He could hear her heart speeding up. He could smell the change in her scent at the pleasure he gave her.

She desired him. She knew what he was, and she still desired him.

He fought to keep his kiss tender so his fangs wouldn't cut her. When her tongue found his canine, they both jumped.

He started to pull away. But her arms twined around his neck, and she sucked on his fang. He groaned and closed his hand around her buttocks, yanking her against him. She let out a whimper. Her tongue laved his canines, one after the other. She ground softly against him.

He pulled her deeper into his veils and forgot about everything except her taste and touch.

She still wanted him.

When she pulled back and gasped a breath, reality returned. They had to escape Gerrian's castle. Iskhyra waited for them in the shadows.

Maerea lifted her hand to her swollen mouth and licked her fingers. She pinched the candle flame. The little light winked out.

Then she linked her hands behind his head and pulled his mouth down to hers again.

He stopped worrying about escape. He was a Hesperine. He could spirit her away in a heartbeat. He could stand here in his enemy's stronghold and hold her as long as he pleased. No one would tear her from his arms again.

Magic cracked in the air. Before he could untangle himself from Maerea to see what had happened, something splashed over his head and poured down his back. An acrid odor choked him. Then Maerea darted out of his arms.

He spun around. Bria stood there with an empty jug in her hands. Daughter Pherakia clung to the back of a chair, her face ashen. Next to her, Master Eusebios brandished a torch, but Iskhyra's hand manacled his wrist.

She held him and his fire at arm's length. "Case in point. Humans who aren't war mages will still try to light you on fire."

He struggled against her grip. "The sorceress is with him! All is lost!"

"Oh, hush." She gave his arm a deft twist.

He dropped to his knees, releasing the torch. She caught it, tossed it, and it landed neatly in the fire. Bria staggered back from the shower of sparks, while Daughter Pherakia sank against the chair.

Iskhyra had been right. It had been a trap. Had Maerea known?

He made himself look at her. She stood as far away from him as she could, tears streaming down her face. Now he could sense in her aura what he had chosen to ignore before. She had never intended to leave with him. She had distracted him with pleasure while the mages arrived.

She had held him in her arms while she planned to kill him.

The pain of that knowledge had just hit him when an answering pain consumed his body. Countless tiny, excruciating points flared to life all over his skin and spread together into agony. With a scream, he crumpled to the floor. Maerea's face was the last thing he saw before everything disappeared in fire.

chapter fourteen

INTO HESPERA'S REALM

It all happened so fast. Maerea stood frozen in horror at what the others had tried to do. Alcaeus convicted her with a gaze.

Then Daughter Pherakia stirred. A draft breathed through the room. The embers in the hearth gave a pop.

It only took a few. Perhaps seven tiny sparks. They landed on Alcaeus's soaked clothing. And then he was consumed.

A scream tore from Maerea's throat. She didn't think. She raced forward to try to catch him as he fell.

Powerful arms closed around her. She kicked and fought, but she couldn't break the hold. Just like when the commander had taken her from Alcaeus.

She was about to lose him again.

"Watch," the sorceress said in her ear.

Shadow descended over him. Darkness itself smothered the flames.

Maerea's captor released her. She stumbled, righted herself, then went to Alcaeus, dropping to her knees beside him.

Master Eusebios made a dash for the hearth. With a hiss, he caught hold of the torch handle and yanked it out.

Maerea threw herself over Alcaeus's unmoving form. "You promised to cure him! Not destroy him!"

"It's for the best, dove." Bria took a step toward her.

"There is no cure for Hespera's curse. I won't let Alcaeus suffer like this for eternity." Daughter Pherakia raised her hands.

Master Eusebios pulled back his arm.

"Enough." The sorceress's voice silenced the room.

The shadow that protected Alcaeus swept outward in a wave. Master Eusebios threw the torch. Something unseen rippled from Daughter Pherakia's hands.

Fire and force collided with the shield of darkness. The mages staggered back.

The shadow engulfed the hearth room and swept Maerea away.

~

Maerea felt as if she had tripped through a doorway into a place she didn't recognize. Stone pillars, spell light, a thick rug under her knees. The smell of paper and Alcaeus's burnt flesh.

The sorceress knelt on the other side of him. "Are you going to help or hinder?" Her voice was calm.

Somehow it also calmed Maerea. "Help."

The sorceress nodded. "We have to get his clothes off and cleanse the potion from his wounds so it doesn't poison him."

Cloths and a jug of clean water appeared beside them, as if the sorceress had conjured them. Maerea ignored the strangeness of it all and soaked a cloth in the cool water.

When she touched the cloth to his arm, he didn't cry out in pain. Was it already too late? Was he…?

"He's unconscious," the sorceress said. "We need to work quickly."

Could the sorceress read her mind? Maerea had no time to be afraid of that. They worked in swift silence to soak his clothing off.

Watching patches of his skin go with it, she wept. "What did they do to him?"

"An alchemical concoction made from two common plants. I'm sure you're familiar with the flowers called Anthros's fire and the herb sunsword."

Maerea swallowed. Every Tenebran warrior's household grew Anthros's fire and sunsword. She had placed them on her father's bier herself to ward off Hesperines. "They really are harmful to you."

"Skin contact or fumes won't give us worse than a headache, but if they get into our blood, they're poison. They also make us burn faster."

"I didn't know. I asked the mages to help me—" *Free him from you.* "—cure him."

"I believe you."

Maerea wasn't sure why that mattered so much to her. Because she was afraid of the sorceress's revenge? Or because the sorceress was the one helping her save Alcaeus's life?

When they had completely stripped and cleansed him, the sorceress stretched him out on a blanket on his stomach. The burns ran from his shoulders, all over his back, and halfway down his thighs. The angry wounds were tinged the burnt orange of Daughter Pherakia's potion.

"Well done," the sorceress said.

"What else can we do for him?"

"There's a room upstairs where he can rest more comfortably."

"Between the two of us, can we move him without hurting him?"

The blanket levitated off the floor with Alcaeus on it. The sorceress didn't even wave her hands or chant a spell. Like a floating litter, the blanket carried him between the columns and up the steps cut into the wall. Maerea followed the sorceress up.

The staircase ended in a round chamber. The blanket sank down on the single, modest bed, settling Alcaeus there.

"How long will it take him to heal?" Maerea asked.

"That depends. He needs blood. Mine will do, but human is better." She looked at Maerea again. "Will you help or hinder?"

For the third time that night, Maerea had to choose her side. When fire had threatened to take him from her, she had run to him without thought. Just now she had tended his wounds without hesitation.

Now her thoughts confronted her, inescapable.

She had helped them do this to him. Lured him, distracted him, trapped him so the people she had trusted could try to destroy him.

In some part of herself, she had felt sure that Bria and Master Eusebios would listen to her pleas because they cared for her. She had believed Daughter Pherakia would help because Alcaeus was important to her.

Maerea had also believed Gerrian would sheath his sword out of love for her. She had wasted years making excuses for him. She had refused to see how harmful he could really be.

Alcaeus was the only person she had ever known who had chosen love above all else.

"I will give him my blood," Maerea said.

The sorceress gazed at her with unmistakable approval.

"I've made my decision," Maerea went on, "but you must tell me the consequences. People's lives are at stake, and I must be in some condition to help them after this. I want the truth, no matter how harsh."

"Will you take me at my word?"

"I will judge that by what you tell me."

"There are no consequences." Her voice was…kind.

"I don't understand."

"After tonight, do you trust anything mages have ever told you about Hesperines?"

Maerea shook her head.

"Then forget everything you think you know," the sorceress said. "No harm will come to you if he drinks from you. It won't turn you into one of us."

"It won't…put me under your power?"

"No, it won't create any connection between you and me. But it could draw you and Alcaeus closer, since you have a bond already."

Maerea had promised him everything at their wedding and given him her all on their wedding night. "He spilled his blood for my sake. I will not shy from doing the same for him."

"Then I will give you two some privacy. Just start by putting the inside of your wrist to his mouth. He'll know what to do."

The sorceress turned to leave. She moved so fluidly, eerily graceful, her black robes making her elegant figure seem even taller. Hooded and shadow-eyed, she was beautiful, in a haunting way.

"What is he to you?" Maerea asked.

The sorceress looked at him, affection apparent on her face. "A friend." Her gaze lifted to Maerea's. "Thank you."

"What is your name?" Maerea finally thought to ask.

"Iskhyra. Well met, Maerea. Alcaeus's praises of you were not exaggerated."

With that, she disappeared, leaving Maerea alone in a secret chamber with her wounded husband…a hungry Hesperine.

Pain sizzled over his back and through his veins. But he could bear it, because of that fragrance. Sweet and dark, the scent promised the end of all hurt.

Maerea's blood.

"Alcaeus?"

Maerea's voice. What dream was this?

"Alcaeus. You must drink."

Impossible. Maerea had betrayed him. This couldn't be real.

But that felt like her hand in his hair, gently adjusting his head. That felt like her skin against his lips. The perfectly smooth, tender skin on the inside of her wrist. He remembered the taste of it from their wedding night.

But now he could hear her pulse beating beneath. He sensed the vital currents of her blood in the lush, delicate veins beneath that fragile layer of skin.

She massaged his jaw until his teeth parted. The moment the tips of his canines touched her, he was lost.

His fangs shot out of his gums. He sank them into her soft, giving flesh and fastened on. She cried out as if he had touched her body.

Blood welled into his mouth, bringing flavor to life on his tongue. Oh, Goddess. This was what Maerea's blood tasted like.

A summer festival dance under an ancient tree's cool, spreading shade. A wild ride under the open sky. A lily bloom, a bluebird's song, a long, tender tryst and a sudden, consuming pleasure.

Her hand flexed, renewing the font of blood for him. With every swallow, his pain faded. She tangled her other hand in his hair, holding him to her wrist as she pillowed his head on her lap. He rested there and enjoyed the greatest feast of his life. It was a moment of pure perfection.

Her hand slid out of his hair, only to drift over his back. He shivered at the pleasure of her touch. His skin was impossibly sensitive, almost raw with sensation.

"Your burns are gone. You're going to be all right."

He heard tears in her voice. The last thing he had seen were her tears… at what he had become.

No. Had those tears been for his sake?

"She said my blood would heal you. It worked. Thank…I don't know which goddess. I don't care. You're all right."

He lifted his head, trying to understand. Blood slipped out of her wrist. He dropped his mouth to her wound again. He licked and laved the opening until her skin sealed under his tongue.

She gasped, a breathy sound that caressed his ears. Her hand kept trailing over his back.

He turned his head to get a look at her. Red-rimmed eyes, blood and water on her gown. She was curled up on the bed with him in the upstairs chamber of the Sanctuary.

She was here. She had given him her blood.

"Maerea?" His voice came out weaker than he expected. Something still sapped the strength from his veins.

"I'm so sorry," she sobbed. "I went to them for help—for a cure. They promised they would make you human again. They lied to me. I would never have agreed to their plan if I'd known they would do this to you."

"You didn't want me dead?"

"I just wanted you back."

He wrapped his fingers around her wrist. "Here is my cure."

"Do you need more?" Her guileless invitation made his gums throb and brought his body to life.

"Did it hurt?" He had to know.

She shook her head, her tousled hair falling around her face.

"How much more may I take?"

"As much as you need."

He bit her wrist where he had just healed it. It felt as good as sheathing himself in her body. His arousal pressed into the blanket beneath him.

This was *nothing* like drinking from his Gifter.

A shudder moved through Maerea. The air filled with the scent of her blood and desire. "Is it supposed to feel like this?"

"I don't know. I've never felt this way before."

"It's not like this with…her?"

He made himself kiss her vein closed again. He rolled onto his back, looking up at her. "Never. I would never break my vows to you, in death or immortality."

Her gaze swept down to his erection.

He held out a hand. "May I drink from your neck?"

Her lip between her teeth, she pulled her hair away to reveal her throat. Then she took his hand and let him pull her down to him.

The deep throb of her pulse banished his reason. But he kept his hand gentle as he cupped her neck and brought her throat to his mouth.

When he buried his fangs inside her, a roar swept out of him, and his body arched beneath her. She cried out with him, her pulse soaring. He grasped a handful of her skirts, taking hold of her hip as she squirmed against him. He listened to her panting in time to his swallows.

Her hips rocked harder. "Alcaeus. I'm about to—oh, Goddess. *Oh.*"

A new flavor burst through her blood. He jerked under her, his teeth clamping harder.

Climax. He could *taste* hers.

It was enough to make him spill right then, but with an effort of Will, he held onto his control. He would give her so much pleasure first that she would beg for him to climax inside her.

He slipped his hand under her skirts. Her hand found his, and she guided him to her sheath. As he palmed her there, she held him to her, rubbing herself against his hand.

"I thought…" Her voice came out husky between exultant gasps. "…I would never feel your touch again. Now this…"

Their rhythm was still perfect. Their hands on her body. His sucks at her neck. She moved more and more urgently, wetter and wetter against his hand.

Suddenly she put her hands on his chest and pushed away from him.

She wanted him to stop.

He unlocked his jaw, letting her free.

She sat up, blood trailing down her neck and over her collarbone to drip between her breasts. All he could think about was licking her blood from her cleavage, and he hated himself for it.

She pushed her cloak off her shoulders. Then she took her gown in both hands and yanked it over her head.

A joyous laugh overtook him. She wasn't pulling away to tell him no.

She straddled him. Looking into his eyes, she positioned herself over his cock. His head touched the warm wetness at the rim of her sheath, and he discovered just how much more sensitive Hesperine flesh was.

"*Maerea.*" His fingers dug into her hips.

She braced her palms on his chest and lowered herself, slowly at first. He sank into her a measure and groaned. Then she lifted back, adjusting her angle, and tried again.

"Beautiful," he encouraged her. "My passionate bluebird. That's right—just like that—oh, *Goddess.*"

She had found the perfect approach. Eagerly, she covered him to the hilt. Her jaw dropped, her head fell back, and she rode him.

Pleasure scathed him and became the most exquisite pain. His vision hazed until all he could see were those red droplets sliding over the inner curves of her breasts as they swung with her motions. All he could hear was her heartbeat and the undulation of blood in her veins.

He locked his hand around the back of her neck. As he guided her back down to him, she stretched out over him, splaying her knees wider. They moaned together as the fresh angle awoke fresh pleasure.

He realized he was baring his fangs. She stared at his mouth. Her sheath tightened around him, sending a delightful shock through him.

He placed a lingering kiss at her throat and listened to her sigh. This time he sank his fangs into her slowly, tenderly.

Her scream echoed off the walls. He sucked hard, dragging her blood into his mouth. She rode him faster, clawing at his chest. With his free hand, he took hold of her leg, pulling her knee higher.

They drove each other to the brink, and his reward was the foretaste of her release. He would not last this time. He clamped his hand over buttocks, holding her to him.

She writhed on his cock. Emotion and sensation crashed over his senses. His body gripped, then released, thrusting up into her on a powerful crest of ecstasy.

His climax pulsed, again and again, pouring him into her. He felt their joining in his body, tasted it in her blood, sensed it in a Union unlike anything he had ever known. Every throb of their completion seemed to sink them deeper into the current that flowed through them both.

When at last they fell still together, the Union remained. It shone unseen, swirling around them, calm and fathomless.

He healed her throat with soft kisses, then relaxed under her. He breathed, just for the pleasure of her scent. He propped his head on his arm to watch her stroke his chest. She traced a finger over the scratches she had made, as if she could smooth them away.

"I'm sorry," she whispered.

He put his hand over hers. "Those are not the first words you need to say after what you just did for me."

"I never wanted you to get hurt."

"You healed me."

As they watched, the scratches faded and disappeared.

Her tears dripped onto his chest hair, and she hid her face against him. He stroked her hair as she wept.

"How did you get here?" he asked.

"Iskhyra brought you here—with magic—and I didn't let you go."

He smiled up at the shadowy ceiling. It blurred through the tears in his eyes. "Thank you for not letting me go."

Their Union was a double-edged sword. Now it revealed her grief and regret.

"I know it's hard," he tried. "I know there is still so much to decide. But I meant what I said. I will do whatever I must for your happiness."

She lifted her head and pressed kisses to his mouth. He sensed her pushing away her fears and reaching for what was right here in front of them.

SOMETHING INSIDE MAEREA HAD shattered. A lifetime of dutiful days and prayers at a silent goddess's feet had ended. That seemed like another world. Now she was in this world with him, and she couldn't find the discipline to refuse him anything.

She didn't want to.

Deepening their kiss, he rolled with her until she was on her back beneath him. He raised up on his arms and relaxed his weight into where their bodies joined.

She gasped to feel him already hardening and lengthening inside her.

"There are advantages to being a Hesperine," he said.

She surrendered, letting her legs slide apart, letting his thickness fill her. She moaned.

"Trust me, bluebird."

He thrust, long and hard and slow, gliding through her flesh that was so raw from riding him. Like a wanton, she lay back, naked and splayed there beneath him, greedy for the next thrust, and the next…

He arched his back, driving into her as he lowered his head. She imagined having his teeth in her flesh again and almost whimpered with longing. But it was only his lips and tongue he touched to her flesh.

He licked a slow trail between her breasts, lapping up the blood drying there. "Mmm."

His deep, gravelly sound of enjoyment made her sheath quiver around him. "Do you need more blood?"

His tongue moved across her nipple. Her toes curled in her boots.

He lifted his mouth, letting cool air touch her breast. "I've never felt so satisfied in my life, actually."

"Then…I've given you enough?"

He drew her other breast into his mouth and sucked. Within moments, she was gasping for breath again, trembling on the brink of another release.

But before he pushed her over the edge, he pulled his mouth away. He stopped moving inside her and went perfectly still. She whimpered aloud now, rotating her hips under him.

He braced both hands on her knees and pushed them back to the blanket, holding her still. "Do you want to give me more blood?"

His fangs gleamed over her in the spell light. They were magnificent, she realized. As fascinating as his cock that even now impaled her.

He watched her breasts rising and falling with her breaths. "Are you asking me to bite you?"

"*Yes.*" The confession rose out of her. "I want to feel your fangs inside me again. I want to feel my blood rushing into you. Alcaeus—I want—I want—"

She watched his head descend, knowing he would give her what she craved.

He struck her throat. No pain. Not once had his fangs hurt her. She felt only the pleasure, driving deep, laying her open.

"*Yes.* Alcaeus. More. Please—"

He lifted his head and pierced the other side of her throat.

The twin penetrations flooded her body with heat that crashed into a single tide of pleasure, ebbing and flowing between her throat and her sheath. He pumped into her release, still holding her knees down. Her climax buffeted her, tossing her head back to bare her throat, bowing her hips up for his cock.

One wave flowed into another as she lay there, pinned beneath his fangs and cock and strong hands. She didn't want to escape. She wanted to drown in this darkness.

It felt more wondrous and yet more familiar than anything she'd ever known.

Her body was bucking with another climax when he gathered her close. He wrapped her legs around him. Slid one arm under her breasts. Another under her shuddering hips.

Holding her completely, he came apart again. He pounded into her with breathtaking strength.

And she felt his seed streaming into her. She didn't understand his new body. Didn't know what to do with their broken hopes for the future. But this felt the same. Warmth, life, a vital connection with him.

When at last he lifted his head, he looked into her face. His brown eyes, hooded with satisfaction, reflected the light at her like a cat's, turning it gold. His fangs had receded, their sharp lengths tamed, if only for the moment.

"You are mine," she said. "Even if I have to follow you into Hespera's realm to stake my claim. I will not lose you again."

He turned his face into her hand, his eyes drifting shut. "Have faith in me, bluebird."

"You've always been the only one I can trust. Then and now and tomorrow, come what may."

chapter fifteen

THE HIDDEN GODDESS

"Dawn is coming." Alcaeus's tongue felt heavy.

"How can you tell?"

"I can feel it." He took a deep breath, fighting the drowsiness. The heavy fragrances of their passion filled the room. Maerea smelled like screams of pleasure. There were still streaks of blood on her breasts.

It was a good thing he'd veiled this chamber earlier, although he'd not dared hope they would need privacy for this reason. With as much concentration as he could muster, he attempted a cleaning spell.

She yelped. "What was that?"

He grinned. "Did it tickle?"

"Yes." Her nose wrinkled, and she giggled.

His grin widened. "I've never heard you giggle."

"Apparently you can cause me to do all sorts of things I never do."

"I'll be sure to use magic on you more often, then."

She blinked at him. "That was magic?"

"A cleaning spell."

"I never considered Hesperines would have something so practical. If that's what your magic feels like, it won't take so much getting used to, after all." She peered at him. "Your face will, though."

He frowned. "What's wrong with my face?"

She giggled again, tracing the bridge of his nose with her fingers. "Your nose is healed, as if it was never broken. But it's still the Salicinian nose."

"Oh. That's all right, then." He forced his drooping eyelids open. "I will fall into the Dawn Slumber at any moment. I wish I could stay awake with you, but I won't be able to rouse until nightfall."

A furrow appeared between her brows. "That sounds dangerous."

"You'll be safe here."

All traces of her humor were gone. "I meant dangerous for you."

"Only if an enemy happens upon me while I'm asleep."

She brushed his wild hair back from his face. He found her tenderness as gratifying as her blood. "I will watch over you."

A sigh escaped him, and he fell into Slumber with Maerea's arms around him.

A SINGLE BREATH RUSHED out of Alcaeus. Then silence fell.

Instinctive horror came over Maerea. He wasn't breathing. Had the poison…?

She clutched a hand to his chest. There. His heartbeat. Powerful and steady.

Relief made her relax against him. He looked peaceful in the strange slumber that had overtaken him. Did Hesperines not breathe in their sleep? They didn't need air, she supposed. Only blood.

He trusted her enough to let her remain with him while he slept. Once again, he placed his heart and his life in her hands.

She would keep him safe there for now on.

A short time later, Iskhyra's voice drifted up from downstairs. "A word with you, Maerea, if now is a good time?"

"Just a moment." Maerea rose and tucked the blankets around Alcaeus, then looked around for her clothes.

Her boots were still on her feet. Her cloak lay in a pool at Alcaeus's feet. A few paces away on the floor, she found her gown.

Splashes of fiery poison disfigured the yellow velvet. The concoction had already burned through the gold girdle, leaving it in shreds. Anthros's fire and sunsword had destroyed her wedding gown. It slipped from her hands.

A wrought iron chest drew her gaze. She scrubbed her hands at a nearby wash basin before opening the trunk. Garments of strange and wondrous fabric slid between her fingers. Things she imagined a queen might wear. She chose a robe of the thickest, softest wool. The luxurious blue garment was embroidered in silver, black, and indigo, but it was also warm.

Maerea went downstairs on legs shaky from her and Alcaeus's thorough use of each other.

Iskhyra sat at a low table in the center of the room. "How is Alcaeus?"

"His wounds healed. He's sleeping now."

"I'm sorry to disrupt your time together, but I want to make sure you have everything you need before I Slumber." The Hesperine gestured to the cushion across the table from her.

Maerea took a seat. The feeling came over her that this was a negotiation table. She didn't know the true extent of the Hesperine's power. All she had to rely on were her own wits and courage. And the prize? Alcaeus's future—and her own.

Iskhyra put dark brown powder and water into a filigreed pewter pot, then set it on a matching pewter plate that emanated warmth. A day ago, the magical device would have surprised Maerea, but now it simply seemed like another feature of this strange landscape.

"May I ask how long you've been a Hesperine?"

"You may ask."

"Longer than Alcaeus."

"I have quills older than the two of you."

Maerea looked around at the scroll racks that lined the room. "You are a scholar?"

"Yes." Iskhyra filled another pot with water and some kind of dry mix of plants, then put that on the warmer as well. She caught Maerea looking at her. "It's trail stew. Alcaeus wouldn't want you to go hungry. This geomagical warmer will keep your food and drink hot all day."

"Oh."

One side of Iskhyra's mouth tilted up. "I think we've all had enough of alchemy for one night, don't you?"

"Definitely."

"Since we have little time before I fall asleep, let's get to your questions. I'm hopeful you'll find my answers helpful, since you seem to have taken me at my word about the consequences of giving Alcaeus your blood."

Actually, Iskhyra's vague warnings had left Maerea completely ignorant of the consequences. But she wouldn't have wanted to discuss anything so intimate with the Hesperine, and she didn't want to now.

"You must have turned Alcaeus for a reason. Perhaps if you explain your terms, we can come to an arrangement."

"I gave him Hespera's Gift because he asked me to. He'd rather be a Hesperine than go to Anthros's Hall and leave you."

Maerea tried not to betray her emotions. "What does he owe you in return?"

"Nothing. It's called the Gift for a reason. I would like to help you two break the siege, though."

Maerea leaned forward. "You would help us do that? Why?"

She glimpsed Iskhyra's fangs. "I'll enjoy it. Besides, I know you two will never have a moment's peace until your people are safe. Coffee?" She offered a cup.

Maerea's expectations scattered, and along with them, her negotiation tactics. This wasn't a bargaining table at all.

"Not what you expected from a Hesperine sorceress?" Iskhyra poured herself a cup of coffee.

"You told the truth. He…drank my blood, and…" Curse it. She was blushing. "…I am still in my right mind. So I doubt anything in this cup will put me under a spell."

The Hesperine's only comment was, "In fact, coffee will help you feel more alert. You'll need it."

Maerea took the cup and let it warm her hands.

"A word of advice," Iskhyra went on. "You're not trapped here, and you're free to come and go as you please. But the path outside is treacherous. It leads along the cliffs below Castra Lapidea. You wouldn't want to fall, get lost—or encounter any search parties your brother may have sent out."

Maerea swallowed. "We're so near?"

"This Hesperine Sanctuary has lain hidden under your ancestors' noses for generations. Stay inside its magic, and you'll be safe from anything."

"Master Eusebios can't find us, can he?"

"He couldn't find his own torch if it burned his ass." Her eyes flashed. "I want to apologize. No harm should have come to Alcaeus tonight, not with me standing right there. I am more than a match for those three. The Kyrian mage shouldn't have been able to take me by surprise. But I thought her defeated by the traversal and underestimated her."

"So did I."

"But they will not underestimate you again, I think."

"What was that magic? That shadow that smothered the fire and protected Alcaeus from the mages?"

"That was warding magic. Not like the shiny things you may have seen temple mages raise. Hesperine blood magic makes shadow wards."

"You're a protector," Maerea realized.

"That is my calling. Only the Goddess can decide if I have honored my vows."

Maerea knew that look. That struggle. Waking and rising day after day and wondering if you had done enough.

"I think you're beginning to understand," said Iskhyra.

Perhaps she was.

Iskhyra rose from the table, as coordinated as before. If she was on the verge of sleep, it didn't show. Taking her coffee with her, she strolled between two of the columns. She downed the contents of the cup before stretching out on a bedroll there.

"Does coffee help Hesperines feel alert?"

"I wish." Iskhyra lay on her stomach, pillowing her head on her arms. "I'll wake before Alcaeus. Let me know then if you need anything."

And then the only breathing Maerea could hear in the Sanctuary was her own.

Iskhyra trusted her, too. Perhaps it was time she trusted Iskhyra.

Maerea lay beside Alcaeus for a long time. She needed to feel his body against hers and his heartbeat under her hand.

She had not lost him.

She expected exhaustion to claim her, but energy suffused her limbs. She hadn't drunk the coffee yet. This strength in her had somehow come from what she and Alcaeus had done together.

His bite had changed her. It *had* deepened their bond, but in ways she had never imagined.

She ran a hand over the inside of her wrist, where her skin felt more sensitive than before. She felt as if some part of him ran through her veins. What they had done had not felt strange or frightening. New and thrilling, yes. But natural, too.

Everything she had done with him had always felt right.

At last the restlessness drove her to her feet. She ran a hand over the bas relief that ringed the room, which seemed to surround her in twining vines and thorns and five-petaled flowers. She drifted downstairs and learned the forms of the gargoyles carved into the columns.

She knew that outside the Sanctuary, the summer sun reigned. But here, hidden from Anthros's gaze, it was easy to forget he rode his chariot across the sky.

She peered at the scrolls without touching. The only literate women she knew were mages who lived in the confines of a shrine or temple. But Iskhyra could read these and even write. Was it difficult to learn?

What heresy did these scrolls contain? Would the secrets in them help Maerea understand all of this?

When she came to the votive statue, she stopped. So this was Hespera. Maerea had never seen a depiction of the goddess of night. Lurid tales had conjured images in her mind of a wild-haired woman with claws and blood dripping from her teeth.

This statue was beautiful. She was made of the same stone as the Sanctuary, the cliffs, and the castle. She had been hidden here all along, forgotten.

Her face was uplifted, as if to catch the light. Her hair draped around her all the way to her bare feet, concealing, revealing. Her body was sensual, her gaze intelligent, her lips curved in a joyous smile.

Red petals lay scattered at her feet. They must have come from roses, the thorned flowers associated with Hespera. Growing roses was so forbidden in the Tenebrae that Maerea had never seen one.

Rose petals looked just like pieces of festival ribbon. More red tinged the ends of Hespera's hair. Layers of bloodstains, offered over years, perhaps centuries.

Maerea touched her hand to the blood at the goddess's feet. Then she filled her hands with the petals and brought them to her face. The fragrance was sweeter than anything she had ever smelled.

Maerea went back upstairs to where her cloak lay on the end of the bed. Searching through the folds, she found her bluebird box. She filled it to the brim with Hespera's sacred flowers, and her festival ribbons began to smell like roses and blood.

Maerea realized night had fallen when Iskhyra joined her at the statue. The Hesperine pricked her finger on one fang and placed a fresh, bright libation of blood at the Goddess's feet.

"Did you sleep?"

Maerea shook her head. "I had a decision to make."

"Have you found the answers you sought?"

She looked at Iskhyra. "Can you give me the power that you have?"

"Warding?" Iskhyra asked. "Or the Gift?"

"I am sick of it." The words spilled out of her like the poison from a lanced wound. "I give every last drop within me, and it never makes a difference. I want no one to drag me away from the battle again. I want no locked doors to hold me. When people need me, I want the power to protect them. And if anyone every threatens Alcaeus again, I want to fight them with something more powerful than a sword."

"Hespera can give you that power and more."

"Why must I turn from the gods for anything I do to matter?"

"Ask rather why the gods turned us away. Hespera once held an honorable place in her brother Anthros's pantheon. All revered her as the goddess of Mercy and Sanctuary until his mages declared us heretics and began to persecute us."

"Why?"

"If you held the power, how do you think your brother would feel?"

Maerea met Hespera's gaze. "Afraid."

"You would make a worthy Hesperine. We would value you. Among our people, females can be anything we wish. Warriors or scholars, crafters or Queens. Above all, we have magic in our own right. Upon your Gifting, your unique power would manifest, whatever shape it might take."

"I want to know what my power is."

"As you have learned, there is no way to reverse the transformation. This decision is eternal. It's very important for you to be sure."

The thing she had worried away at all day, here at Hespera's feet, became a pearl. Her prize, hard-won. "I am sure. I want to become a Hesperine."

⁓

Maerea's touch coaxed him out of the Slumber. She was still here.

Half-asleep, he managed to find the important question and say it aloud. "Have you changed your mind?"

"No. I will not change my mind."

"That's all I need to hear, Maerea. I can bear everything else."

Her caresses roused him and dispelled his stupor. They rested together in silence for a long moment, and he savored it.

Her aura took on a gleam, hard and lustrous with decision.

His brow furrowed. "Maerea?"

"Alcaeus, there's something I need to tell you." Despite her serious tone, a smile spread across her face.

He sat up, cupping her face in his hand. A thought stole over him, one he dared not voice, whether out of hope or despair, he didn't know. What if…could she be with child?

She took a deep breath. "I want to become a Hesperine."

He sat back on the narrow bed, speechless.

"Iskhyra has said she will do it for me…but that you could, instead. I want it to be you. After we break the siege…after we've done all we must… we can have a future together like this."

He hadn't thought past rescuing her and protecting Salicina. He hadn't let himself. "The thought that I could still spend the rest of my life with you…it's more than I could ever ask for. I won't ask. Not for the price you would pay."

"You're not asking."

"You don't have to do this."

"I know. I want to."

He scoured his hair with his hands, swallowing the lump in his throat. "You mustn't do this for me."

Surprise flickered through her. "I thought you would be happy."

"I did what I had to, but you have a choice. You could still have a human life."

She gave her head a shake. "What is there for me in the human world?"

"You could go to my mother's side of the family. They are not invested in the feud. I'm sure they would welcome you in my memory. You could have a home, a family, all our traditions…"

"What home would there be for me, where I must beg for entry? What family could I have as a widow? And our traditions? The ones that turned my brother's heart to steel and sent your father and brother to their graves? I want no part in it."

"You could keep faith with the gods. You have not lost your place in Anthros's favor. He would still welcome you among Mother Kyria's handmaidens in his Hall."

She let out a disbelieving laugh. "I doubt he welcomes women who have lain with Hesperines—and enjoyed it. I will not go contrite to his domain. Not when my heart would still roam this world with you."

"There's still hope. Maerea, you could see your mother again one day."

Sudden tears spilled down her cheeks, and she closed her eyes tight.

"You don't have to make that sacrifice," he said.

Her eyes flew open. "My mother wasted away in that castle. Lapidea slowly destroyed her. She wouldn't wish that fate upon me. She wanted happiness for me."

"I will secure your happiness, just as I promised."

"How can you imagine I would find it anywhere but at your side?"

He knew his bluebird. She would try to follow him into darkness in the name of their vows. She held to duty to the last. But he had promised her more than that. "What happiness can there be for you in eternal night?"

"The happiness we had just found together. That endures."

"How can it?"

She shrank back from him. "I thought your feelings hadn't changed. I thought you still…"

Loved me. Her unspoken words throbbed in the Union. She yearned for him to return them, her aura pining, although he was right here next to her.

He had to hold her. Had to kiss her with all the ferocity of what she meant to him. Had to feel her holding him as if she would never let him go. Even though he knew she must.

"I love you," he swore. "I will love you every moment of every night of eternity."

"So will I. I'm still in love with you, Alcaeus."

Her priceless gift, granted twice. This time, with no secrets between them.

She loved him. Just as he was. Even now.

"Maerea. This transformation cost me everything else, but not your love. That is all I need to endure this life."

"You don't have to endure it. You can enjoy it—with me."

"I will not let the strangeness of this existence and the burden of time wear away at your sweet hopes until it extinguishes your spirit."

"That's not how I feel."

"Not now. But one night, you would. I'm so sorry, Maerea. I made a bargain with Hespera for the strength to rescue you. But it's not within my power to give you the future I promised you. Our life together was the price I paid."

"Are you saying you would go back to the way things were, if you could? That you would still choose our human life over what you have become?"

"Wouldn't you?"

Her aura gleamed brighter. "No."

He stared at her. "I don't understand."

She took his hands. "I know how sudden this must seem, after the way

I reacted when I learned you're a Hesperine. But you know how I feel now. I hope I proved that with my blood. The past night and day have changed how I see everything."

"Even our *marriage?* I thought you were happy."

"That was the only happiness in my life. And we can still have that."

"All the plans we made…" They had felt so real, for so short a time.

She pulled his hands a little closer, her gaze alight. "We can make new plans."

He saw before him no woman in mourning. She made it look easy to cast aside the life they had lost. Maerea, who had held every other memory in reverence, who had lived by her grief. "You would come to miss it. If not tonight, then one night soon. And there will be many, many nights—an eternity of them, and no going back."

"I wouldn't want to go back to having no power."

"Power?" The word sounded like a foreign tongue, coming from her. "That's not why I chose the Gift. It was never about that."

"I know. But that's why I want it."

He pulled his hands slowly from hers. "I never thought that was important to you."

"Is that so strange? That I would want to no longer be at men's mercy? That I would want to be powerful like Iskhyra?"

"What has she been saying to you?"

"Only answers to the questions I asked her. This is my decision. By every goddess, I have a mind of my own! I want power of my own to match it. You do not understand what it was like after Gerrian took me back to Castra Lapidea. What he did to me while I was his prisoner. I will never endure that again."

He couldn't find an answer to that.

She got to her feet, so sure of herself, more regal than he had ever seen her. A blue robe that shone with Hesperine embroidery swirled around her. "I'm not doing this for you, Alcaeus. I'm doing it for me. Will you Gift me or not?"

His sweet wife, a Hesperine? His bluebird, with no chance of happiness in the human world? "I cannot bear the thought."

Hurt shattered her aura, but on her face, she showed him only her certainty. "I see. You don't wish to be a part of this. Iskhyra will be my Gifter, then."

"Maerea, I beg of you. Wait—"

"I've spent my life waiting."

Desperation and unquenched thirst burned in his throat. This was his fault.

But not only his fault. The true blame lay at one man's feet.

"I will give you back your human life, even though I cannot share it with you. I'll make this right."

"What are you talking about? Alcaeus—"

The lid of the chest banged open before his Will, and she jumped. Rich garments flew out of the trunk and scattered. Robes fit for Hesperines. He blasted them aside and donned the last fighting robe in the pile.

He stepped to the library. By the time Maerea made it down the stairs, he had already levitated his mail over his head. His armor settled over the robe, cold through the fabric. It held none of its reassuring weight. It felt too light on his immortal body.

"Alcaeus, what are you going to do?"

His family sword flew into his hand. "It is time I ended the feud once and for all."

She reached out, clutching at his arms, but she could not hold him. Focusing all his Will on the object of his rage, he stepped.

chapter sixteen

THE PILLARS OF THE SANCTUARY

ISKHYRA NEVER NEEDED HELP. She was always the one who came to the rescue.

She had no illusions, however, that she never made mistakes. And as powerful as she was, they occurred on only one scale: devastating. This one could have cost her newgift his life, so soon after Hespera had saved him.

She kept recalling every moment of the confrontation with the mages. By the Goddess, she had dueled war mages and lived to tell the tale. A puff of telekinesis from an exhausted healer should never have gotten past her.

It wouldn't have, if she'd been using all her power.

She could break the siege. If she stopped holding back. But that would draw too much attention. Tales would carry…and eventually reach the First Prince's ears. If he found out about her, she would be in trouble.

Now she faced a choice. She could wield her magic to the fullest, then pick up the pieces. Or she could admit she needed help.

Standing on the porch of the Sanctuary, Iskhyra looked up at the moons that pushed and pulled the tides of her life. When she had undertaken this quest, she had made an effort to ensure no one would get hurt except her. That was why she traveled alone.

But her search for the library had led her to Alcaeus. His suffering had led her to the library. Somehow he and Maerea had become Iskhyra's quest, too.

She wouldn't fail them. She put a fist over her heart in a Hesperine salute before the Goddess's Eyes. It was time to seek allies.

She would find out if any other Hesperines errant were within hailing distance. She levitated up to the top of the cliffs. Flaring her nostrils, she scented the air.

"Bleeding thorns," she swore.

There was no mistaking the distinctive musk on the wind. Every Hesperine knew what that smell meant: they were coming for you.

Liegehounds.

The fighting man's one and only effective weapon against Hesperines. Gerrian wanted Maerea back.

He could not have her.

Holding her magic close, Iskhyra stepped to a position upwind of the beasts. Darts of fire shot through the night. In the glare of the flames, seven liegehounds leapt. Their handlers stood at their backs, shouting commands and firing flaming bolts from their crossbows.

At the center of the battle, two powerful auras shone within a shadow ward. Fellow Hesperines. The hounds circled them, closing in.

Iskhyra whipped a ward around herself and stepped into the fray. A spray of flaming bolts ricocheted off her spell as she landed between the other two immortals.

"Welcome!" A male Hesperine towered beside her, an open scroll levitating in front of his hand.

"Excellent. Another warder." The shadow ward emanated from the female on Iskhyra's other side.

It was almost a shock to hear friendly voices speaking the Divine Tongue, the mother tongue of immortals, the language of Orthros.

She joined her magic to her fellow warder's in time for the liegehounds to make a lunge. They braced themselves. The dogs' teeth raked through their magic.

The warder grimaced. "We should step out of here. Now."

Light shone from the scroll, illuminating the scholar's hooded face and casting his rich black skin in sorcerous blue. His travel robes whipped around him as if in an invisible current. Half the crossbow bolts extinguished.

He let out a laugh. "I crossed half the world to go errant here! I will not allow a few dogs to run me off."

"Stubborn scrollworm," muttered the warder, who wore a fighting robe. She pushed more power into her and Iskhyra's spell. The tears in their shield shrank.

"Seven liegehounds are nothing." The scholar's voice was deep and educated. He spoke with the cosmopolitan Imperial accent of a Capital University professor. "Did I tell you I once had to defeat seven dozen undead to retrieve an enchanted toe ring from a necromancer's underground palace?"

"Only seven dozen times. But defeating necromancers is your specialty. These liegehounds' specialty is defeating Hesperines." The warder's accent was Imperial, too, like her smooth brown skin and silken black braid.

Many Hesperines came from mortal origins in the Empire, the human lands far from here where immortals were welcome. The Empire was more than Orthros's ally. It was one of Orthros's two hearts, their greatest poet had written.

Something warm and fierce rose in Iskhyra. These two Hesperines reminded her so much of…

She channeled her emotion into her magic and layered more power into the ward. But not too much power.

The scholar flicked his fingers at the men trying to relight their bolts. Fires snuffed out here and there. "Where are my manners? With whom do we have the pleasure of educating these uncouth miscreants?"

The warder spared her a glance. "I would remember your aura if we'd met in the Prince's Charge."

Well, this grew more complicated by the moment. They were members of the Prince's Charge, the force of Hesperines errant under the command of the First Prince. The very Hesperine Iskhyra must avoid at all costs. "No, I'm not a Charger."

"An independent Hesperine errant, then. No easy path." The warder gave her a salute. "Fortress Master Jaya, at your service."

"Fortress Master Baruti." The scholar managed a bow while whipping another scroll out of his sash.

Cup and thorns. Not just Chargers. Two of the Fortress Masters, the First Prince's seconds-in-command, who answered only to him.

It wasn't too late for Iskhyra to help them defeat the liegehounds, wish them well, and be on her way.

But where would that leave Alcaeus and Maerea?

"Your reputations precede you, Fortress Masters. But I thought you usually remain on guard at Castra Justa. What brings you so far from the Prince's stronghold?"

Master Baruti's aura lit up with enthusiasm. "It's true I usually remain at the Castra in my capacity as the Charge's librarian. Safeguarding our collection of magical texts usually requires my undivided attention. But in this case, it was necessary for me to come looking for the scrolls myself."

Master Jaya drove the ward down into the dirt where the liegehounds were trying to dig under it. "You can tell how he loathes field assignments. Hard to pry this one out of his reading chair, to be sure. Too bad there's no one else qualified to handle the scrolls and artifacts our Hesperines errant run across in the field."

Iskhyra struggled not to smile. She eyed Master Baruti. He was all honed muscle and elegant poise. He looked like he could break a liegehound in two with his bare hands, but would rather devote them to calligraphy.

She buried another section of the ward. "Are you here as his protection, Master Jaya?"

She snorted. "Our current errand requires a warder."

"If anyone can uncover the Sanctuary, Jaya can."

They were looking for scrolls…and a Sanctuary that needed a powerful warder to uncover it.

Iskhyra would have to even more careful than she had imagined.

Master Baruti's second scroll sent up tendrils of black, as if the ink leapt off the paper. The dark threads from his arcane text leapt into the ward, strengthening Iskhyra and Jaya's spell.

The influx of magic from the two Hesperines made Iskhyra's heart pound and her veins sing.

Master Baruti's aura quieted with reverence. "We're searching for a library from fifteen and a half centuries ago. Records indicate it's in this area, but no one has found it. When Hespera worship was outlawed, the Sanctuary mages who tended the library sealed themselves and their scrolls inside to protect our knowledge from our persecutors."

"They gave their lives," Master Jaya said, "rather than let our sacred texts fall into the hands of the mages."

"Now their cause is ours. We must retrieve the documents and secure them at Castra Justa so the knowledge will survive and benefit our people."

"I hope to detect the wards and open them to us without compromising the protections."

"Yes, we must ensure our discovery does not put the scrolls at risk of deterioration."

The First Prince's confidants, and they were looking for the library.

The knowledge had survived. The wards had opened. And Iskhyra had found what she'd been looking for. Now they wanted to take all of it to the Castra.

Where it would benefit their people.

The hounds' handlers shouted more commands in their strange old training tongue. The dogs opened their jaws and scoured the ward again. Iskhyra and Master Jaya pushed their barrier outward, knocking the hounds back. Dark cords of magic from Master Baruti's scroll wound around the hounds' jaws.

When Iskhyra continued her quest, the library would do no one any good if it was once more lost to history.

It belonged to all Hesperines. And there could be no better stewards than the Hesperines beside her. Of course the First Prince would send such worthy experts to complete their people's search for the lost trove of wisdom.

When the liegehounds crouched to spring, Master Jaya raised the ward higher above their heads. Iskhyra followed her lead, helping her heighten the barrier.

The dogs lunged, making one of their infamous leaps. Iskhyra watched them jump high enough to snatch a levitating Hesperine from the air. A drop of their spittle hit her forehead.

She slammed her power into the ward, colliding with Jaya's. The barrier sealed in a dome over their heads just as the darkness at Master Baruti's command coiled around the beasts' paws. The inky snares dragged the hounds back down to the ground.

"If you insist on staying, Baru, we should disable the handlers. That will make the hounds easier to defeat."

"Very well. Seven non-mages will be easy for you."

"Are you sure you don't want to knock a few heads together yourself?"

"That's what you warriors are for."

The Fortress Masters laughed, and Iskhyra with them. So this was what life was like at Castra Justa.

Her humor faded into something wistful and painful she chose not to examine. Such feelings were hazardous to her quest.

"And you?" Master Jaya asked. "Warrior or scholar?"

"Whatever the occasion demands," she offered. "I am Iskhyra."

Master Baruti smiled. "To what do we the owe the good fortune of meeting with you at such an opportune place and time?"

"I came looking for reinforcements. My newgifts and I ran into some trouble last night, courtesy of the lord who sent these hounds, and we would be very grateful for your assistance."

Their auras changed, reverent joy charging the small circle they formed.

Iskhyra couldn't help but smile, too. "Most nights, they ask for the Mercy. But Alcaeus asked for the Gift. Now his wife wishes to join him."

"Two to welcome among our people," Master Baruti marveled.

"They need that. I'm sorry their first impressions have been the hardships of life as a Hesperine errant Abroad."

"Where are they now?" Master Jaya watched the hounds wrest free of the ink traps. "We can't let these beasts find them."

Iskhyra readied her power for the next attack. "When I rescued Alcaeus from the battlefield, I feared I wouldn't find a safe place to Gift him before his wounds claimed his life. But a Sanctuary I had never encountered opened for us, deep in the Lapidean Cliffs. There's a chamber full of scrolls inside."

An incredulous laugh escaped Master Baruti.

"The wards opened to his need?" Master Jaya's magic swelled.

Master Baruti unfurled his scrolls. "Sanctuary magic is inherently sacrificial. By its very nature, it responds to the needs of others. When confronted with a person in danger, the spells on the library rose to the occasion."

Iskhyra looked from the warrior to the scholar. "Care to break a siege with me, then settle in for some reading?"

"There's a siege?" Master Jaya's aura all but sparkled.

"Well, Iskhyra, you know how to win over a warrior and a scholar in one fell swoop." A wooden orb levitated out of Master Baruti's pocket and spun in the air.

Bolts emptied from the men's loaded crossbows. The liegehounds scattered in confusion. Their handlers shouted after them, running off in different directions to round up their wayward beasts.

Iskhyra looked Master Baruti up and down. "I've never seen artifacts like you use in battle."

"I pick up all sorts of useful things here and there." With a satisfied smile, he pocketed the orb. "Let us leave these fools to their fruitless hunt. Show us the library."

GERRIAN HAD ALREADY BEGUN to build himself a new life on the ashes of Alcaeus's. The bastard had set himself up in a commander's pavilion out of the reach of Salicina's archers, but with a good view of the siege. Firelight glowed from within the tent, and the night wind lifted his banners high.

Tonight Alcaeus would teach Gerrian to be careful what he wished for.

Armored and veiled, he marched through the camp. The soldiers on watch drank and sang and stuffed themselves with fetid game as if death did not stalk in their midst. The others snored, trusting that the god of death and dreams would not snatch them before they woke. It was not Hypnos they had to fear tonight. Alcaeus strolled up to Gerrian's pavilion and stepped through the flap without lifting a finger. He swept his veil around the entire tent.

Gerrian slept fully clothed atop the blankets of his cot, one hand wrapped around his blade, the other around a charm of Anthros's fire and sunsword. So he did not rest so easily tonight. Alcaeus flared his nostrils and drank in the scent of the man's fear.

He tried levitating the charm out of Gerrian's hand, but the herbs stung his senses, as if hostile to his magic. He would have to watch out for those. But he had survived poison and fire worse than Gerrian's little protective charm.

He rested the tip of his sword at the base of Gerrian's pale, weak throat. "Well met, brother-in-law."

Gerrian jerked awake. The motion pressed him against the sword tip, and he hissed in pain. He shrank back, his eyes widening.

Alcaeus smiled, letting Gerrian see his fully extended fangs.

The smell of Gerrian's fear grew rich and thick. White rimmed his eyes. He let out a hoarse yell. "Guards! To me!"

Alcaeus laughed. "Scream as loud as you like. No one will hear you."

"Commander! Hesperines! Loose the dogs!"

"No one is coming to save you."

He kept screaming until Alcaeus pressed the sword tip a little closer against his throat. At the first droplet of blood that squeezed out, Gerrian fell silent. The stuff in his veins stank of malice. Alcaeus's stomach turned.

Where in this wretch was the brother who had once shown Maerea love? How had he come from the same blood as she?

"Well, Gerrian, everything is going exactly according to your plan. You're getting everything you wanted. Or are you?"

Sweat glistened on Gerrian's lip.

Alcaeus smiled wider. "Did you expect Hesperines to prolong my death, then desecrate my corpse? That would have been so much easier and more satisfying for you. Alas, now you have a problem. Your worst enemy is immortal—and he has come for you."

Gerrian lifted the charm and began reciting prayers. His entire body went stiff, braced for the bite of Alcaeus's steel.

Alcaeus listened to the incantations and sniffed the air. The charm's odor made his nose burn, but he felt no other ill effects. "Well, you're no mage, are you? Perhaps not much of a devout, either."

"I've been faithful to the god of war all my life! Anthros favors me! He showed that when he blessed me with victory over your father, your brother—and you."

Alcaeus stepped back, lifting his sword. "Prove it."

Gerrian just stared at him.

"On your feet. Raise your father's sword to meet my father's. Or are you too much of a coward to face me in battle now?"

Gerrian's face went from pallid with fear to ruddy with anger. He leapt to his feet, bringing up his blade with his infamous speed and precision.

Alcaeus had watched that steel cut short his father and brother's lives. He'd felt its power for himself when it had broken through his mail. It had seemed as if Anthros himself imbued Gerrian's strike with godly power, directing the blade to just the right place to perform the unlikely feat.

But now Gerrian's movements seemed slow. Alcaeus parried without effort.

Gerrian might be rash and arrogant, but when it came to swordsmanship, he was no fool. Instead of launching into his characteristic, devastating attacks, he feinted. He was trying to test Alcaeus's defenses and reevaluate him as an opponent.

Alcaeus batted his enemy's sword away, another smile coming to his face. They circled each other in the confines of the pavilion to the sound of Gerrian's tense breathing. Alcaeus's steps were silent, not even rousing a clink from his mail.

"Where is my sister?" Gerrian demanded.

"If not for you, she would be safe in her home."

"What have you done to her?"

She had offered herself so willingly. Alcaeus should never have given into the temptation. Never drawn her deeper into the darkness with him. Shame at how he had feasted on her made him falter.

Gerrian's blade came too close to Alcaeus's neck. He parried at the last instant. Their blades locked at the hilt, bringing their faces so close he could smell the rage and wine on Gerrian's breath. "I have only ever tried to keep her safe and happy. Because I love her more than you do."

"How dare you!" Gerrian's spittle landed on Alcaeus's blade. "Even as a mortal you stole her, violated her, took her from the future she could have had. And then when I got her back, you took her from me again! I should cut your tongue from your head for invoking her name!"

"If you truly loved her, you never would have made her mourn. You would have spared me for her sake."

"I struck you down because I love her. To save her from you. I had to protect her from herself."

"You're such a fool. All these years, she has been protecting you. She's the only reason anyone in your domain still lives. You should have listened to her."

Alcaeus gave Gerrian a little shove. The man staggered back as if hit by a battering ram. He righted himself and he charged, putting all the power of his body behind the opening move Alcaeus recognized. The first of the series of strikes that had brought all the men of his family to their knees.

Alcaeus held fast to their sword.

The blows rained down. His sword leapt to block or parry every one. He withstood the deadly dance that had destroyed his family.

When it was over, Gerrian retreated, his chest heaving.

"Not feeling so victorious now, are you?" Alcaeus taunted.

With a single swing, he sent Gerrian's blade flying from his hand. The sword that had destroyed Alcaeus's life clanged to the ground. Gerrian held nothing but impotent herbs, his hair plastered to his head with sweat.

With a flick of levitation, Alcaeus dropped Gerrian at his feet. He planted his boot on the wrist of Gerrian's sword arm and pressed the tip of his own blade to the man's throat once more.

"What do you want?" Gerrian rasped. "I'm sure we can come to some agreement."

"How soon the mighty warrior abandons the way of Anthros and stoops to cunning bargains like Hypnos. But you remember the temple stories, don't you? Hespera always outwits Hypnos, in the end."

"What use to you is revenge? Will it really satisfy you to send me to my rewards in Anthros's Hall, where you cannot follow? Surely there is something more you want."

Alcaeus leaned closer, baring his fangs. "I wanted my father to grow old in peace. I wanted my brother to raise my nephew. I wanted my sister-in-law to spend her days with the man she loved. For myself, all I ever asked for was Maerea. You've already taken everything I want, and there is no power in this world that can restore it."

The Thirst gnawed at him, and a shudder wracked him. No matter. His enemy was down.

"I'll save her from you again!" Gerrian ranted. "My men are already in the forest, tracking her with liegehounds. They'll hunt you down and tear you to shreds for what you did to her."

"They'll never find her. She is beyond your reach."

"I won't abandon her to whatever fate you have in store for her!"

"You won't live to see it. With you dead, Lapidea will be hers. The one who is worthy of the domain will hold it in her own right. I already paid for her future with my blood. Now it's your turn. We are the price of her happiness. So be it."

"She wants the title? Faithless bitch."

Alcaeus kicked Gerrian in the ribs and listened to them crack. "Watch your tongue. All she ever wanted was to keep your sorry hide safe."

Alcaeus looked down upon the shivering coward who was all that remained of Maerea's loved ones. Gerrian's fragile heart pounded hard, his aura flickering with panic.

He stared at the damaged links of Alcaeus's mail. "What are you waiting for?"

If you truly loved her…you would have spared me for her sake.

Why did Alcaeus hesitate?

I had to protect her from herself.

This is my decision. By every goddess, I have a mind of my own!

"Send me to Anthros's Hall!" Despair soured Gerrian's scent and the Blood Union.

Another shudder made Alcaeus's blade tremble in his hand.

You should have listened to her.

I wouldn't want to go back to having no power.

"Anthros is pleased with my deeds," Gerrian whimpered.

You've already taken everything I want, and there is no power in this world that can restore it.

The happiness we had just found together. That endures.

Alcaeus flicked his blade across Gerrian's throat. The precise cut marked his jugular, but left it intact. That would scar. "I will not kill you. Let that stand as testament to my love for Maerea. Don't waste the life you owe her."

An eerie howl tore through the night. A cunning gleam appeared in Gerrian's eyes.

Alcaeus knew that sound. The baying of a hound who has scented his prey. Six more joined the chorus.

The liegehounds.

Their excited barks closed in fast. Before he could muster the focus to step, the dogs burst into the tent.

～

Maerea paced the porch of the Sanctuary and counted every helpless moment until Iskhyra's return.

When the Hesperine finally appeared, Maerea rushed to her, only to hesitate. They were not alone.

Two other Hesperines flanked Iskhyra. They looked nothing like the deathly pale creatures the horrid tales described. The Blood Moon shone russet on the slender, muscular female, while the night cast the tall, powerful male in indigo and black. The world of Hesperines was more complex than Maerea had ever imagined. They gave her kind, fanged smiles.

"What's wrong?" Iskhyra asked.

"Alcaeus is gone. I don't know what he planned to do, but we have to stop him."

Iskhyra uttered something in Divine that must be a curse. "What happened? Did he give you any idea where he might have gone?"

"When I told him I want the Gift, he reacted in the last way I expected. He doesn't want me to do it. He still thinks I should have a human life. He took up his sword and stepped away."

"We must divide our forces and search the area," Iskhyra said.

"We must find him before the liegehounds do," the male Hesperine said.

"A newgift is no match for one of them," said the female, "much less a whole pack."

Maerea's heart lurched. "Liegehounds? Where?"

Iskhyra gripped Maerea's shoulder. "I believe your brother sent them to look for you."

"Hypnos take him. He must have gotten the dogs from his ally."

"Maerea, this is Master Baruti and Master Jaya. They are our people, and we will help each other."

Masters? They sounded important—and powerful. Maerea resisted the urge to curtsy to her new allies. That wasn't right. After a moment's hesitation, she extended a hand. All she knew of a lady's proper conduct gave her no idea of what to say.

"Fortress Masters," Iskhyra addressed them, "Newgift Maerea, who awaits her transformation."

"Don't be afraid." Master Baruti put back his hood. The moons shone on his bald head and compassionate, bearded face. Instead of clasping her wrist, he gently took her hand in both of his huge ones.

Master Jaya rested a hand on Maerea's other shoulder. "We'll help Iskhyra find Alcaeus."

How could humans be so wrong about Hesperines? They didn't even know her, and yet they gave her protection. Honesty. Respect. "Thank you so much. What can I do?"

Iskhyra gave her shoulder a squeeze before releasing her. "Stay here and stay safe, I'm afraid. The last thing we want is for the liegehounds to scent you and their handlers to take you back to your brother yet again. Don't set foot beyond the pillars of the Sanctuary."

"I hate it. I hate not being able to lift a finger."

"That won't be the case for much longer," Master Baruti reassured her.

"You'll make a fine Hesperine," said Master Jaya.

With that, the three immortals faced different directions and disappeared.

Alcaeus felt the hounds' hot breath on his neck.

He stepped away and landed hard. As he rolled to his feet, his head spun with thirst. He scented the air, glancing around.

The tent was a scant distance away. How could that be? He had aimed for the Sanctuary.

Seven massive shadows raced out of the camp, eating the distance.

He took off running through a field of rye. Trees neared ahead. The pack's jaws snapped behind him. There were human footfalls, too, barely keeping up with the beasts. The crackle of torches. The howls echoed behind him, the jubilant bays of hunters who would soon taste blood.

Alcaeus focused his Will on the Sanctuary. The magic, the refuge. Maerea. He stepped again.

And landed in the woods. The liegehounds crashed into the underbrush not far behind him.

What was wrong with him?

He raced at Hesperine speed around and between the trees, levitating over thickets and logs. The howls split the air behind him again. Closer. Closer.

His tongue was dry, his throat hoarse, his veins aching with the need for blood. The forest lurched around him. He couldn't muster the concentration to try stepping again.

He would have to keep running.

chapter seventeen

A BETTER HESPERINE

I*F HE DIED HERE* while Gerrian still breathed, Alcaeus would fail Maerea after all.

He clung to the thought. It had kept him on his feet for…how long? Hours?

The dogs were strange, torturous sounds in the night. Always behind him. Driving him onward.

Misshapen shadows swooped past him. Trees. The world was loud, the night bright, his senses so keen it pained him, although his thoughts were a blur.

And always, the Thirst. No. Hunger. It wracked him, stealing the strength from his limbs, dragging at his legs.

His armor weighed on him. He struggled out of it, half levitating it, half wrestling with it. He cast it aside, and the hounds were on it in an instant. But it bought him that instant. He ran on, his fingers going numb around the grip of his sword.

He had to have Maerea's blood. Just one more time. His mouth watered, but it wasn't enough to wet his tongue. Just a sip of her…her bright, vibrant spirit filling his veins…her warm body welcoming him…

The cacophony of the hounds was closer now.

He tried to run faster and stumbled. His gums throbbed. He scented a deer nearby. The smell of its blood sickened him, but he needed it. If only there was time to stop and drink.

One liegehound made a leap and came within arm's length. He levitated out of its reach.

He made it only a pace off the ground before he dropped like a stone. His legs folded under him. He heard something crack. But he dragged himself to his feet again and ran on.

Pain lanced his ankle with every step. Nothing compared to the pain of his thirst. His sword became his crutch.

How had it come to this?

His good foot caught on a branch and sent him flying. His sword flew out of his hand. He skidded across the underbrush and collided with a tree. His head snapped back against the hard trunk, pain shooting through his neck, and his teeth sank into his tongue.

Stunned, he could only watch the oncoming beasts.

Fur like armor. Broad, dripping maws. Paws the size of his face. The air was ripe with their musk. All he could hear now were their panting breaths as they closed in.

A shadow blazed to life between him and the onslaught. Heavenly darkness stood before him. Magic hammered in the Union. Amidst the powerful spell, he recognized her. Iskhyra, his Gifter, as he had never sensed her before.

Then all his senses went dark.

"You look like Hypnos used you for target practice."

Alcaeus pried his eyes open.

Iskhyra scowled down at him, her wrist before his mouth. "Drink, you fool."

He tried to look around to get his bearings. Pain seized him. He was still plastered to that godsforsaken tree. "Is it already too late? Has she begun her Gifting?"

"No, I was too busy saving your fresh blood from the liegehounds."

"The liegehounds—!"

"I took care of them."

No more howls. But Alcaeus didn't smell any bodies. "How?"

Iskhyra yanked his jaw open and jammed her wrist onto his fangs. Then she put a hand to his throat and did something that made him swallow.

His stomach heaved. She pulled her wrist away and turned him over in time for him to empty his stomach into the underbrush.

"Bleeding thorns," she muttered. "Try again. Slowly."

He knew it was no use arguing with Iskhyra. He drank one small sip at a time. His thirst went from pure torture to mere horror. His thoughts cleared enough for him to realize something was very wrong.

"I don't know what's happening to me."

She examined him with efficient, careful hands, identifying his wounds. "You drank from Maerea last night?"

He grimaced. "Yes."

"And tonight when you awoke?"

"No…we quarreled."

"Then what happened?"

He dragged in a breath.

"I'm here to help you, Newgift."

"I went to kill Gerrian."

"Oh? And how did you do?"

"I couldn't."

"Was it a difficult fight?"

"No. So easy. My speed, strength. Magic."

"So you exerted significant energy."

"Then the liegehounds…"

Anger tinged her aura. "Why didn't you step back to the Sanctuary?"

"Tried. Couldn't."

She ceased her exam. "Your wounds aren't healing. My blood isn't nourishing you properly. Your power, even your essential magic, is inhibited." She pulled back his lip and examined his fangs, then looked into his eyes. "Overextended canines, dilated eyes, fever, and chills."

"What does it mean?"

"You're a blessed vulture."

"Uh?"

"Hmph. That Hesperine expression doesn't translate very well. I think men would call you a lucky bastard."

He snorted a laugh and quickly regretted it. "Lucky to be alive."

"That's not what I mean." Iskhyra sat back on her heels. Her cleaning spell rid him of half the forest floor, bloody vomit, dog spittle, and the stink of Gerrian's fear. "Do you remember when I explained the only things that can make Hesperines ill?"

"Poison," he spat. "How could it still be in my body after…" After Maerea's blood, sweet and pure, had cleansed him. The thought made another shudder rattle his body and pushed his fangs painfully far from his gums.

"It isn't. Maerea's blood has completely cured any and all damage from the mages' attack."

Maerea's blood… "You didn't prepare me. At all."

Iskhyra grinned. "I did warn you."

"Not that she would taste like that…that it would feel like…"

"That is what we call the Feast. I don't think you need a lesson in how it differs from the Drink."

Emotions he couldn't name surged in him. He yearned for Maerea. Not just thirst. Not just lust. If he didn't taste her again, and soon, it would destroy him more painfully than men had ever tried to do.

"What besides poison can sicken a Hesperine?" Iskhyra asked.

Alcaeus gasped a breath. "The Craving."

Iskhyra spoke in a reverent hush. "May Hespera's Eyes gaze with joy upon your love." She cleared her throat. "That one translates rather well, I think, but I mean to say congratulations."

"Maerea is my Grace?"

Iskhyra put a finger to her lips. "As your Gifter, I count as your only immediate family. Announcing your Grace to anyone else is legally binding. You wouldn't want to formally invoke your bond without Maerea's participation."

"This can't be."

"I've seen the symptoms of Craving before. There's no doubt."

"I only had her blood once."

"Once is all it takes, when your love is true."

"But it hasn't been that long."

"How long it takes the withdrawal symptoms to manifest varies based on a Hesperine's power, age, and self-control."

"I have excellent stamina!" he protested.

"You've been a Hesperine for less than a month, and you're still learning discipline. Given a newgift's hunger and your untrained power, it's not surprising it took barely a night for you to notice the symptoms, especially a night that taxed you so."

"I can't be addicted to her blood already. My life can't depend on her. I can't…" Die without her?

Of course he would. He had known all along he was prepared to die for her. And without her, what did he have to live for? Once she and Salicina were safe, he would have nothing but his honor.

Of course Maerea was his Grace. She had always been the only one for him, and she always would be. As a man, he had needed her strength and her love, her keen mind and passionate body. As a Hesperine, he needed all that and more. Her blood filling his veins. Her spirit filling their Union.

"You mustn't tell her," he implored.

"I wouldn't presume. This news is yours to share with her. But Alcaeus, it is wonderful news. Consider how fortunate you are. Many Hesperines wait centuries to find their Grace. You two embrace immortality at each other's sides. You will know abundance every night of your lives."

Alcaeus blinked up at his Gifter, trying to clear his vision. "You said you've seen the symptoms of Craving before."

She nodded. "You can take my word for it."

"But you've never experienced them."

"No," she answered neutrally.

"How long have you been waiting?"

"It's just as well," was her reply. "I have work to do, and I couldn't do it if I had a Grace pestering me to stay at home."

"What if you had a Grace who would help with your work?"

"I think that's a question Maerea would very much appreciate if you asked her."

"I can't. If she finds out about my Craving, she'll do anything to become a Hesperine to save me. I misunderstood her decision…but I'm still certain that she shouldn't become a Hesperine for my sake."

Iskhyra helped him to his feet, half carrying him. "Come. I'll step you back to the Sanctuary. You need her blood, and then you need to talk to her."

"I'm not sure she's ready for me to take her blood again yet."

"You must drink from her. You need a clear head. This may be one of the most important conversations you have in your very long life."

He nodded, although it made his head pound. "I have to speak with my Grace."

⁓

THE FRAGRANCE OF MAEREA'S blood hit him like a gale. She leapt to her feet from where she had knelt at the statue of Hespera. Her face streaked with tears, she raced to his side.

He looked into her eyes. "I promised I would never make you cry."

"No, you promised you would only make me cry for good reasons." She laughed through her tears, her relief brighter than the spell lights, and put his other arm around her shoulders.

Suddenly they were in the upstairs room. Iskhyra and Maerea lowered him onto the bed.

"What happened?" Maerea was asking.

"Don't worry about me, bluebird. I'll be all right now."

"The liegehounds nearly ran him into the ground," Iskhyra said, "but I found him in time. Nothing your blood can't mend. I'll go find the Fortress Masters and let them know all is well." She departed and left them alone.

Alcaeus drew a labored breath, gazing up at his wife. His Grace. "There is so much to say…"

"Not yet." Maerea put her mouth to his.

She kissed him with tender desperation, and his Craving roared up. He grasped her shoulders to push her away from this hunger he had become. But she deepened the kiss, devouring his tongue, licking his fangs. He groaned and yanked her down to him.

She dragged her mouth away, and the next thing he knew, the soft flesh of her throat pressed against his fangs.

"Feast," she commanded.

He could only obey. His wild fangs fastened onto her throat, and he consumed her sacred offering of blood.

Her anger and love, declarations and unsaid words filled his mouth and veins and the Union. Blood and spirit poured into him. His pulse came to life, and his heartbeat surged.

She had saved him again. She had been saving him all along.

Her strong, slender hands pushed his fighting robe up past his waist. Her own soft robe scoured his skin as she dragged the fabric out from between them. The insides of her thighs caressed the outside of his. Soft, warm velvet skin. She gripped him between her knees, trapping him beneath her.

Hot wetness descended upon his cock, and he let out a cry against her throat. His hips jerked, reaching for what his body craved. Lust had never been so agonizing and wondrous.

She claimed his body in hard, fast strokes. A feast of arousal and gratification with every roll of her hips and each tightening of her sheath.

Everywhere her blood reached, his power returned. Magic filled his dry veins. The next thing he knew, they were levitating an arm's length off the bed. Maerea gasped and wrapped her legs around him.

He spun them around midair and pushed her against the wall. She arched into him with a cry, scouring his shoulders. He grasped her thighs in his hands and pumped into her with every pump of her blood into his mouth. He heard her feet slap against the stone as she braced herself. She raked her fingers through his hair and held him to her vein, levering herself on the wall to grind against him.

She climaxed twice while he had his fill of her. Her cries echoed off the walls of the chamber, another satisfaction that stoked his Craving. The flavor of her peak pushed him closer to the edge each time. He shuddered on the precipice. Then he was flying with her, great bursts of pleasure driving him, soaring, into their Union and into her body.

At last he could think, move, breathe again. He gathered her close, his trembling, gasping savior. He rolled onto his back, cushioning her on his body, and carried them back down to the bed.

Her lips were swollen from their feast, her eyes fierce with determination. Her love throbbed in her aura, the lifeblood of their Union, tender and ferocious. "I won't lose you again."

"I'm sorry." Alcaeus ran his hand over Maerea's hair, as much to comfort himself as her. "I never meant to cause you more fear."

"Where did you go? How did the liegehounds find you?"

"I…confronted Gerrian."

She pressed her face against the front of his fighting robe, right over his heart. "Thank Hespera you're safe."

He stared up at the ceiling. "I didn't challenge him after he destroyed my family. When I faced him in battle, I couldn't defeat him. And tonight, I could not end him. Every time our swords cross, he wins."

"No, Alcaeus. He is no victor."

"I'm a failure as a man."

"That is nothing to be ashamed of, if Gerrian is man's definition of success."

"I came close to his level tonight. It all seemed so clear to me when I left. If I killed him, then Lapidea would be yours."

"Oh, Alcaeus—"

"You would have your home, your future, your rightful power."

"That's not what I want. Perhaps I should. But I never want to go back there. And if I did, what would it accomplish? How could I feed my people any better than I did before? How long would I have before Domitia came for her revenge?"

"I should have realized all that. But all I could think about was…trying to make things right."

Maerea lifted her head and looked at him, unflinching. "There may come a night soon when we must choose between Gerrian's life and Aemilian's. Between a man and a child. Between my brother and peace. It is clear what the right choice is. But if he must die, I don't want it to be for me."

He met her gaze. "I understand."

"Don't you see? That's why I've always loved you. Because you are the one who does not draw his sword."

"You are not ashamed of me."

"Never. Are you ashamed of yourself?"

He took a deep breath. "Not anymore. I'm realizing I am a better Hesperine than I ever was a man."

Hope bloomed in her aura. "You don't regret it, then?"

"No." He twined his fingers in hers where they rested upon his chest. "You understood before I did. I must ask for your forgiveness."

"I had hours, terrible hours, to think about what you said. About how this choice was forced upon you, and you did what you must. Of course you would still be coming to terms with the sacrifice you made. Of course it was more difficult for you than for me. You're right that I have the luxury of choice."

"But I should never have questioned your choice."

She looked away. "I thought you were ashamed of me."

"No, my love." He turned her face back to him, stroking her cheeks. "Never. I would not think less of you for wanting the Gift. I am not that much of a hypocrite. I just couldn't bear the thought of you giving up what was taken from me, from us. I let myself believe you could still have it."

"You were still mourning our old lives."

"So much that I couldn't envision the new one you're offering me." His heart gave a painful thump in his chest. "Is it too late? Do you still want a Hesperine future for us?"

"With all my heart. But this future will be different. I will not be your lady for you to shelter. You cannot charge into battle alone. We must stand beside one another in all things and face every challenge together."

"I'll never stop trying to protect you."

"I know. But you must accept that I will protect you just as fiercely."

"How can I deny that? You saved my life tonight. Again." He took both her hands. "I will always listen to you and respect your judgment. I will never be cruel and call it protection. And I will never deny you your rightful power."

"I love you."

Once more, she offered him her love. This time, he knew it wasn't too late. This time, he knew he didn't have to return her to the human world. As if invoking a magical law, her third declaration worked a spell upon the rules they had once lived by. Her love was more powerful than time and defied the boundaries of the world.

"I love you too, bluebird." He pulled her mouth to his.

They shared a kiss as long as a promise. He thought he could taste the future itself on her lips.

Those three sorcerous words, *I love you,* had already bound them together for all time. Grace was just the way it was written in his veins.

"Maerea, I have something to tell you. About the bond lovers can have as Hesperines."

"It's something I wanted to ask. We…cannot be husband and wife anymore, can we?"

"No. We can be more."

A beautiful flush darkened her cheeks. "Like what we feel when you feast on me."

"Yes, but even more than that. It's something Hesperines experience when their love is true. A bond magical and physical, known as Grace."

"Hesperine magic can bring us even closer?"

"It already has. Or at least, I feel it. But you will not, unless you become a Hesperine."

She slid higher on his body, bringing her face closer to his. "I want to feel it."

He ran his hands down her sides. His strong, beautiful Maerea. She had already endured so much. He would do anything to give her only pleasure and spare her every pain. Why couldn't he, even in this? "I want you to know what will happen to you, so you can be sure. When you have tasted your Grace's blood, you can no longer live without it. Deprivation for even a few nights can be agony. It's called the Craving. There is no antidote except your Grace's blood, and if you are without it…if you are separated, or one of you dies…the other cannot survive."

She sank back. "That's what happened to you tonight. It wasn't the liegehounds. It was because I didn't give you my blood before you left."

"I deserved that. I would endure much worse for such a blessed revelation. You're my Grace, Maerea. My vows to you hold true, even in this life. But I want you to understand the cost to you. Grace is always mutual. If you become a Hesperine, your life will depend on my blood as well."

She brought his hand to her, holding it between her breasts. "When I met you, I felt alive for the first time in years. I also know what it feels like to lose you. This Grace bond does not surprise or frighten me. The mortal world condemned our bond, but Hespera vindicates it."

Hope lodged in his breast, finally there to stay. "Live with me, Maerea.

Not in the name of peace or in spite of the feuds. Not for title or land, for family or ancestors. For us. I promise I will devote the rest of my life to making you happy. Eternity might be long enough to give you all the happiness you deserve."

"I will."

"Will you have me as your Gifter?"

She threw her arms around him, embracing him hard. "Thank you."

He held her to him. This time, he knew he did not have to let her go. Ever.

chapter eighteen

ALKAIOS AND NEPHALEA

THE FRAGRANCES OF WINE and coffee were heady even to Maerea's mortal sense of smell. The spell lights had never seemed so cheerful. Sitting in Alcaeus's arms around the table with Iskhyra, Baru, and Jaya, she felt as if she were at a festival. A mystical and secret one few mortals ever glimpsed.

Iskhyra looked around and nodded. "This is beginning to resemble a proper Gift Night celebration."

Alcaeus looked at Maerea, his eyes full of emotion. What would those emotions feel like in the Blood Union? "I'm glad we can mark Maerea's Gifting with the fanfare she deserves."

She stroked his arm. "You never had the chance to celebrate your transformation. I want tonight to be for you, too."

"It is, bluebird."

"Baru," Jaya asked, "where did you get this wine?"

He winked at Maerea and Alcaeus. "Stepping in and out of a mage's wine cellar is much easier than rescuing a cursed codex from a flooded temple."

They laughed and raised their goblets to the scholar. He bowed.

Maerea could hardly believe she'd only met the three elder Hesperines a few nights ago. They felt like lifelong mentors and friends after the time they'd spent helping her and Alcaeus prepare for her Gifting. "You have all done so much for us. I promise I will honor our bond of gratitude once I have the power."

Jaya clinked her goblet against Maerea's. "We look forward to having you at our sides in the field one night. But you have honored our bond already."

"Never forget you are a gift to our people," said Baru.

Jaya nudged Alcaeus's shoulder. "So, are you feeling ready, lad?"

"No performance anxiety?" Iskhyra asked.

Baru held up a finger. "Stamina is very important."

Maerea gave him a significant smile. "My love has nothing to prove."

The elders laughed, and Alcaeus dropped a kiss on Maerea's lips. Hesperines did not consider such displays indecent, she had learned. The life they would have together among their new people would be so different. She felt as if the weight of an entire castle had lifted from her chest, and she could breathe.

Iskhyra took a swig of wine. "So, what's the first thing you want to do as a Hesperine?"

None of them mentioned the siege. This one night of revelry meant so much, amid the darkness they had all faced together. "I want to find out what kind of magic I have, then learn to read."

"I could help." Alcaeus was the first to support everything she suggested now, as if eager to prove his change of heart about her choice. "I was taught to read and write Vulgus. After speaking it throughout our lives, you'll find it's not difficult."

"I do want to be able to read the vulgar tongue, but…" Maerea frowned at the racks and racks of documents around them. "Most Hesperine scrolls will be in the Divine Tongue, won't they? Those of us who aren't mages can't even speak it, although we hear it all our lives at shrine rituals."

Baru scowled. "Making an entire language a secret. What a despicable practice. The mages should be as ashamed of keeping Divine to themselves as they should be of hoarding magic."

"Divine is Hesperines' common language," Iskhyra said. "All we have to do is talk for the mages to get their robes in a twist. We love committing heresy every time we open our mouths."

Baru grinned. "You'll master it in no time, Maerea. Then you should start on at least two of the most widely spoken Imperial languages."

Iskhyra nodded. "You'll hear them more often than Vulgus in Orthros."

A scroll levitated out of one of the racks and into Baru's hand. "Here is a primer on Divine I ran across last night. We can start as soon as you like."

Maerea clasped her hands around her goblet. "This room is full of ancient wonders you've been seeking for years. Are you sure you don't mind taking time away from your work?"

Baru held out the scroll. "Clearly, our lesson would please the library's original stewards. Why else would they have stored beginner reading primers among the sacred scriptures?"

"I could study the primer on my own while you catalog the more important texts."

"I can do my research and teach you at the same time. I'll tell you something I've discovered in my long years as a scholar." He cast a glance at Jaya and lowering his voice. "Don't tell the warriors, or they will think me sentimental. There is only one thing in this world more exciting than a new scroll: a new student."

Laughing, Maerea leaned forward and accepted the scroll. "Thank you so much for doing this."

Jaya cleared her throat. "If you wanted your enthusiasm for teaching to be a secret, you should've named yourself something else when you became a Hesperine. The name he chose for himself means 'born to be a teacher.'"

Maerea sat up straighter. "You get to choose your name when you become a Hesperine?"

"Yes," Baru answered, "if you desire a new name for a new life. My parents burdened me with a dreadful martial epithet that does not bear repeating. At last, upon my Gifting, I could take a name that suits my true purpose in life."

"What about you, Jaya?" Alcaeus asked.

"I kept my human name. It looked so good on my commission papers when I became an officer in the Imperial army. I was rather too fond of it to let it go."

Baru shook his head. "Glory-seeking warrior. You couldn't resist your name living on forever, could you?"

"It *was* the rallying cry of my soldiers and the curse of my enemies." Jaya showed her fangs. "Still is."

Iskhyra half smiled. She appeared to enjoy the two colleagues' banter. In fact, she seemed to like the company very much.

Jaya lifted her goblet again. "Time for a Gift Night tradition. Everyone must tell the story of why they became a Hesperine. Youngest goes first."

"Elders can't resist having the last word," Iskhyra muttered.

Jaya snickered. "Yours an overbearing bloodline?"

"Aren't they all?"

"Let us begin with tonight's celebrant." Baru smiled at Maerea.

"You all know my story. My true love sprouted fangs, and I decided I wanted them too." She batted her eyelashes at Alcaeus.

He grabbed her close and kissed her again, to their companions' laughter and whistles. "I'm not your only reason, of course."

"Well, there is the fact that no one in the Tenebrae listens to women about a godsforsaken thing. I think if I have blood magic from the goddess of night, people might pay attention when I talk."

"If that fails," Jaya added, "you can always knock their heads together."

"Your turn." Maerea settled back against Alcaeus.

He gave her a squeeze. "I failed at the only thing a mortal man is good for—cutting people up with swords. So I decided I would make a better Hesperine."

She tilted her head back. "I like you much better with fangs than a sword."

"So do I, I've found."

Iskhyra glanced between her fellow elders. "All right, confess. Who is the greener recruit?"

Baru wore a humble smile.

Jaya sighed and raised her hand. "He got his fangs a few months before I did. Don't let his pride inflate any bigger."

"It's hard to believe that was forty-six years ago, isn't it, dear colleague?"

"Huh. Now we've both been Hesperines longer than we were mortals. You don't look half bad for a ninety-year-old."

"What's that you just said about my pride?"

"I'll throw you a bone in this case, old codger. As a young eighty-five-year-old, I should be generous to my elders."

Maerea couldn't help being surprised. She'd known they might be ancient, but all the Hesperines looked like adults in their prime. "Is that why you wanted to leave the Empire? For the longevity? From all you've said of your mortal homeland, it sounds like a wonderful place to live."

Jaya settled back on her cushion. "The Tenebrae and Cordium are dreary little cesspools by comparison. In the Empire, women can achieve great things. That's what comes of the Imperial throne passing down through the female line for countless generations. I came from nowhere, but the Empress's army afforded me opportunities. They needed warders to become mage-engineers, so they paid for my training and my travels all over the world."

"My colleague is too modest," Baru put in. "She rose in the ranks on her own merit to become one of the most respected siege defenders in the Empress's service."

Jaya swirled her wine in her goblet. "I was casting wards during a siege to bear up a curtain wall. When the enemy breached it, I was buried under the rubble. We won, but it was hours before anyone could get me out. The army sent me to Orthros to see if the Hesperine healers could do anything for me. It was too late to reverse the damage, though. So I chose the Gift."

"I'm so sorry, Jaya." Alcaeus shook his head.

"You and I have that in common. We fell in battle."

"To that honorable pathway into eternity." Iskhyra led a toast.

Maerea didn't want to pry, but the wine loosened her tongue. "Jaya… do you miss your human life?"

She seemed to struggle for words. "Giving up your Imperial citizenship for any reason is…"

"A great sacrifice." Baru nodded.

"Do you wish things had turned out differently?" Alcaeus asked.

"I'll leave that sort of agonizing to the philosophers. Things happened the way they did."

"Gratitude is a choice we make every night," Baru said.

Jaya pointed at him, mouthing *philosopher*. "Your turn."

He picked up the next bottle of wine, and the cork levitated out of it with a *pop*. "I taught myself to read shortly after I learned to walk. The Goddess made me to be a scholar. And yet, for reasons only she understands, she had me born into a family of warriors. My parents decided my destiny in the womb. They had a mural of spears painted in my nursery. As my physical characteristics developed, they took it as a sign."

Iskhyra held her goblet out for him. "I assumed you were Gifted in childhood, and that's where you got your height. You were this tall as a human?"

He leaned close to her to pour. "Alas, I didn't fit in the chairs at the local school. But more importantly, all the lessons there fit in my head with room to spare. I learned everything our local instructors could teach me, many years ahead of my peers."

Iskhyra gave his bald head a significant glance. Jaya shook with silent laughter.

He sighed. "Yes. I am one of the few Hesperines who does not sport long, glorious locks. I was bald as a human, I remain bald as a Hesperine, and if the Goddess sees fit that my immortal life should one night end, I will go to her eternal Sanctuary *proudly* bald."

"The Gift doesn't change who you are…" Iskhyra said.

"…it turns you into your best self." Jaya patted Baru's arm.

"Clearly, Baru's best self is bald," said Maerea. "You have a very nice beard, though."

He ran his fingers over the groomed lines of his beard, which framed his face to handsome advantage. "Thank you, Maerea. I'm happy to see there are females who can appreciate a man for more than the hair on his head."

Alcaeus looked down at her. "Must I now grow a beard to keep your eyes from wandering, my love?"

She swatted him. "Nonsense. I am smitten with you, in mortal life and immortality, clean-shaven or bearded."

"If you want a beard," Baru said, "start now. They take *forever* to grow out. The slow pace of Hesperine physiology has its downsides."

Alcaeus rubbed his stubbled chin. "I wondered why I hadn't needed a shave since my Gifting."

Jaya gestured to the coffee pot. "The last sack of Imperial roast says he doesn't have the patience."

Iskhyra chuckled. "I'll take that bet."

"You must come to the Castra to give me my coffee beans. We'll all enjoy a pot together in the mess hall."

"You were going to tell us how you ended up in the Charge," Iskhyra said to Baru.

"Ah. My parents' dream came true, and the king selected me for training as his heir's personal protector. They looked at me and saw a body they could place between the crown prince and his enemies." Baru sniffed. "I left for university that very night."

"Capital University?" Iskhyra's face actually lit up.

He tilted his head at her. "Why, yes. My parents refused to support my education, so I had neither the funds nor the references to enter the Empress's own institution, Imperial University. I attended Capital University, that haven of higher learning open to every citizen of the Empire."

"Well, all the truly advanced research takes place at Capital, where they aren't afraid to take chances. Imperial is too set in the old ways, in my opinion."

"Did you attend?"

"Yes." She seemed to check herself.

"What was your area of study?" Baru leaned closer. "Do you have friends or relatives who are also alumni? Perhaps I know them."

"Many of my friends and family are from the Empire. Some of my happiest memories are there." Iskhyra didn't entirely answer the question, Maerea noticed.

Jaya groaned. "They'll go on like this for hours if we don't stop them now."

"We will return to the topic of our alma mater," Baru promised. "In any case, I earned my degrees—"

"Several of them," Jaya supplied.

"—and became an independent researcher attached to the University, traveling far and wide, wherever there was a need for someone of my specialty."

"Now who's being modest? Baru was so eminent a scholar in the Empire that even a warrior like me had heard of him. He's a theramancer, a mind healer trained in the Imperial tradition of banishing evil magic. His expertise is such that the First Prince sought him out and offered him who knows what as incentive to join the Charge."

"After years of delving into ancient ruins in search of lost knowledge, I decided I'd had my fill of adventure in my mortal life. Castra Justa sounded like a nice change of pace."

"Of course." Jaya nodded. "A forbidding fortress, the only stronghold of civilization in a hostile land where liegehounds, heart hunters, Gift Collectors, and war mages roam. What a lovely place to retire."

Iskhyra's face was hard to read again. "You became a Hesperine just to join the Charge, at the First Prince's invitation?"

"The truth is, I couldn't resist having the rest of eternity to finish everything on my to-be-read list."

Baru and Iskhyra both burst out laughing. They shared a glance Maerea recognized, like you forgot anyone else was in the room for an instant.

"The prince still owes Baru…how many favors?" Jaya poured herself yet another goblet of wine.

Baru waved a hand. "We make a point to assist each other whenever the need arises. After all, Ioustin is a fellow alumnus of Capital University."

Iskhyra gave a start, her amusement fading. "'Ioustin,' eh? That's what you call First Prince Ioustinianos of Orthros, Royal Commander of the Charge?"

"They're thick as thieves," Jaya said. "Always going off into esoteric discussions of mind healing."

Baru savored a swallow of wine. "Of course he is an excellent partner for discussing our mutual affinity for theramancy. Queen Soteira trained him."

"Admit it." Iskhyra smiled at him over her goblet. "That's another reason you became a Hesperine—to study with Queen Soteira."

"I hoped for a single audience with her, but it proved to be the first of many. She and Queen Alea have been kind enough to welcome me into their scholarly circles."

"That's our Queens," Iskhyra said. "You ask them for a thorn, and they give you a rose garden."

"Have you met them?" Alcaeus asked.

"All of us meet the Queens." She looked at him and Maerea. "You will too, one night, and you will understand their love for you."

"What are the Queens like?" Maerea wondered.

Iskhyra's gaze drifted to the arches above. "Queen Alea is like this Sanctuary. She is, in fact, the only Sanctuary mage who has survived the persecution of Hespera worshipers. Queen Soteira is like deliverance in the deepest night. They call her the great healer, for she can mend any hurt of the body or mind. They founded Orthros on their love and have ruled together ever since."

Maerea was prepared to forget every horrible lie she had ever heard about them, but it sounded as if one tale in particular might have some truth to it. "They are…" Lovers probably didn't capture it. "…Graced?"

"For over fifteen centuries now. They were the first Graces, and their Union is what all Hesperines strive to emulate."

Jaya's lip curled. "That's forbidden in this cesspool, too, isn't it? Imagine, the little mages thinking they can declare the most epic love in history illegal."

Just days ago, such a bond between two women would have shocked Maerea. But that had been her other life. Before good and evil had realigned. Before she had understood the mages' betrayals and the Hesperines' kindness.

This was her Gift Night, when Hespera would decide where on the line between good and evil Maerea stood. She would bring none of the hateful teachings of her human life into eternity with her.

In truth, the thought of Orthros being ruled by two females who needed no king seemed… "Beautiful. What a love for the ages."

But so far, there had been many aspects of this new life that Alcaeus had not accepted so easily. Would she see censure in his eyes?

No, only warmth and determination. "One and a half thousand years of love. That is something to emulate."

She tangled her fingers in his. "I'll still love you one and a half thousand years from now."

He pressed a kiss to her forehead.

"Patience, Newgifts," Jaya teased. "Before you depart, we must have one more tale. Well, well, Elder, have the last word."

"Thorns," Iskhyra muttered. "I'm not some mossy ancient."

Baru regarded her. "I think you are too much on the move to gather moss."

"I am curious, Iskhyra," Alcaeus said. "You've never said what your human life was like."

She shrugged. "I don't remember a thing about it, I was so young when my parents Gifted me." She raised her eyebrows. "You look surprised."

"I admit, I didn't realize…"

"We Solace children—we take in orphans in accordance with the Equinox Oath. I was an orphan. My Hesperine parents raised me on their blood. I grew up in Orthros. Typical story."

Maerea felt Alcaeus tense against her. He would not get squeamish now, would he?

No, there was pure wonder on his face. "So although Hesperines cannot birth children, they can be parents."

Maerea smiled, sharing that private look with him. They *could* have children.

"Enough about me," Iskhyra said. "The two turtle doves are looking besotted enough from wine and celebration to begin tonight's endeavor. I think we mossy elders must soon let them get to it."

The laughter and conversation quieted, and a hush descended over them.

It was time. Maerea was about to face her entire past. All her griefs. All her choices. What she had done to others—and failed to do.

But she had chosen her side. Hespera must know where she stood now.

"Newgift Maerea," Iskhyra asked, "will you take a new name for your new life? Let it be spoken now before those who love you, that we may acknowledge you among us."

"I do want a new name," she realized. "I don't want to be grieving Maerea anymore."

"I will love you by any name," Alcaeus said. "As a mortal or Hesperine, in marriage or avowal, you will always be my bluebird."

She blinked back tears and caressed his face. "Thank you."

"Thank *you*, my love."

She turned back to the elders. "Will you help me choose a Hesperine name?"

"Something in Divine, perhaps?" Baru suggested.

Iskhyra nodded, considering her. "You are a woman who has faced every challenge with vigilance and a clear mind. In every crisis, you have remained calm."

"I didn't feel calm."

"No, but you acted it. You found that inner reserve of temperance that helped you make astute decisions. Perhaps you would like a name that captures this: 'Nephalea.'"

"Nephalea." The beautiful name rolled off her tongue. It felt right. Like someone she could become. "Yes. Nephalea is someone others will listen to."

"It is good enough for you," Alcaeus said.

She smiled at him again. "And what about you? Shall I call you a new name in our new lives?"

Iskhyra gave him an encouraging look. "You never had a chance to consider that decision, but now you can."

"Is there an equivalent of Alcaeus in Divine?" he asked his Gifter.

"Alkaios," she replied. "It means the same: strength."

He nodded. "Alkaios."

"Alkaios and Nephalea," said Iskhyra, "may the Goddess's Eyes light your path for all of time…"

"And her darkness ever be your Sanctuary," Baru and Jaya echoed.

Their words and their welcome seemed to fill the ancient cliff with something powerful. She knew she would never be alone again. She had more family than she could count, bound to her by blood, and all of eternity to learn their names and stories.

And she would do it all with the one she loved at her side.

He got to his feet and held out his hand. "Are you ready, Nephalea?"

She took his hand and rose to stand beside him. "I am ready for my Gifting, Alkaios."

They climbed the stairs together. Iskhyra, Baru, and Jaya sent them off with a cheer and a round of Hesperine applause.

chapter nineteen

THE TASTE OF SUNSET

WHEN SHE SAW WHAT he had prepared for her, she stopped a pressed a hand to her heart. He had transformed the bare room into a luxurious bedchamber. In the intimate glow of the spell lights, she could see that he had covered the floor in layers of rugs. The narrow bed was gone, a lavish pile of blankets in its place. To one side, her bluebird box rested on a small table, as if on its own altar.

"It's divine," she said.

"There is only one thing missing." He halted her near the center of the room, then went to the side table. He rested one hand on the box, as tenderly as he always touched her. "I would like to open this, with your permission, bluebird."

"You can always look inside now, my Grace."

Oh, the smile that lit his face when she said that. With careful fingers, he unfastened the lock he had once mended for her and opened the box.

He held her gaze. The rose petals and scraps of festival ribbon levitated from her treasure chest and scattered across her Gifting bed. "Tonight will be the first of the happiest nights of your life. That is my promise to you—Nephalea."

She went into his arms. "I love you, Alkaios."

"And I love you, my bluebird." He tilted her face back to look at him. "I'll be with you every step of the way tonight and make it as comfortable for you as I can."

"You've told me what it was like for you…"

"But your Gifting will be so much easier, under far better circumstances."

"I wish I had been there." It was a pain lodged in her heart that could never be removed. "I should have been with you."

"How could you have been?" He smoothed her hair back from her face. "I will never regret that you were spared seeing me in that condition."

"I will always wish I could have held you and given you comfort."

"You do, every time you give me your blood. It's incredible, tasting you…making you a part of me…I hope you enjoy feasting on me as much as I do feasting on you."

"Tonight I'll finally get to know what it feels like. If it's anything like our wedding night, I think we'll do quite well, don't you?"

"Very, very well."

His mouth descended to hers. His kiss was heavy and warm and slow. If his intent was to relax her, it worked. How quickly he could reduce her to sighs and make her melt against him. With each consuming stroke of his tongue, her fears eased, until their pleasure and closeness had taken over her thoughts.

Cool air caressed her ankles. He was disrobing her. She lifted her arms so he could remove her robe.

"Are you cold?" He trailed his warm hands up and down her arms.

She shook her head.

"Good. The Sanctuary magic should keep it comfortable in here, even for mortals." His fingers teased her skin, the delicate touches raising goosebumps of pleasure. "Soon, you will be a Hesperine, and nothing will feel cold to you."

"I can't wait."

He smiled and held out his arms. Offering himself to her. Her strong, gentle Grace. "My Grace," she said aloud, tasting the word. She ran her hands down his body to the hem of his short robe.

"I thought nothing could give me as much pleasure as hearing you call me husband. Until now."

"My Grace," she said again. She pulled his robe over his head to reveal his tall, lean, muscular body. She was coming to know his Hesperine body even more intimately than she had his mortal one. He felt so familiar to her, yet wonderfully new.

He sat down on their bed with his back propped against the wall, which he had lined with cushions. He held out his hands to her. "Come here."

She knelt in front of him.

He turned her around and eased her back against him. "Relax."

She lay back, supported by the strength of his chest, her hips framed by his hard thighs.

He coaxed her head against his shoulder, baring her throat. "First, I will drink from you, so that when you drink from me, your body will absorb the magic faster. That will avoid prolonging the difficult parts of the transformation." He kissed her throat.

She reached up and threaded her fingers through his hair. He and the other Hesperines had explained the Gifting to her in detail. But hearing him repeat each step to her now was deeply reassuring. She focused on his voice, his touch, her guides through what was to come.

"After your first drink of my blood, the visions will begin. The more blood I give you, and the faster I give it to you, the easier it will be for you. My power will strengthen you through the trial. Do not fear what the Gifting will reveal of your life, bluebird. You have lived with honor and tried only to protect those you love."

"There has been anger and hatred inside me too. All of us have some ugliness within us. But I will face that as well. It is my ugliness, mine to own and master."

"You will come through it, and then the hard part will be over. After that—pure pleasure for us, my Grace. You know the Gifting is not always erotic—mine certainly wasn't—but between us, it will be. As a new Hesperine, your thirst for my blood will be powerful, and so will your hunger for my body. Your Craving for me as your Grace will awaken at the same time, and that will be even stronger. But I will give you anything you want. Everything you need."

"I want it all."

He smoothed a hand down her belly, pressing her against him. He showered kisses on her throat as his fingers traced tantalizing circles below her navel. Her anticipation built. She rubbed back against him, wanting more.

"We will take it very slow." His murmur in her ear sent a shiver through her.

"I want everything."

He grinned down at her. "You are so much more eager than you were on our wedding night."

She felt a flush spread over her cheeks, her neck, her breasts. "I was so afraid you'd think me indecent if I showed how much I wanted you. I didn't want to ruin our first night together by earning your censure."

"I hope I showed you how I treasured your passion."

"Oh, you did." The memory of his mouth on her and the feel of his body against her now filled her core with liquid warmth.

"I'm sorry I didn't make that clear when you asked me for the Gift."

"No more regrets, Alkaios. Not after tonight."

"I need to know, before we do this, whether I have your forgiveness."

"You do." She swallowed. "And I need to know I have earned yours. Can you forgive me for rejecting you when you first returned to me? How I treated you when I found out you were a Hesperine is one of my worst regrets. How I must have made you feel…"

"You had my forgiveness the moment I awakened here in your arms and realized you still wanted me. Then you told me you wanted me forever. You've banished any pain I felt that night or any night since my transformation." He stroked her skin again, tracing the line of her hipbone to the top of her thigh, as if she were a great miracle he was trying to understand. "You have cured all the grief of my mortal life."

"You have done the same for me. With you, I've learned to stop mourning."

"No more duty," he reminded her, smiling.

"I am going to become *very* dangerous."

"I love it when you're dangerous…and indecent. Let us be very indecent now."

His fingers slipped to the inside of her thigh, and on instinct, she parted her legs. They came up against the firm embrace of his thighs.

His hand drifted oh, so slowly toward her curls. But then his fingers went no further, drifting back and forth in place on her thigh.

She thought she would die longing for him to touch her.

A slow, seductive smile spread across his face. "Tonight, why don't you tell me where you want me to touch you?"

She slid her buttocks along his erection and watched the tense angles of pleasure on his face. "Very well, but you must learn the Hesperine words, for those are the only ones I shall use."

He raised his brows. "When did you learn what Hesperines call such things, my shameless Grace?"

"I've been talking about…female things…with Iskhyra and Jaya," she informed him. "Hesperines talk about bodies so differently. Those are some of the first Divine words I learned, actually."

"How fitting, for your body is divine."

She guided his hand to her sheath. "I want to feel your finger inside my *krana*."

His finger delved between her curls. He explored the wet folds of her krana, tracing brilliant pleasure through her. "Where inside your *krana* would you like me to touch you?"

She moved his finger to her point of pleasure. "My *kalux*."

His touch circled the nub of sensation. She sucked in a breath. He flicked the bud of nerves with his finger, sharpening the pleasure. He kept teasing her kalux as his fangs pierced her.

His new name flew from her lips. "Alkaios—!"

He lifted his head from her vein. Her blood stained his lips and dripped down his chin, and the sight fascinated her. "I loved hearing you say my name in your passion on our wedding night. I didn't want to change it. I want to hear it over and over for the rest of time."

"Alkaios…" Her hips quivering under his touches, she caressed his jaw. Her fingers came away red. "Will you whisper my new name to me in our bed?"

"I will say it will pleasure, and every time, I will feel grateful that you chose this life with me."

She leaned up and captured his mouth. Her blood was tangy on her tongue. He kissed her back, hungry, before he dragged his mouth to her throat once more.

"Nephalea," he whispered.

His fangs sank deep. He drank from her hard and fast. Her neck ached as she felt herself flowing out into his mouth. Her core ached with desire as his deft hand drew pleasure from the depths of her body. Her head spun, and she panted for breath.

She shivered and shifted against his hand, reveling in his thorough strokes through her intimate folds. He found every little place that could please her and used them all relentlessly. His other hand came to her breast and lifted it, squeezing gently, while his thumb pressed across her nipple in time to his caresses between her legs.

He delved deeper into her krana. Curling his finger, he dragged it out of her, and with it, a low cry. She braced her heels on the blankets and rose up and back against him. He held her down with his fangs, supporting her with his hand on her breast. He kept sliding his finger in, hooking it, drawing it out, as he dragged the warm heat from her vein and applied the perfect pressure to her nipple.

In a delirium of pleasure, she forgot everything except his fangs pleasuring her throat and his hands feasting on her body. She writhed for him, this new, sensual Nephalea, and she scarcely recognized her husky, rhythmic moans echoing around them.

She felt the thickness of his arousal behind her, evidence of all the pleasure still to come. Rocking back against his hard length, she named it in Divine. "I want to feel your *rhabdos* thrusting inside me."

"You will," he promised, "inside your new body."

The flood of pleasure swelled, crested, and her climax crashed upon her. Her body broke free as never before. She grasped his knees, throwing her head back, and rode the wondrous transformation inside her. His jaw clenched harder on her, even as his hands continued their worship, heightening her ecstasy until she screamed.

She collapsed against him, heaving for breath, sweat trickling down her skin. He eased his fangs from her flesh. Limp from pleasure, she lay against him and watched him lift his wrist to his mouth. His fangs flashed, and his blood welled, mingling with her own.

He brought the gleaming red offering to her lips. "I am yours."

She took his wrist in both her hands. With this irreversible act, she would change forever.

What would he taste like?

She brought his vein to her lips and opened her mouth.

The hot elixir struck her tongue and sent a shock through her. She tasted strength and kindness. White lilies and vivid sunsets. Passion and gentleness and power. So much power.

She swallowed. Raw pleasure pounded through her, as if their bodies were joined. She arched in his hold, digging her teeth into his flesh.

"Yes," he growled. "Goddess, yes."

Voices, images flashed in her thoughts, distracting her from the taste of him. Sudden fury whipped through her, drowning out the pleasure, even as fear descended like a blade, and grief knocked the air from her lungs.

Her own emotions filled her up, carrying her to another time and place on their inexorable tide.

~

A girl must keep her spindle turning, come what may. That's what Mama and Bria said. Maerea knew it meant she shouldn't give up, even when it was hard.

But she wasn't sure how to keep going now that she was at the bottom of the ravine, and her leg folded up every time she tried to stand.

She would never be able to climb out.

Her throat hurt from calling for help. There was no one to hear her.

She was getting colder by the moment. Night would fall soon. What if there were wolves? What if no one found her until tomorrow?

What if no one ever found her?

"Merry!"

At the sound of her name, she gasped. That was her brother's voice.

"I'm here!" she cried, as loud as she could.

"Merry!" Gerrian called back.

Tears of relief ran down her cheeks. "Down here!"

His tousled head appeared at the top of the ravine. "Are you all right?"

She sniffed. Yes, she was all right. He was here now. "I—I might need some help climbing out."

In the fading light, she watched him sling his legs over the side of the ridge. He eyed the steep incline between them.

"No, you can't come down that way!" she warned. "There's fire nettle."

"By the time I hike over to the other path down, it will be night. And it will take too long for the other search parties to get here. I won't leave you alone in the dark."

"Oh, no, Gerrian—it will hurt you—"

He didn't heed her. Didn't even hesitate to half-crawl, half-scramble down into the ravine.

A new rush of tears came to her eyes at the thought of how his skin would hurt him after this. But when he landed beside her and wrapped her in his arms, she was so very glad he was there.

But night was falling. Another night. Another year. So many years, so much of life, rushing by on the current of blood, withering away.

She missed the safety of her brother's arms. He was out of reach in the chair beside her. They sat and watched the mage close the curtains around Father's bed.

Now he was gone too.

Exhaustion weighed her down. She thought she might never get up from this chair. She felt as if she could sink into the earth.

A girl must keep her spindle turning.

Even lifting a finger to turn a spindle felt like too much effort.

She was mother and father, daughter and son, lord and lady to Lapidea. She carried all their burdens. Alone.

Who could blame her if she finally surrendered? If she donned mourning clothes and installed herself in this chair forever and allowed herself to be tired?

No. Their people needed her. If she did not get up, there would be no one left to keep the god of death away from Lapidea's door.

But how would she ever climb out of this deep, dark place?

Gerrian stood. Her brother. She still had him. His love withstood fire nettle, and he never hesitated to come to her rescue.

If only he would offer her a hand and pull her out of this chair, she would be back on her feet and able to go on.

He didn't look at her. He disappeared into those curtains. And when he re-emerged, he was holding Father's sword.

She looked into his eyes. Cold as death.

Oh gods. She had to get up. Whatever he was about to do, she had to stop him.

There was no one else to keep the spindle turning but her. She could let it all come to a halt. So easy. Or she could do the hard thing and stand.

She pushed to her feet and held out her arms to Gerrian. "Come here. Stay here with me, brother. We need not mourn alone."

He moved for the door. She blocked his way, clutching his arms. "Please, Gerrian. I don't know what you intend, but no good can come of it. All we need is some peace. Just a moment of peace. And then there's so much work to do—but we can manage it, if we do it together—"

He set her away from him with astonishing ease. When had he become so strong? So hard?

He spoke no words of comfort. Shed no tears. He charged out of the sickroom to carve his mourning on the world with his sword.

And left her holding the spindle that must keep turning at any cost.

She would not give up. She would hold onto the threads of their lives.

The pattern of their fates was in her hands.

chapter twenty

CHERISHED SHADOWS

S HE HAD THOUGHT HER eyes were open, until her lids lifted, and she saw his face.

She was here, now. All that was past.

"Alkaios." Saying his name anchored her to their present.

"Nephalea. My bluebird. It's over. All is well."

His words echoed around her. The air felt strange in her lungs, potent with smells. Blood. Roses. Stone. Wool. *Alkaios.* He was all male, a carnal, alluring musk that promised divine things.

Him against her. Skin and hair. Hard and soft. He was all around her and within her. She felt him in her veins. He was like a light glowing inside her chest, a thought in her mind.

Blood Union. She meant to say it aloud, but she wasn't sure the words made it past her thoughts.

Grace Union, he answered.

His voice touched her mind like an intimate caress. She could more than hear his words. She could feel them inside her. *Alkaios? Can you hear me?*

Joy warmed her from the inside out. Everywhere in it, she could feel him. It was his joy. *Nephalea...I had no idea we'd be able to speak like this. I never imagined this is what magic could give us.*

I need you this close. Closer.

Her body felt light, her tongue heavy. A vicious fire snaked through her veins, burning everything in its path, parching her mouth, making her core clench with frustrated need.

Now the pleasure, he promised.

Holding her on his lap, he brought his wrist to her mouth once more. The dry blood on her lips cracked as she opened them. She felt a pleasurable pressure and stretching in her gums.

He smiled down at her. She sensed that smile like light shining around him. *Those fangs are the most beautiful thing I've ever seen.*

Her body knew what to do. She sank her fangs into his wrist.

The flavor of his blood wrung a moan from her. So good. Better than anything she'd ever tasted or imagined. She devoted herself to his wrist.

On impulse, she swiveled her hips, riding the pleasure of every swallow. She devoured his blood as she would his mouth, his touches. If only he would touch her.

But he didn't. He held her close, his hands still, letting her slake herself at his vein.

She heard his voice with her ears now, a gravelly whisper. "This is what your Grace's blood does to you. My blood alone."

Her muscles rippled, tightened, and let fly. Her spine flexed in a sinuous arch. Pleasure was a thousand pinpoints of light, burning forever.

She felt her power in every grip and release. Limitless.

Even as her first climax as a Hesperine eased, her body pounded, ready for the next.

And he hadn't even touched her yet.

She needed more. He understood. His arm came around her waist, and he sat up, pushing her forward onto her hands and knees. She dug her fingers into the blankets, her mouth still fastened to the hot rush of blood from his wrist. She would never get enough.

His hard body cupped hers, chest to back, thigh to thigh. His strong hand splayed on the blankets beside her slender one. His breath was warm at her ear, shivering over her skin. "We'll take it slow."

The head of his rhabdos barely touched her entrance. Her entire body came alive with sensation. Exquisite. Unbearable.

He nudged a little deeper. She whimpered against his wrist, sucking harder at his vein.

"How does it feel?" he asked.

She bowed her back, opening herself to him, begging.

His rhabdos entered her new body. So tender, so slow. Impossibly thick and hard. Her krana was too tight. But she was so wet. Measure for measure, he pressed inside her and stretched her.

Tears trailed down her face. She trembled beneath him, not daring to move as she tried to adapt to how sensitive her body was.

He filled her to the depths of her body. They both went still. Only her mouth moved at his wrist. Her krana quivered. She would climax again. The pleasure would be intense. She held on, breathless on the brink.

Nephalea. Emotion throbbed through her as he said her name. *It's even better than I imagined, being inside you with your fangs in me…*

She had the power to give him more pleasure now. She slipped her fangs out of him, then bit down again to begin her feast anew.

He shuddered against her, his rhabdos penetrating deeper. She shattered. Her krana clenched on his thickness inside her. Her back arched, flush against his chest, his skin hot against hers as the waves of pleasure wracked her.

Goddess. Nephalea. His body was strung tight, but still he did not follow her over the edge.

The climax swept her down into hunger again. Compelled her to move. He gasped, holding steady but for the small, tight motions she could manage trapped beneath his body. She bit him harder.

Are you ready for me to move? he begged.

She nodded wildly.

Are you ready for us to feast together?

His fangs in her. Hers in him. Their bodies joined. She would break. She needed it all.

She reached up with one hand and tangled her fingers in his hair, bringing his mouth closer to her.

He slid his rhabdos halfway out of her, her krana clutching at him as he retreated. Then he drove deep, burying his fangs in her throat.

This was everything. Their bodies pumping together. Her blood pumping out of her into him. His into her. An eternal cycle that whirled them closer, deeper, until they were no longer two, but one.

She sucked wantonly at his wrist, bucking beneath him. Braced on all fours, she spread her legs wider and lifted her hips, baring herself to his thrusts. He took her over and over, driving long and hard and deep.

That place where their bodies joined felt like the source of all pleasure itself. She lost herself in their endless rhythm, not sure where her body ended and his began.

She tasted his love under her skin and felt it on her tongue. He spoke it again and again with every motion of his body and every beat of his heart.

A new flavor enriched his blood. So intense, her krana clenched and slicked with a surge of moisture. Oh Goddess. What was it?

His climax.

His rhabdos slammed into her. He pulsed against her inner walls. His seed surged within her, and his climax surged in his blood, hers to feast on.

She felt it to the tips of her nipples and the bottoms of her feet. The room spun. She fell forward onto her elbows, another climax of her own ripping up through her. His fingers dug into her hip, and her keen ears filled with the sound of their flesh slapping together.

He collapsed over her. His weight felt good. She lay there cradled under him, willing to never move again.

The last thing she remembered was him stroking her hair and saying her new name. Then the deepest sleep she had ever known welcomed her into its embrace.

Her breathing ceased, and Alkaios knew his Grace had fallen into her first Slumber.

He didn't move for a long moment. He sheltered her small, powerful form under his body, his rhabdos still within her now soft and pliant krana.

He finally eased out of her and rolled them onto their sides, tucking her against him.

They had done it. She was a Hesperine.

He would fall into Slumber with her in his arms and wake to her hunger. Tonight and every night after.

He spent his last wakeful moments praying to the Goddess who had brought them here. And imagining Nephalea's next feast.

∽

Midnight had passed, and all Iskhyra sensed from upstairs were the heavy veils over her newgifts' chamber.

"It's high time I have a look at the siege we are to break."

At Jaya's pronouncement, Baru looked up from his scrolls. "I'm surprised you resisted the temptation this long."

She cast a glance upward. "Well, it's not every night we are called upon to stand by during a Gifting. But if anything had gone wrong, they would have let us know by now."

"I think everything is all right," Iskhyra said.

Jaya set aside her coffee cup and got to her feet. "You two have fun with your scrolls."

She stepped away. Comfortable silence descended over the library. Iskhyra sat back against the cushions and took another swallow of coffee.

"You can breathe a sigh of relief now," Baru said. "Your newgifts are well on their way."

"Thank the Goddess." She was more relaxed that she had been in… she couldn't remember how long. Her newgifts were both safe. And she had to admit, Baru's presence was…pleasant.

"You aren't working any theramancy on me, are you?" she asked lightly.

"It wouldn't be the first time I used my magic to comfort a nervous Gifter on the momentous night. But no, I just have that effect on people."

She laughed. "And so modest, too."

"When it's the truth, it's no boast."

"Truth. I see why the Charge could not do without you."

"Is that what you see?"

She glanced up from her cup to find him looking not at his scroll, but at her. His gaze warmed her. She hadn't realized she was so cold. "No. That is far from all I see, Baru."

He carefully rolled the scroll closed, then joined her at the coffee table, lowering his powerful body gracefully to the cushions beside her.

She would rather not ask him what he saw when he looked at her. Mind healers had a tendency to see too much. She checked that her veils were in place.

He refilled her coffee cup. "When was the last time you passed the night in good company?"

"I would ask you when was the last time you passed the night in a library like this, but I know the answer is never." She waved a hand at the scroll racks. "You needn't keep me company. Go enjoy yourself, fellow scholar."

"I am enjoying myself." He stretched out and lounged beside her, leaning on an elbow. The rich, masculine layers of his scent enveloped her. Imperial soap. Beard oil. Incense.

In another time and place, she would have been enjoying herself thoroughly. Her conversation skills wouldn't have been rusty, and she wouldn't have smelled like grief and wandering.

Baru took a sip of her coffee, briefly shutting his eyes. "Mm." He handed the cup to her.

She drank, tasting where his mouth had touched the cup. "I confess… I've spent the past few nights with more people than I've seen in a year. I'm afraid my only conversation partner for a long time has been the Goddess." She sighed. "Your scrolls are honestly much better company than I at the moment."

"Why don't you let me be the judge of that? I have the impression you're actually very good company who is simply focused on other matters right now."

"You're being generous. I would be remiss if I didn't at least try to be good company for you." Goddess, what was she doing? He was much too easy to talk to. All mind healers were, but that was far from the only reason. She opened her mouth to wrestle the conversation in a different direction.

He spoke first. "What were your favorite pastimes, before you became so distracted rescuing newgifts from Tenebran squalor?" There was a faint smile on his full lips. He *was* enjoying himself. Goddess knew why.

Reading. That was a safe topic. "I have an enviable collection of poetry in my library at home, if I do say so myself."

No, not a safe topic at all. *Home* was the least safe word of all, and even the thought of her books gathering dust was full of traps, waiting to awaken old pain.

"Hmm," he said. "I brought the word 'past' to the table with me. It can often be an unwelcome guest. Forgive me."

"Don't apologize. The past is pleasant to most people. The fact that we don't get along makes me most unwelcome at festivals."

He laughed at that. "It won't always be so, Iskhyra. There will be plenty of festivals with the future as the guest of honor."

There was only one version of the future that would be acceptable to her—the success of her quest. It was far from guaranteed. But she couldn't bear to imagine the alternative.

At that moment, she felt very grateful to Baru for reminding her the future existed, and that it might hold some possibility for good. "Thank you."

"We have dis-invited the past, and the future has not arrived yet. It is just you and me and the present at our little gathering."

"What are your pastimes, when you aren't rediscovering long-lost libraries?"

"I enjoy a good game of Prince and Diplomat."

"Oh, it's a shame we don't have a board."

"You play?"

She grinned. "When I sit down to the board, I never play."

His gaze lingered on her fangs. "How unfair of you to issue such a challenge, when we have no board."

She laughed again and drank some coffee to escape his gaze. Thorns, she had laughed more in the last few minutes than she had in ages.

She passed him the coffee. "So, reading and games of strategy. Are there any physical pursuits that interest you, scholar?"

Oh, Goddess. She was more than rusty. How obvious could she be?

Baru only smiled and shared her cup again. "To be sure. Just not the arts of war."

As he passed the coffee back to her, their fingers brushed. The sensation of his smooth skin sent brilliant shocks through her.

When was the last time she had touched someone? And not to drag a dying man off a battlefield or disarm an enemy mage.

In another time and another place, she would never have denied herself. Temperance was not one of her strengths.

So why was she denying herself now? Why should she deny him, if this was what he wanted?

For a moment, she recalled what it felt like to enjoy someone's interest and return it. She remembered how it had been when drawing close to someone did not carry complex layers of risk, and mutual pleasure was a pure, uncomplicated gift.

"The arts of love?" she asked him.

"Only two things truly matter. Love and wisdom."

"And while you are in the field in pursuit of wisdom, is there someone back at Castra Justa who holds your love?"

"I am a heart-free adventurer. Like you?"

"Like me."

His thumb found the inside of her wrist, caressing her pulse. "When was the last time more than animals sustained you?"

She gave a humorless laugh.

He made a sympathetic hum in his throat.

"Not all skills grow dull with disuse," she said, "unlike my abilities as a conversationalist."

"I availed myself of the Charge's human retainers before departing Castra Justa. You might enjoy the benefits of my recent drink of mortal blood."

"Baru. I would enjoy you if all you'd had to drink was a grudging sip of goat."

His laughter made his chest shake and lit up the Union.

She stretched out on the cushions, facing him. "You'll enjoy me too. I promised to be good company."

"Oh, I'll enjoy you." He traced the line of her jaw. Then her throat. That feather touch of his fingers on her vein felt more intimate than anything that had happened to her in so, so long. "I always enjoy a mystery."

A mystery she must remain. He was a Charger. He was the prince's personal friend. If he mentioned one too many details when he went back to Castra Justa, the prince would know where she'd been and come after her.

This was a very bad idea. But she really never had been temperate.

She leaned closer. Goddess, he smelled amazing. In the middle of this bloody land of suffering, suddenly this kind, cultured, powerful Hesperine.

His power was irresistible. As their faces drew nearer, and their breaths mingled, his latent magic flowed in the Union and washed over her.

He sucked in a breath. "There is something about your aura, Iskhyra. How you shine."

"I haven't entirely lost my touch, then."

"Touch me, and I'll assure you you haven't."

Nephalea woke with a scream.

"Shh, my love. I'm here for you."

She clawed at her throat, at her wrists, trying to find the source of the fire.

He held her hands still. "Do not fear the Craving. I have what you need."

Craving. Starving. She was starving. This hunger was killing her.

She had fought long and hard to get here. She had survived so much. She refused to die.

She let out a wordless shout of defiance, and something else rose out of her with it. She had felt it all along. When all seemed lost, she reached deep into it. When she thought she'd given all she had, it kept her on her feet. That fierce, nameless thing inside her had tried to stop the bloodshed and was still fighting for peace.

It was real. It took shape, tingling at the ends of her fingers. Then it surged through her veins and erupted from her chest. She threw her head back, spread her hands and welcomed it.

Darkness fell. Night itself seemed to dance over her skin and embrace Alkaios, turning him into a cherished shadow. It radiated out and out, a fortress of darkness between them and the world.

The Hunger staggered back before her power. Although the Craving still ravaged her, she felt certain she was safe.

"Nephalea, your magic has manifested."

"My magic. That's my magic."

"It's your ward."

"I'm a warder? I *am* a warder." She wrapped her arms around herself, running her fingers over the tangible darkness on her skin.

"Let us feed that beautiful power of yours." His hands felt warm on her icy skin. He framed her face and brought it against his neck. He massaged her jaw open.

Yes. His blood. That was what she Craved.

Her fangs unsheathed. She sliced her lip in her eagerness to fasten onto him. His flesh resisted her, but the pressure felt good to her gums. Then the points of her fangs broke his skin. Her teeth slid beneath, into flesh.

His vein gave to her. The darkness deepened around them. Her magic throbbed in time to his pulse.

She feasted on his throat until she felt she would not die. She lifted her head, blinking, trying to order her thoughts.

There, his beloved face before her. He was sitting up against the wall. Her on his lap, her legs spread. He had known what she would need when she woke.

"Eventually your head will clear," he said patiently. "You need more blood."

He was right. She went for the other side of his neck. He jerked under her. She felt his heart pounding against her breasts. He needed this too.

Within moments, her agony turned to lust. She clenched his hips between her knees, running her hands over his shoulders, through his hair. He felt so strong and male. He was hers, and she could have as much of him as she wanted.

His arousal was already stiff against her curls. She reached between them and found him with her hands. Silken to touch, steel beneath. Still lapping at his neck, she explored his rhabdos with compulsive, curious touches, enjoying how he felt to her sensitive fingertips. Dark tendrils of her magic followed her hands, wrapping around him.

"Nephalea, you are torturing me."

She lifted her mouth from his neck, licking her lips. She blinked at him, her lids heavy. "How can I make it better?"

He captured her lips, thrusting his tongue into her mouth. She mewled and opened her lips wider for him, fascinated by his invasions. Her toes curled, and her hands tightened around his shaft.

When he took hold of her wrists and pulled her hands away from his body, her magic retreated from him, too. She made a sound of protest in her throat. But then his hands closed around her hips.

He lifted her and set her on his rhabdos, pulling her down as he thrust up inside her. "Ride me."

Oh, yes. She clutched his shoulders, shifting on his rhabdos to gain leverage. He gritted his fangs. She got her knees under her, and his hands guided her into a rocking motion. Oh yes. *Yes.*

She panted for his delicious scent. Pleasure built inside her, and she moved faster. Her magic rose, twisting around their waists and winding their bodies tighter together.

He buried his hands in her hair and dragged her back to his throat. She mouthed his vein, searching for the place it felt so good to bite.

She found it, the perfect fit. As her fangs locked into him again, his locked onto her. Her climax came fast and rough. She rode it out on his hard, unyielding length.

Her mind wasn't clearing. She couldn't think, only feel and devour.

He thrust up into her rapid pace. Without warning, he released inside her. That taste. His pleasure spilling. He had known. He had waited to let go so he could push her over the edge again. Her second climax wrung her, their bodies throbbing together.

She lifted her mouth from his vein only long enough to cry out, "Again."

Bite. Slake. Join. Thrust. She devoured him and let him consume her. The darkness drew them deeper in. Her magic was their Sanctuary, the shadow covering the secret ecstasy they shared, the fortress that protected what they had become.

She would never lose him again.

Alkaios lost track of how many nights they spent alone in that room. They Slumbered. He woke, watching her, waiting for the moment when she and her hunger would rouse. Then her eyes opened, her fangs unsheathed, and they began again.

Nephalea had been passionate as a mortal. As a Hesperine, she was insatiable. He reveled in his ability to gratify her. His immortal strength was ample match for her appetite.

The outside world barely existed for them. They lived in a dream of each other's blood and bodies. They relearned one another, discovering together all the wondrous new ways they could please and be pleased.

As they tamed her hunger, they began to talk. To laugh. To plan.

"I have an important question for you, bluebird."

"What, my love?"

He looked deep into her eyes. "Does my blood taste as good as pork chops?"

She let out a peal of laughter and kissed him. "Better. So much better than the best pork chop known to humankind."

He gave her a cocky smile.

"I will not miss pork chops." She lipped his jugular.

He could no longer resist what he really wanted to ask her. Perhaps it was too soon. But he'd seen the look on her face when Iskhyra had told them about the Solace. "Nephalea…"

"Yes, my Grace?" She propped her head on her hand, trailing the other over his chest hair.

He fondled her thigh where her leg was hooked around his. "We *can* have children."

Her eyes lit up, and a smile spread through her aura. "I told you we could still have everything we wanted."

"You were right. So that is what you still want?"

"Do you?"

"Yes," he confessed. "That feeling of possibility, of knowing we can…"

"Have a family."

"There's still so much we haven't learned about Orthros and what sort of upbringing our children would have. But I feel certain it would be a more peaceful life than we could have given them as humans."

"I want that too. After I learn to wield my magic, read, and fight."

Her power waited in pools of shadow under the spell light. He gazed at her beautiful face, framed in her wild yellow hair. A bit of his blood still lingered at the corner of her mouth.

But her gaze was clear, her aura lucid. His brilliant bluebird. Ready to fly. "I could stay in this room with you forever. I am greedy for this time together. I don't want it to end."

"It won't. My Gifting may be complete, but our feasting has only just begun."

She pressed her face to his chest, sliding her arm around him. He wrapped her close. They lay tangled together for a long moment, holding each other tightly, sharing in that sacred space just a little longer.

"I think it's time," he said at last. "Don't you?"

"Yes. I must greet our companions as their fellow Hesperine—and begin learning to use my power."

chapter twenty-one

TO STAY ANTHROS'S HAND

"Try again," Iskhyra said.

Nephalea clenched her fangs and focused her Will on her magic once more. The shadows rose from around her feet to swirl and dance in front of her. Through the misty darkness, she could still see the ravine, but at least there were no holes in her ward. She held it, her heart pounding with the effort.

On Iskhyra's cue, Alkaios levitated another handkerchief in Nephalea's direction. When it reached her ward, the fabric flattened against her magic, unable to pass through.

"Good." Iskhyra gestured to Alkaios again.

Now he levitated a small stone. It sailed toward Nephalea. Her heart pounded harder. The hazy ward before her pulsed.

Nearing her barrier, the rock slowed. But then the accursed thing embedded itself in the ward and kept pushing through. She tried to gather more shadows around the rock before it could breach her defenses.

It popped out of her ward and thumped her chest before dropping to the ground and hitting her toe.

Alkaios stepped to her side, rubbing her breastbone. "I'm so sorry. I didn't mean to hit you."

"I barely felt it. It's my failure that stings."

"You haven't failed," Iskhyra said. "Mastering your power takes time."

"You've been spending every waking moment teaching me. Why can't I even raise a ward strong enough to repel a pebble?"

"It's not a pebble. It's the size of my fist." Alkaios knelt to examine her toe.

"I'm a Hesperine now, love. It takes more than that to break my toe."

"I don't care. I would never forgive myself if I bruised your toe."

"I'm not bruised. I'm furious."

Iskhyra leaned against a column. "You still harbor a great deal of anger from your human life."

Nephalea frowned. "I thought I came to terms with it during my Gifting."

"The Gifting only purges from us what is unfit for us to carry into eternity."

"You're saying I was supposed to keep my anger?"

"Anger is not always wrong. In fact, it is often right and necessary. But you must learn to use it, just like magic."

It had taken Nephalea most of her life to rise above her grief. How much longer would it take to master her anger? "We don't have time for this. Salicina must begin the harvest soon, and the siege still has them pinned inside the walls."

Alkaios rose to his feet. "I hate what Salicina must endure every day, but the most important thing you can do for Domitia and Aemilian right now is focus on learning your magic."

"If they cannot start getting the crops in, it will be too late. Gerrian is so focused on the castle, he'll let Salicina's harvest rot in the fields while your people and mine starve."

Alkaios took her hands. "Domitia's allies are still on the way. They'll arrive any day now to lift the siege in time for the harvest. And every spell you master is another line of defense when we go to aid them."

She squeezed his hands. "You're right."

"Take heart, bluebird. You're already very good with your innate Hesperine abilities. You mastered levitation in record time." He grabbed her and tossed her over the cliff.

She shrieked in surprise. Then laughed, catching herself with her levitation. She hovered over the ravine, looking down. There were a lot of nettles down there. She needn't fear them now. The long drop was rather exhilarating, in fact.

Without giving him any warning, she swept Alkaios up on a surge of levitation. He flew toward her with an indignant sound, but his aura was full of laughter. She levitated him into her arms.

"You *thoroughly* mastered levitation." He spun her in a circle.

Holding his hand, she spun away from him, then back.

Before she knew it, they were dancing. They twirled and leapt on nothing but magic and air.

She knew one thing about her anger. The weight on the other side of the scales was happiness, and Alkaios always knew just how much to apply.

Their dance carried them round and round. She caught sight of a herd of little goats scaling the other side of the ravine. Then of Iskhyra standing in between the Sanctuary's columns. The moons setting over the opposite cliffs. Baru behind Iskhyra, saying veiled words in her ear. She lifted her face to him.

The dance turned Nephalea's back to them again. *Is he giving her a kiss? Not in front of us newgifts.*
I don't know why they feel they have to be subtle.
Iskhyra is very private.
True. And Baru is very dignified.
Alkaios twirled her in and pulled her against his chest. *I'm glad he's here.*
So am I. Very glad. Catching sight of the Sanctuary again, Nephalea halted midair.

Jaya was back from her latest survey of the siege, and her aura warned of grim news.

⸺

ALKAIOS WATCHED ALL OF Salicina emerge on paper, sketched in logical lines by Jaya's hand. They all gathered closer around the table to study her diagram of the siege.

She pointed to a river some distance from the castle, just inside the borders of Salicina. "Warriors under two different banners are approaching from this direction with supplies—weapons, provisions, medicine."

"Salicina's allies," Alkaios said. "Right on time. What did I tell you, bluebird?"

Jaya shook her head. "They can't reach the castle. Gerrian and Drusus's forces destroyed Salicina Dam and flooded the river."

"Cup and thorns," Alkaios swore. "There's another safe crossing, but it's in the next domain. To march an army that size upriver, across, and back to Castra Salicina will take longer than a fortnight."

Nephalea held his hand. "By then it will be too late to start the harvest."

"And Salicina will run out of supplies," Jaya said. "But there's another problem."

Iskhyra frowned. "The miners can't have tunneled under the walls. Not when you collapse their progress every night."

"No," Jaya replied. "Siege engines."

"They tried that already." Baru smiled. "Until their battering ram mysteriously shattered against a strangely sturdy gate, which you may or may not have reinforced with your wards."

Iskhyra tapped the drawing. "And the ballistae aren't much use to them since you stepped all their ammunition into the latrines."

Jaya leaned over her diagram, sketching. "Lord Drusus' catapults and trebuchets present more of a challenge."

Alkaios watched the little squares take shape and surround the castle. "Goddess. Our walls won't last long under that assault."

Nephalea braced a fist on the table. "Why has Lord Drusus invested so much in this? His alliance with Gerrian should have crumbled without a marriage to seal it."

Jaya straightened, crossing her arms. "From what I overheard in Gerrian's camp just now, he has spread the tale that Daughter Pherakia betrayed her temple oaths and intervened in the feud. He claims she used her magic to kidnap you to weaken Lapidea. Lord Drusus believes you are a prisoner inside Castra Salicina, and that you will be his reward for a successful siege."

A dangerous light glittered in Nephalea's eyes. "We can't wait any longer. It's time to make our stand."

Alkaios took her arm. "You aren't ready. You—"

She put a hand to his mouth. "I will not stay here. I know my wards aren't ready, but I'll use my essential magic."

He started to protest again.

"I have the power, Alkaios."

The thought of letting his wife accompany him onto a battlefield made his every nerve scream. The last time he had done that had been the worst day of their lives.

But she wasn't his wife anymore. She was his Grace.

Her fangs gleamed in the spell lights. Her aura, entwined with his in their Union, pulsed with power. All the strength she had possessed as a mortal was now made tangible by the Gift.

"You are right." He tucked a strand of her hair behind her ear. "I will not hold you back. I will stand at your side."

"And I at yours."

They rested their joined hands on the table.

"All right." Jaya drew herself up. "I want everyone to know their roles in our plan—and adhere to them."

Nephalea smiled, baring her fangs. "I can break the alliance. I'll expose Gerrian's lies and make it clear to Lord Drusus exactly where—and what—I am."

Alkaios traced the distance between the castle and the mark where Salicina's allies were stranded. "Domitia needs those supplies. Now. It won't take much time to step them across the river and behind the walls. I should do it, because I know my way around inside."

"Good," Jaya approved, then turned to Iskhyra. "I want you with me warding the castle against the catapults and trebuchets."

"At your service, Fortress Master."

Jaya smiled. "No matter what they throw at the walls, it won't get through a ward the two of us cast. As for you, scrollworm…"

Baru put a hand to his chest. "You surely have a better use for my talents than knocking the attackers' thick skulls together. Don't do that to me, dear colleague."

"You disable the siege engines. *I* would take out the engineers, but…"

"Catapults and trebuchets are such crude mechanisms. It should be easy for me to make a few alterations to their structures that will compromise their integrity."

Iskhyra grinned at him. "I will enjoy watching this."

He gave her a warm smile in return. "I'll show Salicina's enemies how Imperial theramancers handle a siege."

Jaya looked around the table at each of them. "No one's going into battle thirsty, are they?"

"No." Baru exchanged a glance with Iskhyra.

All the elders' gazes turned to Alkaios and Nephalea.

"Alkaios takes his responsibilities as my Gifter very seriously," Nephalea said primly.

He slipped an arm around her waist and pulled her closer.

Jaya nodded. "I got in a drink from the animals on my way back from scouting. We're all in fighting condition."

"Siege-engine-dismantling condition," said Baru.

She ignored his protest. "Five Hesperines should be equal to this task. Newgifts, I have every confidence in you. But if you run into trouble, step to safety within reach of an elder."

Alkaios lifted Nephalea's chin. "Promise me."

"I'll make it through this alive, I vow. Do you promise me?"

"On my honor."

Iskhyra put a hand on each of their shoulders. "Don't either of you get yourselves killed tonight. Understand?"

"Yes, Gifter," Alkaios answered.

Nephalea smiled. "We have too much to live for."

Iskhyra gripped their shoulders for an instant, then let them go.

Jaya headed for the door. "Make your preparations. We leave in a few minutes." She marched out of the Sanctuary, leaving the two pairs of lovers alone.

"We'll be right down." Alkaios tugged on Nephalea's hand, and she followed him away from the table in silent agreement.

They stepped upstairs to their room. He framed her face in his hands, studying her beloved features, his heart so full words failed him.

She stroked his arms. "This isn't the night we faced Gerrian in the West Field."

"It feels like it."

"I know. But we will never endure that again. No one has the power to take me from you now."

"That day, I didn't even get to make love to you one last time. I wish I could now."

"It wasn't the last time." She pulled his mouth to hers. *After tonight, our future will truly begin.*

I won't let him cheat us out of it a second time. He crushed her to him and feasted on her kiss.

Have faith in our future, my love. In our power. Our eternity.

I have faith in you, bluebird.

She pulled back, her eyes glistening with tears. "I'm glad to hear that."

He stared at her. "Did you doubt it?"

Her disappointment was a bitter taste in the Union. "My wards aren't worth anything in tonight's battle. I feared I couldn't convince you that I'm powerful enough to protect myself—and you. That we can protect each other now."

"My need to shield you from harm does not mean I question your strength. You were always strong. But after all the hardship you've endured, I can't help wanting to make things easy for you."

"You did. You gave me the Gift."

They held each other for a long moment more.

"Be safe outside the walls," he said. "Don't leave me."

"Be safe inside the castle. Come back to me."

Hand in hand, they stepped out to join their fellow Hesperines.

⁓

THE WARMTH OF BARU'S last, generous kiss lingered on Iskhyra's mouth. A luxury from a world they had left a mere instant ago. Now she was in the Tenebrae again.

Jaya had led the five of them to a strategic position overlooking the siege from a nearby rise. Iskhyra stood behind her next to Baru and braced her feet.

The shouts of men. The creak, groan, and *thwack* of the siege engines. The sound of the missile hurtling through the air. Then the sickening impact. Screams.

Behind her, her newgifts shone, Hespera's newly forged stars. How easily they could be knocked from the sky. The night when she must let them come out from behind her shield had arrived too soon.

"You know what to do," Jaya told them all. "Fight with wisdom and strike with Mercy."

Iskhyra looked at Baru. "May the Goddess's Eyes light out paths…"

He held her gaze as he gave the Ritual response. "…and her darkness keep us in Sanctuary."

Alkaios moved forward to stand beside Baru. "All of you have our gratitude."

Nephalea took her place at Jaya's side. "Tonight, Hespera will stay Anthros's hand."

Then came that last moment before the battle, silent and too long, shivering and too short. And they all stepped.

Iskhyra followed Jaya's aura. They landed atop the roof of Salicina's keep. Iskhyra could sense the auras of determined women and frightened children within. She and Jaya crouched there, veiled creatures of fangs and night, an unlikely last line of defense for the mortal families huddling below. Hespera's sacred gargoyles would guard the Sanctuary of Salicina tonight.

Jaya gave Iskhyra a sidelong glance. "I can tell this isn't your first siege."

"Definitely not." Iskhyra tightened her veil to make sure her fellow Hesperine suspected nothing about her past experiences. "But this is your area of expertise, Fortress Master. I follow your orders tonight."

"First ward. Before the walls sustain another blow. Fast but thorough."

Their auras swelled with magic and blurred together. Iskhyra lent her strength to Jaya's mighty, razor-sharp Will.

A barrage of flaming projectiles soared toward the castle. The men on the walls braced themselves.

Iskhyra and Jaya's ward gathered before the soldiers, a rondel of deepening night that swirled and expanded. Iskhyra felt when their magics lifted each other up to the perfect height of power, and they were no longer two warriors, but one force made stronger together. With a silent explosion, the ward blasted outward, a curtain of darkness between the castle and the enemy.

The fiery missiles made impact. Iskhyra felt the satisfying crunch as the projectiles dashed to pieces upon the ward. She snarled a smile, and Jaya let out a wicked laugh.

The soldiers shouted, their auras lighting the walls with fearful awe. But there came no screams of agony, no despairing curses at the state of the walls. They could be as afraid of shadow wards as they wished. Iskhyra would not apologize for saving their mortal necks.

"What is this magic?"

"It's a miracle!"

"The gods have answered our prayers!"

"Well," Iskhyra huffed. "We don't usually get that reaction."

Jaya barked a laugh. "Wonder what the enemy is saying?"

Iskhyra turned her ear to the battlefield beyond the castle.

"Unholy sorcery!"

"Black magic! Heresy!"

"A curse upon their souls!"

Iskhyra and Jaya exchanged a grin.

The first siege engine collapsed in a heap of beams and ropes. Baru's clever laughter echoed up into the night. Then suddenly there he was beside Iskhyra. With an elegant bow, he presented her with a linchpin from one of the catapults' wheels. "I believe you will appreciate this more than flowers."

Iskhyra took it from him and brought it to her nose. "Ah, the sweet fragrance of destruction."

"Stop distracting my reinforcements," Jaya ordered, her aura full of enjoyment.

With another bow, Baru stepped back down into the fray and continued to wreak havoc.

"He should get his overeducated backside out of the Castra more often," Jaya said affectionately.

"I don't think he's the only one who's benefiting from a little adventure."

"Guilty as charged. Ah, next volley. Let's cast over another layer."

They fell silent, throwing all their concentration into the next buildup of their spell. Cast. Volley. Cast. They found a rhythm, two allies marching at the same pace.

"For an independent Hesperine errant," Jaya commented, "you're surprisingly comfortable following orders."

"When lives are at stake, independence can be selfish, and cooperation can avert catastrophe."

"Well said."

Between each assault, they layered over another protective sheet of molten darkness. Their ward hardened into pure, steel night.

But every time the enemy fired their siege engines, they lost another. One trebuchet started rolling backward, sending soldiers fleeing to escape its destructive path. It kept going until it sank into a deep bed of mud. Men swarmed around it, heaving uselessly. The mules they brought to help kicked up their heels and danced off, heading for the fields.

One missile halted midair, turned around, then crashed into the catapult that had fired it, reducing it to splinters. Another catapult swiveled in place, aiming squarely in the direction of the commanders.

"Hold your fire!" came a man's yell. "Hypnos's nails, *hold your fire!*"

"And Baru says he doesn't have a taste for violence," said Jaya.

With every one of Baru's victories, Iskhyra's hand closed around the linchpin a little tighter.

Amid the mortals' confused cries and her laughter with her comrades, the stink of death that still threatened and the sweet pulse of the shadow ward, the truth whispered softly to her.

She had missed this. So fiercely she could weep.

But there was no time for sentiment now. Not when she spotted Nephalea in the middle of the battlefield. Iskhyra's hands fisted with the urge to put a ward around her newgift.

"We can't," Jaya warned. "We must put all our power into holding the ward over the castle. Trust Nephalea. She is more powerful than she yet knows."

Iskhyra gritted her teeth and made herself focus on the castle, while the new Hesperine she was sworn to protect faced the enemy on her own.

chapter twenty-two

LIGHT'S BENEDICTION

DELIVER THE SUPPLIES. DON'T be seen. Alkaios's duty tonight was simple.

Except for the knowledge that this would be the last time he ever set foot in his family home.

Under the cover of his veils, he entered the camp of Salicina's allies. They huddled on the banks of the river, their fires doused to avoid drawing the enemy's attention. The deep tracks in their muddy wake said they had spent a long, slow day trying to get men, wagons, and beasts as far as they could. Not far enough.

The aromas of medicinal herbs, the salty, ripe odor of cured meat, and the metallic scent of weapons drew him to the supply wagons. Here was everything Domitia needed to save Salicina.

This was his last chance to speak to his family.

He shouldn't. Mustn't. It would only increase Domitia's pain to see him like this. It was a miracle the woman he loved had accepted him. His sister-in-law would never have a change of heart like Nephalea's.

Any contact with Aemilian was out of the question.

Alkaios had said his goodbyes to them the day his mortal life had ended. He must reconcile himself to that.

It was a good thing he had eternity to work on it.

He put a hand on one canvas-covered bundle in the back of the first wagon, opening his senses to the smell and weight of the supplies within.

He knew the best place to deliver these, the best person who would see them properly distributed.

He focused on Salicina. That feeling in his chest when he was riding toward the castle after a long day and caught sight of the banners. The shelter of its walls as he came inside. The warm greetings of the villagers. Then the fragrant, fascinating flowers, and that sense of wonder he had felt as a boy in the garden around the shrine.

It took so little Will to step, when the pull was so strong.

He arrived precisely in Daughter Pherakia's garden, careful to set the sacks and crates on the walkways between her precious plants.

Are you all right? His Grace, just a thought away.

I'm delivering the supplies. I wish everything else were as easy.

I know.

You know, my Grace.

It took five trips and only a few minutes to transfer all the supplies from the army's camp to the shrine's garden. Not a soldier stirred. Not a stem or leaf was bent.

Before he could draw her attention, the mage herself shot out of the back door of the shrine. The groans of wounded men sounded from within. Alkaios could smell the blood that stained Daughter Pherakia's arms.

She was headed for a bed of medicinal herbs when she halted in her tracks. She breathed, blinked, then muttered a prayer. Racing to the nearest pile of supplies, she threw back the tarps.

How would she explain this miracle to herself? Alkaios wasn't sure. But she would never imagine he had done it. Would she?

Her arms full of bottles and bushels of medicine, she turned back toward the shrine. He watched the woman who had taught him how to bandage his training wounds, the woman who had tried to kill him, go to save the lives of those who had once been his people.

The stakes of the night urged him onward, even as his Will rooted him to the spot. On the wind came the rich fragrances of the fertile fields and the stench of sweat and fire. He smelled the sweet lilies and souring wounds. The mage's relief gusted through his senses, as the suffering of the dying keened in the Union. Within the castle, all the hearts dearest to him lay under a heavy pall of fear.

One fear, one pulse, grew louder and more cherished with every beat of his heart.

Aemilian.

He was so afraid. But he was surrounded by those sworn to defend and serve him. He was blessed with the most devoted mother any child could ask for. Alkaios had to keep telling himself his nephew would be all right until the night he believed his own reassurances to himself.

But tonight, it still felt like his nephew needed him. He still felt like someone who could protect and comfort the boy.

Alkaios turned toward the castle. To Hypnos with the consequences. He would just make sure Aemilian was all right. One last time.

Fortifying his veils, he honed in on the boy's aura and stepped to him.

The small, innermost chamber of the keep was the eye of a storm. Domitia sat at its center with her son on her lap, pressing one of his ears to her chest and covering the other with her hand. Messengers, soldiers, and householders came in and out as she delivered orders, her voice clear and strong.

"My lady, I'm afraid we must go to quarter rations, if you—"

"We must. See that it's done."

"We only have enough herbs to treat the pain of the wounded or tip our arrows with poison."

Not a moment's hesitation. "Give my men relief. Light your arrows on fire."

"We're out of tar, my lady."

"Then shoot them without. Our men will aim true."

Domitia had dried her tears. While he and Nephalea had become Hesperines, his sister-in-law had also undergone a transformation. She had found her power, all on her own.

A lull came in the demands, and Domitia's handmaiden departed to retrieve the rations reserved for her and Aemilian. Quiet descended. Although they didn't know he was there, Alkaios savored the moment of peace with his family.

"Are you cold?" Domitia wrapped a blanket closer around Aemilian.

He snuggled closer against his mother. "No, mama. But it's so dark in here."

"I'm sorry, sweetling. We can't stoke the fire any higher. We mustn't use up too much wood."

"I understand." He hid his tear-streaked face against her chest and held himself so still, his sobs barely shook his chest.

Alkaios's chest shook. As a mortal, it had always undone him to see the boy's tears. The Blood Union made this unbearable.

"Could we have just one more candle?" Aemilian finally asked.

"We're out of candles, dearest. But I will sing you the candle song, and it will be as if we have plenty."

"Yes, Mama."

Her aura a fortress of determination, Domitia stroked Aemilian's hair and rocked him, singing a favorite old lullaby. Alkaios could hear the memory of his brother's voice, singing that same song in harmony with her to their little boy. Aemilian's sniffles punctuated the verses.

Light crept through the room so gently, Alkaios didn't notice it at first. But soon the glow touched Aemilian's hair like a benediction from the moons.

Alkaios looked everywhere for the source of the light. When he caught sight of himself, he stared.

The light was brightest upon his own skin. It was coming from him.

Alkaios, Nephalea said, *it feels as if moonrise came twice in our Union. Is that…your magic?*

It is. I'm a mage. I'm a light mage.

Does it surprise you, my Grace? You have always been our light.

It seemed the moons came out of his veins to shine within the windowless room. He had known this power for all of a few heartbeats, but it felt so familiar. As if it had been there all along, just waiting for his embrace.

It flowed where he sent his Will. He started with a gleam that chased away the shadows in the corners of the room. Then he gathered it closer. Brighter.

Aemilian lifted his head, his sobs pausing.

Domitia's eyes widened, even as her song drifted into silence.

"Mama? I don't see any candles."

"Neither do I," she whispered.

Alkaios wrapped his family in his magic. Aemilian looked around the room with the fascination only a child could have, looking for the source of his rescue.

Even as his fear faded, his mother's rose.

"Don't be afraid." Alkaios eased his veil off.

Domitia shrank back in her chair, clutching Aemilian closer.

"Uncle Alcaeus." The boy gazed up at him, breathless with emotion.

Alkaios swallowed around the lump in his throat. "I'm here."

Aemilian leapt down from his mother's lap and ran toward him.

"Aemilian, don't—!"

His mother's plea halted him in his tracks. She caught up with him an instant later. Pulling him with her, she retreated across the room.

Alkaios held up his hands. "You have nothing to fear from me, Domitia. Ever."

Her gaze raced over him, fixing on his mouth. But he kept his fangs veiled. He would not subject Aemilian to another instant of fear.

"Uncle Alcaeus, they told me you—they said the enemy had—"

"All is well now."

Aemilian folded his hands in front of him. "Did Grandfather and Papa send you to us with a message?"

Alkaios met Domitia's gaze. Would she reveal his nature to Aemilian?

Alkaios wanted to tell the truth. But that would be selfish and give only him solace. Aemilian would find no comfort in knowing what had really happened to his uncle. At least not until he was old enough to decide for himself what he thought.

Alkaios had a chance to give his nephew a good memory of this moment. He could only pray that would influence Aemilian's judgment upon him one day.

When Domitia did not contradict the boy's assumption, Alkaios took a step closer. Another. Slowly, he closed the distance between them.

He knelt before Aemilian. "Your grandfather and your papa are both very, very proud of you. And so am I."

Aemilian stood up straighter.

Alkaios unbuckled his sword belt. He held the ancestral blade across his hands for a long moment, bidding his mortal legacy a silent farewell.

Then he held it out to Aemilian, his beloved boy, who must still live in the world of men. "This sword is rightfully yours now. Having it with you is just like having your grandfather, father, and me at your side. We will always guide your hand. Do as we taught you and wield your blade with honor." To generations of the wisdom of Anthros, he added Hespera's guidance. "But first, try to solve problems without fighting. You are most powerful when you do not draw your sword."

With great solemnity, Aemilian nodded. "You have my word, Uncle Alcaeus."

Alkaios held the sword out. The boy's little hands closed around it. His mother grasped the hilt, taking the sword's weight, and Alkaios released it.

Aemilian's eyes filled with quivering tears. "Am I allowed to touch messengers from Anthros's Hall?"

Alkaios couldn't keep the smile off his face. "Only with your mother's permission."

Her aura was a silent battle. Could she see the love in Alkaios's eyes? Or were the mages' lies all she saw when she looked at him?

"Domitia…I have a message for you as well. We are all admiration for the woman you have become. You are more than equal to this task. Have no regrets."

"Do you have regrets?" she asked.

"Only two. They will be lighter to carry, if they will give me their blessing now."

Her anguish tore at the Union. "I'm so sorry. We shouldn't have let this happen to you."

"Domitia, no. It was not your fault. There was nothing you could have done. I made a choice. I wanted another chance to help the people I love. Tonight, I have that."

"That's why?"

"Yes."

A sob choked her words. "You did this for us."

"Always."

"And after tonight?"

"I want you to know that my honor is still my guide and always will be. Let my deeds tonight stand testament to the man I was—and who I will always be."

"Thank you, Alcaeus," she said. "For…everything."

He put his hand over his heart, where he would hold those words for eternity. "Do not be afraid anymore."

She released Aemilian. He threw himself into Alkaios's arms. Alkaios held him tight, savoring the feeling of the sweet boy in his arms for as long as he could.

~

Smoke billowed around Nephalea, stinging her sensitive nose, so she stopped breathing. She levitated over the splashes of mud. The din of the catapults and the shouts of men blurred into one roar around her.

"A woman on the battlefield?"

"What in Anthros's name?"

"Someone get her out of here!"

"That's Lady Maerea!"

"Lady Maerea is free!"

Boots splashed and pounded toward her, and there was the commander. "My lady! How did you escape? Let me get you to safety."

"You will not take me anywhere, ever again." She smiled, showing him her fangs.

He staggered backward.

She levitated higher until he had to look up at her. "Try keeping me prisoner now."

A grimace twisted his stone face. "How did this happen?"

"Gerrian lied to you. While you stood guard at my door and refused my pleas to release me, it was no mage, but my Hesperine who came for me and spirited me away."

"I…I…had to do my duty."

"You should have chosen your duty to me. I have always protected you and everyone else from my brother's abuses. Why did you side with him?"

"He is my lord."

"I was your lady."

He wiped his brow, his shoulders hunched, his aura an echo of the battle raging around him. "What have I done?"

She left him to defend the walls of his honor against the siege of his conscience.

Are you safe? Alkaios's voice broke through the noise around her.

She laughed. *They are terrified of me.*

You did warn me it could be dangerous if I encouraged you to misbehave. So very dangerous.

She heard the name that was no longer hers, over and over. Men she had known all her mortal life rushed forward to aid her, only to cower in fear when they saw what she was.

Didn't they recognize her? She had been this person all along. They hadn't seen, hadn't listened.

It had taken the Gift to reveal her to them—and to herself.

They got out of her way, giving her a clear path to the men who drove the charge. Gerrian and Lord Drusus drew rein so fast their horses reared and skidded in the mud. She levitated out of reach of the grime, her pristine blue robe fluttering with the movement.

"S—sister?"

The first word out of his mouth. Not an insult. An invocation of their bond.

"I have returned to you, brother. Isn't that what you wished? Will you not present me to your ally, who would have me for his bride?" She made a perfect curtsy in the air and gave Lord Drusus a most ladylike smile, her long canines on display.

He sketched the glyph of what seemed like every god in the air. "Witch!"

"That is no way to greet the lady you have come to court, my lord."

He backed his horse further and further away. "What's going on here?"

Gerrian gaped.

Nephalea held his gaze as she answered for him. "My brother left my husband for the Hesperines."

His flushed face grew more ashen by the moment.

"When love demanded Gerrian accept my union, he mortally wounded the man I married. When honor demanded he give Alcaeus dignity in death, he made sure a Hesperine could reach him. When compassion demanded he comfort me in my grief, he kept me hostage in my own home to force me into marrying you, Lord Drusus. But Alcaeus has not lost his love, his honor, or his compassion. He listened to my plea for freedom."

"That's why you needed my liegehounds!" Lord Drusus made violent gestures with his hands, his horse skittering backward. "Not to keep any roaming Hesperines away from our dead during the siege, but because you knew Lord Alcaeus had already become one! Because he came for your sister—and you knew he would come for you."

Nephalea smiled and watched their alliance fall apart before her eyes.

Gerrian hauled on his reins, backing away from her. "I thought he was dead! I thought to make an example of him. Letting Hesperines ravage his corpse would serve as a warning to all my enemies. I never expected a sorceress to find him barely alive and take a liking to him."

"You knew all along."

"We're allies. I was doing my part to watch your back. To keep the truth quiet, to avoid panic among the men."

A red-gold flicker at the corner of her eye was her only warning.

Then the rush of heat at her back told her it was almost too late. Her mind, sharpened by the Gift, processed it all in the space of a heartbeat. Lord Drusus's hand signals, a warrior's code she had not recognized. The stench of tar, the hiss of flames, the creak of bowstrings lost under the noise of the siege. The whisper of arrows flying.

She spun in the air, facing the oncoming assault from Lord Drusus's archers. Flaming arrows flew from their longbows, crossing the breadth of the battlefield, homing toward her.

chapter twenty-three

SHADOW'S REIGN

SHE HAD TO STEP. Now.

No. She was done giving in. She was through with letting men silence her with either words or weapons. And she was not through with Gerrian.

Her certainty became an act of Will. Darkness rose in her blood and took to the air, blocking out the sky. Night seemed to fall over the battlefield.

Tears came to her eyes with the joy and power of it. Her magic. Her *magic*. Hers.

She would never be powerless again.

The arrows collided with her ward. Shadow snuffed their flames, and their broken shafts scattered on the ground.

There came a triumphant shout in the Blood Union, and from the front of the battle, she could hear her fellow Hesperines' cheers. Baru and Jaya, treasured allies. Iskhyra, Gifter of her Gifter.

And the beloved voice of her Grace. *Night has fallen twice. Miraculous. That's you, Nephalea.*

It is me.

She faced Gerrian and Lord Drusus once more. They sat unmoving. The siege had frozen, shocked into stillness by her show of power.

She let the shadow reign over them all and reached within her veins to see what more was there. Greater depths of magic came to her

Will. She gathered the shadows around her, strengthening her wards, donning them.

"The feud must end." Her declaration rang across the battlefield. "My wards will stand between Lapidea and Salicina until every last man lays down his weapons. Make peace, or Hespera will do it for you."

Lord Drusus let out a string of foul curses. "Show me a battlefield, Gerrian, and I'll march through entrails to prove my mettle. But Hesperine sorcery? I never agreed to this."

"We'll—we'll call the mages—" Gerrian rasped.

"You've already cost me a bride, my liegehounds, and too many men. I'm finished here."

Lord Drusus shouted commands to his men, drowning out Gerrian's protests. Soldiers mobilized, and the retreat was underway. The army in green followed Lord Drusus off the field, leaving behind anything that might slow their flight. The commander led the footsoldiers in gray toward Lapidea without a glance back at Gerrian.

Gerrian dug his heels into his horse. His mount sprang away.

"Wherever you run," Nephalea called after him, "I can find you. No matter how fast you go, I am faster. We are not finished."

The men with muddy faces and bloodstained armor scurried away below Nephalea, her darkness driving them back into the light. Through her shadows, there emerged a warrior garbed only in a simple robe, his face clean, his light brown hair and white fangs gleaming in the light that cloaked him like a second skin.

She wasn't sure which of them reached first, but they were in each other's arms. The chaos receded below them.

He held her to him, his arms hard and desperate. "When I saw the fire arrows—Goddess. Nephalea, I—"

"I'm all right. You're all right." She stroked his hair, his shoulders, his back, proving to herself he was in one piece.

"You cast your spell just in time. You're so powerful, bluebird, and I'll thank Hespera for it every night as long as I live."

"I heard you cheering for me. I'm so glad you were with me in that moment. And you, my love? How does it feel to be a mage?" She ran her hand down his arm, feeling his magic play between her fingers.

"It doesn't feel wrong, the way I feared it would. It makes sense. I think I understand why Hespera gave me this affinity. And why she chose this moment to awaken it."

"What happened in the castle?"

"I talked to Domitia and Aemilian."

"Oh, Alkaios." She waited, hoping.

His aura filled with the light that still lingered around him. "I'm glad I did."

"Did you say everything you needed to?"

"Yes. Yes, I did." He rested his face on her shoulder. "And now I have you."

"You will always have me."

At last he lifted his head. "But Aemilian and Domitia still aren't safe."

"No. As long as Gerrian breathes, so will the feud. We can't let him escape."

Alkaios took her hand. "This time will be different."

"This time, we will defeat him."

※

In the ruins of the battlefield, beneath the shadow wards that blocked the sky, Gerrian sat on his horse. Alone. Had Alkaios's greatest enemy always been so small?

"Lord Drusus!" Gerrian spun his horse around. "Commander!"

No one answered him.

"At last," Nephalea said. "A meeting, just the three of us. No soldiers this time. Just as I always wanted."

He stared at her and Alkaios for one instant, white around his eyes. Then he whirled his horse around and fled again.

"Coward," Nephalea said.

They levitated after him. He pushed his horse hard, as if Hespera herself were at his heels. For she was.

"I know where I want to end this," Alkaios said.

"Are you sure, my love?"

"Yes. It has to be there."

She squeezed his hand. "I know it won't change his mind, but I need to speak with him."

"You do."

Unspoken understanding flowed between them. Whatever the outcome, tonight was also her last chance to speak with her family.

They hounded him away from the castle and across the fields. He rode breakneck for the boundary of Lapidea. At last, his only escape from Salicina was through the West Field.

Alkaios's ears roared. He sank a little in the air. Moving forward became a strenuous act of Will.

Are you all right?

He wished the Union did not prevent him from putting on a brave face for her. *I thought immortality would make me immune.*

Not to our worst memories.

They crossed into the field.

It looked smaller. The moons shone on the surviving stands of golden grain. The shadows of night softened the bare patches of ground. He could almost imagine no skirmish had ever happened here.

"Think of everything we've already survived." Nephalea's voice in the night, her power in the Union. Eternal. "We'll be all right."

His light magic gathered in his hands. "Yes. We'll get through this, too."

Ready?

Yes.

She disappeared, then reappeared in Gerrian's path. He almost toppled his horse to get away from his personal specter—his sister.

But as he turned, Alkaios was there.

It became a bleak dance. Gerrian pivoted his steed, seeking escape. And every time, Nephalea or Alkaios stepped and blocked his way. They drove him closer, closer.

There. That was where Alkaios had fallen.

He touched the horse's brow. That was all it took. Gerrian's destrier tossed him in the mud and ran for home.

Gerrian landed on his back where Alkaios's mortal life had ended. Alkaios stood over him.

The man rolled to his feet, whipping his deadly blade from his scabbard. Grim determination settled over his aura, weighing down his panic. He held his sword with steady hands. He had chosen how he wished to die—as he had lived, by the sword, fighting to the last.

"There is no glory in clinging to our blades," Alkaios said.

"Maybe not for Hespera's get. But by Anthros's Sword, I will not bow to her meekly."

Alkaios held up his hands, white light shining in his palms and banding between his fingers. "By her thorns, I will fight you only with the strength she has given me."

Cool, sweet darkness snaked around him like an intimate embrace. Pure Nephalea pulsed in every shadow. Her ward coated him, an ephemeral suit of armor, stronger than any steel.

Gerrian swung. Alkaios raised his arm and let her ward stop the blade. His Gift-strengthened body absorbed the force of the blow.

Calm settled within Alkaios. As the man hacked away at him, he parried, blocked and dodged by the light of his magic. No anger drove him to counterattack. No bitter taunts came to his lips.

He let Gerrian battle out his rage. His hate. All of it spewed in his aura and took form in his wicked swordsmanship.

Alkaios let him hack out all the pain and poison of generations of Lapideans and Salicinians.

Nephalea didn't know if her imaginings of their first duel were gentler or more horrific than what had actually happened. Her worst visions of that day rose like fire magic, engulfing tonight's battle.

Alkaios moved so fast he must be a blur to Gerrian's mortal eyes. But Nephalea saw her Grace's every move. The fight was too clean and beautiful to be real.

But it was terribly real. The whistle of that blade was a horrible thunder in her ears.

She fed all her anguish into her magic, and the sweet music of her wards became stronger, sheltering her Grace.

One blow after another, she felt it each time Gerrian's sword aimed at Alkaios's flesh and struck her ward. Those flashes of pain were nothing. The knowledge that her magic would not fail drove back her phantom despair.

⁓

The battle lengthened, but Alkaios's body never tired.

In their first duel, Gerrian's skill had taken time to wear through Alkaios's motivation to survive. Tonight, Alkaios's patience took more time to wear through Gerrian's violence.

Eventually Gerrian's strength flagged. Clumsiness ate away at his swings. Exhaustion dulled his strikes. At last, his own need to fight and fight and fight consumed the last of his strength.

He went down on his knees, catching himself on his sword. The blade sank into the ground. He clung to the hilt, heaving for breath. "I have only one request. That I die by your hand, and not—not some unholy spell."

Alkaios lowered his hands. "Hesperines do not kill cruelly or needlessly. Have your last words with your sister."

That seemed to strike more terror in his heart than the prospect of his imminent death.

⁓

When Gerrian collapsed, Nephalea knew she didn't have to ask Alkaios to stay his hand. Her Grace stepped aside to let her approach her brother.

He looked everywhere but at her.

"Gerrian."

His gaze touched on her, and he swallowed and looked away. "Merry. I failed you."

Those words. Not at all what she had expected. "Yes. Yes, you did."

He let go of the sword to cover his face in his hands. "You are a Hesperine, and I am to blame."

She blinked back the rain that had begun to fall. A sweet smell, cleansing the air, disguising the ugliness of bloodshed.

Gerrian hung his head. "None of this would have happened if I had taken better care of you. How could I have failed you, when I was trying so hard to protect you? I tried so hard, Merry. I did everything Father taught me to do. How has it come to this?"

"Father was wrong."

He looked at her at last, his eyes bleary and lost.

"Our ancestors were wrong," she said. "The feud is wrong. The only right thing to do is to make peace. If you had made peace, you wouldn't have lost me."

"You were right," he whispered.

The world shook, although the ground was utterly still beneath her feet.

"What would you have me do?" he asked.

"Give us cause not to spill another drop of blood in this field."

He looked at his sword as if it were his anchor, and yet some strange, foreign thing. "How?"

"I'm going to ask you to do the most difficult deed you have ever imagined. Will you listen to me?"

He looked at her. Really looked at her. And did not look away. "Will it earn me your forgiveness?"

Her Gifting had not banished her anger. It was up to her to master it. "Yes."

"Then I will do it. You have my word."

Whatever he believed about Hesperines, he had just promised to do anything for her without knowing what she would ask.

In that moment, she knew they had won.

More than the feud. She had won a thread that still tied Merry and Gerrian together. One they had never shared in mortal life.

She laid a hand on his damp head. "Swear your allegiance to Domitia of Salicina."

His entire body flinched.

"Submit yourself to her as your liege lady. Devote your sword to protecting her son and see to it he grows to manhood to become lord of our ancestral lands and his own."

"She will have me executed for making her a widow."

"No," Alkaios said. "She will do what is best for her people. She will recognize that your swordsmanship is of greater use than your death. And when Lapidea's people become her own, she will provide for them without holding your family's deeds against them."

Gerrian's hand closed around his sword, his fingers grasping it like claws. "Sister, you alone of all our line remain in this world to judge me. Is this really what you would have me do?"

"It is."

Rain trailed over his head. "Then it shall be done."

He dragged himself to his feet. They faced each other, him slouching with exhaustion, her levitating over the wet ground, eye-to-eye.

She touched a hand to his cheek. "Fare thee well, brother."

He let go of the sword and put his hand over hers.

Seven Nights Later

IT SHOULD HAVE BEEN hard to focus on Bria's presence, but it wasn't. Veiled and warded, Nephalea stepped into the unknown.

The pleasant room disoriented her for an instant. A spacious chamber with a sturdy wooden table, a broad stone hearth, and aromatic herbs hanging from the ceiling.

Nephalea didn't recognize this place, and she knew every nook and cranny of Lapidea. But there was Bria by the fire, stirring a pot that smelled of savory vegetable stew.

The fragrance of lilies drifted on the night air. Daughter Pherakia appeared in the doorway. She wasn't wearing a veil, revealing steel-gray curls that framed an elegant face with an expressive mouth. "I've told you, you needn't cook for me."

Bria tapped her spoon on the side of the pot. "I enjoy doing things for you."

The mage joined Bria at the fireside. "You spent a lifetime waiting on others. Put that away."

"This is entirely different." Bria turned to face Daughter Pherakia. "Why won't you let me take care of you?"

"I've always taken care of myself."

"I know. For too many years. That was my fault. Let me make it right."

Daughter Pherakia let Bria lift a spoonful of the stew to her lips. "Mm. Mmm. That's not cooking, that's…alchemy. I won't tell the Orders if you make this for me forever."

Bria laughed, shy and free all at once. Her aura was a shower of bright sparks. Had she been hiding herself all those long years at Lapidea?

What had it cost her?

"Forever." Bria said the word like a promise.

"With my magic, forever could last awhile, even for two creaky old ladies like us." Vulnerability twinged in the aura of the confident mage. "Are you certain you can live with me that long?"

Bria answered her with a kiss, a soft meeting of lips that quickly became a passionate embrace.

Nephalea looked away, ashamed to have intruded on such a deeply private moment.

Goddess. She had been so clueless about the one person closest to her. How could she do that to Bria?

"This will be ready in just a few minutes," Bria murmured. "Shall we eat in the garden?"

"I'll set the table," Pherakia replied. "And then you must promise not to spend any more time in the kitchen for tonight. I have better plans for you."

"I promise." Bria sounded like a youthful, breathless girl.

Nephalea waited for Pherakia to leave the room. Now was her chance. Should she do what she had come here for after all? Or just slip away and leave Bria to this surprising new life?

Everyone deserved a choice.

And this was their last opportunity to make peace.

Nephalea kept her aura concealed so the mage wouldn't sense a Hesperine presence. But she altered her veils so Bria could see and hear her.

She took one step forward. Bria turned toward the sound, the spoon in her hand.

She didn't spill a drop of soup. Bria, steady as always. Bria, who had harbored pain Nephalea had never imagined.

"If you're here to harm Rakia, I will spend the last breath in my body trying to stop you. I may not have the power to stand against a Hesperine, but I won't give her up without a fight this time."

"I'm not here for revenge."

"I don't know if what I say means anything to you now, but we were trying to protect both of you. Rakia loved Alcaeus like a son and couldn't bear for him to exist under that curse. And I knew he would bring his curse on you if we failed to stop him."

"You and Pherakia have nothing to fear from me."

Bria took a step back. "I did fear seeing you again. And yet, I was jealous of Gerrian for getting to tell you goodbye."

"I wouldn't leave without telling you farewell."

"You're…leaving?" The two words hung between them, heavy with all Bria's unanswered questions.

"Lapidea and Salicina are finally safe. Alcaeus and I did what we set out to do."

"Peace." Bria's aura felt like a held breath, waiting to release into a sigh of wonder. "Rakia and I were there when your brother came. Lady Domitia refused him entry at first, thinking he might try to do harm. He camped outside the gates for days. His situation became so wretched, she realized he really had come as her supplicant. You should have seen the look on her face when he entered her great hall and knelt before her to swear an oath of fealty to her and Lord Aemilian."

"We did. No one saw us, but Alcaeus and I were there to make sure Gerrian kept his word. Domitia accepted his pledge with great dignity. I can only imagine how difficult that was for her."

"The tasks she has already set him will take him far from Lapidea and Salicina. She intends to make use of him out of sight."

"I think that's for the best. She shouldn't have to endure his presence. But I hope my brother's fall will make him a better man, as he picks himself back up again."

Bria shook her head and put a hand to her mouth. "I can't believe we're talking like this. As if…"

"As if I'm not a Hesperine? As if I'm still the Lady of Lapidea, responsible for all our fates?"

Bria nodded.

"I will always care what happens to my brother, our people—and you."

"I don't understand. Why would you forgive us for what we did?"

Shame, unbearably sharp, sank into Nephalea's heart, a splinter of a thorn that would worry at her for all time. "How many years did you devote to my family, while our feud destroyed your happiness? How many days did you spend with me while you pined for the woman you love?"

Bria drew in a sharp breath. Nephalea could feel her burying it all. Bria pushed it down hard within herself, as if she could make it small, and no one would see. As if she could make herself small, and her pain would somehow be easier to carry.

Nephalea choked back tears. "You owe me no answers, no explanations. But if you wish to speak of love, I am the last person who will judge you. If there is any way I can honor the years you cared for me, I will do it. You do not need my blessing or approval, but if my support has any worth to you, you have it. I want you to be happy."

"You were too young to understand," Bria said stiffly. "Then too proper…"

"Too ignorant. Too wrapped up in my own troubles. I was selfish. I thought I gave every last drop within me to others, but I foolishly gave far too much of it to my brother, and spared not enough for you. I am so sorry."

Just then, Pherakia's voice drifted in from the garden, her words carrying a heady hint of double meaning. "Almost ready?"

"I'll just be another moment," Bria called, her voice admirably normal. "Wait there and let me bring everything out to you."

"I would protest, but I know you will insist."

"I do insist," Bria said lightly.

"Would you like to talk about her?" Nephalea asked.

Bria sank into a chair. "Your mother never suspected, either. I admit, it…eases something, for it not to be my secret anymore."

"How did you first meet her?"

A smile played across Bria's face. "At your parents' wedding. When your mother brought me to Lapidea to help me escape an unwanted marriage, I never expected to find a woman I could love."

"When the feud stopped my mother's visits here, no one realized what it cost you."

"Rakia asked me to stay with her."

"Oh, Goddess. You could have had this happiness all those years ago. Why didn't you?"

"I had to choose between loyalty and love. I would say I made the wrong choice…but I refuse to regret so much of my life. Rakia and I both had important responsibilities. I made the right choice this time, at least."

"She helped you get away from Lapidea?"

"The night you left with Alcaeus. We…found comfort in each other. Rakia gave me a second chance. Everyone thinks I couldn't bear to stay at Lapidea after losing you, and that the local mage of Kyria offered me sanctuary."

"There will be no consequences for you from the temple?"

Bria's eyes twinkled. "The exact wording of Rakia's vow of celibacy is all about men this and men that. No one imagines anything scandalous about two old women living together."

"I could give you and Pherakia time, Bria. All the time in the world. I could make up those lost years to you." Nephalea held out her wrist, where the Gift flowed through her veins.

Bria reached out, slowly at first. But when she placed her hand on Nephalea's wrist, her touch felt the same as all those years she had offered her strength and comfort. "I have exactly what I've always wanted, right here, right now."

"Among Hesperines, you wouldn't have to hide your union."

A lifetime of consideration flashed by in Bria's aura, too complex for Nephalea to fully understand.

"We're Kyria's, through and through. And we're happier in our little shrine garden than we would be wherever Hesperines call home. Mortality is not without its beauties. Growing old—well—" She laughed. "—older with the one you love is a blessing."

"I didn't think you would accept, but…I had to offer. I wish the two of you many happy years of being secretly scandalous."

They shared a smile.

Nephalea's faded. "I'm sorry raising me stole so much of your time. I don't want to be one of your regrets. When you think of me, don't think of the horrible tales you've heard. Think of what Alcaeus and I did to protect everyone. I hope that proves to you I have chosen my better nature."

"I'm beginning to see that."

Nephalea held her hand tight. "Thank you. I will treasure those words always."

"You're leaving," she said.

"The world is so big, and I will no longer live inside the walls, looking out at it all."

"Where will you go? What will you be doing?"

"We'll be in the Tenebrae for a while. Perhaps one day we'll go to Orthros, but for now…I think there are many more places like Lapidea and Salicina that could use our help. That is what Hesperines do, Bria. We give Mercy and Solace wherever we go, to whomever needs it."

"Will I ever see you again?"

"I will come back and check on you," Nephalea promised. "If you ever change your mind about my offer, you have but to ask."

"Don't let Rakia find you here. She wants to believe the best of you and Alcaeus, and I will help her do so. But she is still a mage. She has responsibilities to her temple."

"We will not put her in that position with the Orders. Just…avert her suspicions, when one lily goes missing from her garden each year. You will know I took it, as a reminder that all four of us are happy in love."

chapter twenty-four

NO WALLS OF STONE

Iskhyra watched Baru put the last scroll away. "Your catalog is complete."

He nodded. "Now that I've made a record of every scroll in the Sanctuary, I can be sure nothing will get lost in transfer. After I step all the documents back to Castra Justa, I'll cross-check everything I arrive with against the catalog."

"The scrolls are in the best of hands."

"It's a shame we must remove them from this sacred place. I wish we could keep it as a library. But we can't leave these scrolls in hostile territory."

"They will be of much greater benefit at the Castra, where Hesperines can access and study them."

Baru grumbled. "When the scholarly circles in Orthros hear about this discovery, I'll have visiting academics swarming through my quiet library for months."

Iskhyra laughed. "What a terrible distraction for you."

"Overbearing elders," he muttered.

"You know, once the scrolls are safe in your library, you could leave them for the researchers to argue over. You could sneak out again for another adventure."

He roamed toward her. "Is that an invitation, my heart-free adventurer?"

When he came within reach, she ran her hands down his chest. "Would you like it to be?"

He put his hands over hers, pressing her palms into his chest, sealing them flesh to flesh. But she didn't have to be a mind healer to sense his hesitation.

Some part of her had known, deep down, what his answer would be. She would never have asked him such a dangerous question, unless she'd been sure he would give her a safe answer.

How could safety hurt so much?

He leaned in, his aura laced with regret. "I have made a rather surprising discovery, fellow scholar. I admit, I was not expecting it, but the evidence does not lie."

"What has experience taught you on this journey, Master Librarian, that you had not already discovered in the depths of a scroll?"

He sighed. "I am actually happy to return to the Castra."

She gave him a rueful smile. "Have you finally had enough of the life of adventure?"

"I'm still looking forward to my next foray in the field, but…I'm glad to have my library to go back to. After all these years and all the places I've seen, I've discovered the most elusive location of all. The place that feels like home."

"Castra Justa is…a remarkable place."

"I have never felt this way about anywhere. The Charge feels more like family than my own parents ever did. Even more than my fellow alumni of Capital University."

"Now *that* is high praise."

"Perhaps it has something to do with the prince being an alumnus himself."

"I'm sure that's it."

He pulled her hands up to circle his neck, bringing their bodies closer together. "As an alumna, you would fit right in, you know."

"Oh, I don't know. Not everyone finds me good company."

"Iskhyra." The way he said her name, a lush, throaty purr, made it sound like it belonged to someone else…someone she wanted to become.

She didn't have the luxury of being that person.

And yet his aura swept her in deep, full of intent. "Come back to Castra Justa with me."

He made it sound so easy. He could never imagine why it was not.

She could never remain the lover of the First Prince's friend. She could never set foot in Castra Justa. She could never risk her quest for her wants…her needs.

"You have no idea how much I want to."

His aura heated with cocky amusement, his skin scorching on hers. "Last night convinced me how much you want."

She let out a little groan in her throat. He kissed away the outcry, and she let him. She stole long moments of his heady flavor, tasting sweet companionship, savory passion, and rich courage. The flavors that ran even stronger and more irresistible in his veins.

For just a few moments, she let it all fall away. Her past. Her quest. The reasons why she must not. She let herself drink of this pure thing between them, this shared and shameless desire, this equal giving and taking that was both respect and plunder of each other.

It was how good he was that made her pull away.

"Baru." She rolled his name on her tongue one more time. "I cannot."

"If you expect me to accept that conclusion, make a very compelling argument."

"I made an oath. As long as I am promised to my quest, I cannot make any promises to anyone."

"I'm not asking for promises. Only that on your wanderings, you wander through my library. I have a nice chair. A big chair."

"Sounds like a chair I'd never want to get out of."

"That would be fine, too."

She shared a sad smile with him.

"Your path does not lead through my library, does it?"

She shook her head. "I have a purpose. I must see it through."

He rested his hands on her shoulders. "I would ask you what it is, so that you might shift a little of its weight onto me. But I think you are too stubborn, or perhaps too honorable, to share it with anyone."

"You think of everything I do not wish to confess, mind healer."

"I think you have given yourself to your cause, whatever it may be.

What you cannot give to others is only one of the many sacrifices you have made in that shrine. What of all you cannot give to yourself?"

"I had…everything. But none of it mattered, in the end."

"And at the end of your quest, what will you gain? What will be left for you—left *of* you?"

"If there is nothing left of me, it will have been worth the sacrifice."

"Don't you dare." That tone would teach any enemy to fear his power. "Swear to me you're not going to your death, or I will take you to Castra Justa myself. I *am* a mind healer, Iskhyra. It is my sacred duty to intervene when someone is considering harming themselves."

He watched her, his magic humming around and through her. There was no escaping his perception.

"It's not that, Baru. I'm not a danger to myself. I can't afford to die. Who would finish my quest then?"

"That is not what I hoped to hear."

"I can't afford to imagine what awaits me when…if…I succeed."

He pulled her close again, wrapping her up in his powerful arms. She breathed in deep, filling herself with his scent and the promise of all she might have imagined.

"I should take you to the Castra," he rumbled, "and keep you there for mind healing until you can see moonrise on the horizon."

"But?"

"But I sense the need in you. It is its own sort of Craving, but not for anything so sweet as love. You seek to right a wrong. What you need is to finish your quest, and I doubt anything else could make things right inside you."

"You understand." Her voice came out husky. "Some sacrifices should never have happened. Others are necessary and right. Sacred, even."

He pulled back, looking into her eyes once more with his brilliant brown ones. "I do not believe in coming between a Hesperine and the Goddess's calling."

He even understood this. Why—how—was she letting him go? "You deserve a truly heart-free adventurer, Baru. Someone who will always come home to your library and spend long hours in that chair with you. Someone as generous as you who can give you more than I."

"I will be the judge of what I want and deserve. But I will ask for only one promise from you."

"If I can give it, I will."

"Promise me that if it becomes too much, you will ask for help. You know where to find us, and we will always be there for you." He cupped her cheek in his hand. "For you to complete your quest, your heart must survive, too."

"Thank you," she whispered. "I will give you that promise for one of your own."

"What would you ask of me?"

"As long as there isn't anyone waiting for you at home in that chair… Whenever you leave your library to do fieldwork, make sure you cross paths with me. We'll enjoy it to the fullest."

A slow, gorgeous smile spread across his face. "Promise."

∞

AFTER SHE AND BARU had said their private goodbyes, they joined Jaya and the newgifts in front of the Sanctuary. Jaya and Nephalea were deep in one last lesson on warding magic. Alkaios alternated between hurling boulders for their training exercises and offering his Grace flowery praise like the lovesick youngblood he was.

Iskhyra and Baru stood for a moment in aching, companionable silence, before Jaya spoke.

"Well done, Newgift Nephalea. I'm afraid that's all we have time for."

Nephalea dispelled the wards surrounding her. "I feel like we've only just begun."

"You know you have an open invitation at the Castra. Come join my trainees for lessons with me anytime you like."

"Thank you so much, Master Jaya." Nephalea's aura overflowed with her anticipation of all her future now held.

Alkaios was a mirror of that brilliant light. It filled up the Union, catching every heart within range and buoying them up. Even heavy old elder hearts.

Thorns, who knew youth could be infectious?

Alkaios draped an arm around Nephalea's shoulder. "I look forward to meeting the master light mages of the Charge and discovering what they can teach me."

Baru crossed to Alkaios, offering him a scroll. "In the meantime, you'll need this. It is a peerless text on light magic as practiced by blood mages. It will take you from the basics to powerful, advanced spells—and teach you many long-lost secrets along the way."

Alkaios held the scroll in both hands. "Master Baru, shouldn't you keep this safe at Castra Justa?"

"As the Charge's librarian, I hereby authorize an extended loan. As extended as you need it to be. You can return it whenever you and Nephalea visit the Castra, and we'll enjoy a discussion of it over coffee."

"You have my gratitude, Master Baru." They exchanged a wrist clasp.

Jaya clasped his wrist next. "You really are meant to be a Hesperine warrior."

"High praise, coming from you, Fortress Master. Thank you."

"And to answer a question you asked me before...no, I don't wish anything had turned out differently." She smiled.

"My dear colleague," said Baru, "do you mean to imply that whipping the green recruits at the Castra into shape is actually fun for you?"

"I wouldn't do it otherwise, you overgrown schoolboy. I get to do the work I love, except with even more magic. My enemies are more terrified of me than ever. And the Charge is considerably less regimented than the Imperial army." She winked at Alkaios and Nephalea.

Baru raised his eyebrows. "Is a single title really enough to satisfy a decorated officer with multiple medals to her name? There are no promotions after Fortress Master for you to work toward."

"I know. It's good to be the best, isn't it?"

Iskhyra watched the exchange, looking back and forth between her newgifts and the Fortress Masters. Now Nephalea was embracing Jaya and saying her farewells.

Why were they saying their farewells?

"Thorn-seeking newgifts." She threw up her hands. "You two can't really be thinking of traveling alone. Yes, breaking a siege—with the help of three elders, I might add—was a feat to be proud of at your age. But that shouldn't give you any ideas. You're not ready for the wide world, not without more training and someone to watch your backs. Go to the Castra. Learn everything Jaya and Baru and the other mages can teach you. Then you will be ready for the field."

Her newgifts came to stand beside her.

"We don't plan to travel alone," Nephalea said. "We're coming with you."

"If you'll have us, Gifter."

After all these years, Iskhyra thought she was too world weary for much of anything to surprise her. But these two had. So many times.

She was already shaking her head. "Out of the question."

"Why?" Nephalea asked.

The favorite question of the young. Those who hadn't reached the age when they knew better than to drive themselves mad wondering *why*. "I have work to do."

"We'll help," Alkaios offered.

"Dangerous work. It's no task for newgifts."

Nephalea raised her chin. "As dangerous as being a fragile mortal at the mercy of men?"

Alkaios gestured to his fighting robe. "As dangerous as living by the sword?"

"We are accustomed to danger," Nephalea said, "and we managed to survive it."

"Largely thanks to you." Alkaios leveled that gaze at her, honest as spring snow. "Let us help you, Iskhyra."

"I have told you, you owe me nothing as your Gifter."

"Hesperines don't practice debts." Alkaios's response would have been impudent, if he hadn't been so sincere. "Let us honor our bond of gratitude."

Nephalea smiled. "Or at least keep you company."

Iskhyra's gaze drifted to where Baru and Jaya stood. They weren't far, but that distance already seemed vast. Baru gave her a knowing, encouraging smile.

Then she looked at the two young Hesperines before her. They were eager for her approval. Her acceptance. Newgifts, but strong ones, who could already claim the victory of having withstood being human.

Alkaios held out his hand, light glittering over his palms and fingertips. "I can use my light magic to conceal us wherever we roam, or learn to conjure illusions to misdirect our enemies. Besides, I do know how to fight."

"And my wards are ready now. They will only get stronger and better as I train with you." A shadow rose behind Nephalea, a beautiful shield of fresh, dark magic, snapping with stars of energy. For the first time in a long while, Iskhyra remembered her wards had once felt like that.

She was now on a path gargoyles feared to tread. How could she drag Alkaios and Nephalea there with her? They had lived with such pain. Only now had they begun to shine.

They deserved a happier path than hers. "A much better future awaits you at Castra Justa. Alkaios, I cannot train you in light magic. Nephalea, having Jaya as a mentor is the opportunity of a lifetime."

Alkaios held up his scroll. "You can teach me to read Divine."

"And you can teach me warding," said Nephalea.

Iskhyra shook her head. "It is time for you two to stop sacrificing for others and enjoy everything your new lives have to offer."

Nephalea nodded. "Yes, it is."

That answer should have fill Iskhyra with relief. She still felt as if she were treading over a bed of thorns.

Nephalea tilted her face toward the night sky. "At last, we are free. We can choose any future we want, isn't that right?"

"Free Will is one of Hespera's most sacred tenets," Iskhyra replied.

"So the first steps we take on our journey with her are ours to decide."

"And we choose to share that path with you," Alkaios said, "if you will choose us."

Never had two such raw recruits cornered her so effectively.

"A most convincing argument." Baru raised his brows at Iskhyra.

Waiting for her verdict, Nephalea lowered her wards, gathering the shadows around herself once more. As the darkness came to rest, it revealed the sky behind her. The crystal clear horizon overflowed with cold, bright, guiding stars. The moons were rising.

Iskhyra was many things, and there were many things she no longer was.

But she had always been honest with others—and herself. So were

Alkaios and Nephalea, and they deserved their honesty returned. "I have grown accustomed to your company. I could ask for no better allies, and I have many things to teach you. I would enjoy having you travel with me."

Nephalea's smiles were much more frequent of late, and now Iskhyra discovered she could cause one. Alkaios's aura glowed in that quiet, candid way he had when he was immensely pleased about something.

Iskhyra put her hands behind her back. "Welcome to my errant circle. May our deeds beneath the Goddess's Eyes do her proud."

Eight Nights Later

ALKAIOS WATCHED THE WAVES sweep up over the sand. The ocean caressed his thighs, then darted back, then reached for him again. The water reflected the crescent moons as if Hespera gazed up at him from the depths.

Nephalea emerged from the sea, nothing but the water clothing her, a thousand tiny droplets of moonlight shimmering from her. She joined him in the shallows, twining her arm around his waist. They looked out across the ocean together, connected to each other and that immense, wondrous flow.

"Had you ever seen the sea before tonight?" she asked.

"No, never."

"And I thought I was the only one trapped in the small world where we once lived."

"I seldom gave thought to anything beyond my family's concerns. I never realized I might want more. That I could need more."

"That's as horrible in its own way as knowing you want more and that you cannot have it."

He tangled his hand in her wet hair, tilting her head back, and trapped her mouth with his. The kiss tasted of salt and wild ocean, of welcoming depths and vast new things. Grace tasted different every night, and yet always of her. *We can have everything now.*

She turned to face him fully, molding her warm, slick body to his. The inviting swells of her breasts pressed against his chest. He framed her hips in his hands, savoring the new softness there. She was still his slim, light bluebird, but their new life of plenty was filling her hollows. One night at a time, he undid her years of deprivation with his blood.

Entwined with him, she looked across the sea again, to the horizon where ocean and sky were one. "So this is what it's like—Akanthia, the whole world, which holds the Tenebrae and Cordium, Orthros and the Empire, and more lands we've not even heard of yet. I thought once we were out in it, it might feel smaller than my imaginings. But I was wrong. Akanthia feels bigger."

"It does." They stood with the Tenebrae behind them. Alkaios pointed westward, out to sea. "Just think. If we crossed that ocean, we would reach the Empire."

"So Iskhyra says." Nephalea nodded northward up the coast. "And if we traveled north on this sea, we would reach the shores of Orthros."

"We could go there with a thought."

"Or swim the entire way without tiring."

"Or fly, bluebird." He grabbed her up and swung her around, twirling her all along the shore.

She laughed as the water splashed around them. "Even as a Hesperine, you can make me breathless!"

"Do you want to go to Orthros, my love?"

"Oh, yes."

He set her on her feet again. "But not tonight."

She shook her head, her hair flinging droplets onto his skin. "I'm sure that one night, Orthros will feel like home. But right now, I want no walls of stone. Just the open road and every night different from the last. Is that what you want?"

"For the first time in my life, it is. I love this fine household we have established for ourselves. It is built of you and me."

"That is all we need to make a home."

She levitated to bring her mouth to his, her toes drifting through the surf behind her. His passionate bluebird, now so confident in her desires. She got him drunk on the taste of her and the wide world and their freedom.

She rose higher, wrapping her legs around his waist. He gripped her buttocks, urging her to his rhabdos. She pulled her face back, looking into his eyes. Her fangs had descended, moon-pale and thorn-sharp. Her blue eyes reflected all the lights in the sky, glowing with magic and desire.

She hooked her heels in the small of his back and took him. As he plunged into her, he gave a sharp moan, asking for everything. Knowing they could have it.

There on the remote brink of the sea, under veil spells and the open sky, they made love with rapacious hunger. The tide rose, engulfing them. Their wet bodies slipped and collided against each other, every ebb and flow pounding through their Union.

Light winked at them from the water, and shadows danced on the surface of the sea. The light and darkness surged upon them. The glow of his magic kissed her swollen lips, shone along her throat, gleamed upon her rolling hips. Her wards ran over his shoulders and down his back, pulsing over his skin.

He gathered her hair in his hand and pulled the length of it around his neck, twining them together. She nuzzled his neck, arching on him at an angle that seemed a spell perfectly cast to harrow him with pleasure. He let his head fall back.

She bit his bared throat. Four perfect points of pleasure-pain sent a cascade of stars through his every vein.

He let out a groan at the sky. "My Grace."

He lowered his head to her neck. One rough kiss, another, and he took her vein, joining her in the Feast.

Cheek to cheek, they consumed and fed each other, their bodies rocking in the tide of blood and sea. Her limbs twined around him, her hair and magic binding him, all graceful writhing and slippery lust. The current carried her to him over and over again, adding force to the rhythm of their joining.

Suddenly her bite released, and she tore away from his fangs to throw her head back. She rose on his body, rose from the sea, blood trailing in four rivulets down her neck, over her breasts. Her face to the sky, she let out a glorious call and took flight, carrying him with her. His climax surged out of him, inexorable as the sea, tide after tide that promised forever. He let out his own victory cry.

They stood there in the waves afterward, caressing and licking each other, murmuring to one another about everything they had to look forward to.

"Shall we head back to the Sanctuary?" she asked eventually.

"Yes, we should check on Iskhyra."

Nephalea waded out of the water, treating him to a stunning view of her from behind. He followed her to shore to grab the glistening curves of her backside. Laughing and teasing, they dried each other with cleaning spells. Finding their robes turned into a game of chase up and down the beach.

Hand in hand, they strolled back around the curve of the shore to the Sanctuary nestled in the cliffs there. Ruined columns rose from the sand, worn smooth by wind, surf, and time. The remnants of engravings hinted at forgotten beauty. One pillar bore a carving that was stark by contrast, the rough, sensual shape of a siren, half brought to life from the stone.

Iskhyra had propped her back against a fallen column. A small ward sheltered the scroll on her lap.

Alkaios sat next to her, peering over her shoulder. "I didn't know Baru gave you something from the library."

Nephalea stood near, looking down at the scroll. "Is it about warding?"

Iskhyra lifted her head. In that instant, Alkaios glimpsed something in her gaze that sent a shiver creeping over his skin. Her eyes seemed not to reflect the lights of the night sky above them, but a desolate, moonless place.

Then she focused on him and Nephalea, and he wondered if he had imagined the haunted look. "You two are back early. I told you to have fun."

"We had fun," Nephalea said.

"Plenty." Alkaios grinned and didn't care if he looked like a randy newgift.

Iskhyra rolled up the scroll, wrapping it in yet another ward. Alkaios couldn't make out a thing.

Nephalea raised an eyebrow. "Perhaps it isn't a scroll from the library, but a love letter from the librarian. If it is private, Iskhyra, we shall not pry."

Alkaios studied Iskhyra's face. "No dilated eyes…no overextended fangs…"

"Iskhyra, if you had symptoms, you wouldn't hide them from *us*, would you?"

"Not after I was nearly sick all over you from my Craving?"

The elder's snort sounded dangerously close to a laugh. "Thank you for the concern, you two."

"Well?" Alkaios prompted.

"I should know better than to travel with the newly Graced. You are lovesick and determined to spread the disease to everyone around you."

Nephalea clasped her hands. "Have you caught it yet?"

Iskhyra waved a hand and tucked the scroll into her pack. "Time for warding lessons."

"Iskhyra," Alkaios said. "Are you all right?"

She went still, her hand on the now-hidden scroll. "You and your honesty, Alkaios. I can never meet it with anything other than honesty of my own."

"You can trust us, Gifter."

"I know." She sighed and sat back. "It has been several nights, and I have no Craving symptoms."

Nephalea's face fell. "Oh."

"I'm sorry, Iskhyra." Alkaios touched his shoulder to hers. "I know you've been looking a long time."

"Don't mope, turtle doves. Craving or not, Baru and I will be seeing more of each other."

"Then what has made you so grim tonight?" Nephalea asked.

"This scroll. I suppose there are a few things you should know. If it changes your thoughts on traveling with me, I understand."

Nephalea opened her mouth, then closed it again. *Does she really think she can scare us off that easily?*

I'm afraid if we protest, she'll retreat behind her veils again.

It's so like her to reveal secrets only as a warning.

Let's see how many she reveals while she's feeling protective.

"You two will eventually visit Castra Justa," Iskhyra began. "When you do, it would be best if you said as little about me as possible."

He and Nephalea shared a glance and waited for Iskhyra to continue. When she didn't, Alkaios spoke up. "May we ask why?"

"If the First Prince finds out about my quest, he will try to stop me. That cannot happen."

A ward stirred around Nephalea's hands. "What does he have against you?"

Iskhyra paused, clearly considering her words. "I don't want you to judge him based on my affairs. When you meet him, he will welcome you, as he does all Hesperines. He would not hesitate to lay down his life for you, if there was ever a need. He is our champion of justice."

Alkaios frowned. "How can someone so good set himself against you?"

"Iskhyra, we know your character. You can tell us the truth, and we will not judge you. Are you a fugitive?"

"Let me say it this way. I am old enough to remember a time before Charge Law. The prince established it less than a century ago. The ink is barely dry. If he thinks I will change my ways and follow all the new rules he's come up with to keep the babies safe, he can spend the Dawn Slumber in Cordium."

Alkaios swallowed hard to avoid laughing.

Nephalea crossed her arms. "I love breaking rules."

"No," Iskhyra said firmly.

"We aren't babies that need to be kept safe," Alkaios reminded her.

"But I don't want my conduct to jeopardize what you two can have among our people. I must stay away from the Castra, but you need not. You must spend your Ritual separation there, not somewhere out here in hostile territory."

Alkaios shuddered. "We won't be ready for the Ritual separation for some time."

Nephalea was shaking her head. "We don't want to spend eight nights without each other's blood, even if it is to demonstrate our Craving to our fellow Hesperines and prove we're Graced. Not until we're older and the newgift bloodthirst has calmed."

"You'll want to celebrate your avowal with the Charge," Iskhyra insisted.

Nephalea smiled at Alkaios. "We've decided we want to wait to avow. As you once told Alkaios, we need no one's approval for our love to be recognized by our new people."

He smiled back at her. "And that night will be all the sweeter when the time is right. We want you to be there, Iskhyra, wherever we celebrate it. It will be a much happier occasion than our wedding day."

"We'll see," Iskhyra replied. "The fact remains that one night, you will go to the Castra—and I want you to get to enjoy it."

Nephalea sat down on her Iskhyra's other side. "We will, and we'll be discreet."

Iskhyra propped her arms on her knees. "When they ask you questions, it would be easier for you if you didn't know the answers. Are you certain you wish to hide my secrets?"

"You held our lives in your hands," Alkaios said. "What burden are secrets?"

Iskhyra lifted her face heavenward again for a moment, blinking hard. Then, apparently coming to a decision, she withdrew the scroll from her pack again. "These secrets are a matter of life and death. This scroll is the reason I was searching for the library. It is not in Baru's catalog. One night, when my quest is over, I will apologize to him. But until that time comes, this knowledge is too dangerous, even within the safety of the Castra, and it is too necessary to my cause."

"What does the scroll say?" Alkaios asked.

Nephalea leaned closer. "And what is your cause?"

"And will you teach me Hesperine fighting forms?"

Iskhyra narrowed her eyes at him. "What?"

"I saw you disarm Master Eusebios when he tried to torch me. That wasn't something you learned from reading."

She gave him an exasperated, affectionate look, but her aura shone with something deeper and more powerful.

She was proud of them.

"I will teach you everything I know," she promised.

"We will help you with your quest," Nephalea pledged.

"And along the way," said Alkaios, "I hope we will help many other mortals who need to meet a Hesperine on the battlefield."

epilogue

AN ARROW IN THE GRASS

Twenty Years Later

Alkaios gazed up at the walls of the fortress. It was a different night, a different army in the woods nearby, readying for a siege. A different castle than Salicina. But the same mortal plight.

"This looks familiar, doesn't it?" Nephalea stood close to him.

He put a hand on her back. "Too familiar."

"Who are they?" she wondered.

"It doesn't matter," Iskhyra said at Alkaios's shoulder. "They deserve our Mercy."

Nephalea's gaze fell to the still figures that lay crumpled at the foot of the fortress. "We are too late for them."

Alkaios cocked his head, his eyes sliding shut, and listened with every drop of his strength. "No. There is one heartbeat."

He stepped, and his Grace followed, his Gifter shadowing them. They surrounded the one man whose breath still rattled in his chest. Alkaios went down on his knees in a patch of snow.

The man looked up at him with wide, slow eyes.

Alkaios cradled the broken life on his lap. "Do not be afraid."

He scented Nephalea's tears in the air. He felt her hand on his shoulder, soft and strong, ever his support.

The man's lips moved, his voice so quiet, even Alkaios's Hesperine ears couldn't discern the words. He bent low, putting his ear to the man's mouth.

"Hesperine. Make it quick."

"That does not have to be your choice," Alkaios said. "I can save your life."

"Gave my life. For her. I am ready."

Alkaios swallowed the pain that saturated the Union. "Are you sure?"

"Sure. Proud. Make it quick."

Alkaios made himself breathe. He would remember the man's scent forever—peace, rising above the stench of death.

"I can do it, Alkaios," Iskhyra said.

"No. He asked me. His request is sacred. I will do it."

⁓

ALKAIOS LEANED INTO NEPHALEA. He couldn't look back at the fortress, not yet. The woods beyond the battlefield gave his gaze a welcome escape.

She wrapped him in her arms and her presence and their Union. "You did the right thing."

His Gifter nodded. "You did well."

"Goddess. Why can't we find one person we can save? Just one. That's all I ask for."

Nephalea stroked his face. "Not everyone can be like you."

Just then, he saw a flicker of motion in the trees. "Goddess—a *child*."

A sickening whisper from the walls. The sound of an arrow in flight. Alkaios started forward. Nephalea was a flash of movement beside him.

But Iskhyra was already there. She swept the child into her arms. The arrow struck hard in the grass where two little feet had stood a heartbeat before.

"Bleeding thorns," Alkaios swore. "They fired on a child!"

She was a mite of a girl, wearing nothing in the winter night but a sleep tunica. She kicked with her bare feet as she lashed against Iskhyra's hold.

The three of them gathered around the precious, vicious bundle under the shelter of the trees. Nephalea and Iskhyra surrounded them all in a ward.

Remembering another child who had been afraid of the dark, Alkaios conjured a gentle glow around them. The girl looked only a couple of years older than Aemilian had been that night.

At last, the little girl stopped fighting. Iskhyra knelt down and set her on her feet, holding her steady. Nephalea pulled off her cape and moved to wrap it around the child's shivering body. She and Iskhyra murmured reassurances and asked the child gentle questions.

The girl looked up at the three of them with wide hazel eyes, her freckled face set in an expression of defiance.

The petite, guileless sorceress worked a sudden and powerful spell on Alkaios. She healed the wound that had just opened in his heart when he'd ended the life of a good man with Mercy. That moment sealed into a clean scar.

Tonight, they had saved this little girl. This one life, among the many that had slipped through their fingers. One was an enormous number. What might this little bud of strength grow into? How would this small fighter change the world around her?

"Will you tell me your name?" Iskhyra asked the girl.

"Cassia."

Ready to find out who Cassia grows up to be?
Her epic begins in Blood Grace Book 1, *Blood Mercy*!
Learn more at
vroth.co/mercy

GLOSSARY

Abroad: Hesperine term for lands outside Orthros where Hesperines errant roam, meaning the Tenebrae and Cordium.
Aemilian: Alcaeus's five-year-old nephew, who has inherited Salicina due to the untimely deaths of his father and grandfather, Lords Aemilius the Younger and Elder.
Aemilius the Elder: Alcaeus's late father, Aemilian's grandfather; Lord of Salicina until his recent death in a duel with Gerrian. Lifelong rival of Maerea and Gerrian's father; took the West Field from Lapidea.
Aemilius the Younger: Alcaeus's elder brother, Aemilian's father; would have inherited Salicina, had he not died the same day as his father, Aemilius the Elder.
affinity: the type of magic a person has an aptitude for, such as healing, warding, or fire magic.
Akanthia: the world comprising the Tenebrae, Cordium, Orthros, and the Empire, among other lands.
Alcaeus: second son of Salicina who must unexpectedly take charge after the deaths of his father and elder brother, Lords Aemilius the Elder and Younger; manages the estate for his nephew, Aemilian. Hopes to end the feud with Lapidea. See also **Alkaios**
Alea: one of the two Queens of Orthros, who has ruled the Hesperines for over fifteen hundred years with her Grace, Queen Soteira.
Alkaios: Alcaeus's Hesperine name.
Anthros: god of war, order, and fire; supreme deity of the Tenebran and Cordian pantheon; ruler of summer. The sun is said to be Anthros riding his chariot across the sky. According to myth, he is the husband of Kyria and brother of Hypnos and Hespera.
Anthros's fire: a flower commonly grown in the Tenebrae, used by humans in combination with the herb sunsword to ward off Hesperines. Poisonous to Hesperines when properly prepared by mages.
Anthros's Hall: the god Anthros's great hall beyond the mortal world. Tenebrans and Cordians believe that those who please Anthros in life are rewarded with an afterlife in his Hall with his company of eternal warriors.

avowal: ceremony in which Graces profess their bond before other Hesperines; legally binding and an occasion of great celebration.

Baruti *or* **Baru:** Hesperine scholar and Fortress Master in the Prince's Charge; a theramancer and the librarian of Castra Justa, responsible for dangerous magical tomes and artifacts Chargers discover in the field. Began his mortal life in the Empire and chose to become a Hesperine at the First Prince's request; alumnus of Capital University.

Blood Union: a magical empathic connection that allows Hesperines to sense the emotions of any living thing that has blood.

Bria: Maerea's oldest friend, who was her late mother's handmaiden and promised to look after Maerea when her mother died.

Capital University: university located in the capital city of the Empire, open to all Imperial citizens of any social class; known for egalitarianism and cutting-edge research.

Castra Justa: the stronghold of the First Prince and base of operations for the Prince's Charge.

Charge Law: laws established by the First Prince, which all Hesperines errant must follow, designed to keep them safe when traveling in hostile human lands.

Charger: a Hesperine errant who is a member of the Prince's Charge.

Chera: goddess of rain and spinning in the Tenebran and Cordian pantheon, known as the Mourning Goddess and the Widow. According to myth, she was the Bride of Spring before Anthros destroyed her god-husband, Demergos, for disobedience.

The Commander: the commander of the guard at Lapidea, who has served Maerea's family for many years.

Cordium: land to the south of the Tenebrae, ruled by the Mage Orders. War mages are sent there to train.

Council of Free Lords: a group of the most powerful lords in the Tenebrae, who have influence over the king.

The Craving: a Hesperine's addiction to their Grace's blood. When deprived of each other, Graces suffer agonizing withdrawal symptoms and fatal illness.

Dawn Slumber: a deep sleep Hesperines fall into when the sun rises. Although the sunlight causes them no harm, they're unable to awaken until nightfall, leaving them vulnerable during daylight hours.

Demergos: formerly the god of agriculture, now stricken from the Tenebran and Cordian pantheon. His worshipers were disbanded in ancient times when the mages of Anthros seized power. According to myth, he was the husband of Chera, but disobeyed Anthros and brought on his own death and her grief.

Divine Tongue: language spoken by Hesperines and mages, used for spells, rituals, and magical texts. The common tongue of Orthros, spoken freely by all Hesperines. In the Tenebrae and Cordium, the mages keep it a secret and disallow non-mages from learning it.

Domitia: Alcaeus's sister-in-law and Lady of Salicina; mother of Aemilian and widow of Aemilius the Younger.

The Drink: when a Hesperine drinks blood from a human or animal; a nonsexual act, considered sacred, which should be carried out with respect for the donor. It's forbidden to take the Drink from an unwilling person.
Drusus: Tenebran lord and ally of Gerrian, who aids Lapidea in the feud against Salicina.
The Empire: vast and prosperous human lands located far to the west, across an ocean from the Tenebrae. Comprises many different languages and cultures united under the Empress. Allied with Orthros and welcoming to Hesperines, many of whom began their mortal lives as Imperial citizens.
The Empress: the ruler of the Empire, admired by her citizens. The Imperial throne has passed down through the female line for many generations.
Equinox Oath: ancient treaty between Orthros and Tenebra, which prescribes the conduct of Hesperines errant and grants them protection from humans.
errant circle: a group of Hesperines who go errant together Abroad.
essential magic: Hesperines' innate abilities, such as the Blood Union, self-healing, veil spells, stepping, and levitation. Very powerful, but cost little effort and are impossible for anyone but experts to detect.
Eusebios: master mage responsible for the shrine of Anthros in Lapidea. An old friend of Maerea's family and her spiritual advisor.
The Feast: Hesperine term for drinking blood while making love.
First Prince: see **Ioustinianos**
Fortress Masters: highest ranking officers in the Prince's Charge, his seconds-in-command responsible for the defense of Castra Justa.
geomagical warmer: a magical device created by a geomagus, a mage with an affinity for geological forces; emanates heat and can be used for cooking or brewing coffee.
Gerrian: Maerea's younger brother; Lord of Lapidea since the recent death of their father. An expert swordsman bent on winning his feud with Salicina; killed Lords Aemilius the Elder and Younger in duels.
The Gift: see **Hespera's Gift**
Gift Collectors: necromancers devoted to Hypnos who are professional assassins of Hesperines. Zealots for their cause of collecting immortals' debt to the god of death. They earn lucrative bounties for destroying Hesperines.
Gift Night: the occasion of a person's Gifting, when they are transformed into a Hesperine. Traditionally marked by a celebration among family and friends, when the newgift may choose a new name.
Gifter: the Hesperine who transforms another, conveying Hespera's Gift to the new immortal, and is thereafter a lifelong mentor.
Gifting: the transformation from human into Hesperine.
Goddess's Eyes: Akanthia's two moons, the red Blood Moon and the white Light Moon; associated with Hespera and regarded as her gaze by Hesperines.
Grace: a magical bond between two Hesperine lovers, which frees them from the need for human blood and enables them to sustain each other, but comes at the cost of the Craving. A fated bond that happens when their love is true. It is believed every Hesperine has a Grace just waiting to be found.

Grace Union: the particularly powerful and intimate Blood Union between two Hesperines who are Graced; enables them to communicate telepathically.

heart hunters: warbands of Tenebrans who hunt down and excardiate Hesperines, regarded by their countrymen as protectors of humanity. They patrol the northern borders of the Tenebrae with packs of liegehounds, waiting to attack Hesperines who leave Orthros.

Hespera: goddess of night cast from the Tenebran and Cordian pantheon. The Mage Orders declared her worship heresy punishable by death. Hesperines keep her cult alive. Associated with roses, thorns, the moons and stars, and fanged creatures. According to myth, she is the sister of Anthros and Hypnos.

Hespera's Gift: Hesperines' immortality and magical abilities, which they regard as a blessing from the goddess Hespera.

Hesperine: a nocturnal immortal being with fangs who gains nourishment from drinking blood. Tenebrans and Cordians believe them to be monsters bent on humanity's destruction. In truth, they follow a strict moral code in the name of their goddess, Hespera, and wish only to ease humankind's suffering.

Hesperine errant: a Hesperine who has left Orthros to travel through the Tenebrae doing good deeds for mortals.

The Hunger: a combination of sexual desire and the need for blood, which Hesperines experience with their lovers.

Hypnos: god of death and dreams in the Tenebran and Cordian pantheon. Winter is considered his season. Humans unworthy of going to Anthros's Hall are believed to spend the afterlife in Hypnos's realm of the dead. According to myth, he is the brother of Anthros and Hespera.

Imperial army: the highly skilled and organized army of the Empire, which provides opportunities to citizens from all walks of life and rewards merit.

Imperial University: illustrious university in the Empire. Only students with wealth and the best references gain entry, usually those of noble or royal blood. Known for traditionalism and conservative approaches to research.

Ioustinianos *or* **Ioustin:** First Prince of the Hesperines and Royal Commander of the Charge. Eldest son of the Queens of Orthros. Governs all Hesperines errant Abroad. A theramancer and alumnus of Capital University.

Iskhyra: Alcaeus's Gifter. Honorable but secretive Hesperine errant with powerful warding magic, known as a scholar but capable in battle. Age unknown, but considered an elder by the Fortress Masters. Dedicated to a quest known only to her. Alumna of Capital University.

Jaya: Hesperine warrior and Fortress Master in the Prince's Charge. Warder and siege expert, responsible for the magical defenses of Castra Justa. Began her mortal life in the Empire, where she was a mage-engineer in the Imperial army. Fell in battle and chose the Gift.

kalux: Hesperine term in the Divine Tongue for clitoris.

krana: Hesperine term in the Divine Tongue for vagina.

Kyria: goddess of weaving and the harvest in the Tenebran and Cordian pantheon, known as the Mother Goddess or the Wife. Her season is autumn. According to myth, she is married to Anthros.

Lapidea: Maerea's family's domain. Most of the terrain is cliffs, which provide good defense but poor soil. Due to lack of arable land, Lapidea has fallen on hard times and suffers deprivation.

liegehounds: war dogs bred and trained by Tenebrans as Hesperine hunting dogs. Veil spells do not throw them off the scent, and they can leap high enough to pull a levitating Hesperine from the air. The only animals that do not trust Hesperines.

Maerea: Lady of Lapidea who tries to care for her struggling people and temper her brother Gerrian. See also **Nephalea**

Mage Orders: the magical and religious authorities in Cordium, which also dictate sacred law to the Tenebrae. Responsible for training and governing mages and punishing heretics.

The Mercy: sacred Hesperine practice of caring for dying mortals; easing their suffering, offering them the Gift, and granting them dignity in death if they refuse.

Nephalea: Maerea's Hesperine name.

newgift: a newborn Hesperine, or a person who has decided to transform and awaits their Gifting.

The Oath: see **Equinox Oath**

Orthros: homeland of the Hesperines, ruled by the Queens. The Mage Orders describe it as a horrific place where no human can survive, but in reality, it is safer and more peaceful than mortal lands. Located north of the Tenebrae.

Pherakia *or* **Rakia:** mage with the rank of Daughter, responsible for the shrine of Kyria at Salicina. Has great affection for Alcaeus and his family.

Prince and Diplomat: a board game and beloved Hesperine pastime; requires strategy and practice to master.

Prince's Charge: the force of Hesperines errant under the First Prince's command, based at Castra Justa.

The Queens: the Hesperine monarchs of Orthros; see **Alea** and **Soteira**

rhabdos: Hesperine term in the Divine Tongue meaning penis.

Ritual separation: eight nights that Hesperine Graces must spend apart to demonstrate their Craving symptoms and prove their bond to their people; required before avowal.

Salicina: Alcaeus's family's domain. These fertile lands have enjoyed unusual bounty in a time when the feuds have ravaged much of the Tenebrae.

Sanctuary: a Hesperine refuge in hostile territory, concealed and protected from humans by Sanctuary magic.

Sanctuary magic: a blend of shadow wards and light magic, used to create powerful protections that also conceal. Queen Alea of Orthros is the only person with this affinity who survived the mages' persecution of Hespera worshipers.

The Solace: sacred Hesperine practice of adopting abandoned children.

Soteira: one of the two Queens of Orthros, who has ruled the Hesperines for over fifteen hundred years with her Grace, Alea.

stepping: innate Hesperine ability to teleport instantly from one place to another with little magical effort; a type of essential magic.

sunsword: an herb commonly grown in the Tenebrae, used by humans in combination with the flower Anthros's fire to ward off Hesperines. Poisonous to Hesperines when properly prepared by mages.

The Tenebrae: the kingdom Maerea and Alcaeus hail from, where Lapidea and Salicina are located. Consists of fractured domains under the rule of a weak king, which suffer instability due to the feuds of warring lords. Situated south of Orthros and north of Cordium.

theramancer: a person with an affinity for theramancy, or mind healing. trained in the Imperial tradition of banishing evil magic; expert at combating necromancers.

The Thirst: a Hesperine's need to drink blood, a non-sexual urge like a human's need to drink water or eat food.

traversal: teleportation ability of human mages; requires a great expense of magic and usually leaves the mortal mage seriously ill.

veil spell: magical Hesperine concealment that allows them to hide their presence and activities from humans or fellow immortals; a type of essential magic.

Vulgus *or* **the vulgar tongue:** common language of all non-mages in the Tenebrae and Cordium.

The Will: free will or willpower, held sacred by Hesperines, who are forbidden to use their power to violate a person's freedom of choice.

Blood Mercy
Blood Grace Book I

One human. One immortal. Will their alliance save the kingdom, or will their forbidden love be a death sentence?

When Cassia seeks out a Hesperine, he could end her mortal life in a heartbeat. But she has no fear of his magic or his fangs. She knows the real monster is the human king, her father. If he finds out she's bargaining with his enemy, he'll send her to the executioner.

As a Hesperine diplomat, Lio must negotiate with mortals who hate him. Cassia is different, but politics aren't why she captivates the gentle immortal. He wants more than her blood, and if he can't resist the temptation, he'll provoke the war he's trying to prevent.

Slow-burn, steamy romance meets classic fantasy worldbuilding in Blood Grace. Follow fated mates Cassia and Lio through their epic story of forbidden love for a guaranteed series HEA.

Learn more:
vroth.co/mercy

ACKNOWLEDGEMENTS

June 2022

Love, eternal gratitude, and watermelons to my wonderful word witches in the FaRo Authors coven. Special thanks to Elsie Winters, S.L. Prater, Lisette Marshall, Colleen Cowley, Erin Vere, and M.J. Faraldo for creative input and moral support every step of the way.

Thank you to my amazing artist, Patcas Illustration, for creating this exceptionally stunning cover that expresses the soul of this story.

Huge heart eyes to Kaija and Brittany and my reader team, the Ambassadors for Orthros, for all your support and feedback:

Abi @words_and_dreams	Bridie @northviewcrafts
Abigail @a_reads_alot	Brittany @brittany.wilson1764
Ahana @tohearts_content	Brittany @bookwyvernlovestea
Alex	Carole
Alexa @alexapleasereview	Cheyenne
Alisha	Christine @anxioustattooedandbookish
Amy @halfhorchata	
Angela	Corinne @corinnerichardson
Anshul @stories.buddy	Courtney @mylifeonshelves
Ashleigh	Deborah
Aurora @AuroraLydia	Emily @thehamsterreads
Babs	Erika @theenchantedshelf
Brandy @better_0ff_read	Faigy @Seasonofbooks

Haley @thecaffeinated.reader
Heather @_the_forgotten_books
Isis @inked.fantasy
Jessica @reddoorromance
Jessica @readbelievelove
Julie @1bookmore
Kadie
Kai
Kaija @strictlybookish_kai
Keshia @808bookdr
Kris @a_bookish_dream
Kristen
Kristin @madhattersfolly_reads
Leah @leahlovestoread
Lucrezia @books_in.the.clouds0899
Maddison @landscapesofink
Madhu @mabookyard
Marta @marta.pellegrini__
Megan @bookish_megeen
Melissa
Nadine
Nat
Nicki @starseternal182
Nicole @starsbooksandtea
Nikki @authordanimorrison
Nina
Opal
Patricia @titas.tales
Priscilla @priscillaroseauthor
Raley
Riley @paperroselibrary
Riri @acreativebooknook
Rishma @bookaddict__ril
Sahana @books_and_draws_eclectic
Samantha @bookobsessedandblonde
Sarah @retrogirlreads
Sarah @theheavycrownreads
Sharon
Sherri @sherrisharpe14
Shreya @my_fair_fiction
Sonya
Steph @slpraterwrites
Stephanie
Tammy
Tara @rosereadokie
Taylor @tmo_reads
Tia @tiaisreading
Whitney
Yana

October 2020

THE FIRST person I need to thank is my number one supporter—my dad. Thank you for coffee breaks in the gazebo and anytime movie nights. Thank you for listening to me about my stories and sharing your wisdom by telling me yours. There's no one I'd rather be in lockdown with, and I'm so glad we're in this together. I love you.

Heartfelt thanks also go to my Ambassadors for Orthros. First to my beta readers Nadine and Nancy, who provided such thorough and insightful feedback on this book. You really are superheroes. I'm grateful for your constructive criticism, kind support, and just chatting about books, heat waves, gardens, and tea. To my Ambassadors Tanya, Robin, Doreen, and Kristen, I feel so lucky that among all the things you do with your time and energy, you volunteer to read my absurdly long books. I look forward to working with all of you as beta and ARC readers on upcoming projects!

How do I even begin to thank my readers? Thank you, Caroline, for emailing me to ask when Blood Grace Book IV is coming out. You are the first person who ever sent me fan mail, and I'll never forget it. A very special shout-out goes to Stephi, who started as a Blood Grace reader and became a pen pal. Your love and dedication for this series are humbling and inspiring, and I will always appreciate you taking the time to email with me. I'm so grateful for the people behind every sale, KU page read, review, email, Twitter follow, or StoryOrigin click. You, dear reader, are such a smart, interesting and wonderful person, and trying to write the books you want is the best job in the world.

To all of my author friends and colleagues at StoryOrigin, wow, what an amazing community. Thank you for the group promos, newsletter swaps, and opportunities to build each other up. Kim, your writing books are a joyful source of creativity. Thank you for your kind words and support. I'm so happy we met. To all the authors who agreed to participate in my multicultural newsletter promo while I was writing this book, you're an inspiration, and I'm thankful I can continue learning from you.

Finally, to my mom's author friends who have been there for me during a truly difficult time. Jannine and Tabitha, you are the true friends who remain when the going gets tough. Thank you for your love, understanding, and encouragement about writing and life.

ABOUT THE AUTHOR

Vela Roth grew up with female-driven fantasy books and classic epics, then grew into romance novels. She set out to write stories that blend the rich worlds of fantasy with the passion of romance.

She has pursued a career in academia, worked as a web designer and book formatter, and stayed home as a full-time caregiver for her loved ones with severe illnesses. Writing through her own grief and trauma, she created the Blood Grace series, which now offers comfort to readers around the world.

She lives in a solar-powered writer's garret in the Southwestern United States, finding inspiration in the mountains and growing roses in the desert. Her feline familiar is a rescue cat named Milly with a missing fang and a big heart.

Vela loves hearing from readers and hopes you'll visit her at velaroth.com.